# SALLY BISHOP

## *A ROMANCE*

## E. TEMPLE THURSTON

1st WORLD
LIBRARY
Literary Society

# Sally Bishop

## E. Temple Thurston

© 1st World Library, 2007
PO Box 2211
Fairfield, IA 52556
www.1stworldlibrary.com
First Edition

LCCN: 2007927761

Softcover ISBN: 978-1-4218-4522-7
Hardcover ISBN: 978-1-4218-4438-1
eBook ISBN: 978-1-4218-4606-4

Purchase *"Sally Bishop"*
as a traditional bound book at:
www.1stWorldLibrary.com/purchase.asp?ISBN=978-1-4218-4522-7

1st World Library is a literary, educational organization
dedicated to:

- Creating a free internet library of downloadable ebooks

- Hosting writing competitions and offering book publishing scholarships.

Interested in more 1st World Library books? contact:
literacy@1stworldlibrary.com
Check us out at: www.1stworldlibrary.com

# 1ˢᵗ World Library Literary Society

## Giving Back to the World

"If you want to work on the core problem, it's early school literacy."

**- James Barksdale, former CEO of Netscape**

"No skill is more crucial to the future of a child, or to a democratic and prosperous society, than literacy."

**- Los Angeles Times**

"Literacy... means far more than learning how to read and write... The aim is to transmit... knowledge and promote social participation."

**- UNESCO**

"Literacy is not a luxury, it is a right and a responsibility. If our world is to meet the challenges of the twenty-first century we must harness the energy and creativity of all our citizens."

**- President Bill Clinton**

"Parents should be encouraged to read to their children, and teachers should be equipped with all available techniques for teaching literacy, so the varying needs and capacities of individual kids can be taken into account."

**- Hugh Mackay**

To

GERALD DU MAURIER

*MY DEAR GERALD,*

*Amongst the many things which I anticipate in the reception of this book, is the shrug-shoulder smile of critics at my sub-title—a Romance. There are canons and rubrics to be observed, it would seem, in the slightest action that a man attempts in this Great World's Fair of Conventionality, whose every sideshow is hedged around with the red-tape of the Law. Witness even that delusive proverb—there is honour amongst thieves. So is there an unwritten canon in literature and the making of books, that a Romance must end with a phrase to convey another illusion—namely, the happiness that is ever after.*

*And so, in this respect, I throw canons to the winds—it sounds a herculean feat—wash out the printed red of the rubric, and call, perhaps the saddest story I shall write, a Romance.*

*Yet I profess to have a reason beyond mere contrariness. The world of Romance must be at all times an elusive star—never capable of being put in the exact same place on any one's calendar. And to me it conveys no fixed beginning, no fixed* end, so long as it possesses that quality of dreaming imagination in the mind of the character with whom the circumstances are first concerned. All that we know certainly of life is reality, and of all those myriad things which combine to make up the one great scheme, of which we know nothing, there is the quality of Romance—free to any one who cares to let his mind drift upon the sea of conjecture.

In that this was the case with Sally; in that she made her dream out of Reality itself—I have called it a Romance. The Romance that remains a Romance until the end, is not as yet within the reach of my pen. If it ever should be—then I promise you that book as well.

On all my other anticipations—the attitude of the critical mind towards Chapter IV. in Book I., the sensitiveness of the delicate mind when it closes its eyes on Chapter VI. of Book II.—I will keep silent. As I have said, I anticipate many things, but I only hope for your approval.

Yours always,

E. TEMPLE THURSTON.
LONDON,
January 31st, 1908.

# CONTENTS

# BOOK I

## THE CONSCRIPT

### CHAPTER I

It was an evening late in November. The fog that during the afternoon had been lying like a crouching beast between the closely built houses had now risen. It was as though it had waited till nightfall for its prey, and then departed, leaving a sense of sulkiness in the atmosphere that weighed persistently on the spirits. A slight drizzling rain was wetting the pavements. It clung in a mist to the glass panes of the street lamps, dimming the glow of the light within.

In the windows of all the houses the electric lights were burning. You could see clerks, male and female, bent up over their desks beneath them. Some worked steadily, never looking up from their occupations; others gazed with expressionless faces out into the street. Occasionally the figure of a man would move out of the apparent darkness of the room beyond. The light would fan in patches on his face. You could see his lips moving as he spoke to the occupant of the desk; you might even trace the faint animation as it crept into the face of the person thus addressed. But it would only last for a few moments. The man would move away and the look of tired apathy settle itself once more upon the clerk's features as soon as he or she were left alone.

As it grew later, there might be seen men with hats on their heads, moving about—in the light one moment, lost in the darkness the next. Some of them were pulling gloves on to their hands, or lighting cigarettes, others would be pinning a bunch of violets into their button-holes, or brushing the shoulders of their coats. These were the ones who had finished for the day. It could always be known when they had taken their departure. The heads of the clerks would twist towards the interior of the room. You could almost imagine the wistful expression on their faces from the bare outlines of their attitudes as they turned in their chairs. Then, a minute later, the main door of the house would open, the figure of a man emerge; for a moment he would turn his face up to the sky, then the umbrella would go up and he would walk away into the darkness of the street, for one brief moment an individual with an identity; the next, a mere unit in the great herd of human beings.

There were many departures such as these before, at last, the clerks rose from their chairs. When finally they did move, it was with a lethargy that almost concealed the relief which the cessation of work had brought them. One might have expected to see the slamming of books and the rushing for hats like children released from school. But there was no such energy of delight as that. Ledgers were closed wearily, as though they were weighted with leaden covers; papers were put in tiny heaps as if they were a pile of death-warrants. Typewriters were covered with such slowness and such care that one might think they were delicate instruments of music with silver strings, instead of treadmills for tired hands.

Some reason must explain why these young men and girls, when their superiors took their departure, showed so plainly

E. Temple Thurston

the envy that they felt and now are apparently unmoved by the prospect of their own freedom. It is simply this. Vitality is an exhaustible quality. It may last up to a certain moment, then it burns out like the hungry wick of a candle that has no more grease to feed it. You can incarcerate a man for such a length of time that when at last you do give him his liberty he has no love left for it. It is much the same with these creatures who are imprisoned in the barred cells of London offices. By the time their day's work is ended their vitality for enjoyment has been exhausted. They take their liberty much as a man takes the sentence of penal servitude when he had expected to be hanged.

Stand for a moment in this street that runs out from the Covent Garden Market and watch the office windows before the lights are extinguished. Is there one attitude, one movement, one gesture that betrays the joy of freedom now that the day's work is over? Scarcely one. That boy with the long dark hair drooping on his forehead, contrasting so vividly against his sallow skin—you might imagine from the listlessness of his actions that the day's work was just beginning. At lunch time, when the vitality was yet in store, he might have been seen, running out from the building in the gleeful anticipation of an hour's rest. But now, when all the hours of the night are before him, his nervous energy has been sapped away. You get no spirit in a tired horse. It shies at nothing, but drags one foot wearily after another until the stable door is reached.

This is the actual condition of things that the young men and women find when they have burnt their boats, have left the country for the illusory joys of the town. There may be greater possibilities of enjoyment; but this huge, carnivorous plant—this gigantic city of London—has only displayed its attractions in order to gain its prey. They are drawn by the colours of the petals, they come to the honeyed perfume of its scent; but once caught in the prison of its embrace, there is only the slow poison of forced labour that eats its deadly way into the very heart of their vitality.

In one of these offices off Covent Garden, under a green-shaded lamp that cast its metallic rays on to the typewriting machine before her, sat one of the young lady clerks in the establishment of Bonsfield & Co., a firm of book-buyers. They carried on a promiscuous trade with America and the Colonies, and managed, by the straining of ends, to meet their expenses and show a small margin of profit. You undertake the labour of a slave in Egypt, and run the risk of a forlorn hope when you try to make a living wage in London as your own master. The price of freedom in a free country is beyond the reach of most pockets.

The hour of six had rung out from the neighbouring clocks, yet this girl showed no signs of finishing her work. From down in the street you could see her bent over the machine, her fingers pounding the keys—human hammers mono-tonously striving to beat out a pattern upon metal, a pattern that would never come. The light from the green-shaded lamp above her, fell obliquely on her head. It lit up her pale, golden hair like a sun-ray; it drew out the round, gentle curve of her face and threw it up against the darkness of the room beyond. So well as it could, with its harsh methods, it made a picture. One instinctively paused to look at it. A man coming out of the shadows of the Covent Garden Market stopped as he passed down King Street and gazed up at the window.

For five minutes he stood and watched her, assuming, by looking up and down the street when anybody passed him by, the attitude of a person who is waiting for some one.

It is impossible to say whether it is really the woman herself, or a combination of the woman and the moment, which

E. Temple Thurston

seizes and drags a man's attention towards her. In this case it may have been the combined result of the two. The girl was pretty. In the ray of that electric light, the soft, childish outline of her face and the pale, sensuous strands of her hair were probably lent a glamour such as that given by the footlights. The man, too, was on his way back to companionless chambers. The lower end of Regent Street may be a far from lonely spot in which to take up one's abode; but there is nothing so empty as an empty room, no matter on to what crowded thoroughfare it may look. Say, then, it was a combination of impulses, the woman and the moment—the girl pretty and the man oppressed by a sense of loneliness. Whatever it was, he stood there, without any apparent intention of moving, and watched her.

She was the last, amongst all those workers who could be seen within the lighted apertures of the windows, to leave her post. One by one they performed their weary play of actions, the shutting up of ledgers, the putting away of papers—out went the lights, and a moment later dim figures stole out of the darkened doorways into the drizzling rain, and hurried away into the shadows of the streets. But she still remained, and the man, with a certain amount of dogged persistence, continued to watch her movements. Once he took out his watch, as his impatience became more insistent. Then, with the continual watching of her, the continual sight of her hands dancing laboriously on those keys, the noise of the typewriter at last reached the ears of his imagination. He could hear, above the sounds of the street, that everlasting metallic tapping.

"God! What a life!" he exclaimed to himself.

If there is anything in telepathy; if thoughts, by reason of their concentration, can be borne from one mind to another utterly unconscious of them, then what followed his exclamation might well have been an example of it. For a moment the girl buried her face in her hands. He could see her pressing her fingers into the sockets of her eyes. Then, sitting upright, she stretched her arms above her head. Every action was expressive of her exhaustion. The glancing at her watch, the critical inspection of the bundle of papers, yet untyped, that lay beside her on the desk; all these various movements were like the gestures of a dumb show. Was she going to give in? From the size of the bundle of papers which she had looked at, there was apparently still a great deal of work left for her to do.

The thought passed across his mind that he would give her until he had counted twenty; if she showed no signs of moving by that time, he decided to wait no longer.

One—two—three—four—she stood up from the desk. He still watched her until he had seen her place the wooden cover over the machine; then he crossed to the other side of the road and began walking up and down the pavement, passing the door of Bonsfield & Co. About every twenty yards or so, he turned and passed it again.

Five minutes elapsed. At last he heard the door of the premises close—the noise of it rattled in the street; then he turned and faced her as she came towards him.

Her head was down; her feet were moving quickly, tapping on the pavement. He prepared himself to speak to her, his hand getting ready to lift his hat. If she had given him half the encouragement that he imagined he required, he would have found courage; but without lifting her head, as though she were utterly unconscious of his presence, she hurried by in the direction of Bedford Street and the West.

Was that to be the end of it? Had he waited that full quarter

E. Temple Thurston

of an hour in the drizzling rain for nothing? The man of fixed intent is hardly beaten so easily as that. There was no definite evil purpose in his mind. He was caught in that mood when a man must talk to some one, and a woman for preference. The waiting of fifteen minutes in that sluggish atmosphere had only intensified it. The fact that in the first moment of opportunity his courage had failed had had no power to move him from his purpose, or to change the prompting of his mood.

As soon as she had passed him on the pavement, he turned resolutely and followed her.

# CHAPTER II

All life is an adventure, even the most monotonous moments of it. It is impossible to walk the streets of London without being conscious of that spirit of the possibility of happenings which makes life tolerable. It was not to feast their eyes upon unknown worlds, or drench their hands in a stream of gold, that the old marauders of England set forth upon the high seas. Assuredly it must have been, in the hearts of them, that love of adventure, that desire for the happenings of strange things which spurred them on to face God in the wind, to dare Him in the tempest, to brave Him even into the unknown.

Some of that instinct, but in its various and lesser degrees, is left in us now. For one moment it rose in the mind of Sally Bishop, as she turned into Bedford Street and directed her course towards Piccadilly Circus. It had crossed her mind in suspicion—the uprush of an idea, as a bubble struggles to the surface—that the man whom she had found waiting outside the premises of Bonsfield & Co. had had the intention in his mind to speak to her as she passed. Now, as she looked sideways when she turned the corner, and found that he had altered his direction—was following her—the suspicion became a conviction. She knew.

In the first realization, the thought of adventure thrilled her.

E. Temple Thurston

A life, quiet and uneventful such as hers, looks of necessity for its happiness to the little thrills, the little emotions that combine to make one day less monotonous than another. But when, having reached Garrick Street and, looking hurriedly over her shoulder, she found that not only was he still following, but that he had perceptibly lessened the distance between them, the spirit of interest sank—died out, like a candle snuffed in a gale. In that moment she became afraid.

It is nameless, that terror in the mind of a woman pursued. Yet without it one of the first of her abstract attractions would be gone. Undoubtedly it is the joy of the pursuer that the quarry should take to flight. Would there be any chase without? But long years of study amongst the more advanced of us have made the fact of rather common knowledge. The woman has learnt that to be caught there must be flight, and, in assuming it, she has acquired for herself the instincts of the pursuer. So an army, resorting to the strategy of retreat, is still the pursuer in the more subtle sense of the word. It is this strategy that is cunningly taught in the modern, genteel education of the sex. The virtue of chastity it is called, but over the length of time it has come to be a forced growth; it has altered intrinsically in its composition. Education has learnt to make use of chastity, rather than to acquire it for itself. And, after all, what is it in itself, when the gilt of its glamour is stripped, like tinsel, from the fairy's pantomimic wand?

There is, when everything has been said, only one value in chastity in its ideal sense, so long as we are tied to these conditions of human instinct, and that is in the value that it brings to women. Without it, a woman may be the essence of fascination; she may be the completeness of attraction, but for the need of the race she is undesirable. Without chastity, a woman may be most things to a man, but she cannot be a mother to his child.

Amongst those girls, then, whose desire in life it is to marry, conforming in all ways to the authority of convention, chastity has been taught from the cradle—taught as a means to an end. It is mostly, if not altogether, in the lower middle classes that you will find chastity to be an end in itself. The destructive philosophy of education has not swept out the gentler virtues from them. As yet they have not come under the keen edge of its influence. For their chastity, then, they are interesting; whereas the manufactured virtue of the upper middle class is like the hothouse strawberry—forced in May—a tempting fruit to lay upon a dish, but tasteless, as is wool, between the teeth.

It is this virtue—this real quality, breeding self-respect—that you will find in the mind of Sally Bishop. Here is no strategy of movement, no well-considered campaign. She quickens her steps, and her heart thumps within her, because that virtue, which is her priceless possession, is in danger of being assailed. In the very soul of her is the desire to escape. There are thousands of women whom education has nursed who set the pace as well, whenever a man starts in pursuit; but the course of their flight leads straight to the altar and they run neither too fast, nor too slow, lest by any chance the hunter should weary of the chase. But here you have none of this. The woman is obeying instincts that Nature gave her with her soul. Sally Bishop is pure—the chaste woman. Where men most look for her, she is hard to find.

This journey from King Street to Piccadilly Circus was performed every evening. In Piccadilly she found the 'bus that took her to Hammersmith. It was a pleasurable little journey; she looked forward to it. It amused her to dally on the way, stopping to look in the shop windows. The bright lights lifted her spirits. After a time she had become acquainted with the prints that hung in the print-seller's windows in Garrick Street; they always stayed there long

E. Temple Thurston

enough to grow familiar. There was also a jeweller's shop in Coventry Street; it sold second-hand silver—old Sheffield-plated candle-sticks, cream ewers and sugar bowls; George III. silver tea-services, and quaint-shaped wine strainers—they stood there in the window in profusion. In themselves, for the daintiness of their design, or the value of their antiquity, they did not interest her. She liked the look of them glittering there; they conveyed a sense of the emba-rrassment of riches which touched her ideas of romance. It was the tray of old-fashioned ornaments, brooches in the design of flimsy baskets of flowers, each flower represented by a different coloured stone—old signet rings, old seals, quaint little figures of men and beasts in silver, sometimes in gold; these were the things that caught her fancy; she pored over them, choosing, every time she passed, some fresh trinket that she would like to possess.

But on this evening in November she did not stop. At the print-seller's in Garrick Street, she hesitated, but one glance over her shoulder sped her onwards. The apprehension most prominent in her mind was that if she continually looked behind her, the man might fancy she was encouraging him. Once having consciously decided that, she turned no more until she had reached the protection of the fountain in the middle of the Circus. There she stopped and glanced back. He was gone. In all the hundreds of human beings who mingled and churned like a swarm of ants upon an ant-hill, he was nowhere to be seen. With a genuine sigh of relief, she crossed over to the Piccadilly side and walked beside a Hammersmith 'bus, as if slowed gradually down to the regulated place where the conditions of traffic permit vehicles to collect their passengers.

A little crowd of people, like flies upon fallen fruit, clung about the steps of the 'bus as it moved towards its resting-place. She joined in with them, jostled along the pavement by their efforts to secure an advantageous position by the steps. When finally it did come to a standstill and she had reached the conductor's platform, the announcement, "Outside only," met her attempt to force a passage within.

It was still raining—persistent mist of rain that steals a way through any clothing. Should she wait? She had no umbrella. But she had known what it was to wait on such occasions before. The next 'bus would probably be full up inside, and the next, and the next. Twenty minutes might well be wasted before she could start on her way home, and you have little energy left within you to care about a wetting, when from nine o'clock in the morning until six, when it is dark, you have been beating the keys of a typewriter. Your mind demands but little then, so long as you can secure a peaceful oblivion.

So, in the face of others who turned back, she mounted the stairway on to the roof of the 'bus. There she was alone, and, pulling the tarpaulin covering around her, she seated herself on the little bench farthest from the driver. The little bell tinkled twice, viciously—all drivers and conductors are made vicious by a steady rain—and they moved out into the swim of the traffic, as a steamer puts out from its pier.

On bright evenings it was the most enjoyable part of the journey home, this ride from Piccadilly Circus to Hammersmith. From there onwards in the tram to Kew Bridge, it became uninteresting. The shops were not so bright; the people not so well dressed. It always gave her a certain amount of quaint amusement to envy the ladies in their carriages and motor-cars. The envy was not malicious. You would have found no socialistic tendencies in her. In her mind, utterly untutored in the sense of logic, she found birth to be a full and sufficient reason for possession. But there was always alive in her consciousness the orderly desire to

E. Temple Thurston

also be a possessor herself. It never led her actually into a definite discontent with her own conditions of life, irksome, wearying, exhausting though she found them to be. But subconsciously within her was the feeling that she was not really meant to be denied the joy of luxuries. That instinct showed itself in many little ways. She was sometimes extravagant—bought a silk petticoat when a cotton one would have done just as well, but, oh heavens! it was cheap! You would scarcely have thought it possible to buy silk petticoats at the price. And no doubt the appearance of the silk was only superficial. But it gave her a great deal of pleasure. When any lady stepped down from her carriage to go into one of those West End shops, Sally always noticed the petticoat that she wore. Women will—men too, perhaps.

But on this dismal evening, when whenever she lifted her head the fine rain sprayed upon her face, there was no pleasure to be found in watching the people in the streets below. Carriages were huddled up in line upon the stands and the coachmen shivered miserably on their seats, the rain dripping in steady drops from the brims of their hats into the laps of their mackintoshes. So she kept her head down, and when she heard footsteps mounting the stairway, approaching her, she held out the three coppers for her fare without looking up. When her mind, anticipating the answering ring of the conductor's ticket-puncher, realized the mistake, she raised her head, then twisted back, electrically, as though some current had been passed through her body. Seated on the bench at the other side of the passage-way, was the man whom she had found in King Street outside the premises of Bonsfield & Co.

Her first thought was to get off the 'bus. She made a preparatory movement, leaning forward with her hand upon the back of the seat in front of her. Possibly the man saw it and had no desire to be foiled a second time. Whatever may have been his purpose, he moved nearer to her and held out the umbrella with which he was sheltering himself.

"You'd better let me lend you an umbrella—hadn't you?" he said.

There is a quality of voice that commands. It neither considers nor admits of refusal. He had it. Women of strong personality it irritates; women with no personality it affrights; but the women who are women obey—with reluctance probably, struggling against it, but in the end they obey. There is, again, a quality of voice that hall-marks the man of birth. Long years of careful preservation of the breed have refined it down. It may cloak a mind that is vicious to a thought; but there is a ring in it—a ring of true metal, well tried in the furnace. He had that also. From him, dressed none too carefully, it sounded almost misplaced and therefore was the more noticeable. The effect of it upon her was obvious. Instead of taking his suggestion as an insult, which undoubtedly she would have done had the offer been made in any other type of voice, Sally checked the offended toss of the head, restrained the contemptuous flash of eye, and merely said, "No, thank you." She said it coldly. There was no warmth of encouragement, either in her tone of voice or the unrecognizing eye which she turned upon him without trace of sympathy.

"Isn't that rather foolish?" he suggested. "You'll get wet through. How far are you going?"

"Hammersmith."

He had asked the question with such apparent inconsequence that the thought of denying him the information had not occurred to her. Undoubtedly it was foolish to refuse his offer. She would get wet through before she reached

E. Temple Thurston

Hammersmith. The tarpaulin only covered her skirt, and in the lap that it made was already a pool of water swilling backwards and forwards with the rocking of the 'bus. Through her mind raced a swift calculation, estimating the benefits she would gain by keeping dry. They were not many in number, but they entered the balance, dragged down the scales of her decision. The hat she was wearing—it was not a best hat—but some few evenings before, she had retrimmed it; there was matter for consideration in that. The frame was a good one. It could be trimmed again and again, so long as it met with those requirements which in Sally's mind were governed by a vogue of fashion that she followed reverently, though always, perhaps, some few paces in the rear. A severe wetting might so alter the shape of that frame as to make it for ever unwearable. Her coat was serge—short, ending at the waist; the feather boa that clung round her neck, they would inevitably suffer without protection. For the moment she felt angry with herself. She hoped almost, since he was there, that he would make his offer again. It is these little things—the saving of a feather boa, the destruction of a flimsy hat frame—that are the seed of big issues. Every book, as is this, is in its way a study in the evolution of a crisis, the germ of tiny incident which through a thousand stages grows in strength and magnitude until it takes upon itself the stature of some giant event.

The thought of her clothes that had entered Sally's mind brought her one step further, prepared her for the silent permission she gave him, when he took the vacant seat beside her and shared the umbrella between them.

"By the time you reached Hammersmith," he said, "you know you'd be soaked."

"It wouldn't be the first time," she replied.

"Probably not—but it might be the last."

"How?"

"Influenza—pneumonia—congestion of the lungs—of such are the kingdom of heaven."

She looked at him quickly—that sudden look of one who for a moment sees into another and a new mind, as passing some strange house, you look with curious surprise through the unexpectedly opened door into another's life. The glance was as quick, as little comprehensive. Just as within that strange house you see schemes of colour that you would never have thought of, furniture and pictures that are not of your taste at all, so Sally saw for one brief moment the glimpse of a mind that could casually make a jest of death and holy-written things. A great deal of that servile obedience to the religion in which she had been brought up had been driven out of her by hard work. You might not get the priesthood to admit it, but religion is a luxury which few of the hard-workers in this world can afford. But she still maintained that sense of conventional awe which strict religious training drives deep into a receptive mind.

"Do you think it amusing to speak like that?" she asked.

"Like what?"

"What you said—the sentence that you quoted?"

"Of such are the kingdom of heaven?"

"Yes."

"Well—I don't think it's the best joke I've ever made—but it was meant to be amusing."

At this, she laughed—laughed in spite of herself. His absolute inconsequence was in itself humorous. She snatched a swift glance at him under cover of a pretence to look behind her. As her eyes returned, she was conscious that she was interested.

He was clean shaven. The lines were hard about his mouth, cutting character—the chin was strong, the jaw well-moulded. It was not a type of face that belonged to the class in which she moved. These men were of the unreliable type—some definite weakness somewhere in every face. So far as she could see in that one sudden glance, this man had none. His face dominated, his voice too. The hardness of his features carried with it a sense of cruelty; but a woman is seldom thwarted by that.

Then returned again the spirit of adventure. By the peculiar inconsequence of his conversation, he had succeeded in driving timidity from her. No man whom she knew would, in the first moments of acquaintance, have spoken as he did. The fact of that alone was an interest in itself. This was an adventure. Again she thrilled to it. The unexpectedness of the whole affair, this riding homewards on the top of a 'bus with a man who had come out of nowhere into her life—even if it were only for a few moments. Would not many another girl in her position be delighted with the experience? That thought warmed her to a greater appreciation of the situation.

But why had he been waiting outside the door of the office? Why had he followed her? How had he known that she was employed in the exacting services of Bonsfield & Co.? All these questions gyrated wildly in her mind, swept about, confused at finding no plausible answers to their importunate demands.

Then, lastly, who was he? There are men who suggest to you

that they must be somebody; there is an air of distinction about them that glosses the cheapest coat and creases the poorest pair of trousers. If they are poorly dressed, then it must be that they are masquerading; if their clothes are well-fitting, then it is only what you would have expected. It makes for no definite confirmation of your opinion.

Sally was made conscious of this impression, and, in its way, that thrilled her too. You have little chance with a woman in this world if you are a nonentity. Personality inevitably wins its way, and, in that she was susceptible to the personality of the man beside her, Sally forgot the circumstances of their acquaintance, forgot to review them with that same impartial judgment which she would have exercised had the man conveyed to her mind a more commonplace impression.

Stung then with curiosity to know how he had heard of her, how he had come to be waiting in King Street until she should leave off her work, or whether, as she suspected, it were only that he had been attracted to her as she passed by, she gave herself away with unconscious ingenuousness.

"Why were you waiting in King Street?" she asked suddenly.

The words hurried, tumbling in a confusion of self-consciousness from her lips.

"Oh—you saw me there?" said he.

"Yes."

"You saw me when you passed?"

"Yes."

"Did you know I was walking behind you all the way to

E. Temple Thurston

Piccadilly Circus?"

"N—no—how should I?"

"You looked back once or twice."

"Did I?"

"Why do you want to know why I was waiting in King Street?"

"I don't want to know particularly."

"Shall I tell you?"

"Yes."

"I had seen you through the window—working at that ghastly typewriter—stood there for more than a quarter of an hour—down the street—waiting till you got sick of it. Then I was going to ask you to come and have tea with me—dinner if you'd liked. I wanted some one to talk to; I was going back to my rooms. When they're empty, a man's rooms can be the most godless—"

She stood up abruptly, striking her hat against the roof of the umbrella.

"Will you let me out, please?"

"But you told me you were going to Hammersmith. This is only Knightsbridge."

"I'm getting down here."

He stood up. "I've offended you," he said quietly.

"Did you imagine you would not?"

"No—I suppose I didn't—but I wasn't going to let that stop me from making your acquaintance. There's nothing to be sorry about. You were sick of things—I could see that through the window—so was I. Mayn't two human beings, who are sick of things, find something in common? You're really going?"

"Yes."

She curled her lip with contempt; but it had a smile behind it which he could not see.

"Shan't we see each other again?"

"Certainly not!"

She stood at the top of the steps waiting for the 'bus to stop. He looked up into her face and held her eyes.

"Then I apologize," he said willingly. "And don't be offended at what I'm going to say now."

She put her foot down on to the first step. "What is it?"

"I'll bet you ten pounds we don't. That is to say you win ten pounds if we do."

She laughed contemptuously in a breath and hurried down the steps.

# CHAPTER III

It is all very well to say that there have been movements towards the enfranchisement of women since before the Roman era; it is all very well to point out that these movements are periodical, almost as inevitable as the volcanic eruptions that belch out their volumes of running fire and die down again into peaceful submission: but when the whole vital cause is altered, when the intrinsic motive in the entrails of that vast crater is changed, it is no wise policy to say, "It will pass over—another two or three years and women will find, as they have always found before, that it is better to sit still and let others do the work."

It is the problem of population that is being worked out now, not the mere spontaneous and ephemeral struggle of a few dominating personalities.

It is well-nigh ludicrous to think that Sally Bishop—quiet, virtuous, chaste Sally Bishop, the very opposite of a revolutionary—is one in the ranks of a great army who are marching, they scarcely know whither, to a command they have scarcely heard, strained to a mighty endurance in a cause they scarcely understand. She seems too young to be of service, too frail to bear the hardships of the way. How can she stand out against the forced marches, the weary, sleepless camping at night?

There are going to be many in this great campaign who will drop exhausted from the ranks—many who, under cover of night, when the sentinel is drowsy at his post, will slip out into the darkness, weary of the fatigue, regardless of the consequences—a deserter from the cause that is so ill-understood. There are going to be many who, through a passing village where all is peace and contentment, will hear the tempting whisper of mutiny. What is the good of it all—to what does it lead, this endless forced march towards a vague encounter with the enemy who are never to be seen? If only they might pitch tents there and then—there and then dig trenches, make positions, occupy heights—put the rifle to the shoulder and fire—into hell if need be. But no—this endless, toilsome marching, marching—always onward, yet never at the journey's end.

Who blames them if they fall by the way? Even the sergeant of the division, passing their crumpled bodies by the roadside, becomes a hypocrite if he kicks them into an obedience of their orders. In his heart he might well wish to drop out as they have done. Who blames them, too, if they slink off, hiding behind any cover that will conceal their trembling bodies until the whole army has gone by?—who blames them if they sham illness, lameness, anything that may be put forward as an excuse to set them free?—who blames them if a wayside cottage offers them shelter and, taking it, they leave the other poor wretches to go on? Who blames them then? No one—no one with a heart could do so. The great tragedy lies in the fact that they are left to blame themselves.

And this—this is the way that Nature wages war—a civil war, that is the worst, the most harrowing of all. She fights her own kith and kin; she gives battle to the very conditions which she herself has made. There is very seldom a hand-to-hand encounter. Only your French Revolutions and your

E. Temple Thurston

Russian Massacres mark the spots where the two armies have met, where blood has flowed like wine from the broken goblets of some thousands of lives. But usually it is the forced marches, with the enemy ever retreating over its own ground. And in this position of women, it is the army of Nature that has begun to move. Not the mere rising of a rebellious faction, but the entire unconquerable force of humanity whose whole existence is threatened by the invading power of population.

And Sally Bishop—frail, tender-hearted, sensitive Sally Bishop—has donned the bandolier and the haversack and is off with the rest, just one unit in the rank and file, one slender individual in Nature's army that is out on a campaign to effect the inevitable change in the social conditions of the sex. It makes no matter that she will never reap the benefit; it counts not at all that she will never touch the spoil. The lines must be filled up. When she falls, there must be others to take her place. The bugle has sounded in the hearts of thousands of women of her type, and they have had to obey its shrilling call.

Stand for half an hour in the morning at any of the main termini of London's traffic-ways, and you will see them in their thousands. They little know the law they are obeying; they little realize the cause for which they are working, or the effect it will produce. In another book from this pen it has been declared that the words of Maeterlinck—"the spirit of the hive"—are an inspired phrase. Here, in these conditions, with no need to don the protecting gauze, you may see its vivid illustration, as only the great draughts-manship of life can illustrate the wondrous schemes of Nature.

For two years Sally Bishop had been one amongst them. For two years she had caught her tram at Kew Bridge in the morning and her tram again at Hammersmith at night. Only her Sundays and her Saturday afternoons were free, except for those two wonderful weeks in the summer and the yawning gaps in the side of the year which are known as National holidays.

When—where did the bugle sound that called Sally to her conscription? What press-gang of circumstances waylaid her, in what peaceful wandering of life, and bore her off to the service of her sex?

There is a little story attached to it—one of those slight, slender threads of incident that go to form a shadow here or a light there in the broad tapestry of the whole.

The Rev. Samuel Bishop was rector of the parish church in the little town of Cailsham, in Kent. This was Sally's father. There never was a meeker man; there never was a man more truly fitted with those characteristics of piety which are essentially and only Christian. With charity he was filled, though he had but little to bestow—his whole intellect was subordinated to his faith—and with the light of hope his little eyes glittered so long as one straw lay floating on the tide.

This is the man whom Christianity demands, and this the very man whom Christianity crushes like a slug under the heel. He is bound to be a failure—bound to hope too much, be blind with faith, and give, out of charity, with the witless hand that knows not where to bestow.

For ten years he had held the parish of Cailsham, fulfilling all his duties by that rule of thumb which is the refuge to all those lacking in initiative. Not one of the parishioners could find any fault with him, yet none bore him respect. They blinked through his services. During his deliberate intoning of the lessons, they thought of all their worldly affairs, and

E. Temple Thurston

while he preached, they slept.

Hundreds of parishes are served with men like the Rev. Samuel Bishop. It is half the decay of Christianity that the prospect of a fat living will induce men to adopt the profession of the Church. This is the irony of life in all religions, that to be kept going, to increase and multiply, they must be financially sound; yet as soon as that financial security is reached, you have men pouring into their offices who seek no more than a comfortable living.

There is only one true religion, the ministry of the head to the devotion of the heart. You need no priesthood here, but the priesthood of conscience; you need no costly erection of churches, but the open world of God's house of worship. There is no necessity for the training of voices, when the choir of Nature can sing in harmony as no voice ever sang. There is no call now for the two or three to gather together. The group system has had its day, has done its work. The two or three who gather together now, do so, not in a communion of mind, but in criticism and fear. Each knows quite well what the other is thinking of. Where is the necessity for one common prayer to bring their souls together? Their souls are already tearing at each other's throats.

You would not have found the Rev. Samuel Bishop agreeing to this. How could any man consent to give up his livelihood, even for the truth? This gentleman would have stayed on in his parish, happy in his hopeless incompetence, until his parishioners might have sent in a third request for his retirement, had not the irony of circumstance broken him upon its unyielding anvil.

For ten years, as has been said, he had held the rectorship of the parish of Cailsham. Sally was then fourteen years of age.

Her mother, one of those hard yet well-featured women upon whom the struggle of life wears with but little ill-effect, had endeavoured to bring her up in the first belief of social importance consistent, to an illogical mind, with the teachings of her husband's calling. But she had failed. It was grained in the nature of Sally to let the morrow take thought for the things of itself. The other three children, the boy up at Oxford, the two girls, one older, the other younger than Sally, were different. With them she succeeded. Into their minds she instilled the knowledge that, of all professions, the Church takes the highest rank in the social scale, and though in the world itself they might have found that hard to believe, yet in the little town of Cailsham Mrs. Bishop had discovered her capacity for draining from her husband's parishioners a certain social deference and respect.

By persuading the Rev. Samuel to utilize his priestly influence upon the declining years of an old lady of title in the neighbourhood, Mrs. Bishop had stolen her way into the very best society which Cailsham had to offer. And Sally was the only one of her children who did not thoroughly appreciate it.

With what deftness she had induced her husband to make his spiritual ministrations indispensable to the tottering vitality of Lady Bray; with what cunning she herself had persuaded the old woman to be present at her garden parties over the last five years, though the poor creature was nothing but the head of death and the bones of decay, barely kept together by the common support of her clothes, it would be almost impossible to imagine. But to entertain Lady Bray; to be even a friend of her ladyship was, in Cailsham in those days, a key to the secret chamber of social success. And Mrs. Bishop held it.

The Rev. Samuel himself gave her ladyship a copy of the

Holy Bible, bound in the best Russian leather, with various texts marked, which had never failed to bring her comfort when intoned in the meek monotony of his gentle voice. On the fly-leaf he had inscribed her name—Lady Bray, from her devoted friend and rector, Samuel Bishop.

On Sundays it was quite a feature of the Communion Service to see the state and ceremony with which the Holy Eucharist was carried down the aisle to the Bray's family pew, where the old lady sat, huddled and alone in one of the corners, like a dead body covered clumsily with a black pall. One of the parishioners, who had not that good fortune of being personally acquainted with Lady Bray declared that she really almost objected to this invariable interruption of the service.

"I assure you," she said, "it—it practically amounts to a procession like they have in the Roman Catholic Church."

It was this lady who—whenever the occasion demanded, which was not often—bracketed in a breath Roman Catholics and unfortunate women of the street, and alluded to them jointly as—poor creatures.

To be able to say this, and feel that one is daring convention by one's breadth of mind, is no uncommon standard of Christian intelligence.

But all this dutiful attention to Lady Bray availed the Rev. Samuel nothing. On the anvil of circumstances he was broken, as in the smithy the red-hot metal is bent and severed as though it were but clay.

After ten years' faithful, if somewhat incompetent service, in the parish of Cailsham, the Rev. Samuel Bishop was requested to accept the chaplaincy at some distant Union. It was in this manner that his downfall came about.

E. Temple Thurston

# CHAPTER IV

It was Easter Sunday. The vicar of the little parish of Steynton, just outside Maidstone, was away for his holidays, and the Rev. Samuel Bishop had taken his place as *locum tenens*.

In the small church where the parishioners met every Sunday, it had been the custom for some time past for an earnest and well-known member of the congregation, who had an appreciation for the sound of his own voice, to read the lessons at Matins and at Evensong. This duty, combined with that of warden, was fulfilled by Mr. Windle, an ardent church-goer, a staunch, if somewhat narrow-visioned Christian, and a man rigid in his adherence to the cause of total abstinence.

Before morning service on this Easter Sunday, he met the Rev. Samuel Bishop in the vestry. The organist had already gone to his seat behind the chancel. The first preliminary notes of the voluntary—weak and uncertain, because the organ-blower had come late and as yet there was not sufficient wind in the bellows—were beginning to sound through the building. The two men were alone.

"I should like to know," Sally's father was saying, in his quiet, apologetic voice, "how many people you generally expect to communicate on Easter Sunday. The wine, you know. I want to know how much wine to pour out."

His face twitched as he waited for the answer. It seemed as if some unseen fingers were alternately pinching the flabby flesh of his cheeks, then as swiftly letting it go.

Mr. Windle made a mental calculation, delivering his estimation of the number with a voice confident of his accuracy.

"Sixty," he said. "Not less—possibly more."

"That will take a lot of wine."

"There's plenty in that cupboard," said Mr. Windle.

The gentle rector reverently opened the cupboard and examined it.

"Oh yes; there is enough," he said. He held up a black bottle to the light, and blinked at it short-sightedly. "I—I only wanted to make sure," he added; "it is apt to make one somewhat apprehensive, when one is officiating in a strange church—apprehensive, if you understand what I mean, of any hitch in the service."

"Quite so," said Mr. Windle, sympathetically. He extracted a small, white, potash throat lozenge from the pocket of his waistcoat, and placed it on his tongue. In another twenty-five minutes from that moment he would be reading the lessons. The lozenge would be dissolved and swallowed by that time, and the beneficial effect upon his throat complete when he was ready to begin.

"The bishop is holding early Communion in Maidstone this

E. Temple Thurston

morning," he said, when the lozenge had settled into its customary place in his mouth.

"So I heard," said Mr. Bishop. "What a charming man his lordship is."

"You know him?" asked Mr. Windle in surprise.

"Well—slightly."

"He is doing us the honour of dining with us to-day after morning service. We always dine in the middle of the day on Sundays—only Sundays, of course."

"Indeed?" said the Rev. Samuel, in reference to the first part of Mr. Windle's sentence.

"My wife and I will be pleased if you will come."

Mr. Bishop's face twitched with pleasure. He saw the opportunity of becoming better acquainted with his lordship; of mentioning one or two little alterations in his own parish which he had conceived and approved of, entirely on his own initiative.

"I shall be delighted," he replied—"delighted. Sixty I think you said?" he added, as he commenced to pour the wine into the silver altar jug.

"If not more," replied the other, departing to take his place in the Windle family pew.

Mr. Bishop was left in the vestry, apportioning out sixty separate quantities of wine—quantities, which he deemed would be sufficient to seem appreciable to the palates, spiritual and physical, of those for whom they were intended.

You can see him, tilting up the neck of the black bottle sixty consecutive times, with no sense of the ludicrous. Sixty—when meted out, it did not seem quite so much as he had expected. The silver wine-ewer was only a little more than half full. Supposing there were not enough. He would have to go over the consecration part of the service again. That would make them very late. The bishop might be annoyed if he were kept waiting for his dinner. His lordship was a rigid Churchman, inclined to be somewhat High Church in his ideas. It was certain that food would not have passed his lips since the previous night. It would be a pity to find the Bishop annoyed, just when he had the opportunity of speaking to him about those little alterations of his own invention, which he felt sure would raise him in his lordship's estimation.

Perhaps it would be wiser to add a little more wine. It was Easter Sunday. Many members of the congregation were farmers and farm labourers. He had vivid remembrances in his mind of having forcibly to take the cup from the lips of such as these. They meant no irreverence by it, of course. He imagined it to be habit in great part with them, and a smile flickered over his face as the thought crossed his mind.

Yes—certainly, he had better add a little more wine—just a little. If there were some over, why, naturally it would have to be consumed. Wine once consecrated must not be kept. There is that fear that it might become an object of worship, than which no other thought can seem more fearsome to the Anglican mind. He might have to drink it; but there would only be a little in any case; yet, not being accustomed, with the poor stipend which he received, to the taste of such luxuries, it might perhaps—it might—well, so little as there would be, could scarcely lift his spirits. And if it did, could that really be considered a harmful result? On mature consideration, he thought it better to add a little more wine. It would save them from the contingency of a longer service

E. Temple Thurston

than was already necessary. He poured in the little more, and the silver jug was now a little more than three parts full.

Mr. Windle's lozenge was well dissolved and swallowed before the anthem was finished, and the service went through without a break. The Rev. Samuel preached one of the sermons which he had written in his younger days for the season of Easter. He bade his congregation raise their heads and begin life again with new vigour, new hope in their hearts, for this was the third day, the day their Lord had risen for their salvation. It was, he said, both the day of promise and the day of fulfilment. The anticipation of meeting the bishop flashed across his mind as he said it. He felt sure that his lordship would approve of his little alterations.

When the last voluntary had been played, the reverend gentleman sat in his chair by the altar and watched the congregation filing out of the church. A great many seemed to be departing, but it was impossible to tell as yet the number that remained. Mr. Windle had been so very definite, so confident in his assertion of the number of communicants. He looked at his watch. The service had taken longer than usual. He stood up before they had all gone and poured out the wine into the chalices. From where he had been sitting it was impossible to see those sides of the church that formed the cross upon which the foundations had been laid, and so, though only a few people remained in the centre aisle, he felt no cause for uneasiness. Mr. Windle had been well assured, and he ought to know.

It was when he stood waiting for the communicants to approach the altar and saw all the church empty itself into the chancel like a stream which has been dammed and is set free, that he realized his mistake.

There were not more than twenty people, and with his own

willing and ready hands he had consecrated all the wine which he had poured out into the vessel in the vestry. What was the meaning of it? Why had Mr. Windle told him sixty, or more, when scarcely twenty attended?

He stood waiting in the vestry afterwards with the well-filled chalice in his hand, tremulously anticipating Mr. Windle's arrival. His face was twitching spasmodically. The unseen fingers were busy. They never left him alone.

*"It shall not be carried out of the church, but the priest and such others of the communicants as he shall call unto him shall, immediately after the blessing, reverently eat and drink the same."*

So it alluded in the rubric of the Book of Common Prayer to the leaving over of consecrated wine. In the mind of the Rev. Samuel, Mr. Windle was that other communicant.

"What shall I do?" he began, directly the devout warden entered.

Mr. Windle was beaming with good nature. He had just been talking to a lady—the last to leave the church—who had told him that he had read the lessons with great feeling; and, while he despised all emotion as sacrilegious in the precincts of God's house of worship, he liked to be thought capable of it.

Seeing the cup in Mr. Bishop's hand and the dismayed expression on that gentleman's countenance, he smiled.

"This has to be—be finished," said the distraught clergyman.

"Ah, I'm sorry about that," replied Mr. Windle, easily. "Under ordinary circumstances, there would have been as many as I said; but I understand that a lot of people attended early Communion at the bishop's service in Maidstone. You see, it is not often that he comes, and they like to have his lordship."

"But this is consecrated wine."

"Ah—well—there's not much, I suppose. Is there?"

Mr. Windle looked casually into the chalice. "Oh, there is a good deal. What are you going to do?"

"I shall have to call upon you for your assistance."

"Mine?"

"Yes; I couldn't drink all this myself. I'm not accustomed to taking wine. As much as this would—I am afraid—go to my head." His face was now twitching convulsively. "Especially on a—a somewhat—empty stomach."

"But it's no good asking me," said Mr. Windle.

"Why not? You have just been a communicant? Under extraordinary circumstances like this, I am expected to call upon some one who has communicated, reverently, to assist me."

"Ah, yes; that is all very well—so long as you do not enforce any one whom you may choose to break their own most rigid principles. I'm a total abstainer, you see. Even—er—at the altar—I—I—only permit the wine to touch my tongue, as I hold every communicant should do. But you want me actually to drink this. As much liquid as, I assure you, I should take with a meal. Again, I have taken the pledge—"

"But, my dear Mr. Windle, in such an exceptional circumstance as this—"

"I have openly taken the pledge," Mr. Windle repeated conclusively—"I'm very sorry. I'm afraid, too, that the sacristan has gone. But I think the organ blower was there when I came in; I fancy I heard him."

"Ah, yes; but he was not at Communion."

"Of course not—then I'm sorry. I shall be sure to see some one who was, and I'll send them along. We shall see you up at the house soon. Don't be long—you'll forgive my going on ahead, but I'm afraid his lordship may have arrived already. I'll send you any one if I see them. And I'm bound to meet somebody. They haven't been gone very long."

He had gone. The Rev. Samuel was left alone with the half-filled goblet of noxious wine in his hand. For some moments he continued to stand in the same position, looking down into the crimson depth of liquid that lay, scintillating lazily, in the silver bowl.

At last he raised it to his lips and sipped it—once, twice, three times. Then he waited. "Wine to make glad the heart of man." The words came to his mind. Wine was a terrible power, a fascinating evil. He thanked God that he had never fallen a prey to its fascinations. This wine was very sweet. He liked sweet things. Once he had tasted champagne when dining at the house of Lady Bray. He had thought that disagreeable, though at the moment he had murmured that it was excellent wine; but he had been unable to understand how any man could take of that more than was good for him. This wine, of course, that they used in the church was infinitely more palatable. But how could he possibly drink all this? It was out of the question. He prayed devoutly that

E. Temple Thurston

Mr. Windle would soon find him relief and send some one.

He took another sip and waited, noticing that already there were slight signs of diminution in the contents of the chalice. Then he thought of the bishop. It was possible that his lordship might notice the scent of it in his breath if he took it all. They would be sure to be talking together about his little alterations; and if the bishop were to notice it, it would be disastrous. He looked at his watch. It was already almost the time that they were supposed to sit down to dinner. Oh! why did not Mr. Windle find some one and bring him release from this torture of mind?

He walked to the cupboard where the bottle of wine was kept. Perhaps it would be better to pour it back—really better in the end. They would be waiting dinner for him. He knew that the bishop would be annoyed. It might be better to pour it back.

Then all the force of dogma rose before him like a phoenix from the ashes of his lower nature. This was consecrated wine! He had consecrated it with his own hands at the altar of God, for one purpose and one purpose only—to be consumed by those who believed in the body and blood of Christ. To pour it back again into the bottle of unconsecrated wine—that would be sacrilege! Why had Mr. Windle been so narrow-minded about his foolish pledge of total abstinence? How foolish some good people were! How bigoted! He felt assured that Mr. Windle was a good man; but again, there was no doubt about his being narrow-minded. Ah, why did he not send some one!

Mr. Bishop walked to the door of the vestry that opened on to the little country lane. He looked out. There was no trace of the devout warden. Only a man, carefully dressed, with black leather leggings encasing his legs from knees to the boot-tops—seemingly the type of clerk in a country town— was coming up the lane. A thought flew into the clergyman's head. He beckoned to him. The man quickened his steps and came up to the door.

In the space of two minutes, with nervous, hurried voice, the Rev. Samuel had told him of his predicament. The man looked on amazed, but said nothing.

"Now, have you just come from Communion?" he asked at the conclusion of his explanation.

"Me?" said the man. "No."

"Then I must entreat you to let me read that part of the service to you—I assure you it won't take long—that is necessitated by the taking of the wine. You see I must institute you as a communicant. You are of course a—a Protestant?" he added in sudden afterthought.

"Me?" said the man. "No."

Mr. Bishop stood up dismayed.

"Not a Protestant?" he exclaimed in wonder.

"No, why should I be? Nor anything else. Don't believe in it, 'specially if it can put gentlemen in such a position as you're in now. I'll drink the wine for you if you like. I see no harm in that. I'll drink it reverently too—I don't want to hurt your feelings. But you can't expect me to take it for granted that it ain't nothin' else but what it is—just the juice out of the grape, don't yer know. You see, I know what I'm talking about. I'm a chauffeur now, but I used to be in a brewery— see?"

E. Temple Thurston

"Thank you," said Mr. Bishop bitterly, sarcastically; "but you can be of no service to me." He retired, closing the door and saying "Thank you" again, in the same tone of voice.

When he found himself alone once more in the vestry he took another sip of wine. The sentiments which that man had expressed were half rankling in his mind. They made him feel careless, reckless. He did not really think of what he was doing. He took another sip—it was most palatable—and another—it was certainly very good to the taste. With the little food that he had taken that day, he felt it warm within him. It was considerably more than half-finished now. He waited again, and really he felt no bad effects.

Once more he looked at his watch. They were actually sitting down to dinner now. He walked down the floor of the vestry and back again, and his steps were quite steady; so he took another sip. Then he breathed into his open hand held up against his face—as he had once seen an undergraduate do at Oxford—but he could detect no perfume of the wine in his breath. Possibly it would be all right. And he was looking forward so intensely to meeting the bishop. He felt that he would be able to convince him of the need for his little alterations.

Once again he looked into the cup. Then he finished the wine at a draught—elbow tilted at an angle on a level with his head—and hurriedly put the chalice away.

It was done now. And he felt quite all right. He began to take off his surplice, and when he trod on the end of it and stumbled a little, it seemed quite a natural accident. He smiled—laughed even, but very gently—at the fears he had entertained. Evidently he must have a very good head to be able to take so much wine. His hat dropped from his hand as he was raising it to his head; but that was nothing. It was quite a simple thing to stoop and pick it up again. If a man were intoxicated he could not do that. He would probably fall. Mr. Bishop only knocked his elbow against the vestry table as he stood upright.

He looked round the room. Was everything put away? What a delightful service that was at morning prayer on Easter day. It was quite true what he had said in his sermon—this was a day of promise, of good hope. He felt that within himself.

Ah! the cupboard that contained the bottle of wine had not been locked. He walked across to it, quite steadily, perhaps a little slowly. The bottle was there all right. How much had they used of it? He remembered that it had been full to the base of the neck. Now? He took it out and looked at it. It was more than half empty! He had practically consumed half a bottle of strongly intoxicating wine! How could he be sober? He laughed. He heard the laugh within himself, as though he were standing by, a spectator to his own actions. Then he knew he was drunk. He said so—to himself—aloud.

"I'm drunk."

At that instant the door of the vestry opened, and in walked Mr. Windle, followed by the bishop. They saw him there, standing with gently swaying movements by the cupboard, with the black bottle of wine in his hands.

"Mr. Bishop," said the warden, "I have brought his lordship to your assistance. I could find no one on my way home."

The Rev. Samuel put down the bottle and bowed uncertainly.

"I'm afraid it's too late," he said humbly.

The two men looked at him with growing suspicion, then his

E. Temple Thurston

lordship said in austere tones, "So I should imagine, Mr. Bishop." He turned to his companion. "Shall we get back to dinner, Mr. Windle?"

They moved to the vestry door.

"Mr. Bishop," he said, turning round as they departed, "I would advise you to go back quietly to the vicarage."

Then the door closed and the little man sat down upon the nearest form. The bishop would never hear of his little alterations now; he would never think well of them, even if he did.

He burst into tears, and for some moments sat there with his head buried in his hands. Then he looked up, saw the bread which also had been kept over from the service, and, reaching forward, began pathetically to put the little squares one by one into his mouth.

# CHAPTER V

That incident in itself is sufficient. There is no need to lead a way down the steps that brought the Rev. Samuel Bishop to his final degradation and ultimate death. The generous offer of the chaplaincy of a small union, the withdrawal of his son from Oxford, the dismissal of the tutelary services of the lady who had charge of his daughter's education, the replacing of a better man in the rectory at Cailsham—all these stages of the little tragedy have no intimate importance in themselves, except that they formed the first evolutionary periods of the development of Sally's life. These were the press-gang of circumstances that forced her into the service of her sex; these, the shrilling calls of the bugle that bid her strap the haversack to her slender shoulders and march out to war against the sea of trouble.

In a living and moving institution such as the Christian Church, you cannot afford to be lenient to incompetency. And the Rev. Samuel was incompetent. There is no doubt about that.

In such circumstances as these, assuming them up to the point where the obliging chauffeur had found the door closed in his face, a competent man would have lifted reason above his faith. Calmly, he would have told himself, as did the chauffeur, "This is the juice of the grape; it is in nowise

E. Temple Thurston

altered in composition because these hands of mine—which have done many things—have been laid upon it. It is better to mix it again with unconsecrated wine, than pour it down the sacrilegious throat of an unbelieving chauffeur; I will put it back in the bottle."

So a competent man would have acted, presuming that he had ever allowed himself to be so far caught in such a predicament. But the Rev. Samuel was too fully possessed of that first characteristic of faith, which the Christian Church demands. It only argues that you must take no man absolutely at his word, even when he presumes to speak, inspired with the voice of God. Nothing has yet been written, nothing has yet been said, which can be made to apply without deviation to the law of change, and also indiscriminately of persons.

And so, for this unswerving faith of the Rev. Samuel, Sally Bishop is made to suffer. Very shortly after the removal from Cailsham, she made her declaration of independence.

"Mother," she said, one morning at breakfast, "I'm going to earn my own living." The baby lines of her mouth set tight, and her chin puckered.

Mrs. Bishop laid down her piece of toast. "I wish you wouldn't talk nonsense, Sally," she said.

The young man down from Oxford ejaculated—

"Rot!"

"It's not rot—it's not nonsense!"

Her voice was petulant; there were tears in it. It was not a decision of strength. Here the press-gang was at work driving the unwilling conscript. She was going; there was no doubt about her going; but it was a hard struggle to feel resigned.

"But it *is* nonsense," said Mrs. Bishop.

"How do you think *you* could earn your living?" said the young man. He knew something about the matter; he was trying to find employment himself—he, a 'Varsity man—and as yet nothing had offered itself. "If I can't get anything to do," he added sententiously, "how on earth do you think you're going to?"

"She doesn't mean it," said Sally's eldest sister. "She only thinks it sounds self-sacrificing."

"Is that the kindest thing you can think of?" asked Sally. "I do mean it. I've written to London and I've got the prospectus here of one of the schools for teaching shorthand and typewriting. For eight pounds they guarantee to make any one proficient in both—suitable to take a secretaryship. Doesn't matter how long you'll stay; they agree for that sum to make you proficient, and they also half promise to get you a situation."

"And where are you going to get the eight pounds from?" said her little sister.

"And where are you going to get the cost of your living up in Town?" asked the wise young man, who knew how London could dissolve the money in one's pocket.

"Oh, she's all right there," said the eldest sister bitterly. "I know what she's thinking about. She's going to draw that money that grandmama left her—that fifty pounds. I guessed she'd spend that on herself one of these days."

"And who else was it left to?" asked Sally.

"Yes, my dear child," said her mother; "we know it was left to you, of course; but since we came away from Cailsham"— her mouth pursed; she admirably conveyed the effort of controlling her emotions—the lump in the throat, the hasty swallowing and the blinking eyes—"since we left Cailsham, I'd sometimes hoped—"

"Of course you had, mater," said the young man sympathetically.

"But I'm going to relieve you of all responsibility," said Sally. "I'm no longer going to be an expense to you, and I'm going to do it with my own money—the money I was given and the money I make. I can't see what right you have to think me selfish—all of you—as I know you do. I'm no more selfish than you who expect me to spend the money on you; in fact, I'm less selfish. It's my money."

This, in a word, is the spirit, the attitude of mind that is entering into the mental composition of women. They are becoming conscious of their personality. That phrase may be cryptic; without consideration it may convey but little; yet it sums up the whole movement, is the very moon itself to the turning tide. The woman who once becomes conscious of her own personality is in a fair way towards her own enfranchisement. Away go the fettering conventions of home life, the chains of social hypocrisy are flung aside. She rides out into the open air like the bird from the shattered cage, and if man, the marksman, does not bring her to earth before her fluttering wings are fully spread, then she is off—up into the deep, blue zenith of liberty!

"I'm no more selfish than you who expect me to spend the money on you; in fact, I'm less selfish. It's my money."

In that definite assertion, Sally first expressed the realization of her own personality. The girl of twenty years ago would have sacrificed her little dowry upon the family altar without a word; she would, without complaint, have allowed it to be spent upon her brother's education. But now we are dealing with modernity, and out of the quiet country lanes, from the sacred hearth of the peaceful home-circles, this army of women are rising. Who has taught them? No one knows. Who has inspired them with the vitality of action? No one can say. The spirit of the hive is at work within them; already they are swarming in obedience to the silent command. Pick out a hundred girls as they go to work in the city, and ask them why they are toiling from one day to another. They will all—or ninety-nine of them—give you the same answer—

"I didn't want to stay at home. I prefer to be independent."

There lies the heart of it, the realization of the ego in the personality.

Sally had her own way. In the face of abuse, in the face of reproach, she packed her leather trunk. All those little idols of sentiment, the clock that ticked on her mantelshelf, the pictures that hung on the walls; the books she had collected, even the copy of Browning that she did not understand— they all were stowed away into the leather trunk. She went out of the house, she went out of the home as a moth flies out of a darkened room, and you know that unless you kindle a light to lure it back, it will never return. They knew they could never kindle the light. They knew she would never come back. What love had they to offer as an inducement? And no love of her relations is an inducement to the woman who is seeking her own.

Only the Rev. Samuel shed tears over her. She came into his study one morning after breakfast to say good-bye. He was

E. Temple Thurston

writing a new sermon for the season of Easter, and his mind was raking up the past as a man unearths some buried thing that the mould has rotted.

The sunlight was pouring in through the window as he bent over his desk nursing thoughts that were vermin in his brain.

"You're going, Sally?" he said.

"Yes, father."

He stood up from his chair and looked at her—looked her up and down as though he wished the sight of her to last in his memory for the rest of his life.

"What time do you get to London?"

"Half-past one."

"And you've arranged about where you're going to stay?"

"Yes, I'm going to share rooms with Miss Hallard—"

"The girl who's going to be an artist?"

"Yes; she has lodgings near Kew."

"Ah, Kew. Yes, Kew. I remember walking from Kew to Richmond, along by the gardens, when I was quite a young man. So you're going there, Sally?" His eyes still roamed over her.

"Yes, father. What are you doing? Are you writing a sermon?"

That little interest in his own affairs awakened him.

Animation crept into his eyes. It was the slight, subtle touch that a woman knows how to bestow.

"Yes, I'm writing a sermon, Sally, for next Sunday—Easter Sunday—listen to this—" In the pride of composition, having none but her who would appreciate his efforts, he took up one of the papers with almost trembling hands.

"There can be no hope without promise, and in the rising of our Lord from the dead, we have the promise of everlasting life. For just as He, on that Sabbath morning, defied the prison walls of the sepulchre, and was lifted beyond earthly things to those things that are spiritual, so shall we, if we defy the things of this world—its pomps and its vanities and all the sinful lusts of the flesh—so shall we win to the things that are eternal rather than those which are temporal and void."

He looked up at her, waiting eagerly for the words of her approval to convince him of what he was scarcely convinced himself. Before she could utter them, Mrs. Bishop entered the room.

"Samuel," she said, "I've written my letter to Lady Bray. I've asked her to come on the seventeenth. You'd better write yours and enclose it with mine. You know what to say. I mean you know what sort of thing she likes from you. I've also written and asked the Colles's to come to dinner on the eighteenth to meet her. They're sure to accept if they know they're going to meet her, and I think they ought to be useful. Write your letter now, will you?"

The Rev. Samuel nodded assent. "I will," he added.

Then he turned to his daughter. "Good-bye, Sally."

She put her hands on his shoulders—knowing all his frailty—and kissed him. Then she walked out of the room.

When she had closed the door, the clergyman sat down again to his desk and read again through the sentences he had read to Sally.

"I suppose she didn't think it very true," he said to himself, "but it is—it is true—its pomps and its vanities, ah—"

Then he took out a sheet of note-paper, and picking up his pen, he began—

"My dear Lady Bray—"

# CHAPTER VI

When Sally stepped off the 'bus at Knightsbridge on that November evening, her mind was seething with indignation.

To lay a wager! It was an insult! Did he think her acquaintance was to be bought for a sum of money? It would not be long before he found out his mistake. And what a sum! Ten pounds! It was ridiculous! What man would spend all that money simply upon the mere making of an acquaintance? Of course she knew that if ever she did speak to him again, he would never pay it. It was quite safe to boast like that—it was a boast. Ten pounds! Why with ten pounds she could buy a real silk petticoat, a new frock, a new hat, another feather boa—all of the most expensive too, and still have money in her pocket.

All the amiable and interested impressions that she had obtained of him went when he made that bet. It was so easy to boast—so cheap. But if he thought that the sound of that sum of money had impressed her, he would learn his mistake.

She caught another 'bus on to Hammersmith and tried vainly to forget all about it.

Miss Hallard was home from the School of Art before her. In

E. Temple Thurston

the bedroom which they shared in a house on Strand-on-Green, she was combing out her short hair, her blouse discarded, her thin arms bent at acute angles, and between her lips a Virginian cigarette.

"Wet?" she said laconically, without turning round.

"Dripping." Sally threw her hat on the bed.

"If you bought umbrellas instead of cheap silk petticoats—"

"I knew you'd say that," said Sally.

"Was it raining when you walked from the tram?"

"No. It's stopped now. But it was up in town, and all the 'buses were full up inside."

"Cheerful," said Miss Hallard.

She twisted her hair into some sort of shape and secured it indiscriminately with pins.

This girl is the revolutionary. Hers is the type that has been the revolutionary through all ages. It will be revolutionary to the end, no matter what force may be in power. She has little or nothing to do with the class to which Sally Bishop belongs. Her temperament is the corrective which Nature always uses for the natural functions of her own handi-work—Sally Bishop is Nature herself, enlisted into this civil warfare because she must. In her revolutionary ideas, Miss Hallard follows the temperament of her inclinations. Whatever position women might hold, she would have disagreed with it. She is one of those of whom—like some strange animal that one sees, following instincts which seem the very reverse to Nature's needs—one wonders what her place in the scheme of things can be.

Of this type are those whom the straining of a vocabulary has called—Suffragette. They are merely Nature's correctives. Of definite change in the position of women they will effect nothing. They are not regulars in the great army; only the wandering adventurers who take up arms for any cause, that they may be in the noise of the battle. It is the paid army— the regular troops—who finally place the standard upon the enemy's heights; for it is only the forces of Life itself that, in this life, are unconquerable.

This, then, is Miss Hallard—adventuress in a great philosophy. Her thin lips, her shifting, disconcerting eyes, set deep beneath the brows; the long and narrow face, the high forehead on which the hair hangs heavily; that thin, reedy body, that ill-formed, unnatural breast which never was meant to suckle a child or nurse the drooping of a man's head—all these are the signs of her calling. A woman—by the irony of a fate that has thwarted the original design of Nature.

Sally Bishop is a woman before everything. Miss Hallard is a woman last of all. How these two, in their blatant contrasts, were brought together, is an example of one of those mysterious forces in the great machinery of life which we are unable to comprehend. It is like the harnessing of electricity to the needs of civilization. We can make it do what we will; but of what it is, we know nothing. So we are just as ignorant of that law which governs the contact of personalities. It cannot be luck; it cannot be chance. There is too much method in the mad tumble of it all, too much plot and counter-plot, too much cunning intent—which even we can appreciate—for us to think that it has no meaning. Why, the very wind that blows has its assured direction and carries the pollen of this flower to the heart of that.

E. Temple Thurston

But there is no need to understand it. The thing happens—that is all. Miss Janet Hallard and Sally are intimates; that is really sufficient.

Yet they were not really intimate enough as yet for Sally to sit down on the bed directly she came into the room and break into an excited description of her adventure. She knew the cold look of inquiry in Janet's eyes. She could foresee the disconcerting questions that would be asked. Janet's questions, coming dryly—all on one note—from those thin lips of hers, drove sometimes to a point that was almost too deep for Sally's comprehension. And Sally is a woman of sex, not of intellect.

"You can have the glass now if you want it," said Janet, moving away to her bed.

Sally rose wearily and began to take off her things.

"I am fagged!" she exclaimed.

Janet said nothing. The blue lines under Sally's eyes, that indescribable drawing of the flesh of those round cheeks, had told her that long ago.

Sally gazed at herself in the glass. "Look at my eyes!" she exclaimed.

"I know."

"Awful, aren't they?"

"Pretty bad. Can't think why you don't stick out for more money when they work you overtime."

"It's no good—they'd get somebody else."

"Let 'em."

"Well then, what should I do?"

"Go on the stage."

Sally looked critically at herself again in the little mahogany-framed glass that stood on the dressing-table. With an effort she tried to forget the lines under the eyes, tried to efface the look of weariness. The thought of being an actress did not enter her thoughts. It was her appearance she considered.

"Do you think I look well enough?" she asked.

"Fifty per cent. of them are a good deal worse in those musical comedies."

"How much should I get?"

"Two pounds a week."

"That's as much as you."

"Yes; but you'd have to work for it. I don't."

"Oh yes; but what sort of work? Nothing to typewriting."

"Perhaps not. But they'd probably expect more than work out of you."

"What do you mean?"

"Well, when a stage manager gives an unknown girl a walk on in the chorus of a musical comedy, he looks upon it in the light of a favour. I suppose it is too. He puts her in the way of knowing a lot of well-to-do young men, and he pays her two pounds a week for doing nothing but look pretty under the most advantageous circumstances. There are women who would pay to get a job like that."

Sally's face puckered with disgust. "I think life's beastly," she said.

Janet smiled. "That's not life," she said; "that's musical comedy."

Then she lit another cigarette and sat there, watching Sally take off her wet clothes; smiled at her, catching the garments with the tips of her fingers, and shuddering when they touched her skin.

"You're too sensitive for this business, Sally," she said at last. "You're too romantic. Why don't you get married?"

"I wish I could," said Sally.

"Well, you don't take your chances."

"What chances?"

"Mr. Arthur—"

They both laughed. Mr. Arthur Montagu was a bank clerk, lodging in the same house on Strand-on-Green. He had had the same room for over three years and had, through various stages of acquaintanceship, come to be addressed by the landlady as Mr. Arthur.

For the first few weeks after the arrival of Sally and Janet, he had chosen to take his meals in the kitchen—where all meals were served—after they had finished. His, was a bed-sitting-room, the only one the house contained, and, in social status, the possession of it lifted him in rank above any of the other lodgers who shared the general sitting-room with the land-lady, Mrs. Hewson, and her husband.

But one evening, Sally and he had returned together from Hammersmith on the tram. They had walked together from the bridge along that river way, with its tall houses and its little houses, its narrow alleys and its low-roofed inns, which is perhaps the most picturesque part of the river that the shattering march of time has left. He had made intellectual remarks about the effects of the sunlight in the water. He had drawn her attention to the beauty of the broad stretch of stream as it bent away towards Chiswick out of sight. He felt that he had made an impression of mentality upon the little typewriting girl. And, after that, he had suggested to Mrs. Hewson that it might seem churlish on his part not to have his meals with the rest.

Janet Hallard he did not like. When he talked about art her eyes hung upon him and, waiting until he had finished, she then talked about the Stock Exchange.

"Oh! I hate talking shop," he said one day.

"But you do it so well," she replied quietly. "It seems so much more interesting than art when you talk about it. After all, art is only some one person's idea about something they generally don't understand."

There is no wonder that the man hated her. But for Sally, he formed a deep attachment that was only kept in check and controlled by the remembrance of the superiority of his position. Class bias is universal, and is based almost entirely upon possession. The school-boy who has more pocket-money, the lodger who has the only bed-sitting-room in the house, and the man who has the largest rent-roll, are always

E. Temple Thurston

socially above those in their immediate surroundings. Possession being nine points of the law is also nine points of class superiority. That Mr. Arthur should have stepped down from his high estate and condescended to have his meals with them, was proof enough that the man was in earnest. But his interest in her was not reciprocated.

"I couldn't marry Mr. Arthur," she said; "not even if he was the manager of his old bank."

"But why not?"

"Because I could never love him; not even respect him."

"That's what fetters women."

"What?"

"That idea that they've got to marry the man they love. They've grown to think—unconsciously almost—that to give him love, blinded, is a fair exchange for his provision of a home. They'll never win their independence that way."

"I don't want my independence," said Sally.

"Then why do you work for it?" asked Janet.

"Because I didn't want to be a clog on my own people—because I wanted to be free to answer to myself."

"Then why don't you carry that idea further? Why make yourself free, simply to tie yourself up again at the first chance you get?"

"I don't call it tying myself up to marry a man I'm in love with and who loves me. That's happiness. I know I shall be perfectly happy."

Janet lifted her head and in a thoroughly professional manner blew a long, thin stream of smoke from between her lips.

"How long do you think that happiness is going to last?" she asked.

"I don't know."

"You chance it?"

"Yes."

"And then when the end comes you have not even got yourself to fall back upon. You're done for—sucked dry. You fall to pieces because you've sold your independence."

Sally left the dressing-table and crossed to Janet's bed. Sitting there, she put her bare arms on Janet's shoulders.

"It's no good your talking like that," she said gently. "You think that way, and right or wrong I think the other. If I loved a man and he loved me, I'd willingly sell my independence, willingly do anything for him."

"Supposing he wasn't going to marry you?" said Janet, imperturbably.

"Then he wouldn't love me."

"Oh yes; he might."

"Then I don't know what you mean."

Janet stood up from the bed. "I can smell bloaters for

E. Temple Thurston

supper," she said; "if you don't hurry up, Mr. Hewson 'll get the best one. I can see Mrs. Hewson picking it out for him. Come on. Put a blouse on. There's a woman who's sold her independence. She doesn't get much for it, as far as I can see. Come on. I'm going to talk to Mr. Arthur about art to-night."

# CHAPTER VII

It is one thing to say you could never marry a man, and it is another thing to refuse him when he asks you.

That very afternoon Mr. Arthur had received the intimation at his bank that he was shortly to be made a cashier. He glowed with the prospect. His conversation that evening was of the brightest. The poisoned shafts of Miss Hallard's satire met the armoured resistance of his high spirits. They fell—pointless and unavailing—from his unbounded faith in himself. A man who, after a comparatively few years' service in a bank, is deemed fitted for the responsible duties of a cashier, is qualified to express an opinion, even on art. Mr. Arthur expressed many.

"Don't see how you can say a thing's artistic if you don't like it," he declared.

"I think you're quite right, Mr. Arthur," said Mrs. Hewson. "If I like a thing—like that picture in one of the Christmas Annuals—I always say, 'Now I call that artistic,' don't I, Ern?"

Her husband nodded with his mouth full of the best bloater.

"Well, you couldn't call that thing artistic, Mrs. Hewson, if

E. Temple Thurston

you mean the thing that's over the piano in the sitting-room?"

"Why not?" asked Janet; "don't you like it?"

"No," said Mr. Arthur emphatically, "nor any one else either, I should think. I bet you a shilling they wouldn't."

"But Mrs. Hewson does," Janet replied quietly. "Doesn't that satisfy you that it must be artistic, since some one likes it?"

Mrs. Hewson, finding herself suddenly the object of the conversation, picked her teeth in hurried confusion. Her husband surveyed the company over the rim of his cup and then returned to his reading of the evening paper.

During the weighted silence that followed Janet's last remark, he laid down his paper.

"I see," he said, "as 'ow there are some people up in the north of England 'aving what they call Pentecostal visitations."

Mrs. Hewson laughed tentatively, the uncertain giggle that scarcely dares to come between the teeth. She knew her husband's leaning towards the arid humour of an obscure joke.

"What's that, Ern?"

"Well, 'cording to the paper, they get taken with it sudden. They can't stand up. They fall down in the middle of the service and roll about, just as if they'd 'ad too much to drink."

Mrs. Hewson's laugh became genuine and unafraid, a hysterical clattering of sounds that tumbled from her mouth.

"Silly fools," she said; "the way people go on. Read it—what is it? Read it."

Mr. Hewson picked some bones out of the bloater with a dirty hand, placed the filleted morsel in his mouth, washed it down with a mouthful of tea, and then cleared his throat and began to read.

Mr. Arthur seized this opportunity. "It's quite fine again now," he said in an undertone to Sally.

She expressed mild surprise—the lifting of her eyebrows, the casual "Really." Then it seemed to her that he did not exactly deserve to be treated like that and she told him how she had got wet through, coming home.

"Changed your clothes, I hope," he whispered.

"Oh yes."

"You might get pneumonia, you know," he said.

She smiled at that. "And of such are the Kingdom of Heaven."

He gazed at her in surprise. "Why should you say that?" he asked.

"Don't know—why shouldn't I?"

He looked down at his empty plate. There was something he wanted to say to her. He kept looking round the table for inspiration. At last, with Mrs. Hewson's burst of laughter at the paper's description of the Pentecostal visitations, he took the plunge—head down—the words spluttering in whispers out of his lips.

E. Temple Thurston

"Would you care to come for a little walk down the Strand-on-Green?" he asked. "It's a lovely night now."

In the half breath of a second, Sally's eyes sought Janet's face across the table. Janet had heard and, with her eyes, she urged Sally to accept. This all passed unknown to Mr. Arthur. He thought Sally was hesitating—the moments thumped in his heart.

"I don't mind for a little while," she said.

He rose from the table, conscious of victory. "I'll just go and get on my boots," he said, and he slipped away.

Sally mounted to her room followed by Janet.

"He's going to propose," said Miss Hallard.

"He's not," retorted Sally.

"I'm perfectly certain he is. He's been excited about some-thing all the evening. He's come into some money or something. He talked to-night as if he could buy up all the art treasures in the kingdom."

"You think he's going to buy me up?"

"He's going to make his offer. What'll you do?"

"Well—what can I do? Would you marry him?"

"That's not the question. There's no chance of him asking me. You can't speculate on whether you'll marry a man until he asks you—your mind is biassed before then."

"I don't believe you'd marry any one," said Sally.

"It's quite probable," she replied laconically.

Sally began to take off her hat again. "I'm not going out with him," she said. "I shall hate it."

"Don't be foolish—put on that hat, and see what it's like to be proposed to by an earnest young gentleman on the banks of a river, at nine o'clock in the evening. Go on—don't be foolish, Sally. It does a woman good to be proposed to—teaches her manners—go on. You may like him—you don't know."

Sally obeyed reluctantly. In the heart of her was a dread of it; in her mind, the tardy admission that she was doing her duty, sacrificing at the altar upon which every woman at some time or other is compelled to make her offering.

In the little linoleum'd passage, known as the hall, Mr. Arthur was waiting for her. He had exchanged his felt slippers for a pair of boots; round his neck he had wrapped an ugly muffler and a cap was perched jauntily on his head. The impression that he gave Sally, of being confident of his success, stung her for a moment to resentment. She determined to refuse him. But that mood was only momentary. When the door had closed behind them and they had begun to walk along the paved river path, the impression and its accompanying decision vanished.

Sally was a romantic—that cannot be denied. She could talk reverently about love in the abstract. In her mind, it was not a condition into which one fell, as the unwary traveller falls into the ditch by the roadside, picking himself out as quickly as may be, or, in his weariness, choosing at least to sleep the night there and go on with his journey next morning. In the heart of Sally, whether it were a pitfall or not, love was an end in itself. She directed all her steps towards that destination, and any light of romance allured her.

E. Temple Thurston

That evening, walking up towards Kew Bridge, the lights of the barges lying in the stream, looking themselves like huddled reptiles seeking the warmth of each other's bodies, the lights of the little buildings on the eyot, and the lamps of the bridge itself, all dancing quaint measures in the black water, brought to the susceptibility of Sally's mind a sense of romance. For the moment, until he spoke, she forgot the actual presence of Mr. Arthur. The vague knowledge that some one was with her, stood for the indefinite, the unknown quantity whose existence was essential to the completion of the whole.

As they passed by the City Barge—that little old-fashioned inn which faces the water on the river path—she looked in through the windows. There were bargemen, working men who lived near by, and others whose faces she had often seen as she had walked to her tram in the morning, all talking, laughing good-naturedly, some with the pewter pots pressed to their lips, head throwing slightly back, others enforcing a point with an empty mug on the bar counter. And outside, ahead of them, the lean, gaunt willows, around whose very trunks the hard paving had been laid, shot up into the black sky like witches' brooms that the wind was combing out.

Bright, cheerful lights glowed in every cottage window. In some it was only the light of a fire that leaped a ruddy dance on the whitewashed walls, and caught reflections in the lintels of the windows. In others it was a candle, in others a small oil lamp; but in all, looking through the windows as she passed, Sally saw some old man or woman seated over a fire. There is romance, even in content. Sally was half conscious of it, until Mr. Arthur spoke; then it whipped out, vanished—a wisp of smoke that the air scatters.

"Let's lean over that railing and watch the boats," he suggested.

There were scarcely any boats moving, to be seen. He spoke at random, as if the river swarmed with them; but only a little tug now and then scurried like a water-rat out of the shadows of the bridge, and sped down along towards Chiswick. In its wake, spreading out in ever-broadening lines, it left a row of curling waves that came lapping to the steps below them. These sounds and the occasional noise of voices across on the Kew side, were the only interruptions to the silence. For some moments they stood there, leaning on the railing, saying nothing, watching some dull, dark figures of men who were moving about on the little island that belongs to the Thames Conservancy.

"I—I've got something I want to tell you, Miss Bishop," Mr. Arthur said at length with sudden resolve.

Sally caught her breath. If it were only somebody she could love! What a moment it would be then—what a moment! Her lips felt suddenly dry. She sucked them into her mouth and moistened them.

"What is it?" she asked.

Mr. Arthur coughed, pulled out a handkerchief and blew his nose loudly. The sound, intensified there in that still place, jarred through Sally's senses. She roughly told herself that she was a fool.

"You know I'm in a bank?" he began.

"Yes; of course."

"It's a private bank."

"Really?"

E. Temple Thurston

"Yes; what I mean is, they pay better than most banks usually do."

"Really?"

"And they're going to make me a cashier."

"Oh, is that good?"

"Well, there's hardly a fellow of my age in any bank that's got to a responsible position like that, in the time I have. I bet you a shilling there isn't."

"Well, I can't afford to bet a shilling on it."

"No, of course not; I didn't mean that. What I mean—"

"I understand what you mean," said Sally. A sense of humour might have gone far to save him at that moment. She accredited it against him that he had none. "You might just as well have bet ten pounds," she added with a smile, "and I should have known what you meant. Ten pounds always sounds better than a shilling—even in that sort of—of—transaction."

"Ah, you're only joking," said he.

"No, I'm not," she replied. "I'm quite serious. I like the sound of ten pounds better. There's a nice ring of bravado about it. A shilling seems so mean."

For a few moments he was silenced by the weight of her incomprehensibleness. Such a moment comes at all times to every man, whatever his dealings with a woman may be. Mr. Arthur stood leaning on the railing, looking out at the black water and thinking how little she understood of the seriousness of his position, or the meaning that such an uplifting of his financial status conveyed to a man. She did not even know what he was about to propose. It would steady her considerably when she heard that; she would be less flippant then. Out of the corners of his eyes, he watched her face—the little, round, childish face almost perfect in outline—the gentle force, petulance almost, in the shapely chin, and the lips—tantalizing—they looked so innocent. In another few moments he would be kissing those lips; in another few moments he would be feeling the warmth of that hand that lay idly over the railing. He wondered if he were really wise. Was he being carried away by the first flush of triumph which his success had brought him? There was time to draw back yet.

"Well," she said, "was that what you were going to tell me?"

He turned round and met her look; his eyes wandered over her face. Those lips—they were indescribably alluring. It seemed impossible to give up the delight of kissing them; yet, of course, that was foolish, that was weak. He was not going to let the whole of his life hang upon a momentary desire like that. If she did not appeal to him in other ways, if he did not find admiration for her character, respect for her numerous good qualities, he would certainly not be so wanting in control as to let a passing inclination sway him to a momentous decision. He recounted those good qualities to himself reassuringly. Her innocence, her gentleness, her apparent willingness to be led by any one stronger than herself. Mr. Arthur dwelt long on that. That was a distinctly promising characteristic. He would consider that essential in any woman whom he thought to make his wife. Then she was demonstrative. He had often seen her show signs of deep affection to Miss Hallard. At the moment, that seemed a very necessary quality too. He felt just then that a little demonstration of affection on her part—if she put her hand

E. Temple Thurston

in his, or leant her head up against his shoulder—would make him intensely happy. And those lips! He half closed his eyes and his hand shook.

"No; that wasn't all," he said emotionally. "That was only preliminary to what I'm going to say."

Sally kept her eyes away from him. She did not want to watch his face. She knew he was very good, very honourable, very conscientious in his work; she knew that he would make a reasonably good husband, that he was about to offer her a position in life which it was incumbent upon any girl in her circumstances to consider well before refusing. But she could not look at his face while these things were weighing out their balance in her mind. It seemed hard enough to be compelled to listen to the sound of his voice; the weak, uncertain quality that it possessed, that faint suggestion of commonness which did not exactly admit of dropped aitches, but rang jarringly in her ears.

"I'm listening," she said rigidly. Her eyes were fixed without motion on the quiet water.

"Well, I want you to marry me," he exclaimed impulsively.

She said nothing. She waited.

"After next month, I shall have two hundred pounds a year. We could be very comfortable on that—couldn't we?"

"Do you think so?" she asked.

"Well, I'll bet you a shilling there are a good many men in London—married—who are comfortable enough on less. Besides, next year it'll be two hundred and twenty."

"And you want me to marry you?"

"Yes. I'm offering you a comfortable home of your own. No more pigging it like this in lodgings. You'll have your own house to look after—your own drawing-room. I don't want to boast about it, but don't you think it's a good thing for you?" He felt himself it was a big thing he was offering—and so it was—the biggest he had. "What I mean to say," he continued, "I'm a gentleman, you're earning your own living. I'm going to make you your own mistress—"

"But I don't love you," she said quietly, overlooking with generosity his insinuations about the position she held.

He gazed at her in amazement. "Why not?" he asked.

"Why not? Oh, why should you ask me a hard question like that?"

"'Cause I want to know. What's the matter with me? I bet you—"

"Oh, don't!" she begged, "I don't love you; that's all. I can't say any more."

"Then why did you come out with me this evening?"

"I don't know. Of course, I ought not to—I suppose I ought not to."

"But you haven't said you won't marry me."

"No. But haven't I said enough?"

"No."

"You'd marry me, knowing that I didn't love you?"

She turned her eyes to his. The pathos of that touched her. His senses swam when she looked at him.

"Yes," he said thickly. "You might not love me now—you would."

There, he spoilt it all again. She was so certain of its impossibility; he was so confident of his success. With the sentiment of his humility, the unselfishness of his devotion, he might have won her even then. The pity in a woman is often minister to her heart. But pity left her when he made so sure.

"Oh, it's no good talking like this," she said gently; "I know I shouldn't."

He leant nearer to her, peering into her face. "Well, will you think about it—will you think it over?" He felt certain that when she thought of that home of her own, she would be bound to relent—any woman would. "Let me know some other time."

"If you like. I don't know why you should be so good to me."

Passionately he seized her arm with his hand. "Because I love you—don't you see?"

"Yes; I see. I shouldn't think there's much to love in me though."

"Wouldn't you? My God—I do! Will you give me a kiss?"

One would think he might have known that that was the last thing he should have asked for. One would think he might have realized that passion was the last thing he should have shown her at such a moment as that. But he fancied that any woman might want to be kissed under the circumstances. He had a vague idea that his passion might awaken emotion in her; that with the touch of his lips, she might drop her arms about his neck and swoon into submission. He did not know the fiddle string upon which he was playing; he did not know the fine edge upon which all her thoughts were balancing.

She drew quickly away from him; freed her arm and turned towards the house with lips tight pressed together.

"I'm going in," she said.

E. Temple Thurston

# CHAPTER VIII

But she had promised to think it over. He kept her to that. Again it was the hunter, the quarry, and the inevitable flight. The thought of her possible escape quickened his pulses. He became infinitely more determined to make her his own. The recollection of her saying that she did not love him was humiliating, but it stirred him to deeper feelings of desire. When he thought of her—as at first—readily accepting him and his prospects, he had not formed so high opinion of her as now, being at her mercy.

She stood before his eyes that night as he lay in bed. One vague dream after another filled his sleep, and Sally took part in them all—kissing him, scorning him. His mental vision was obsessed with the sight of her.

With Sally herself, sleep came late—reluctantly—like a tired man, dragging himself to his journey's end.

Janet was seated up in bed, reading and smoking, when she returned. While she was taking off her clothes, Sally told her all about it—word for word—everything that had passed between them. This is a way of women. They have a marvellous memory for the recounting in detail of such incidents as these.

"Thinking it over means nothing," she said when Sally had finished—"thinking it over'll only fix your mind on refusing him all the more. His one chance was this evening. You know that yourself—don't you? You'll never accept him now."

Sally crept wearily into the bed and pulled the clothes about her.

"Will you?" Janet repeated.

Sally muttered a smothered negative into the pillow, and stared out before her at the discoloured wall-paper.

"Sally"—Janet shut up her book, and threw the end of her cigarette with accurate precision into the tiny fireplace—"Sally—"

"What?"

"Is there anybody else? Some man up in Town—some man who comes into the office—some man *in* the office—is there?"

Sally turned her pillow over. "No," she replied. She kept her eyes away from Janet's, but her answer was firm and decided.

For a few moments, Miss Hallard sat upright in the bed and watched her. Her mind was keyed with intuition. She was conscious of the presence of some influence in Sally's mind—probably more conscious of it than Sally was herself. You could not have shaken her in that belief. Even a woman cannot act to a woman, and that decided "No" from Sally had only served the more to convince her. When one woman deals in subtleties with another, fine hairs and the splitting of them are merely clumsy operations to perform.

"Are you tired?" asked Janet presently—"or only pretending to be?"

"Why should I pretend? I am tired—frightfully tired."

"You want to go to sleep, then?"

"Well, I don't feel like talking to-night; do you?"

They talked every night, regularly—talked about dresses, about religion, about other people's love affairs, and other women's indiscretions. Sally described hats she had seen on rich women shopping at Knightsbridge; Janet told questionable stories about the lives of models and art students, Sally listening with wondering eyes, needing sometimes to have them explained to her more graphically in order really to understand. So they would continue, in the dark, till one or the other asked a question and, receiving no answer, would turn over on her side, and the next moment be oblivious of everything.

"What's particularly the matter to-night?" persisted Janet. "Sorry you told Mr. Arthur you didn't love him?"

"I don't know."

"I believe you are."

There was no such belief in her mind. She knew it would draw the truth. She used it.

"No, I'm not," said Sally, decidedly. "I'm not sorry."

"Then what are you so depressed about?"

"Am I depressed?" She sat up again and turned her pillow. "Oh, I haven't said my prayers yet." She began to throw off the bed-clothes.

"Well, you're not going to get out of bed, are you?"

"Yes."

She slid off the bed on to the floor, shuddering as her feet touched the cold linoleum carpet. Habit was strong in her still. She believed in no fixed and certain dogma, but she had never broken the custom of saying her prayers; never even been able to rid herself of the belief that except upon the knees on the hard floor prayers were of little intrinsic value. That she had always been taught; and though the greater lessons—the untangling of the entangled Trinity, the mystery of the bread and wine—had lost their meaning in her mind, ever since her father's predicament, yet she still held fondly to the simple habits of her childhood.

When Janet saw her finally huddled on her knees, her head, with its masses of gold hair, buried in the arms flung out appealingly before her, she turned and blew out the candle. Sally never answered questions when she was saying her prayers, though Janet frequently addressed them to her, and took the answers for granted.

There she knelt in the darkness, while Janet dug the accustomed grove in her pillow and went to sleep.

What does a woman pray for—what does any one pray for—whom do they pray to, when the composition of their mental attitude towards the Highest is a plethora of doubts? Yet they pray.

Instinctively at night, by the side of their beds, their knees

E. Temple Thurston

bent—or there is some genuflexion in their heart which answers just as well—they drop into the attitude of prayer. And they all begin in the same way—O God— And not one of them has the faintest notion of whom or what or why that God is.

Whoever, whatever, wherever He is, His power must be supreme to make itself felt through the thick veil of doubt and despair that hangs so heavily about His identity.

Sally Bishop, who could not say the Apostles' Creed with unswerving conscience—to whom the story of the Resurrection was fogged, blurred with a thousand inconsistencies— even she could not dispense with that moment in each day, that moment of abandonment—the flinging of one's burden of questions at the feet of a deity whose identity it would be impossible to define.

For many minutes she stayed there on her knees, her arms wound round about her head, her shoulders rising wearily with each breath that she took.

Long after Janet had fallen asleep, and when the cold was numbing in her limbs, she stayed there, pouring forth her importunate questions—the woman begging guidance, when she knows full well what course she is going to adopt.

# CHAPTER IX

The life of the Bohemian in London is no brilliantly coloured affair. The most that can be said for it is that it has its moments. The first flush of a full purse and the last despair of an empty pocket are always sensations that are worth while. With the one you can gauge the shallow depth of pleasure and find the world full of friends; with the other you can learn how superfluous are the things you called necessities and you may count upon the fingers of your hand the number of friends whom really you possess. In their way, these moments are true values—both of them.

But the life of the Bohemian, wherever it may be, has one advantage that no other life possesses. It is a series of contrasts. With his last sovereign, he may have supper at the Savoy, rubbing shoulders with the best and with the worst; the next night, he may be dining off a *maquereau grille* in a Greek Street restaurant, jogging elbows with the worst and with the best. It is only the steady possession of wealth that makes a groove; but steady possession is an unknown condition in the life of the Bohemian. And so, drifting in this sporadic way through the wild journeys of existence, he comes truly to learn the definite, certain uncertainty of human things. This he learns; but it is no sure guarantee that he will follow the teaching of the lesson.

E. Temple Thurston

For in the heart of human nature is a common need of bondage. To this, no matter what movement may be afoot, a woman still yields herself willingly. To this, in deep reluctance, with dragging steps, but none the less inevitably, man yields as well. The desire for companionship, the desire to give, albeit there may be no giving in return, the shuddering sense of the empty room and the silent night come to all of us, however much we may wish for the former conditions of solitude when once they are ours.

It was this common need of bondage, this hatred of the silent emptiness of life that caught the mind of Jack Traill, arrested and held it in the interest of Sally Bishop.

You are never really to know why a man, passing through life, meeting this woman, meeting that, some intimately, some in the vapid chance of acquaintanceship, will in one moment be held by the sight of a certain face. The table of affinities is the only attempt at regulating the matter, and in these changing times one cannot look even upon that with confidence.

There is a law, however, whatever it may be, and in unconscious obedience to it, Traill kept the face of Sally Bishop persistently before him. After she had left him at Knightsbridge, he too descended from the 'bus and walked slowly back to Piccadilly Circus.

Casting his eyes round the circle of houses with their brilliant illuminations, he decided, with no anticipation of entertainment, where to dine. A meal is a ceremony of boredom when it has no pleasurable prospect. Indeed, the gratification of any appetite becomes a sordid affair when the mind is stagnant and the body merely asking for its food. But in the last three years, Traill had gone through this same performance a thousand times; a thousand times he had looked out of the little circular window on the top floor of the house in Lower Regent Street where he lived; a thousand times he had taken a coin out of his pocket and let the head or the tail decide between the two restaurants which he most usually frequented.

On this night there was no tossing of a coin. He had not even so much interest in the meal as that. Making his way across the Circus, he entered a restaurant in Shaftesbury Avenue, and passed down the stairs to the grill-room.

The music, the lights, the haze of smoke and the scent of food were depressing. The whole atmosphere rolled forward to meet him as he came through the doors. He had no subtle temperament. It did not offend his imagination, but it sickened his senses, even though he knew that in five minutes he would be eating with the rest and the atmosphere would have taken upon itself a false semblance of normality.

All the tables had one occupant or another. He was forced to seat himself at the same table with some man and a girl, who were already half through their meal. He did so with apologies, quite aware of the annoyance he was causing. But he was not sensitive. He had the right to a seat at the table. The rules of the restaurant offered no restrictions. With it all, he was British.

"Hope you'll excuse my intrusion," he said shortly.

The man, a clerk, with slavery written legibly across his face, offered some mumbled acceptance of the inevitable. Traill himself would not have borne with any such intrusion. He would have called the manager—insisted upon having the table to himself; but he intruded his presence with only a momentary consciousness of being in the way.

E. Temple Thurston

His manner with waiters was peremptory. He gave them the recognition of the position which they occupied, but beyond that, scarcely looked upon them as human.

"Look here," he began, "I want so and so—" he named a dish that was unknown to the companion of the young clerk. She felt a certain respect of him for that. Her friend had ordered the most ordinary of food and had tried to do it in a lordly manner. There was no lordliness about Traill. He wasted no time with a waiter; he had never met a German waiter who was worth it. All this gave the impression of brusqueness. The girl liked it. She looked at her friend and wished she was dining with Traill. But Traill took no notice of her. Except an occasional glance, he ignored them both. As soon as he could, he ordered an evening paper and sat concealed behind it—truly British in every outline. The music in the place was good, but no music appealed to him. It came as a confused wreckage of sounds to his ears as he read through the news of the evening; and when the girl rattled her spoon on the coffee cup and the young man clapped his hands vigorously at the conclusion of a selection, he looked over the top of his paper with annoyance. What music had ever penetrated his understanding of the art, had come in the form of chants of psalms and old hymn tunes, which a constant attendance at church in his youth had dinned into him—the driving of soft iron nails into the stern oak. He sang these laboriously with numberless crescendos as he dressed in the mornings.

He finished dinner as quickly as he could. The young people opposite him were insufferably dull. Apparently they had never met each other before and were at a loss to make conversation to suit the occasion. Accordingly, they listened intently to the string band while the young man smoked a long cigar, and in the natural course of things, they applauded after each piece to show that they had heard it. Traill bolted his meal, glad to leave them.

He came out of the restaurant and thanked God—filling his lungs with it—for the clean air. Then he stood on the pavement contemplating the next move. Should he go back to his rooms, read—smoke—fall asleep? Should he turn into a music-hall? When you live alone, the greatest issues of life sometimes resolve themselves into such questions as these.

Finally, scarcely conscious of arriving at any definite decision, he walked slowly back across the Circus in the direction of Lower Regent Street.

Over by the Criterion he heard the sound of footsteps behind him, hurrying; then his Christian name in a woman's voice. He turned.

"I was up nearly at the Prince of Wales's," she said out of breath, "when I saw you crossing the Circus. My—I ran!"

"What for?" he asked laconically.

"Why to talk to you, of course—what else? Where are you going?"

He looked at her coloured lips, at the tired eyes with their blackened lashes, at the flush of rouge that adorned her cheeks. Involuntarily, he remembered when she was charming, pretty—a time when she required none of these things.

"Where are you going anyway?" she repeated. "You haven't been to see me these months. Where are you going now?"

"I'm going back to my rooms."

A look of resigned disappointment passed like a shadow across her face. The first realization in a woman of her

E. Temple Thurston

failure to attract is the beginning of every woman's tragedy.

"Never seen my rooms, have you?" he added.

"No; never expected to."

"Come in and see them now and have a talk."

"You don't mean that?" Eagerness dragged it out of her.

"Come along," he said; "they're just down here—in Regent Street."

She followed him silently—silently, but in that moment her spirits had lifted. There was a wider swing in her walk. But he took no notice of that; he was not observant.

She hummed a tune with a rather pretty voice as she walked up the flights of stairs behind him.

"Gosh! it's dark," she exclaimed.

"Oh, it's none of your bachelor flats with lifts and attendants and electric lights," he replied.

On the third landing she stopped—out of breath again.

"Tired?" he said.

"There—" she laid a hand on her chest and breathed heavily. Then she moved a step nearer to him.

"Give us a kiss, dearie," she whispered.

He retreated a step. "My dear child—I didn't want you for that. Come up to the next floor when you've got your breath.

Sally Bishop                                                      91

I'll go on and light the candles."

He left her there in the semi-darkness, the thin light from the landing window just breaking up the heavy shadows. When she heard him open the door upstairs, she moved close to the window, took a small mirror from her little reticule bag and gazed for a moment at her face in its reflection. Then from some pocket of the bag, she produced a powder-puff and a box of powdered rouge, applying them with mechanical precision.

"S'pose he thought I looked tired," she muttered to herself as she mounted the remaining flight of stairs.

The room was a bachelor's, but it showed discrimination. Everything was in good taste—taste that was beyond her comprehension. She stood there in the doorway and stared about her before she entered. She thought the rush matting that covered the floor was cold; she thought the oak furniture sombre. Without realizing the need for tact, she said so.

"You want a woman in here," she said, thinking that she was paving the way for herself—"to warm things up a bit—you know what I mean—make things more cosy."

He put a chair out for her by the fire. It had a rush-bottomed seat to it, and for the first few moments she worried about in it, trying vainly to make herself comfortable.

"What would you do?" he asked quietly, filling a well-burnt pipe from a tobacco-jar.

She took this as encouragement—jumped to it, as an animal to the food above it.

"Do? Well, first of all I'd have a nice thick carpet." There

E. Temple Thurston

was no need to force the note of interest into her voice. She was already absorbed with it. She confidently thought that she could impress him with the comfort that she could bring into his life. Her eyes, quick to grasp certain facts, had shown her that he lived alone. Long study of men from certain standpoints had made that easy for her to appreciate. This moment to her was as the gap in the wall of riders before him is to the jockey; in that moment she saw clear down the straight to the winning-post. She took it. Ten minutes before she had not known where to turn. The race had seemed impossible. Two or three times she had opened her reticule bag and counted the four coppers that jingled within the pocket. She had had no dinner. No music hall was possible to her with such capital. You know something of life when you have only fourpence in the world and vice is the only trade for which your hand has acquired any deftness.

"I pray God no man 'll offer me ten bob to-night," she had said to another woman.

"Why?"

"Why? Gosh! I'd take it."

Here then, out of nowhere, in the dull impenetrable wall was torn the gap through which she saw the chance, such a chance as she had never been offered by the generosity of circumstance before. She seized it—no hesitation—no lack of inspiring confidence. It did not even cross her mind that she looked tired. She was in no way thwarted by the knowledge that she was not so young, not so pretty as when first she had known him. The opportunity was too great for that. It had fallen so obviously at her feet, that she felt it was meant for her.

She shuffled her feet on the cold clean matting and said again, "I'd have a nice thick carpet—"

"What colour?"

She looked up to the ceiling to think—not at the room around her.

"I don't know—Turkey red, I think—that's warmest. You know my carpet—well, it used to be nice. It's worn a bit now and there's not so much colour in it as when it was new. That was Turkey red."

"And what else?" He sat on the corner of an old table and smoked his pipe—swinging his legs and looking at her.

"Well, I'd have electric lights instead of these candles—you can't expect a woman to see with candles;—'lectric light's twice as cheap and it's much brighter. And they make lovely new fittings now—quite inexpensive—oxidized copper, I think they call it; I like brass best myself."

"You think brass is better?"

"Yes; don't you? Those brass candlesticks that you've got are all right, only they're so plain."

"You like things more ornate?"

"More what?"

"More ornate—more highly finished—more elaborate?"

"Yes; don't you?"

He took no notice of that question. "What else would you

E. Temple Thurston

do?" he asked. The smoke curled up in clouds from the bowl of his pipe as he sat listening to her.

She looked round the room contemplatively.

"Oh—lots of things," she said. "I'd have a sofa—one of those settee sort of things—"

"Upholstered in red?"

"Yes—to go with the carpet. And a comfortable armchair—really comfortable, I mean—something that you could chuck your legs about it—less like a straight jacket than this thing I'm sitting in."

"Upholstered in red?" he repeated.

"Um—of course."

"Then how about this wall-paper?" he questioned. "It's green—do you think that would go with all the red?"

She looked round the walls, then tried to blur her eyes in an effort to give scope to her imagination. She put her whole heart into it. This was the chance of her life. Thrilling through her, like some warm current that forces its way through cold water, was the consciousness that she was making him seriously consider the benefits of having a woman to live with him, to look after his needs, attend to his comforts, as she pictured herself so well able to do. After due deliberation, she delivered her opinion.

"I don't think the green would go so badly as you'd think," she said slowly—"I suppose it would be expensive to change. But red would look better of course."

He took his pipe out of his mouth and blew a long scroll of smoke from between his lips as he looked at her.

"In fact," he said at last—"you'd like to make this little room of mine look like hell."

It was a brutal thing to have said. Yet he knew her mind no more than she knew his. He knew but little of women. Her knowledge of men was limited to one point of view. When her flat had been newly decorated, newly furnished for her, she had boasted of its comforts to every man she met. Nearly all of them had said that they liked it. It was clean then, and all they had appreciated was the cleanliness. But she had not known that. She thought they had approved of her taste. So, with this narrow knowledge of the sex, she had made her bid for security and failed.

And he, when he saw the drop in her face, when he saw features and expression fall from the lofty height of anti-cipation as a pile of cards topple in a mass upon the table, he was sorry. Her mouth opened—gaped. She looked as if a flat hand had struck her.

"I don't mean that unkindly," he said—"but it would be hell—red hell—to me."

She sat and stared at him. "Can't understand you," she said at last.

"Why not?"

"What did you let me go on talking for?"

"It was rather amusing to compare your taste with mine."

"Amusing? God!"

She lifted herself to her feet and went across to the mantel-piece, leaning her elbows on it, her head in her hands. All her exhaustion had returned. She felt a thousand times more tired in that moment than when she had rested on the landing. All that afternoon she had been walking the streets—all that evening too. From Regent Street to Oxford Street, from Oxford Street to Bond Street, from Bond Street through the Burlington Arcade into Piccadilly, then over the whole course again, smiling cheerfully at this man, looking knowingly at that—all a forced effort, all a spurious energy; and pain throbbed in her limbs—a dominant note of pain. She could feel a pulse in her brain that kept time to it. These are the ecstatic pleasures of vice—the charms, the allure-ments of the gay life.

At last she turned round and faced him. "I don't want any of those damned red carpets and things," she said,—"if you'll let me come and live with you—look after you."

She crossed the room and laid her hands heavily on his shoulders; bent towards him to kiss his lips.

"We should be sick to death of each other in a week," he said, meeting her eyes.

"No, we shouldn't."

He gazed steadily at her for a moment. "What makes you think I want any one to live here with me?" he asked curiously.

"I don't know—you do. I saw it the first second I entered the room. I felt it the first moment you asked me to come up here. You know you do yourself. You're sick of this—aren't you?"

"You're right there."

She nodded her head sententiously—proud of her perceptive ability. She wanted to go on saying other things that were just as true, showing how well she understood him; but she could think of nothing. Then she made the fatal mistake. She threw a guess at a hazard.

"And you thought when you saw me that I was just the girl you wanted. I saw that in your face when you turned round."

He smiled. "You've lost the scent," he said, drawing away from her hands. "Lost it utterly. And why do you want to come and live here? You're not fond of me. You don't care a rap for me. Are you hard up?"

Pride—self-respect—they are lost qualities in a lost woman. You must not even look for them. For the moment, she was silent, saying nothing; but there was no moaning of wounded vanity in the heart of her. Two questions were weighing out the issue. If she said she were hard-up, then all opportunity of gaining the chance would be lost. He would give her money—tell her to go. That would be all. If she refused to admit it, the opportunity—slight as it had become—would still be there. Which to do—which course to take? For a perceptible passing of time she rocked—a weary pendulum of doubt—between the two. Then she gave it.

"I'm dead broke," she said thickly.

She saw the last hope vanish with that—looked after it with a curl of bravado on her lip. Lifting her eyes to his, she knew it was gone. There, in the place of it, was the calculation of what he could spare—what he should give.

"How much do you want?" he asked.

The question was ludicrous to her. She wanted all she could get. Now that she had thrown away her chances of the future, her whole mind concentrated with uncontrolled desire upon the present.

"What's the good of asking me that?" she exclaimed bitterly. "I'll take what I can get. Reminds me of a girl—a friend of mine. She's an illegitimate child. Her father's pretty well off. She was down to the bottom of the bag the other day, so she went to her father and asked him for some money. 'My dear child,' he said—'I can't spare you a cent—I've just spent seven hundred and fifty pounds on a motor car—is a sovereign any good to you?'"

There was a bitter sense of humour in the story. She laughed at it—loud, uncontrolled laughter that rang as empty and as hollow as an echo.

"Give me what you can," she added. "Anything above a shilling's better than fourpence."

"Is that what you're down to?"

"Um—"

He took three sovereigns out of his pocket, and gave them to her. She let them lie out flat in the palm of her hand—the three of them, all in a row. They glittered—even in the candle-light. They were her own.

"When are you coming to see me?"

She still looked at them.

"I'm not coming."

Her head shot up; her eyes filled with questions.

"Why not?"

He opened his hands expressively. If there were any answer to that question, she learnt that she was not going to get it.

"Are you going to be married?" she asked slowly.

He shook his head—laughing. Then understanding shot into her eyes, and a flash of jealousy came with it.

"I know," she exclaimed between thin lips.

"What do you know?"

"You're going to keep some woman here—some girl you're fond of."

It was the moment of intuition. She had struck deeper into his mind than even he was aware of himself.

"What makes you think that?"

"What you said."

"What did I say?"

"You admitted that you were sick of being here alone."

"Well—?"

She burst out laughing. "Well—?" She turned to the door. "Good Lord! Isn't every blooming man the same!"

She opened her bag and dropped the three gold pieces into a

pocket—one after another. You heard the dull sound of the first as it fell, then the clinking of the other two, when the metal touched metal. She shut the bag—the catch snapped sharp! Then she went.

# CHAPTER X

You sow an idea—you sow a seed. It grows upwards through a soil of subliminal unconsciousness until it lifts its head into the clear air of realization. There is no limitation of time, no need for watchful dependence upon the season. Only the moment and the husbandry of circumstances are essential. With these, perhaps a single hour is all that may be required for the seed to open, the shoots to sprout, the plant itself to bear the fruit of action in the fierce light of reality.

In Traill's mind the idea was sown when he stood outside the office of Bonsfield & Co. in King Street. The soil was ready then—hungry for the seed. It fell lightly—unnoticed—into the subconscious strata of his mind. He had not even been aware of its existence. Then, with the woman who had accompanied him to his rooms, came the husbandry of circumstance. She fed the seed. She watered it. Before her foot had finished tapping on the wooden staircase, before the street and the thousand lights had swallowed her up again, his mind had grasped the knowledge of the need that was within him.

On Monday morning he went down to the chambers in the Temple where his name as a practising barrister was painted upon the lintel of the door. This was a matter of formality. Numberless barristers do it every day; numberless ones of

E. Temple Thurston

them find the same as he did—nothing to be done. He had long since overcome the depression which such an announcement had used to bring with it. There should be no disappointment in the expected which invariably happens. The sanguine mind is a weak mind that suffers it. Traill turned away from the Temple, whistling a hymn tune as if it were a popular favourite.

From there he made his way down into the hub of journalism. The descent into hell is easy. He rode there with a free lance—known by all the editors—capable in his way—a man to be relied upon for anything but imagination. From one office to another, he trudged; climbing numberless stairs, filling in numberless slips of paper with his name, saying nothing about his business. They knew his business—the ability to do anything that was going. He had written leaders on the advance of Socialism—criticized a play, reviewed a book. It says little beyond the fact that one is ready and willing to do these things.

So, until the nearing hour of lunch time, he went about—a scavenger of jobs—sweeping up the refuse of the paper's needs, as the boys in Covent Garden search through the barrows of sawdust for the stray, green grapes that have been thrown out with the brushings of the stalls.

If one knew how half the men in London find the way to live, one would stand amazed. Life is not the dreadful thing; it is the living of it. Life in the abstract is a gay pageant, the passing of a show, caparisoned in armour, in ermine, in motley, in what you will. But see that man without his armour, this woman without her ermine, these in the crowd without their motley and the merry, merry jangling of the bells, and you will find how slender are the muscles that the armour lays bare, how shrivelled the breast that the ermine strips, how dragged and weary is that pitiable, naked figure which a few moments before was dancing fantastically, grimacing with its ape.

Traill took it as it came; the man forced to a crude philosophy, as Life, if we get enough of it, will force every soul of us. You must have a philosophy if you are going to accept Life. Even if you refuse it, you must have a philosophy, call it pessimistic, what you wish, it is still a point of view. The "temporary insanity" of the coroner's court is most times a vile hypocrisy, invented to soothe a Christian conscience.

So long as he found enough work to do, his spirits were light. He had a normal contempt for the temperament that is known as artistic, despised the variability of mood, ridiculed its April uncertainty. This is the man who hews his way through Life, making no wide passage perhaps, no definite pathway for the thousands who are looking for the broad and simple track; but cuts down, lops off, with the sheer strength of dogged determination, the hundred obstacles that beset his progress.

When the clock at the Law Courts was striking the half-hour after twelve, he came up out of that depth of journalism which lies like a hidden world below the level of Fleet Street and made his way along towards the Strand. There was a definite intention in his movements. He walked quickly; turned up without hesitation into Southampton Street, and again into King Street. There the speed of his steps lessened and, walking past the premises of Bonsfield & Co., he kept his eyes in the direction of the window at which he had first seen Sally Bishop at work.

She was there, her fingers more lively now than when he had seen them before, in their eternal dance upon the untiring keys. In the lingering glance he took at her as he walked

E. Temple Thurston

slowly by, there was much that was curiosity, but a greater interest. Thoughts had swept through his mind since the previous Saturday night. He saw her now from a different point of view. He still found her attractive-compellingly so. There was something exquisitely naive about her, an innocence that was precious. In all the sordid side of life that he had seen—that was his daily portion to see, for the journalism of a free lance can be sordid indeed—he found her fresh. That had been the swift impression which he had formed in the few moments that he had seen her, spoken to her, on the top of the 'bus from Piccadilly Circus. At this second sight of her, he was not disillusioned. Even there, in the midst of offices, chained to the machine at which she worked, she seemed cut out from her surroundings—a personality apart.

He walked past the book shop, down the street, until he came within sight of the clock in the post-office in Bedford Street. It was ten minutes to one. He turned back again. It was a practical certainty that she would be going out to lunch at one. The only question that arose as a difficulty in his mind was the possibility of her being accompanied by some other member of Bonsfield's staff. He knew that it would be inconsiderate to approach her then.

Finally he decided to a wait her coming in one of the arches of Covent Garden market, from whence he could survey the entire length of the street. He had scarcely taken up his position when she came out into view. She walked in his direction, She was alone.

Traill felt a sensation in his blood. It was not unaccountable, but it was unexpected. A combination of eagerness and timidity, that he would have ridiculed in any one else, had mastered him for the moment. Years ago, he would have understood it, expected it. Now he was thirty-six. A man who has lived to his age, lived the years moreover in his way, does not look to be moved to school-boy timidity by the sight of a woman. He pulled a cigarette-case out of his pocket, extracted a cigarette and lit it before he was really conscious of this action.

She passed down Southampton Street into the Strand without noticing him. Then for the second time he followed. It was an easy matter to keep the blue feather in her hat in sight in the crowds of people all hurrying to get the most of the hour for their mid-day meal. He let her keep some yards ahead. Then she vanished into a restaurant at the corner of Wellington Street. He smiled. The matter was as good as done now. In another three minutes he would be ten pounds in her debt.

He allowed a couple of minutes to go by before he entered the restaurant; then he pushed open the doors and his eyes took in the room with a swift scrutiny.

Everything was in his favour. She was seated at a table in the corner of the room, herself the only occupant of it. He walked across to her without hesitation—no timidity now. That had vanished with the need for a show of determination. Here he must dominate the situation or fail utterly.

"There's no need to move to another table," he said as he pulled out a chair for himself and sat down opposite to her. "If you really strongly object to my having my lunch opposite to you, I'll move away."

"I do object," she replied.

"But why?"

"I don't know you, I don't know who you are."

E. Temple Thurston

"That's not a great difficulty," he said, smiling.

"I think it is."

He laughed lightly. "Not a bit of it. It can easily be over-come. My name's Traill. I'm a barrister—briefless—the type of barrister that populates the Temple and all those places. One of these days I may come into my own; I may be conducting the leading cases at the criminal bar; I may be— but it's not even one of my castles in the air."

She smiled at his inconsequence. "You seem to take it very lightly," she remarked.

"Why not? Do you imagine I sit in chambers all day long, pining for the impossible which no alchemy of fate can apparently ever alter? I'm also a journalist. That's why I've come to see you." He spoke utterly at random.

"To see me?"

"Yes."

The waitress was standing impatiently by the table, tapping her tray with her fingers.

"What are you going to have?" he asked.

Sally snatched a swift glance at him. Was he conscious that he was overruling her objections? She saw no sign of it. He looked up at her questioningly, waiting for her answer.

"I don't mind at all," she replied. She felt too timid to say what she would really like, too ashamed perhaps to say what she usually had for her lunch. The best course was to let him choose. "I'll have whatever you do," she said agreeably.

He gave the order, a meal for which she could never have afforded to pay. Then he turned back with a humorous smile to her.

"The objection, the difficulty's overcome, then," he said.

Sally allowed herself to smile, eyes in a swift moment raised to his.

"I never said so."

"No, no; but surely this is tacit admission. However, the point is not the saying of it." He saw the look of doubtfulness beginning to show itself in her eyes. "What's the good of talking about it? We're here for the purpose of eating, not discussing social conventions. You know who I am, I shall know who you are in another two or three minutes if you'll be kind enough to tell me. Why, good heavens! life's short enough, without surrounding everything we want with social restrictions. I'm a barrister, I told you that before. In some sort of legal directory you'll find out exactly when I left Oxford and was called to the bar. In *Who's Who?* you'll find out exactly where I live, though I can tell you that myself—" he mentioned the number of his chambers in Regent Street. "They'll tell you in *Who's Who?* that my sports are riding, fishing, and shooting—that describes a man in England; it doesn't describe me. I don't ride; I don't fish or shoot; I used to; that's another matter. I only ride an occasional hobby now—fish for work on the papers, and shoot—Lord knows what I shoot! Nothing, I suppose. I belong to the National Liberal Club for the Library, to the Savage where you pass along an editor as you would a christening mug, and to the National Sporting, because there's a beast in every man, thank God!"

He had won her. The rattle of that conversation had driven

E. Temple Thurston

all thoughts of doubt out of her mind. She would not have denied herself of his company now for any foolish pretext of convention. In that hurried summary of himself and his affairs, proving himself by it, without any pride and conceit, to be a man of very different stamp and interest to Mr. Arthur Montagu, he had marked her in her flight for liberty. Nothing was binding her—no interest in life but to be loved. Had there been any such bond—the prospect of an engagement which was not distasteful to her—he would have found it no easy matter to win her to interest then. But she was free, in the midst of her flight, and he had marked her. She looked into his eyes as the sighted bird blinks before the glittering barrel of the gun, and she knew that he could win her if he chose.

"Well," he said, "I've got nothing more to tell you. How about you?"

She took a little handkerchief out from the folds in her coat, then put it back again, apparently with no purpose.

"I thought you had something to tell me?"

"I?"

"Yes; you said when you came up to the table that you had."

"That? Oh yes, that's business. We'll talk about that later. I want to hear something about yourself first. You're engaged to be married."

He rushed blindly at that—knew nothing about it. A ring on her finger had suggested the thought, but whether it were on the proper finger or not was beyond his knowledge of such little details.

"What makes you think that?" she asked.

"The ring on the finger."

"But that's not the right finger."

"Isn't it?"

"No. My grandmother gave me that."

He held her eyes—forced her to see the comprehension in his.

"Then you won't help me?" he said.

"Help you? How?"

"You don't want to tell me anything about yourself?"

"But I have nothing to tell. I'm a very uninteresting person, I'm afraid."

This was shyness, this dropping into conventional phrases. He led her deftly through them to a greater confidence in his interest, as you steer a boat through shallow, rapid-running water. He wanted to get to the woman beneath it all, knowing that the woman was there. So he made for deep water, guiding her through the shoals. Before they had finished their second course, she was telling him about Mr. Arthur.

"And you don't love him?" he said.

"No."

"Respect him?"

She paused. The pause answered him. The tension of the moment lifted.

"Yes. I respect him. I know he's honourable. He must be reliable. After all he's offering me everything."

You would have thought, to hear her, that the matter was yet in the balance, swaying uncertainly before it recorded the weight. There is the instinct of the woman in that. She felt the shadow of his apprehension; knew that she raised her value in his eyes by the seeming presence of debate. Yet none realized better than she, that Mr. Arthur had been stripped of all possibility now. The fateful comparison had been made—the comparison which most women make in the decision of such momentous issues—one man against another. Their emotions are the agate upon which the scales must swing. In favour of the man before her, they swung with ponderous obviousness.

"Then you'll marry him?" said Traill.

She looked at him questioningly—raised eyebrows—the look of mute appeal. You might have read anything behind her eyes—you might have read nothing. Traill studied them wonderingly.

"You'll marry him—of course," he repeated. He was taking the risk. He might be forcing her to say yes. He prepared himself for it. To take that risk, knowing one way or another, rather than blindly groping to the end, this was typical of him. But he could not force her to the answer that he sought for.

"Do you think I ought to?" she asked.

He drummed his fingers on the table and looked through her.

"Why do you ask me?"

"I'm sorry." She returned sensitively to the food that was before her—"I thought you had seemed interested. I'm sorry—I took too much for granted."

He knew the danger of all this—so did she. But danger of what? That dancing upon the edge of the precipice of emotion is in the normal heart of every woman—and he? He sought it out; to the edge he had brought her, knowing the way—every step of it. She had only followed blindly where he had led. Once there, she knew well the chasm on whose edge she was balancing. Natural instinct alone would have told her that. The height was dizzy. She had known well that if ever she gazed down, it would be that. Her head swam with the giddiness of it. She kept her eyes fixed rigidly on the plate before her, not daring to look up, or meet his glance.

"Suppose you haven't taken too much for granted," he suggested quietly.

"Well?" she raised her head—tried to look with unconcern into his eyes—failed. Then her head dropped again.

"I should say—don't marry him—not yet—wait. The harm that is done by waiting is measurable by inches. Wait. How old are you? Is that rude? No—of course it isn't. It's only rude when a woman's got to answer you with a lie. How old are you? Twenty?"

"Twenty-one."

"Twenty-one! I was fifteen when you first woke up and yelled."

She threw back her head and laughed.

"Why do you laugh?"

"You say such funny things sometimes."

"I remember the first joke I made you thought was bad taste."

She looked at him. There was excitement in her eyes. The rush of the stream had taken her; an impulse for the moment carried her away.

"I repeated that joke afterwards," she said quickly, "the same evening to shock Mr. Arthur."

The moment she had said it, came regret. It was showing him too plainly the impression that he had left upon her. But he seemed not to notice it.

"Was he shocked?" he asked.

"Yes—terribly."

She looked at her watch. That moment's regret had brought her to her senses. The blood came quickly to her face, as she thought how intimately they had talked within so short a time. Reviewing it—as with a searchlight that strides across the sky—she scarcely believed that it was true. In just an hour, she had told him as much—more than she had told Miss Hallard. Had she changed? Was the freedom of the life she lived altering her? She had known Mr. Arthur for a year and a half before he had thought of speaking with any intimacy to her. The thought that she was deteriorating—becoming as other women—passed across her mind with a sensation of nausea. She rose to her feet.

"I must get back," she said.

"But it's only just two," he replied.

"I know, but then I came out five minutes early."

"Are they so fierce as that?"

"Yes, I daren't be late. Mr. Bonsfield gives me his letters directly after lunch. I think he'd tell me I might go, if I was late. You see it's very easy for them to get a secretary, the work's not difficult though there's a lot of it; and there are hundreds of girls who'd be ready to fill my place in a moment."

He watched her considerately. "Thank God, my lance is free," he said. "Well—I suppose you must—if you must. I've enjoyed the talk."

Her eyes lighted, smiling. "So have I—immensely—it is very good of you. Good-bye." She held out her hand.

"Do you think you get off so lightly?" he asked.

"How do you mean?"

"I mean—do you think I'm going to let you go without some chance of seeing you again?"

"But—"

He checked that. He could not guess what had been passing through her mind, yet the note in her voice on that one word was discouraging.

"You are going to come to dinner with me one evening."

She was full of indecision. He gave her no time to think. It was not his intention to do so.

"But how can I?" she began.

"By coming dressed—just as you are. No need to go home and change. I'll be ready to meet you outside the office at six o'clock. You don't get out till a quarter past? Then a quarter past. We go to dinner—we go to a theatre; music-hall if you like—then I drive you down to Waterloo, put you in the last train to Kew Bridge—and that is all."

She laughed in spite of herself.

"I'll write to Strand-on-Green, and let you know what evening. Miss Bishop—what initial?"

"S."

"What's S. for?"

"Sally."

"Miss Sally Bishop, 73 Strand-on-Green, Kew Bridge. And I owe you ten pounds."

For a moment she smiled—then her expression changed.

"That's perfectly ridiculous," she said.

"I wouldn't have you think it anything else," he said; "but, nevertheless, that's a legally contracted debt."

## CHAPTER XI

Before she left the office that evening, Sally picked up the volume of *Who's Who?* kept there mainly because Mr. Bonsfield had a brother whose name figured with some credit upon one of its pages. She turned quickly over the leaves, until the name of Traill leapt out from the print to hold her eye.

"John Hewitt Traill"—she read it with self-conscious interest—"barrister-at-law and journalist. Born 1871; son of late Sir William Hewitt Traill, C.B., of Apsley Manor, near High Wycombe, Bucks. Address: Regent Street. *Clubs:* National Liberal, and Savage. *Recreations:* riding, shooting, fishing."

That was all—the registration of a nonentity, it might have seemed—in a wilderness of names. But it meant more than that to her. Each word vibrated in her consciousness. Reading that—slight, uncommunicative as it was—had made her feel a pride in their acquaintance. Her imagination was stirred by the name of the house where his father had lived, where he had probably been brought up. Apsley Manor; she said it half aloud, and the picture was thrust into her mind. She could see red gables, old tiled roofs, latticed windows, overlooking sloping lawns, herbaceous borders with the shadows of yew trees lying lazily across them. She could

E. Temple Thurston

smell the scent of stocks. The colours of sweet-peas and climbing roses filled her eyes. In that moment, she had fallen into the morass of romance, and through it all, like a gift of God, permeated the sense that it belonged to this man who had dropped like a meteor upon the cold, uncoloured world of her existence.

This is the beginning, the opening of the bud, whose petals wrapped round the heart of Sally Bishop. Romance is the gate through which almost every woman enters into the garden of life. Her first glimpse is the path of flowers that stretches on under the ivied archways, and there for a moment she stands, drugged with delight.

After supper that evening, Mr. Arthur followed her into the sitting-room.

"Can you spare me a few minutes?" he asked.

His method of putting the question reminded her of Mr. Bonsfield's chief clerk—the son of a pawnbroker in Camberwell. He assumed the same attitude of body. Certainly Mr. Arthur did not fold his hands together before him—he did not sniff through his nostrils; but her imagination supplied these deficiencies in the likeness.

She agreed quite willingly. The prospect of what she knew was coming, held no terrors for her. The only real terror is that of doubt. She knew the course she was about to take. There was no hesitation in her mind. The fate of Mr. Arthur in moulding the destiny of Sally's life was weighed out, apportioned, sealed. It had only to be delivered into his hands.

If this is a short time for so much to have happened, it can only be said that Romance is a fairy tale where seven-leagued-boots and magic carpets are essential properties of the mind. In a fairy tale you are here and you are there by the simple turning of a ring. Matter—the body—is a thing of nought. It is the same with Romance; but there you deal with magical translations of the mind. From the grim depths of the valley of despair, you are transported on to the summit of the great mountain of delight; from the tangled forest of doubt, in one moment of time you may be swept on the wings of the genie of love into the sun-lit country of content.

Happening upon this fairy tale—as every woman must—had come Sally Bishop. It would seem a foolish thing to think that Apsley Manor, in the county of Buckinghamshire, should play a part in so great a change in the life of any human being; it would seem strange to believe that out of a two hours' acquaintance could arise the beginning of a whole life's desire; yet in the fairy story of romance, all such things are possible; nay, they are even the circumstances that one expects.

When she walked out along the river-side that evening with Mr. Arthur, there was an unreasoning content in her mind. The lights from the bridge danced for her in the black water, reflecting the lightness of her heart. She was in that pleasant attitude of mind—poised—like a diver on a summer day, before he plunges into the glittering green water. A few more days, another meeting, and she knew that she would be immersed—deeply in love. Now she toyed with it, held the moment at arm's length, and let her eyes feast on the seeming voluptuous certainty of it. And when Mr. Arthur began the long preface to the point towards which his mind was set, it sounded distant, aloof, as the monotonous voice of a priest, chanting dull prayers in an empty church, must sound in the ears of one whose whole soul is struggling to lift to a communion with God Himself.

E. Temple Thurston

"I only want to know if you have made up your mind?" he said, when he had finished his preamble.

"Yes, Mr. Arthur, I have."

"You can't?"

He took the note in her voice. It rang there in answer to the apprehension that was already in his mind.

"No, I can't."

"Why not?"

"The same reason I gave you before."

"You don't love me?"

"No; I'm sorry, but I don't."

"That'll come," he tried to say with confidence.

She thought he was really sure of it; but instead of being angry, she felt sorry for him. He hoped for that—he had every right to hope—but oh, he little realized how impossible it was—how utterly, absolutely impossible it was now. There is no rate of exchange for Romance in the heart of a woman; she gives her whole soul for it, and nothing but Romance will she take in return.

"It's no good saying that," she replied; "things don't come when you expect them to. It surely can't be right for people to marry when they are only hoping that one of them may love the other."

"But you seem to forget the position I'm offering you," he

said. "Is that no inducement?"

"No; I'm not forgetting it. But do you think position is everything to a woman?"

"No; but she likes a home."

"Then why do you think I gave up mine?"

"I didn't know you had given it up. I thought you had been compelled to earn your living."

"No; not at all. My father was a clergyman down in Kent. He only died last year. My mother still lives there and my two sisters. I could have a home there if I wished to go back to it."

He looked at her in a little amazement. "I suppose I don't understand women," he said genuinely.

She looked up into his uninteresting face—the weak, protruding lower lip, the drooping moustache that hung on to it—then she smiled.

"I suppose, really, you don't," she agreed. "I think we'll go back; I'm getting cold."

They walked back silently together, all the night sounds of the river soothing to her ears, jarring to his. A train rushed by, thundering over the bridge from Gunnersbury way; he looked at it, frowning, waiting for the noise to cease; she watched it contentedly, thinking that it had come from the Temple where Traill was a barrister-at-law.

"Then I suppose it's no good my saying any more," said Mr. Arthur, as he stood at the door with his latch-key ready in the lock. He waited for her answer before he turned it.

"No, no good," she replied gently; "I'm so sorry, but it isn't. I hope it won't be the cause of any unfriendliness; you have been very good to me, and I do really appreciate the honour of it." The same phrases, with but little variation, that every woman uses. It is an understood thing amongst them that a man is conscious of paying them honour when he asks them in marriage, and that it is better to show him that they are sensitive to it. He thinks of nothing of the kind—certainly not at the time. That last appreciation of the honour is the final application of a caustic to the wound that smarts the most of all—though in the end it may heal.

Mr. Arthur turned the key viciously in the lock, and pushed the door open.

"I suppose you have to say that," he exclaimed, "but of course there's no honour about it to you. If your father was a clergyman, you probably look down on me. My father was in the grocery business. He got me into the bank because he had an account there."

He stood by to let her pass him into the hall.

"You're really quite wrong," she began, then she saw that he was not following her. "I thought you were coming in," she said.

"No; I'm not coming in yet. Good night."

He closed the door behind him, and left her abruptly in the darkness of the hall.

She stood there for a moment, listening to the departure of his footsteps as he slouched aimlessly away. He was nobody—nobody in her life—but she felt sorry for him. On the verge of love—in love itself—is a boundless capacity for sympathy. She turned to go upstairs, still feeling pity for him in the pain she had unavoidably caused him. She did not realize that this was simply a reflection, the first shadowing of her love for Traill, that sought any outlet in which to find expression.

In the bedroom, Janet was making a strange costume for a student's fancy dress ball. She did not look up when Sally entered. With her inexperienced needle, the work occupied her whole attention. Sally stood and watched her laborious efforts with a smile of gentle amusement.

"Let me do it for you," she said at last—"those stitches 'll never hold."

In her mood she was willing—anxious to do anything for any one. She felt no fatigue from her day's work. In the everlasting routine, it is the mind that makes the body tired. Her mind was lifted above the ordinary susceptibility to exhaustion.

Janet stuck her needle into the material on her knee, and looked up searchingly.

"What's the matter with you to-night?" she asked.

"Nothing's the matter. Why?"

"You're so officiously agreeable."

Sally laughed.

"You wanted to help Mrs. Hewson to make that mincemeat," Janet continued; "now you want to help me; and you were the soul of good-nature to Mr. Arthur. I'm sure he thinks you're going to accept him."

"No, he doesn't."

"How do you know?"

"I told him after supper. He asked me to come out with him. I told him I couldn't marry him."

Janet looked at her with curiosity, her eyes narrowed, judging the tone of the words rather than the words themselves, as if they were subject for her brush.

"How did he take it?" she asked, gaining time for the maturity of her judgment.

"I feel awfully sorry for him. He went out again when I came in."

"Takes it badly, then?"

"I'm afraid so."

"You're sorry for him?"

"Yes."

"Why? You haven't thrown him over. He's taken his chance—he'll get over it. You're very soft-hearted. It's all in the game. You'll have to take your chance as well, and no one'll be sorry for you if you come worst out of it."

Sally looked at her thoughtfully. "I don't believe you've got a heart, Janet," she said.

"Don't you?"

"Well, have you?"

"It's not a weakness I care to confess to."

"That's as good as admitting it."

Janet was slowly driving to the point. In another moment, she knew that she would have the truth.

"If having a heart means wasting one's sorrows on men like Mr. Arthur, I'm glad I haven't." Janet threw her work over the end of her bed, and looked up at Sally.

"Who is he, Sally?" she asked abruptly. "What's his name? Where does he live?"

"Who?" She tried to lift her eyebrows in surprise, but the blood rushed to her cheeks and burnt them red. "Who?" she repeated.

"The man you're in love with. I asked you before if there was some one in the office; it's silly going on denying it. You'd never have told Mr. Arthur so soon. You'd have hung it on and hung it on for heaven knows how long. No, something's happened, happened to-day. Do you think I can't see? You're bubbling over with it, longing to tell me, and afraid I'll laugh at you." She rose to her feet and stuck her needle into the pincushion, then she put her arm round Sally's waist, and hugged her gently. "Poor, ridiculous, little Sally," she said, the first soft note that had entered her voice. "I wouldn't laugh at you. Don't you know you're made to be loved—not like me. Men hate thin, bony faces and scraggy hair; they want something they can pinch and pet. Lord! Imagine a man pinching my cheeks—it 'ud be like picking up a threepenny

E. Temple Thurston

bit off a glass counter. Who is he, Sally?"

Sally lifted up her face and kissed the thin cheek.

"Let's get into bed," she whispered.

They undressed in silence. Once, when Sally was not looking, Janet stole a glance at her soft round arms; then gazed contemplatively at her own. They were thin, like the rest of her body—the elbows thick, out of proportion to the arm itself. She bent it, and felt the sharp bone tentatively with her hand. Sally looked up, and she converted the motion of feeling into that of scratching, as though the place had irritated. Then she continued with her undressing.

When once they were in bed and the light was out, Sally told her everything. Janet made no comments. She listened with her eyes glaring out into the darkness, sometimes moistening her lips as they became dry. The unconscious note in Sally's voice thrilled her; it was like that of a lark thanking God for the morning. She felt in it the pulse of the great force of sex—nature rising like a trembling god of power out of the drab realities of everyday existence.

It wakened a sleeping animal in her. She felt as though its stertorous breaths were fanning across her cheeks and she lay there parched under them.

"What's that?" exclaimed Sally under her breath when she had finished her relation.

"What's what?"

"That noise."

They both listened, breaths held waiting between their lips, their heads raised strainingly from their pillows.

On the other side of the wall was Mr. Arthur's room, and from their beds they heard muffled sounds as of a person speaking. They waited to hear the other voice in reply. There was none. He must be speaking to himself. Sometimes the voice would stop. Then came one single sound like a groan, only that it was more exclamatory. For a few moments there was silence; then again a clattering noise. That was recognizable—a boot being thrown on to the floor. It came again—the second boot. Then another single sound of the voice, a sudden violent creaking of springs as a heavy body was thrown on to the bed; then silence.

"That's Mr. Arthur," said Janet. "He's drunk."

And whereas Janet found sympathy for him, Sally lost that which she had.

E. Temple Thurston

# CHAPTER XII

The dinner was fixed some few days later for seven o'clock in a little restaurant in Soho.

*"Don't think because I chose this place,"* concluded Traill's letter, *"that I am considering the fact that we are not dressing, and that, therefore, it ought not to be some ultra-fashionable place. You shall come to those another time if you wish. This particular evening I want to be quiet, and this is the quietest place I know. I leave the theatre to your choosing. Anything will suit me, I have seen them all."*

Janet watched her across the breakfast-table as she folded the letter and crumpled it into her pocket. Their eyes met and they smiled.

"I shan't be in to dinner this evening, Mrs. Hewson," Sally said presently.

Mrs. Hewson looked up from a plate of shrimps which had been left over from the last evening's supper. Her sharp little eyes criticized Sally. Janet often stayed out for the evening; that was by no means an uncommon occurrence. Art students are convivial souls; they love the unconventionality of the evenings in each other's company. Sometimes Sally went with her to a small impromptu dance or a musical at-home in the purlieus of Chelsea. But never before had she announced that she was going out by herself. Mrs. Hewson did not profess to have any control over the morals of her lodgers, so long as they did not reflect in any way upon her own respectability; but she could not refrain from that British desire for interference in other people's affairs in the cause of morality itself.

Morality itself, not as any means to an end, but just its bare superficial display of conventional morals, is treasure in heaven to the average English mind. And their morality itself is a poor business—cheap at the best. To be respectable, to do what others expect of you, is the backbone of all their virtue. It has been said, we are a nation of shopkeepers. If that is true, then all the shops are in one street, packed tight, the one against the other. For we are a nation of neighbours too, prone to do what is being done next door, and a lax king upon the throne of England could turn our morals upside down. All things are fashions—even moralities—they take longer to come and longer to go, but they change with the rest of things nevertheless, and we follow, doing what is at the moment the thing to do.

In Mrs. Hewson's eyes, as she looked up at Sally, was a considerate inquiry blent with curiosity, touched with suspicion which she tried in vain to conceal.

"Going out to dinner, Miss Bishop?" she asked.

"Yes."

"Oh—that's nice for you—isn't it?"

"Very."

Though Janet had finished her breakfast, she waited on with

E. Temple Thurston

amusement concealed behind an expressionless exterior.

"Of course, Mr. Arthur can afford it," Mrs. Hewson went on. Sally made no reply. Mr. Hewson simpered affectedly. "Of course, I'm only supposin' it's Mr. Arthur. P'raps I may be quite wrong." Sally still resorted to silence. "Are you going to a theayter with him?" She shot the last bolt—went as far as decency in such matters and such surroundings would permit, and it succeeded—it forced Sally to retort.

"It's not Mr. Arthur, Mrs. Hewson—there is no need to worry yourself." She snapped the words—broke them crisp and sharp with pardonable irritation and spirit.

"Oh—indeed—I'm not worrying meself. I'm sorry to have made you so offended like—it's no affair of mine. I'm quite aware of that—only that I thought, seeing you've been here nigh on two years and never gone out by yourself before like—I was only just making—whatcher might call—friendly inquiry about it—see?"

She brushed the heads of the shrimps into the slop-basin with her hand and stood up, evidently offended, from the table.

"Of course, it's no business of mine, and I have no cause to complain of anything you do; you give no offence to me, I must say that. I never had better be'aved lodgers than I've got at present."

"But you felt curious?" suggested Janet.

"Me? Curious? Well, I think that's the last thing you could accuse me of. I've got enough affairs of me own without worrying about other people's. Me? Curious?" She laughed at the impossibility of such a thing, and began to clear away the breakfast things with more noise than was actually necessary.

"Well, there's nothing to be excited about, then," said Janet.

Mrs. Hewson laid a cup and saucer with such gentleness upon a pile of plates that the absence of noise was oppressive.

"I'm not excited," she said with crimson cheeks.

"Sorry," said Janet, laconically; "thought you were. If there's a thing more hateful than another, I think it's the vexation of a person who can't satisfy their curiosity about some other body's business. Don't you think so, Mrs. Hewson?"

"I'm sure I don't know. Those abstruse matters don't worry me."

"No? Well, that is so, and it's about the commonest weakness of humanity. If I thought you worried about our affairs—of course, I know you don't, you're most reasonable—I wouldn't stay here another minute."

The colour in Mrs. Hewson's cheeks went from red to white.

"But you said I was curious," she said in a reserved voice.

"Oh yes, that was only fun! Hadn't you better get a key, Sally, if you're going to be late. Can you spare Miss Bishop a key, Mrs. Hewson?"

"Certainly; of course; I'll go and get it."

They both laughed when she had gone out. Sally told Janet that she was wonderful.

"She'll never meddle again," she said. "I couldn't have done it like you did."

"Of course you couldn't."

"But why not? I wouldn't be afraid to, but simply I shouldn't think of things; and why shouldn't I?"

"Because you're not meant to fight, you have to be fought for, like Mr. Arthur fought for you in his own particular way, like this man you're going to meet to-night is fighting for you too."

Sally's eyes looked wonderingly before her. "Do you think things are really like that?" she asked.

"I'm sure of it."

"But why?—why, for instance, are you meant to fight?"

"Do you want me to answer the riddle of the Universe?"

"I don't see why it should be such a riddle."

"Well, it is. I don't know who arranged these things, no more than any one else, though a good many make a comfortable income by telling you that they do. But it's pretty obvious that it is so; that's enough for me."

"I don't see why it's obvious," Sally persisted.

Janet stood away from the table and held out her arms—the thin, fleshless arms—straight, no deviation to the ungainly shoulders. There was unconscious drama in it. Yet she was the last person in the world to act.

"Well, *look* at me," she said.

Sally only looked at her eyes, and her lips twitched compassionately.

"You may be all wrong," she said. "I may have to fight as well—you don't know—and somebody, you can never tell, may fight for you."

Janet took the round, warm cheeks in her hands and caressed them with the long, sensitive fingers.

"That'll never be," she said quietly—"never—never. I know it right away in here." She laid her hand upon her chest.

"But why?" Sally repeated petulantly, as though wishing it could alter the truth.

"Because I suppose I really want to do the fighting, however much I may think differently, when I see you and hear you talk, when your heart's going and there's all the meaning of it in your eyes. I've got to fight, and away inside me I want to. I suppose that's the compensation."

Then Mrs. Hewson brought the key, saying words over it— an incantation of half-hearted rebuke—and following Sally with her eyes as she walked out of the kitchen.

# CHAPTER XIII

There is Bohemianism still—there will always be Bohemianism. But the present will never wear the same air of fantasy as the past. It is the same with all things. Every circumstance take its colour from the immediate surroundings, and you cannot expect to get the same light-hearted Bohemianism in the midst of an orderly, church-going, police-conducted district. What hope is there for a troubadour nowadays with the latest regulations upon street noises? We must dispense with troubadours and get our Romance elsewhere. So everything has to suit itself to its own time— Bohemianism with the rest.

One essential quality there is, however, in this Vie de Boheme that will never alter. It demands that those who live it, shall be careless of the morrow; it expects an absolute liberty of soul, let manners and conditions be what they may. You will still find that; you will always find it. Certain souls must be free and they always seek out the spots of the earth where social restrictions, social exigencies, are least of all in force. They live where life is freest; they eat their meals where it is not compulsory for them to be on their best behaviour. You cannot expect the Bohemian to be a slave, and to customs least of all. The only well-ruled line that he can follow is the customary prompting of his own instinct.

Such a spot—an ideal corner of all unconventionality—is Soho. They say that Greek Street is the worst street in London. You must say something is the worst, to show how bad and good things are. Then why not Greek Street? But for no definite reason. It is really no worse than many another and, with a few more lamps to light its darkened pathways, it might earn that reputation for respectability which would endear it to the most exacting of British matrons. All the doubtful deeds are only done in dark streets. Light is the sole remedy; you will see crime retreating before it like some crawling vermin that dares not show its face. Therefore, why blame Greek Street and those who live there? The county council are to blame that they do not cleanse the place with light.

Bad or good, though—whatever it may be—it is part of Soho; the refuge of Bohemianism to which district Traill brought Sally Bishop on that Thursday evening.

Outside the restaurant in Old Compton Street with its latticed windows, and its almost spotless white lintels and the low-roofed doorway, a barrel-organ was twirling tunes to which two or three girls danced a clumsy step. In the doorway itself, at the top of the precipitous flight of stairs that led immediately to the room below, stood Madame, the proprietor's wife—ready to welcome all who came. Her round, French, good-natured face beamed when she saw Traill, and her little brown eyes gleamed with genuine approval as they swept over Sally.

"Bon soir, Monsieur; bon soir, Madame."

Every lady is Madame, however many during the week Monsieur may choose to bring, and she makes a romance of every single one of them. Her own days are memories, but, being French, she still lives in the romance of others.

"Good evening," said Traill; "how's the business—good?"

"Mais, oui, Monsieur; les affaires vont assez bien."

They climbed down the narrow little staircase, made narrower and almost impassable by the pots of evergreens placed for decoration upon some of the steps. There, in the flood of light, the little room papered in gold, hung with pictures advertising the place, all done by needy customers— mostly French—who had given them to the establishment for a few francs, or out of the fullness of their hearts, they were greeted in welcome again by Berthe, the little waitress.

"Bon soir, Monsieur; bon soir, Madame."

It was like the cuckoo hopping from the clock to sing his note at every quarter.

There were little tables in every corner, all covered with virgin-white cloths and, in the centre of each, a vase full of chrysanthemums. It was all in order—all spick and span— French, every touch of it.

"Ou voulez-vous asseoir, Monsieur? Sous l'escalier?"

Under the staircase by which they had just descended, two tiny tables had been placed—babies, thrust into the corner, looking plaintively for company. An Englishman would probably have made a cupboard of the place for odds and ends.

Traill consulted Sally. She did not mind. Anything in her mood would have pleased her. The atmosphere of all that was foreign in everything around her had lifted her above ordinary considerations. Under the stairs, then, they sat, Traill's head almost touching the sloping roof above him.

"Well, what do you think you'd like to have?" he asked. And Berthe stood by, patiently waiting, content to study the little details that made up Madame's costume; her eyes were lit with the same romantic interest which the proprietress had shown on their arrival.

"I don't mind."

"Well, will you have escargots?"

"What's that?"

"Snails."

Sally shook her head with a grimace and smiled. Berthe tittered with laughter.

"Monsieur is funning, he would not eat escargots himself." She smiled at Sally, the smile that opens confidence and invites you within; no grudging of it between the teeth, ill-favoured and starved, as we do the thing in this country.

"However did you find this lovely little place?" asked Sally, when the girl had gone with Traill's order.

"Deux consommes, deux!" shouted Berthe through a door at the end of the room. "Deux consommes, deux!" came the distant echo from the kitchen.

Traill leant his elbow on the table and looked at her—let his eyes rest on every feature, last of all her eyes, and held them.

"By not looking for it," he said. "By passing it one evening at about the time for dinner, seeing the new-old bottle-panes in the leaded windows, looking down these stairs and getting a rough-drawn impression that the place was cosy, a rough-drawn impression in which the bottle-panes suggested that they had some sort of ideas in their heads, these people—and the little pots of evergreen down the stairs with the ugly red frilled paper round them that made you think that they had known the country—lived in it. All that blurred together in a mazy idea that it was sure to be cosy. Then I came downstairs, saw all these little tables with their vases of flowers, the spotless serviettes sticking up like white horns out of the wine-glasses, saw the beaming face of Berthe over there; was greeted with, 'Bon soir, Monsieur;' and so I dined. That's a year and a half ago. I've had my dinner, on an average, three times a week here ever since."

"It must be nice to be a man," said Sally.

"Why?"

"Oh, I don't know; to dine where you like, find out these quaint little places, never to have to think of the impression you give by what you do."

He leaned back in his chair, and smiled at her. "We have to think just as much as you do, in most of the things we really want to do. I didn't want particularly to dine in such a place as this, that evening I came here. It seemed no liberty to me. There are things I might give the world to be able to do, yet haven't the liberty. What do you want with liberty—the liberty to come and go wherever you please?" He smiled at her again. "What good would it do you?"

Sally wondered what Miss Hallard would say if she were to hear this. She wondered what she would have said herself, had the expression of such ideas come from Mr. Arthur. There was no doubt that she would have repudiated them with vehement denial. With Traill she said nothing—felt that he was right. Why was that? She could not tell. It was beyond her power to analyze the situation as closely as it required. It was beyond her ability to realize that a man may say he is the son of God, if it be that he has behind the words the power of the personality of a Jesus Christ. Traill had the personality—the dominance behind him in what he said—that was all. He might have told her that women were only the chattels of men, born to slavery, the property of their masters, and she would not have denied it to him.

"What in the name of God are women?" he had said more than once in his life—"Is one of them ever worth all the while?" And he thought he had meant it. To a great extent, he acted up to it as well. These are the questions that men of the type put to themselves over and over again—but there are Cleopatras to mate with Antonys, Helens of Troy and Lady Hamiltons who can snap their fingers in the face of such odds and win. But Sally was not of this blood. She is the lamb that goes willing to the slaughter, the woman, whom a man like Traill, when once he holds the trembling threads of her affection, can drive to the uttermost.

"Then you give no liberty to a woman?" she said.

"No—not the liberty she talks about. Not the idea of liberty that she gets from these suffragist pamphleteers."

"I'd like you to meet my friend, Miss Hallard," said Sally.

"Why? Who's Miss Hallard? What is she?"

"She's an artist—I share rooms with her."

"Why would you like me to meet her?"

"I'd like to hear you two argue. She thinks just the opposite. She thinks—"

"I never argue with a woman," Traill interrupted.

"You think so poorly of us?" She tried to say it with spirit—struck the flint in her eyes, contracted her lips to the hard, thin line.

"As women? No—the very best." Her looks did not worry him. Water pouring over marble runs off as smoothly. "You want to be judged as men—you never will be till you can cut your hair short and dress the part. Clothes have the deuce of a lot to do with it. I can love a woman, but, my God, I can't argue with her."

He leant back to let Berthe put the plates of soup before them, and Sally watched his face. It was very hard—high cheek-bones from which the flesh drooped in hollows to the jaws, the grey eyes well set, neither deep nor prominent, but flinching at nothing. There was no great show of intellectuality in the forehead—it was broad, smooth, but not high; yet none of the features were small. The jaw was square, the upper lip long. At one end the mouth seemed to bend upwards in a twist of irony, rather than humour, and the lips themselves were thin—lips that could cut each word to a point if they chose, before they uttered it, a mouth by no means sensitive to the hard things it could speak.

To Sally it both feared and fascinated. Whenever he was not looking, she could not take her eyes away. In the pictures in her mind, it showed itself most often in ironic rage; yet he could look at her with an expression that wooed the softest of thoughts in her heart. Then she felt a slave, and would have given him the world, held in her fingers, the gift would have seemed so small.

He looked up quickly from his plate—all motions of his head were alert. "Why don't you begin your soup?" he asked.

She laughed quietly, and commenced at once with childlike obedience.

"Has Mr. Arthur said anything to you since?" he inquired presently.

For a short moment she hesitated—then she admitted it.

"When?"

"Monday evening."

"Oh—the day you had lunch with me."

"Yes."

"What did he say?"

Again she hesitated.

"What right have I to ask—eh?" he interrupted before she could frame the words to reply. "Isn't that what you're sticking over? Of course I've no right but interest. You brought me the interest, you know—but I apologize for it all the same. Berthe!"

"Oui—Monsieur."

"Maquereaux grilles; and I want something to drink."

Berthe went to the bottom of the stairs, leaning on the third step with her hand and calling up to the room above.

"Alexandre!"

"Why does she do that?" inquired Sally.

"She's calling for Alexandre, the waiter who runs out across the street—obediently but slowly—with your pennies to buy your wine. They don't have a license here."

Alexandre made his appearance with a big red cardboard cover in his hand, which looked as if it held a copy of a weekly paper. This was the wine list. Traill gripped it from him, giving the number almost at the same moment.

Alexandre waited patiently for a moment, then deferentially suggested that he should be given the money, having received which, the little staircase swallowed up his tall, thin body again. It was all like playing at keeping restaurant, only everything worked without a hitch, which would never have happened if it had really been only a game.

"I apologize," Traill repeated, when Alexandre had disappeared.

"But there's no need to," said Sally, quickly. "I think it's very kind of you to take the interest that you do. And I suppose"—her eyes roamed plaintively round the room, rather than at that moment meet his; "I suppose I should have told you without your asking."

"Why?" he leaned a little forward.

"I don't know. Because I wanted to, I expect."

Her eyes fell to the table. She made tiny pellets of bread between her fingers and placed them one by one in a row, knowing that his eyes were searching through her. In that little moment, the silence vibrated with the current of their thoughts. Traill pulled himself together—laying hand upon anything that came within his reach.

"Look at this knife," he said in a dry voice, picking up the nearest to him. "Ever seen such a handle? it's shrunk in the wash." The bone handle of it was bent round, twisted like a ram's horn. "I generally get this about once a week. It's an old friend by this time."

She looked at it, scarcely seeing, and forced a smile that could not quite remove the furrow of silent intensity from her brows. Traill saw that. He could not take his eyes from her face. Her almost childish passivity was like a slow and heavy poison in his blood. It crept gradually and gradually through the veins, leaving fire wherever it touched.

Alexandre came back with the wine, and broke the spell of it. He spread the change out on the table, and the sound of it then, at that moment, was like the breaking of a thousand little pieces of glass, over which his presence walked with clumsy feet.

"Well, what did Mr. Arthur say?" Traill asked when Alexandre had disappeared again and Berthe had brought them their second course.

Sally looked up and smiled at his encouragement, a smile that lit through him. He could feel it dancing in his eyes.

"He asked me if I had made up my mind," she replied.

"Made up your mind to marry him?"

"Yes."

The pause was heavy, it seemed to swing against them.

"And you? What did you say?"

He tried to conceal the burning of his interest to know. His voice was steady—each note of each word quiet, true, subdued; but when the brain is tautened, vibrating as was his, it gives out of itself unconsciously. She felt the strain in her mind as well, just as though a wire, drawn out, were stretched between them. She heard the note, half-dominant in his speech. However quiet his voice, he could not dull her ears to that.

"Oh, I told him I couldn't; it was impossible. I don't love him, I never should love him. How could one take a step like that on no other basis than wanting a home? What a home it would be! I should be miserable."

These were her beliefs. She placed love before everything— lifted it to the altar as you raise a saint and worshipped with bent knees and silently moving lips. To understand the great-hearted love of a greatly loving woman, you must know the joy of greatly giving. She loves to give; she gives to love. Out of her breast, out of her heart, with arms laden to the breaking—dragged down by the weight of her gifts, she will give, and give, and give, holding nothing back, grudging nothing, forgetting all she has ever given in the blind joy of what is left to be bestowed. This, when it comes to a woman, is what she means by love as she kneels down in the silent chapel of her own heart and worships. This was the passion as Sally understood it. Her whole desire was to give, and to Mr. Arthur she could have given nothing.

"What did he say?" asked Traill, quietly. A man always speaks somewhat in awe, somewhat in deference, of another whose hopes have been flung to the ground; speaks of him as if he were a prisoner in a condemned cell—fool enough no doubt, but made a man again by the meeting of his fate. "What did he say?" he repeated.

Across Sally's mind pictures were rushing in kaleidoscope. The remembrance of Mr. Arthur as he had left her at the door and turned away, shuffling his steps along the pathway—the sight of Janet and herself, with heads raised from the pillow, listening to the muffled, disordered sounds in the next room—the recollection of Mr. Arthur's face the next morning as she had passed him in the hall, the eyes dull—steam, as it were, upon a window-pane—and the unhealthy shadows beneath. He had grudged her a good morning, but that was all, and she had scarcely seen him since then. He had been out every evening.

"He said very little," she replied, "but I know he felt it very much."

"How do you know?"

"Well, that night when he came in—" the words refused utterance. She looked up quaintly, appealing to him, desiring to be understood without further explanation.

"Drunk?" said Traill.

She nodded.

"Poor devil!"

A thousand apprehensions fled—darkening—across her face. So pass a flight of starlings with a thousand whirring wings that sweep out light of the sun.

"You think I treated him badly?"

"No, I didn't say so."

"But you think it?" She begged eagerly, importunately.

"No, no, my dear child; no. What else could you do?"

"But you felt sorry for him?"

"Do you forbid it? I was putting myself in his shoes, feeling for the moment what he must have felt. Sift it down and you'll find at the bottom that I really said poor devil for myself." He laughed as he looked at her. "Well, now," he went on, "we're getting more than halfway through dinner and we haven't decided where we're going to yet. What's it to be?"

"Really, I don't mind a little bit."

"Oh, you never give any help at all."

She laughed light-heartedly. "I find I get along quite all right if I let you choose."

"You're satisfied?"

"Absolutely."

"Well, then; I'm not going to offer inviolable judgment. I'm only going to make a suggestion."

"What is it?"

"My rooms are in Regent Street—"

"I know; I looked up the number the other day in the *Who's Who?* after we'd had lunch."

"Was that to know if I'd told the truth?" He held her eyes for the answer as you put your metal in the vice.

"No, of course not! How could you think I'd dream of such a thing?"

"Many women might."

"I certainly shouldn't."

A look of tenderness as it passed across his face freed her. She turned her eyes away. He was finding her so absolutely a child, and on the moment paused. There is a moment when a pause holds possibility laden full in its two hands. He let it slip by—it rode off like a feather on the wind. He lost sight of it.

"Well, what's your suggestion?" she asked.

"That we should come back to Regent Street, sit and talk; we'll have our coffee there; I'll show you how to make it."

He tried to run the whole sentence through. Set it on its feet, and pushed it to the conclusion that it might seem natural, unpremeditated. She saw nothing forced; but his ears burnt to the stumbling sounds. The breath caught in his nostrils as he waited for her definite refusal.

"I think that would be lovely," she said with genuine interest.

He let the breath slowly free, checked, curbed, the bearing rein upon it all the way. He imagined he had found country innocence in London, and for the moment stood aghast at it; could not see that it was her trust in him, blindly, implicitly placed, against all knowledge of the world. He stood for a gentleman in her eyes—that Apsley Manor, the late Sir William Hewitt Traill, C.B., they all helped to conjure the vision in her mind. She knew the world well enough in her gentle way; but this man was a gentleman.

E. Temple Thurston

Yet he saw little of this and, in a broadness of heart, warned her.

"I say nothing for or against myself," he said, "and this has not been put to you as a test; I want you to come, I really hope you'll come. But you'd be foolish beyond words if you indiscriminately accepted such an invitation from any man."

"I know that," she replied firmly.

"And you'll come?"

"Yes; I've said I would."

"Why do you make the exception?"

"Because I know you're a gentleman. I trust you implicitly."

That went to the heart of him—drove home—the words quivering where they struck.

# CHAPTER XIV

There was much ceremony when they departed—much French *politesse*, and many charming little attentions were paid. Marie assisted Monsieur on with his coat, which, being British, he strongly objected to. Berthe brought Madame a beautiful chrysanthemum from the vase on one of the vacant tables and, when Sally proposed wearing it, insisted upon pinning it in herself, her eyes dancing with delight as she stood back to admire its effect.

Berthe and Marie stood at the bottom of the stairs as they ascended.

"Au'voir, Monsieur—merci—au'voir, Madame."

Now it was like a duet of little cuckoo clocks, both in unison, both in time, both with that fascinating touch of the nasal Parisienne voice. Sally was enchanted with it all.

Last of all there was Madame—Madame smiling—Madame rubbing her fat, homely hands together—Madame's twinkling brown eyes dancing upon the two of them.

"You had a good dinner, Monsieur?"

"Excellent, thank you, Madame."

E. Temple Thurston

"Oh, Monsieur;" she caught Traill's arm and detained him as Sally went out in front. "Oh—monsieur—elle est charmante!" Her eyes lifted and her hands carried the words upwards—to heaven, if need be.

Traill threw back his head and laughed. "Madame—vous etes trop romanesque pour ce monde."

"Ah, non, Monsieur—je suis ce que je suis. Je suis trop grosse peut-etre, mais pas trop romanesque. Au'voir, Monsieur—merci—prenez garde d'elle, Monsieur." She held up a fat warning finger. "Au'voir, Madame. A bientot."

They left her bowing there against the background of the old bottle glass, lit yellow by the light within, her smiles following them down the street.

"Well—there you are," said Traill, as they walked away. "That's the terrible, shameless Bohemian life in anarchist quarters. What a thing it is to be thankful for, that only the English manners *are* manners, and couldn't afford to show their face in Soho."

# CHAPTER XV

They walked in silence through the little bye-streets of Soho, and followed their way down Shaftesbury Avenue. At the crossings, he lightly took her arm, protecting her from the traffic, freeing it directly they reached the pavement. Inwardly she thrilled, even at the slight touch of his hand on her elbow. She had never been quite so happy before. Nothing needed explanation. She defined no sensation to herself. When the sun first bursts in April after the leaden winter skies, you bask in it, drench yourself in the fluid of its light, and ask no questions. It is only the smallest natures that are not content with the moment that is absolute.

But in the mind of Traill, there swung a ponderous balance that could not find its equilibrium. She had called him a gentleman; was he going to act as one? Into her side of the scale, with both her little hands, she had thrown in her implicit confidence. Was there any weight on his side which he could put in to equalize? He hunted through his intentions as the goldsmith hunts amongst his drachms and his counter-poises; but he found nothing that could balance the massive quality of her faith—nothing!

In his most emotional dreams of women, he had never conceived himself in the drab light of the married man. Possibly because he had never moved amongst that class of

E. Temple Thurston

women with whom intimacy is obtained only through the sanction of a binding sacrament. His contempt of the society to which his birth gave him right of entrance, had always kept him apart from them. But he scarcely saw the matter in that breadth of light. Intimacy with the women he had known had always been possible—possible in its various degrees, some more difficult to arrive at than others, but always possible. And, until that moment, when Sally had told him that she knew he was a gentleman, he had placed her no differently to the rest. Cheap, sordid seduction, there had been none of that in his mind; but he had tacitly admitted within himself that if their acquaintance were to drift—she willing, he content—into that condition of intimacy, then what harm would be done? She was a little type-writer; he, a man, amongst other men. A thousand women pass through the fire that way and come out little the worse.

So had he assessed her, until that moment when she had unthinkingly, unhesitatingly accepted his invitation to come and see him in his rooms. He had thought it innocence, he had imagined it a purity of mind that, in a city such as this, was almost unthinkable. It was his better nature then that had prompted the warning, the opening of a kitten's eyes before it is to be drowned.

Then the last position of all, the position that made the whole thing impossible. She was not innocent! She was not ignorant of the world! She did know the pitfalls in life— knew the luring dangers that lie concealed in the hedges of every woman's highway! No, it was not that. She knew everything—but she knew him to be a gentleman.

There is no more disarming passe in the everlasting duel between a man and a woman than this appeal—whether it be made intentionally or not—the appeal to his honour as a gentleman. Up flies the glittering rapier from his hand, he is weaponless—and at her mercy. For every man, even more especially when he is not one, would be thought a gentleman.

Traill, disarmed, defenceless, weighing every possibility, every intention, was still faced with the unequal balance, her gentle faith in the best of him dragging down the scale. By the time they had reached the stairway to his rooms, he had forged his mind to its decision. This once he would let her come to his rooms—this once, but never again. He knew his instincts and refused to trust them. If she thought him a gentleman, she should find him one. That was owed to her. We give the world its own valuation of us. This is humanity. It is therefore wisest to think well of a man. Those who think badly will find themselves surrounded by the impersonation of their own minds. It is wisest to think well, for even thinking has its unconscious effects. But say evil of a man, tell him to his face, without thought of punishment, merely in candid criticism that you find him ill and, besides giving him a bad name, you will make a dog of him.

She had said he was a gentleman—bless her heart!

"This staircase is confoundedly dark," he said; "I'll strike a match."

She waited, heart beating, listening to the scratching of the match-head against the woodwork. When it flared, he raised it above his head and strode on before her, grim shadows falling round him, following him like noiseless ghosts. Sally kept close behind.

"I used to live on the top floor," he said, "until the day before yesterday; I've moved down now to the first. There's not so much difference in the rooms, but those four flights of stairs in this sort of light were a bit too much." He thought of the

E. Temple Thurston

last woman who had climbed the stairs with him. All she had said that evening, the first day he had met Sally, trooped through his mind in slow and vivid procession. He compared her life with that of Sally's, the ghastly hollowness of it in contrast with this child's simplicity of faith. The picture was an ugly one. He shuddered before the first, no less than before the second; for whereas one repelled, the other drew him to itself with all its subtle fascinations.

"Now," he said, forcing a smile and turning round to face her with his hand upon the handle of the door, "these are only bachelor's quarters, remember; no soft cushions, no mirrors—nothing. And if you'll stay there one second, I'll light a couple of candles. You'd far better have the room chucked at you all at once, than let it grow slowly to your eyes as I stalk round with a match. Do you mind?"

"I? Not a bit!" She laughed and turned with her back to the door, looking down the staircase which they had just ascended. Her heart was still beating, throbbing with unwonted excitement and anticipation. She knew she could trust, but there was a spring—a vibration in the thought that they played with fire. Yet what a harmless fire! No stake in the marketplace at which the soul, the honour, the life of the victim is burnt! No! Nothing like that. Only that fire which, when once it is lit, soothes, warms, nurses the hearts of men and women into love, and when once it is glowing white in heat, moulds them, forges them into the God-sent cohesion of unity. What need had she to fear in playing with so tenderly fierce a fire as that? None, and there was no trace of fear in the heart of her; but her pulses hammered; she felt them even in her throat.

"Now—you can come in now!" Traill called, and he came to the door, opening it wide for her to pass through.

Sally entered—two or three steps; then she stood there looking round her. The old oak chests, carved some of them, worm-eaten here and there; the clean, pale, straw-coloured matting, no rugs of any description: the dark green walls and the rough, heavy brass candle sconces that glittered against them, reflecting the candle flames in every polished surface: it was almost barbaric, more like a reception room of a presbytery than a living room; but a presbytery decorated to convey the best of a strong and self-reliant mind, rather than to pander with a taste ornate to the futile conception of a God.

Except for two rush-seated armchairs, there was no suggestion of providing any recognized forms of comfort. The chair at the open bureau, with its case of books above it, had a wooden seat; all the rest of the smaller wooden chairs were wooden-seated as well. There was no visible and obvious sign of any desire for luxury; yet luxurious it all seemed to Sally, every corner of it, as she gazed around her. It was a luxury conveyed by the intrinsic value of every article of furniture he possessed; a luxury far more lasting, far more complete, than any to be found in down cushions and gently shaded lights.

Austerity was the note through it all, austerity even in the pictures upon the walls. They were prints, old prints, coloured or plain, representing boxers of the old school, stripped to the waist, the ugly muscles flexed and bulging as they raised their lithe arms in the attitude of defence. There were no other pictures but these; nothing to show that he had a heart above boxing. There was one thing. In their journey around the walls, Sally's eyes fell on a little coloured miniature in a plain gold frame that hung by the side of the bureau. At that distance, she could distinguish that it was a girl, a girl with fair hair that clustered on her shoulders. The beating of her heart dropped to a whisper when she saw it, all

E. Temple Thurston

the pulses stopped, and she felt a cool, damp air blowing across her face.

"Well," said Traill, with a smile, "I suppose you think it is confoundedly uncomfortable?"

She turned, faced him, forcing strength to master her sudden apprehension.

"I think it's absolutely lovely," she said, with simplicity. "I've never seen a room like it before."

"And you don't find the want of soft things, cushions and all that sort of business?"

"No, oh no! they'd spoil it. One doesn't want cushions to be comfortable, one wants surroundings. These are perfect."

He looked at her with appreciation; then, as a thought swept over him, it altered to an expression of tenderness. He put his heel on that, churned it round, and strode over to the fireplace.

"Here, come and sit down here and get warm while I make the coffee," he said. "It's frightfully cold outside, you know. I shouldn't wonder if it isn't freezing."

She followed obediently, and took the chair he had drawn out for her. Then he hurried about, opening cupboards and drawers, producing a saucepan here, a coffee-pot and a milk-can there, until all the things were laid on the table. And all this time, while she made sure that she was not being observed, Sally's eyes wandered backwards and forwards to the little miniature. She was nearer to it now and could more clearly distinguish the features. They reminded her some-what of herself. There were the same round cheeks, the same small childishness of lips and nose and chin, the same pale complexion tinged with fragile pink, the same big, blue eyes. Had he taken an interest in her because she was like this girl, this girl whose miniature he had allowed to be the only breaking note in the whole symphony of his scheme of decoration? They were like each other, a likeness sufficiently apparent to suggest the thought to her mind. The miniature was painted in a fashion common to all such works of art a hundred and fifty years ago. She could not tell from its style when it had been done. But the fact that it hung there alone, the one gentle spot in otherwise austere and hard surroundings, was sufficient for her to give it the highest prominence in her mind.

It must be that, it must be what she had thought. He was lonely. He had said as much to her on that first evening when they had driven on the 'bus together as far as Knightsbridge. The girl was far away, in another country perhaps, and he had seen her, Sally, had seen the likeness, been reminded of her in some slight way, and had sought to ease his own solitude with the half-satisfying pretence that she was with him.

There was no thought of blame in Sally's mind. He meant no evil by her; but it was hard. The bitterness of it struck at her heart. After all, there was no fire to be playing with. The coldness of being absolutely alone again chilled through her whole body, and she shivered.

"Now," said Traill—everything was ready at his hand. "The making of coffee's the simplest thing in the whole world; that's why everybody finds it so deucedly difficult. We'll put this kettle on first." He thrust the kettle on the flame, pressing the coals down beneath it to give it surer hold.

"I'm awfully glad you like my room," he said, looking up

E. Temple Thurston

from his crouching attitude by the fire. "I should have been sorry if you hadn't."

"Why?"

"Oh, I don't know. If you hadn't liked my room, you wouldn't have liked me. My friend and his dog, I suppose."

She tried to smile. "Well, I like it immensely. I think it's so awfully uncommon. I suppose you could never get a piano that would go with the rest of the things?"

For the moment his expression hardened. A piano! He hated the sight of them.

"No, never," he said.

"P'raps you're not fond of music?"

"No, not a bit. Are you?"

"Oh yes; I love it."

His eyes lost their steel again to the tone of her voice when she said that.

"Well, that's as it ought to be," he remarked. "Religion and music are two things a woman can't do without. Are you very religious?"

"I don't know exactly what you mean by that. I'm afraid I hardly ever go to church, and in that sense, I suppose, I'm not religious. But I always say my prayers every night and morning."

Traill smiled at her gently. "That's all right," he said;

"churches are nothing, only monuments that fulfil the double purpose of reminding the more forgetful of us that there are a class of people who believe in things they can't prove, and that also provide employment for those who have to look after them. I don't pray myself, but I should think it's the nearest thing you can get to in a combination of religion and common sense. Is that kettle boiling, do you think? Looks like it. Oh, of course, I ought to have known you were religious."

"Why?"

"Do you remember the way you took that impoverished joke of mine about the occupants of the kingdom of heaven?"

She laughed lightly at the recollection. But it was the lightness only of a moment. Her head turned, and she found again the eyes of that miniature looking into hers. Questions then rushed to her lips—a chorus of children fretting with intense desire. She could not hold them back—they would speak. Each one held her heart in its hands.

"Why do you have that miniature—amongst all the other pictures?"

"That?" He turned round, following her eyes, the boiling kettle steaming in his hands. "Pretty, isn't it?"

They both looked at it—he, without distraction—she, with eyes wandering covertly backwards and forwards to his face. Of course, she admitted its charm. Could she do otherwise?

He poured the hot water into the strainer over the coffeepot, then shutting the lid, he laid the kettle back in the grate and walked across to the miniature, looking long and closely into it. Sally watched him, nostrils slightly distended, lips tightly pressed. In that moment an unwarranted jealousy almost charred her softer feelings with its burning breath.

"There are a good many points in it, you know," he said, turning round, "that bear a strong resemblance to you."

"Oh, but she's very pretty," said Sally.

"And you're not?" He came back to the fireplace; stood there, taking regard of every one of her features with no attempt to conceal the direction of his eyes. "And you're not, I suppose?" he repeated.

She smiled with an effort. "If I were, it 'ud scarcely be for me to say. But I don't think I am. I suppose I'm not ugly. When I'm in good spirits, I sometimes go so far as to think I'm not actually plain. But she's pretty—really pretty." Her eyes pointed in the direction of her last remark.

Traill leant forward, facing her, putting both hands on the arms of the chair in which she was sitting. "So are you," he said quietly, "really pretty."

She was locked in, his hands on the arms of her chair and his body making the bars, against which, even had she wished it, escape were impossible. She tried to take it with a little smile, the ordinary compliment in the ordinary way. But the note in his voice refused to harmonize with that. Her smile was forced, her expression unnatural. And there she was caged, locked in by his eyes and, like a bird in the first moments of its captivity, her heart beat wildly against her breast. It was not because she was afraid—the trust in her mind never failed her for an instant—but she knew that she was captive. Whoever the other woman might be, if his honour, his heart, his whole soul were plighted to her, yet Sally knew that she must love him. There was all the giving, all the yielding, all the passive abandonment in her eyes; and when he saw that, Traill shot upright, forcing his hands to anything they might do.

"That's my sister," he said hurriedly, breaking into conversation—the man pursued and seeking sanctuary. He could not trust himself to look closely at her again. The boiling of the milk was an action of refuge; he crushed the saucepan down on to the glowing coals. She had said he was a gentleman.

"Your sister?" Sally whispered. He did not turn; he did not see her lips twitching in the reaction of relief. He had known nothing of the whirlwind that had been sweeping through her mind. All that play he had lost and yet was no loser. Had he seen the jealous hunger in her heart, it would have pointed the rowels of the spur that was already drawing its blood.

"Yes; she lives down in Buckinghamshire. My father left her the place. She's married. That was done of her when she was twenty."

"Apsley Manor?"

"Yes," he twisted round. "How did you know the name of the place?"

"I saw it in *Who's Who?*"

"Oh—" He laughed—laughed hard. "Of course, you told me. Yes, Apsley Manor. It's a fine old place."

"I'm sure it is. I've often—tried—to picture it."

"I'll take you there one day to see it."

E. Temple Thurston

It was out! Ripped from him on the impulse. How could he take her to see it, if they were not going to meet again after this? But he had never determined that they were not to meet again; only that he would not bring her to his rooms. It amounted to the same thing. He was not the man to let his inclinations fool him. If they met, what was there to keep him from bringing her here? Nothing! He knew he would do it. He hoped then that she would take no notice of his remark; but he hoped in vain. She leapt to it, eyes glinting with delight. To her that offer conveyed everything. She saw herself down there in the country with him, the spring just lifting its promise of life, like a child, out of the cradle of the earth. She heard him telling her that he loved her. She felt herself pledging the very soul that God had given her into the open hollow of his hands. Take no notice of his remark? Her whole instinct lifted to it.

"I don't believe there's anything else I should like so well," she exclaimed intensely.

He inwardly cursed his impulsiveness. "Oh, well, that'll be splendid," he said soberly. "Only it's no good going down at this time of the year. The country now's a grave, a sort of God's acre where only dead things are buried. I can't stand the country at this time of the year."

"No, of course not. It's much too cold now; but in the spring—"

"Yes," he jumped at that—"in the spring. That's the time."

Then he thought so too. Perhaps the same fancies were shaping in his mind as well. She threw back her head, resting it on the chair behind. There was complete happiness in the heart of her. Every breath she took was an unspoken gratitude.

"Do you see your sister often?" she asked, as he handed her her cup of coffee.

"Often? No, once a month perhaps." His lips shut tight, as though the question had been a plea that he should see her more frequently and he were determined to refuse.

"But why is that?" she asked sympathetically. "Doesn't she often come to Town?"

"Oh yes—most part of the year. They've got a small house in Sloane Street, and live there all the winter."

Sally looked at him with troubled eyes—troubled in sympathy because, with the quick wit of a woman in love, she had felt here the need of it. His sister lived in Sloane Street—lived there for the most part of the winter, and he saw but little of her; yet he kept her miniature lovingly in his room. If there is but one woman pictured on his walls, you may be sure a man rates her high. Sally knew all this—knew there was more behind it, yet hesitated to intrude. Another gentle question was rising to her lips, when he volunteered it all.

"My sister and I differ in our points of view," he said without sentiment. "We look at life from hopelessly opposite quarters. That's why I live here. The house, the grounds, they were all left to me when my father died. She was given her legacy in a round sum—not very round either. He wasn't particularly well off. Whatever it was, at any rate, it meant little or nothing to her. The house—the property—they were the only things worth having. I was the eldest son—I got 'em. P'raps this bores you?"

She shook her head firmly—an emphatic negative. "How could you possibly think that?"

E. Temple Thurston

"Well, anyhow," he continued, "she was disappointed. She's become—since she married—a woman to whom social power is a jewelled sceptre. Before then, she was what you see in that miniature—a little bit of a child with a pretty face that wanted kissing—and got it. Got it from me as well as others. I was fond of her, even after she married this man—a soldier; he's in the Guards, and after dinner sometimes thinks he has an eye to the situation in politics. Even after that, when she began to lift her head so that you couldn't kiss her and wouldn't have wanted to if you could, I was fond of her. But I hate society—I wouldn't come to her crushes—I wouldn't go to her dinners. These things sicken me. They're as empty as an echo. We fell out a bit over that; but I was living down at the Manor then, and so it didn't actually come to a split. But when the governor died and she found that I'd been left the house which was worth no end to her—socially—and she'd been left the money which really wasn't worth a damn—sorry—that slipped out"—Sally smiled—"she came back to me, arms round the neck—head quite low enough to be kissed then—and did her best to patch the business up. I suppose that rattled me. I could see the value of it. It was just as empty as all the rest of her social schemes. I took her at the valuation, told her she could have the house and I'd take the money, and behaved generally like a young fool. I was only—what? Only twenty-six then. And sham seemed to me the most detestable thing on earth. So Apsley Manor went over to her and I came up to live in London. I don't know really that I regret it so very much. This life suits me in a way, though sometimes it's a bit lonely. That's, at any rate, the gist of the whole business. We see each other sometimes; but her continual efforts to get me to don the uncomfortable garments of social respectability make the meetings as uninviting as when you go to be fitted at a tailor's. I suppose that's a sort of thing you like—you're a woman—but I'm hanged if I do. I'd buy all my clothes ready made if I could be sure that nobody else had worn 'em before. Anyhow, I won't be fitted for social respectability any more often than I can help. By Jove! What's that? Do you hear that noise? It's at the back!"

They strained their ears; lips half parted on which the breath waited, to listen. The sounds, muffled, were broken at moments by a subdued chorus of men's voices.

Traill crossed the room to the door that opened into his bedroom; unlatched it, held it wide. Sally watched his face with half-expectant eyes.

"There's a yard at the back," he said; "my bedroom looks on to it. Excuse me a second." He disappeared. She heard him throw up the window, when the sounds increased in volume. Now she could distinguish individual voices—voices taut, strained to a pitch of excitement. Then Traill's voice, with a strange, stirring voice of vitality keyed in it.

"Sally—here!"

It was not thinkingly said. That there had been no thought, no premeditation, was the fact that stirred her most. In his mind she had been Sally, and in a moment of tensity he had let it shape on his lips. She felt the blood racing through her like a mill-dam loosed. She thought when first she rose to her feet—and it was as though some strong hand had lifted her—that her limbs would refuse obedience. A moment of emotion, that was passivity itself, obsessed her. Then she hurried through into the other room, across to the open window where he stood expectant. There was no thought that it was his bedroom in which they stood—no consideration in her mind of the observance of any narrow laws of propriety. He had asked her. She came.

"This is the cleanest bit of luck," he said, with scarce

E. Temple Thurston

controlled excitement.

"What is it?" She pressed nearer to the window.

He explained. "This yard at the back belongs to some railway company and two of their men are going to settle a difference of opinion—that's putting it mildly—as far as I can make out they mean business."

"What are they going to do?"

He answered her question by putting another. "You know I told you I belonged to the National Sporting?"

"Are they going to fight?" She caught her breath, forcing back the sense of nausea.

"Yes; bare fists with a definite end in view. Why look here—" He took her arm and gently pulled her to the window where he was standing. "Look here, you see they've even got assistants—those two chaps with towels over their arms. The men are over in that shed—stripping, I suppose. By Jove, if I had thought of an entertainment, I couldn't have got anything more exciting than this for you. Ever seen a fight?"

"No." The word struggled through cold lips.

"P'raps you'd rather not look at this? Don't you hesitate to say so if you think it'll be disgusting."

She caught the note of disappointment. There was no mistaking it. In this moment of excitement, he had become a child—scarce content with seeing the passing show himself, but must drag others with him to share his delight and thereby intensify it.

"I can easily go away if I don't like it," she said.

"Yes—of course you can—of course you can. But you ought just to see the beginning, you ought to really. They'll be as quaint as two waltzing Japanese mice. All these preparations will put them right off at first. They'll be funked utterly and look as if they were trying to break bubbles, then they'll warm up a bit. You should see the novices at the National Sporting on Thursday afternoon. They make the whole house roar with laughter. Talk about Don Quixote and the windmills! You must just see the beginning!"

How could she disappoint or refuse him, though the prospect was a moving horror in her mind? She could close her eyes. He had called her. He wanted her to see it with him. How could she refuse, lessen herself perhaps in his opinion? She leant out upon the window-sill and looked bravely below. Their shoulders were touching—she found even consolation and assistance in that.

"Do you think it'll be long?" she asked in a low voice.

"Don't know; it all depends. I hope it won't be too short. Sure you don't mind?"

She was possessed of that same motive which induces a woman to make light, to make nothing of her pain and her suffering to the man she loves. In such moments—loving deeply—she looks upon it, speaks of it, as a visitation of which she is ashamed. Begs him to forgive her that she suffers. It is an entire abnegation of self. It was so in this matter with Sally.

"I'm quite sure," she replied, as she held, with tightening hands and knuckles white, upon the window-sill.

# CHAPTER XVI

The two men emerged from the shed where they had put away their coats. They were stripped to the waist. The couple of lamps that the yard provided, lit up their skin—sickly yellow—and the surrounding houses flung shadows in confusion.

"They'll have a job to hit straight," said Traill, tensely. His eyes were riveted before him. He did not look at her, did not see her white, drawn face. She raised her head, gazing at the black, leaden patch of sky that was to be seen through the muddle of roofs and walls. A wondering crossed her mind of all the horrible sights and scenes that were being enacted under that same impenetrable curtain of darkness which hung over everything. She rubbed her hand across her eyes, but could not wipe it out.

When she looked back again, the men were surrounded by their little groups of supporters—not more than half a dozen in each party. All but the two combatants were talking in excited undertones—giving advice—saying what they would do—standing on tiptoe and talking over each other's shoulders—pushing those away who came between them and the expression of their own opinions. And in the centre of each of these groups stood the two who were about to be at each other's throats. Except for their bared shoulders, dazzling patches of light against the dark clothes of the men surrounding them—they looked the least aggressive in the crowd. They said nothing. Their heads bent forward listening to the medley of voices that hummed unintelligibly in their ears, and their eyes roamed from one face to another, or through the clustering of heads to the other crowd beyond.

"Told you they'd be funked by all this ceremony," said Traill. "They're beginning to wish it was over, I should think. Hang it, why don't they begin? They'll get so cold it'll be like beating frozen meat."

Sally looked at him in amazement. All the hardness, all the cruelty, she saw then. But it did not succeed in turning her from him. She stood wondering at her own passive consent, yet could not bring herself to risk his offence by declaring that she would not stay. Of his selfishness, she saw nothing. Had his attitude in the affair been pointed out to her as frankly inconsiderate, she would have denied it with fervour. Inconsiderate? It was only her weakness of spirit. Why should he be blamed for that? If she loathed the sight of what was taking place before her, then just as surely he revelled in it. Why should he be expected to give way to her? She would give way to him—willingly—freely—without question or doubt.

Now, as she looked again, a man had stepped out of the crowd holding a watch in his hand. There was a tone of command in his voice. It was evidently he who was the master of ceremonies.

"I've seen that chap at the National Sporting," said Traill, quickly. "I guessed there must be some system about this. You see, he's going to act as timekeeper and referee."

"Come on," exclaimed the man referred to. "I ain't goin' to

wait 'ere the 'ole bloomin' night. Get a move on for Gawd's sake. If you ain't made all yer bets, yer'll 'ave ter do it after the show's begun. Come on an' bloody-well shake 'ands and start."

Even when that word was uttered, loathsome enough in itself for a woman's ears, yet indicative of many worse that were to come, Traill did not think of Sally. She glanced at him when she had heard it, remembering what he had once said to her—"I belong to the National Sporting—because there's a beast in every man—thank God!"

The two combatants sifted their way out of the little crowds. They came slowly towards each other, rubbing their bare arms to encourage the circulation. Neither the one nor the other seemed anxious for what was to come. Sally looked tremblingly at their faces and shuddered. One of them was clean-shaven, the other wore a moustache. Both had the deep blue shadows of the day's growth of beard upon the chin and, in that morbid yellow lamplight, their eyes were sunk in hollows dull and black as charcoal.

"Now, who's attending to Morrison?" said the master of ceremonies.

Two men stepped forward out of the crowd.

"Well—get over there at that side. Got yer towels? And the men for Tucker? Come on! Come on!"

He relegated them to their positions, and the little group of men fell away, leaving the two antagonists alone in an open space.

"Now shake 'ands, gentlemen, please," said the master. "'Urry up for Gawd's sake—I'm getting stiff, I am."

They made no motion of obedience, and he looked from one to the other. Even from their window, they could see in his face the clouds of the storm that was about to burst.

"Oh, I can understand now," exclaimed Traill, in an undertone. He addressed the remark to Sally, but his face scarcely turned in her direction. "You see, these chaps have a quarrel and they're going to fight it out under rules and regulations. They've got this fellow who knows something about boxing—at least I presume he does—to come and manage the affair. Probably he knows nothing of the quarrel. He expects them to shake hands, but I'm hanged if they're going to. By Jove! There'll be a mess here if the police get to hear anything."

"But why should they shake hands if they're going to fight?" asked Sally, forcing spurious interest. So she bled herself—sapping vitality to give him pleasure. And he took it—as a man will—unconscious of receiving anything.

"Why? Oh—it's the rules of boxing. The whole thing is supposed to be done in a friendly spirit. These chaps down here would probably cut each other's throats for a song. What's the good of their shaking hands?"

The combatants were still standing reluctant. It seemed for the moment as if the whole affair were about to topple over into a state of confusion.

"Go on, Jim," urged one man in the ring; "shake 'ands wiv 'im. Damn 'is eyes—'e's a gen'leman—ain't 'e? Go 'arn, shake 'ands."

"Look 'ere," said the master, "if there's any of yer blasted bunkum about this, yer can damn well see to it yourselves. I won't touch yer bloody money."

The words shuddered through Sally's ears.

"Go 'arn, Jim, shake 'ands. Can't yer see 'e'll drop the 'ole bloomin' show if yer don't, an' damn it, I've got a couple o' bob on yer. Shake 'ands, can't yer!"

Jim came reluctantly forward into the centre of the ring with a knotted hand held grudgingly before them. The other took it and dropped it as if it were filth.

"That's right," said the master, "now, come on. Two minutes a round—minute wait. Not more 'n ten rounds. And God save us if the coppers don't 'ave us by then. Come up—up with yer flippers! Time!" He tipped a leering wink to the crowd.

The two men edged together, their arms bent in defensive, one clenched fist held menacingly before them. Sally tried to take her eyes away, but a morbid fascination held them. The anticipation of that first blow dragged her as the butcher drags his sheep to the shambles. Every glance she stole in their direction was reluctant; but all power of volition seemed to have left her. The sight of those two half-stripped bodies, gleaming in the gas-light, had concentrated in her eyes. At that moment they filled, obsessed her vision.

"There's not much style about them," muttered Traill. He was leaning far out now, his elbows on the window-sill, his hands supporting his face—the attitude of concentrated interest. "You'll see, they'll go on dancing round each other like this for the whole of the first round. Just what I said—Japanese dancing mice."

So they sidled, ridiculous to see, had it not been in such vivid earnest. Now one feinted a blow, then the next. At each lurching attempt Sally caught the breath in her throat. It freed itself automatically with the lack of tension.

At last in a moment of over-balance—a blow from one of them that struck air and pitched the striker forward—they rushed together, each grunting like swine as the breath was driven out of them. Sally clutched the curtain at her side. Her fingers tore at the fabric.

"Break away, break away!" called the master; and when neither of them loosed his hold for fear the other would strike, he took him whom they called Jim by the shoulder and pushed him bodily backwards. The other followed him with a blow like the arm of a windmill in a gale. Traill chuckled with delight between his hands.

"Time!" called the master, and Jim, striking a futile blow that glanced harmlessly off the shoulder of his opponent, at which the little ring sent up its titter of laughter, they returned to their attendants.

Traill looked round. "What I said, you see," he remarked; "not one blow went home in the first round. Yet they're fanning them with towels—ridiculous, isn't it?" In the excitement of his interest, he spoke to her as though she were as well acquainted with the manners of the ring as he.

Once more they were called into the open. Once more they slouched forward with the advice that their backers had poured into their ears still gyrating in a wild confusion in their minds. That one minute had seemed interminable to Sally; yet she realized how small a speck of time it must have appeared to them.

"Do you think they'll hit each other this time?" she whispered.

E. Temple Thurston

"Well, let's hope so," said Traill. "It's pretty dull as it is. There isn't much sport in this sort of thing if you can't hit straight. Oh, one of them'll land a blow presently. They want warming, that's all."

His words sounded far away but absolutely distinct. She scarcely recognized in them the man whom she had been talking to but half an hour before. His whole expression of speech was different. The lust of this spirit of animalism was uppermost. He was a different being; yet still she clung to him. "There's a beast in every man, thank God!" Just those few words chased in circles through her brain. They had meant nothing to her; she had barely understood them before. Now they lived with reality, and so deeply had his influence penetrated into the very heart of her desire, that she knew she would not have had him different.

Then her eyes dragged back to the scene below her. The men were still sparring; waiting—as Traill had said—for the first falling blow to heat their blood to boiling. At last it fell. Jim Morrison, in a false moment of vantage, rushed in, head down, arms drawn back like the crank shafts of some unresisting engine, ready to deal the crushing body blows. Sally's eyes were wide in a gaping stare. She expected to see the other fall, waited to hear the grunt of the breath as it crushed out of him. But it did not come. She did not try to think how it happened; she only saw Morrison's head shoot upwards from a blow that seemed to rise from the earth. For a moment he poised before his man, head lifted, eyes on the second dazed with the concussion. And then fell Tucker's second blow—the heavy lunge of the body, the thump of the right foot as it came down upon the stroke, and the lightning flash of that bare left arm as it shot through the ugly shadows and found its mark. Sally heard the thud, the void, hollow sound as when the butcher wields his chopper on the naked bone. She saw one glimpse of the bloody face as it fell out of the circle of light into the shadows that hung about the ground, and the little cry that drove its way between her teeth was drowned by Traill's exclamatory delight.

"Good left!" he called out excitedly; "follow it up, man! Follow it up! Don't let him forget it!" Through the fogged haze of sensation, in which for the moment she was almost lost, Sally heard the sudden cessation of voices below. She heard the scurrying of feet and Traill's low chuckle of ironical laughter.

"It's all right!" he called to them. "Go on as far as I'm concerned. I'm nothing to do with the police. You know your own job better than I do. I don't want to interfere with it. Go on."

The voices commenced their chattering again, through which excitement, like a wandering bee, hummed a moving note.

"You won't make any fuss, will yer, mister?" the master's voice could be heard saying.

"I? Make a fuss? No; why the devil should I? Go on!"

"Third round!" said the master.

Then for a moment Sally's eyes opened. In one of the corners sat Morrison on the knee of an attendant, who was sponging the blood from his face, whilst another flapped a towel before him. She took a deep breath as he rose slowly to his feet and came forward to meet his man. Directly the shuffling sound of feet began again, she closed her eyes once more, holding with fingers numbed and cold to the fringe of the curtain beside her. All the sounds then trooped in pictures before her mind. When she heard the stamp of the foot, the dull slapping thud of the heavy blow, and the moaning rush

E. Temple Thurston

of breath, she saw that bleeding face falling out of the sickly lamplight into the sooty shadows.

At last she could bear it no longer. Her imagination was gloating in her mind over the horrors that it drew. She forced her eyes to look. It was better to see the worst than conjure still worse terrors in her mind. She let her sight rush to those two half-naked bodies; it sped unerringly to the spot like a filing of iron to the magnet's teeth.

Now Tucker had regained the advantage which that momentary interruption of Traill's had lost him. His man was swaying before him as a sack of sawdust swings inert to the vibrating motion of speed. His blows were falling short and fast. No great force was behind them. He had no time to give them force. But they were bewildering—the stones of hail upon the naked eyes. Morrison dropped slowly and slowly backwards, one staggering step at a time; his defenceless arms held feebly like broken straws before his face. From nose to chin, from chin to neck, and from the neck in a spreading stream across his chest, the blood—black in that light—trickled like molten glue. In his eyes, she could see that questioning glare, the stupid senseless gaze of a man drunk with exhaustion. And still the blows fell to the murmuring accompaniment of that gloating crowd—fell steadily, shortly, tappingly, like the beating of a stick upon dead meat.

"He's got him now, by Jove! he's got him now," she just heard Traill muttering, and then the yellow lamplight slowly went out into the shadows; the deep, black curtain of the sky slowly descended over the whole scene; she felt a cold wind full of moisture fanning gently upon her forehead and her lips; she heard the muffled sounds going further and further away as though some great hand were spreading a black velvet cloth over it all; then Traill heard her uncomplaining moan, and felt the dead weight of her senseless body as it lurched against his own.

E. Temple Thurston

# CHAPTER XVII

There are men of a certain type in this world whose judgment is exceedingly sound when their instincts are not in play, but who, in certain channels, when the senses are at riot, become puerile; the good ship, rudderless, which only rights itself when the storm has passed. They are men without the necessary leaven of introspection. Of themselves, in fact, they know nothing, learn nothing even in the remorse when the deed is done. For first of all, they are men of strength—men who can over-ride, with determination, rough-shod, the hampering results of their follies. Fate and circumstance have no power over them. They make their own destiny; cutting, if necessary, the knots they have tied, with a knife-edge of will that needs but the one clear sweep to set them free.

Of this type—a vivid example—is Traill. The lust of animalism and the determination to possess the woman he once desired, were the two channels, swept into which, he became ungovernable. All clear judgment which he displayed in the management of his work, all foresight which he possessed to a degree in the arrangement of common, mundane affairs, were in such a moment cast out of him. Brute instinct hugged him in its embrace. He lost all sense of honour, who could in other matters be most honourable of all. All sense of pity he left, to become the animal that scents its prey, and stretches limbs, strains heart to reach it. In those moments when the hunger held him, he took the cruelty of the beast into his heart, and drove all else out before it.

When Sally's inert body fell, crushing him against the window recess, he looked down at her white face in the first realization of what he had done. Then he came readily to action; picked her up bodily—a tender, listless weight. In the bend of his arms, he carried her into the other room. An uncushioned settle, no springs, the seat of plain wood, was where he laid her, propping her head, because he knew no better, with a pillow which he brought from the inner room. The sounds from the yard at the back still reached his ears. He strode through to the window and closed it; brought back with him a glass of water, and stood beside the settle, looking down at the slowly disappearing pallor of her face. Her hat was crushed against the pillow as she lay; he sought with blind and clumsy fingers for the hat pins, extracting them gently, with infinite slowness, as though they were fastened in the flesh. When it was free, he took the hat away and laid it on the table. Then he stood again and watched her. She looked asleep. The loosened hair clustered over her ears—soft silk of gold; his hands touched it. Where a few curls fell out, and the candle-light struck through them, the hair was pale yellow—champagne held up to the sun.

Presently, he picked up her hand, the arm hanging a dead weight from her shoulder, the knuckles touching the floor. His fingers closed over the pulse to find it faintly beating. He had been a fool to let her stand there and watch the fight. He might have known. The thought thrust itself into his mind that he would like to meet the woman who could watch the whole thing out, take the lust of it as he did. She might be worth while. But this child—she was nothing more than a child—who fainted at the sight of blood; he felt a tenderness for her. Looking down at her as she lay on the settle before

E. Temple Thurston

him, he could not conceive himself actually doing her harm. She had called him a gentleman. It seemed as if that stray phrase of hers had taken away all the sting of the desire. She expected him to act as a gentleman; then her expectations should be fulfilled to the letter. The woman who moved him to the deepest force of his nature, was she who knew the brute, not the gentleman in him, and bowed herself in supine submission. And as he stood and watched her there, slowly creeping back through the faintest tinges of colour to consciousness, he little imagined that Sally was the very woman who would so yield herself rather than lose him from her life.

At last she opened her eyes, the dazed, wondering stare that comes after the period of forced unconsciousness.

"Where—where am I?" she whispered.

"Here—my rooms—you fainted."

"Fainted? Why?"

"I don't know;" he knelt down beside her, all tenderness and apology. "The fight, I suppose; we were looking on at that fight outside, at the back. I never thought—I was a brute—it never entered my head for a moment. Here, take a sip of this water, while I go and get you some brandy."

He put the glass in her hand, laced her cold fingers round it, and hurried across to a cupboard in one of the oak cabinets. She was sipping the water bravely when he returned. He took the glass from her, emptied nearly all the contents away into the coal-scuttle—the first receptacle that came to his hand—and poured in the neat spirit.

"Now drink a few sips of this," he said.

She put it to her lips, then lowered her hand again.

"You're really very kind to me," she said in gratitude.

"Kind! Not a bit. Go on—drink it."

She drank a little, obediently, and the points of light came back again into her eyes, the colour burnt once more with a little fevered glow in her cheeks. Then she sat up suddenly with the glass gripped tightly in her hand.

"Oh, what a fool you must think I am," she exclaimed bitterly, "to make a scene like this, the very first evening that you bring me to your rooms. I am so sorry, so awfully sorry."

He looked at her in wonder. "Great heavens!" he said. "There's nothing to be sorry about. If any one should be sorry, it ought to be myself. I let you in for it. I suppose it is a filthy sight, when you're not accustomed to it."

"Yes, but you must think me so weak. And I'm not weak really; I'm very strong."

He saw part of the pathos of this, but not all of it. He did not realize that she was pleading for herself with all the earnestness of her soul. He had no subtlety of mind, and the fact was too subtle for him to grasp that the whole scene which had taken place with that other woman in his rooms upstairs was being re-enacted, but with a different motive. That woman had fought for his money, his protection for her future. Sally was warring against the frailty of her body for his love. Of his selfishness, she had seen nothing. His cruelty, that she had seen; the beast in the every-man, that she had realized as well.

But in the components of a woman there may always be

E. Temple Thurston

found that unswerving subjection to the lower nature of the man. It is a passive submission—for which we have much to be thankful—taking upon itself in its most extreme form, no more definite expression than the parted lips, eyes glazed with passion, and the body inert in its total abandonment.

It is foolish, therefore, to say that man, in that lower animalism of his nature, is alone in the supposed God-creation of his likeness to the divinity. The very instinct itself would die out were there not in woman the passive echo to answer to its call. Divine he may be; in every man there is the possibility, the nucleus, of divinity; but it has not yet shaken off the beast of the fields which blindly, obstinately, without intelligence, hinders the onward path of its progress.

It was this part of her nature, then, in Sally that answered to the display of the lower instincts in Traill. By reason of that part of her, she understood it; by reason of it also, and because she loved him, she was neither thwarted nor dismayed in her desire to win him to herself.

"I do hate myself for doing that!" she exclaimed afresh, when she had finished the brandy he had poured out for her. "Did I say anything foolish, silly—did I? Oh, I hope I didn't. What happened?"

Traill laughed good-naturedly at her apprehension.

"You didn't say a word; you just moaned and tumbled off. Pitched against me. If I hadn't been there, you'd have fallen clean on to the floor and perhaps hurt yourself."

She sat up, then rose unsteadily to her feet. "I am much better now!" she declared eagerly.

He watched her incomprehensively as she walked across the

floor, her knees loose to bear her weight, her lips twitching, and her hands doing odd little things with no meaning in them. It was forced upon him then, the wondering why she was trying so hard to hide her weakness. He would have imagined that a woman would like to be made a fuss of, petted, looked after; to be allowed to lie prone upon a couch, emitting little moans of discomfort to attract sympathy. And he, himself, would have been quite willing to give it. But now, he came to the conclusion more than ever that she was not a woman who cared for the closest relationship. Such a moment as this had been an excellent opportunity for a woman to have forced sentiment into the position, and dragged it on from there to intimacy, to have put out her hand to touch him, seemingly for comfort, but in reality with an hysterical desire for some demonstration of affection. Sally had done none of these things. With a giant effort she had struggled against her inertia. There she was before him, walking up and down the room, talking anything that came into her head with forced courage, feigning a strength which any fool could see she did not possess.

At last his wonder dragged the question from him. "Why are you going on like this?" he asked suddenly.

She stopped abruptly in her walking, turned and faced him with lips trembling and fingers picking at the braid upon her dress.

"Like what?"

"Like this. Walking up and down the room. Trying to talk all sorts of courageous nonsense, and showing how utterly unnerved you are in everything you say."

"I'm not unnerved!" Her hand wandered blindly to the table near which she was standing. She leant on it imperceptibly for support. "I'm not unnerved," she repeated.

"But you are, my dear child. And why should you want to hide that from me?"

She stood there, swaying slightly, taking deep breaths to aid her in her effort.

"Well, I assure you I feel absolutely all right now. I'm not a bit weak now! I know I was ridiculously foolish—"

"Yes, that's the point I want to get at," he interrupted; "that's just the point I want to get hold of." He did not even appreciate his want of consideration then in pressing her to answer. "Why do you call it foolish? It was I who was foolish; I, entirely, who am to blame. I ought to have known that that was not a fit sight for any woman not accustomed to look on at such things. And because you can't stand it, you call yourself foolish."

Sally walked with an effort across to the armchair with the rushed seat and sank quietly into it.

"I only mean it was foolish," she explained, "because it was a silly thing to do, the first time that I come to your rooms, for me to faint like that. Do you think you'll feel inclined to ask me again? Isn't it natural that a man should hate a scene of that kind? I only hope that you won't think I easily faint; I don't; I've never—"

Traill leant forward on his knees. Understanding was dawning in him, it burnt a light in his eyes.

"Do you want to come again, then?" he asked.

So keen was he upon getting his answer, that he could not

see the climax of hysteria towards which he was bringing her. But against that she was fighting, most fiercely of all. Like the rising water in a gauge, it was leaping in sudden bounds within her. But to break into tears, to murmur incoherently between laughter and sobbing that it could not be helped, but she loved him, wildly, passionately, would give every shred of her body into his hands if he would but take it—against this, in the sweating of her whole strength, she was battling lest he should guess her secret.

"Do you want to come again, then?" he repeated, when she continued to look at him with frightened eyes, saying nothing.

"Yes, of course; of course I do."

"But why—why?" he insisted.

This reached the summit of his cruelty—blind cruelty it may have been—but it dragged her also to the climax of her mood. Like the falling of the Tower of Babel, with its crumbling of dust and its confusion of tongues, she tumbled headlong from her pinnacle of strength.

"Oh, don't, please!" she moaned, and then in torrents came the tears; in an incoherent toppling of sound, the little cries of her weeping rushed from her; and Traill, hurled from the sling of impulse, was kneeling at her feet.

"I'm awfully sorry," he kept on saying; "I'm awfully sorry."

Even then he but vaguely understood, had not rightly guessed the verge upon which she was treading. It was not that she feared he might guess the secret in her heart. If, as she half believed, he loved her too, what real harm could be done by that? It was the fear that, in this unsexing moment of

E. Temple Thurston

hysteria, she might lose all control, pitch all reserve and modesty into the flood-tide of her emotions, and lose him for ever in the unnatural whirlwind of her passion. Against that she fought, needing only the release from the tension of his questions. When he began, in his futile efforts to make amends, to ply them again, she rose hurriedly to her feet.

"Can I go into the other room for a moment?" she asked; "or will you go and leave me here alone—just for a minute or two?"

He stood up. "I'll do anything you like," he said.

"Then, go—just for a moment."

The door had scarcely closed behind him before she sank back again into the chair, shaking with the passion of tears. When they ran dry, she rose and crossed the room to the window, throwing it open. The cold air blew refreshingly on to her face. She pressed back the hair from her temples to let it reach her forehead. It was like ice-water on the burning pulses of her nerves. She took deep breaths of it, thankful from her heart for the release. When, at last, Traill knocked upon the door, she could turn with brave assurance and bid him enter. He came in with questioning eyes that lost their querulousness the moment they had found her face.

"You're better?" he said at once.

"Yes." She smiled reassuringly. "I'm absolutely all right now."

He looked at her eyes, red with weeping. He knew she had been crying—had heard her sobs from the other room. Part of her secret then, at least, he had realized. She was fond of him. How fond, it would be more or less impossible to divine; but it must be nipped there—strangled utterly—if he were to fulfil her expectations of him. What it was that pressed him to the sacrifice, he could not actually say; unless it were that it appealed to his better nature as a thing of shame to do otherwise. She would marry him, he felt sure of that. But marriage, with all its accompanying conventions and indissoluble bonds—indissoluble, except through the loathsome medium of the divorce court—was a condition of life that his whole nature shrank from. He refused it utterly. This girl—this little child—perhaps saw no other termination to their acquaintance than that of marriage, and either this thought had become a brake upon his desire, or he wished, in the honesty of his heart, to treat her well; whatever it was, there was not that in his mind which made him determine to be the one to teach her otherwise.

"Well, now sit down, don't stand about," he said kindly. "You can't be really as strong as you think yet, and I've got something I want to say to you. Take this chair, it's about the most comfortable there is here, and I'll get that pillow for your back."

His voice was soft—gentle even—in the consideration that he showed. To himself, he was striving to make amends; to her, he was that tenderness which she knew lay beneath the iron crust of his harder nature.

When she was seated, when he had placed the pillow at her back, he took a well-burnt pipe—the well-burnt pipe that he had smoked before under other circumstances than these—and filled it slowly from a tobacco jar.

Sally watched all his movements patiently, until she could wait for his words no longer.

"What have you to say?" she asked.

E. Temple Thurston

He lit the pipe before replying; drew it till the tobacco glowed like a little smelting furnace in the bowl, and the smoke lifted in blue clouds, then he rammed his finger on to the burning mass with cool intent, as though the fire of it could not pain him.

From that apparently engrossing occupation, he looked up with a sudden jerk of his head.

"You mustn't come here again," he said, without force, without feeling of any sort.

She leant back against the pillow, holding a breath in her throat, and her eyes wandered like a child that is frightened around the room, passing his face and passing it again, yet fearing to rest upon it for any appreciable moment of time.

When she found that he was going to say no more, she asked him why. Just the one word, breathed rather than spoken, no complaint, no rebellion, the pitiable simplicity of the question that the man puts to his Fate, the woman to her Maker.

"Why?"

He at least was holding himself in harness that she knew nothing of—the curb and snaffle, with the reins held tightly across fingers of iron.

"Why?" he repeated. "If you don't know human nature, would it be wise, do you think, for me to spell it out to you?"

She knit her brows, trying to see, trying to think, but finding nothing save the blank and gaping question. Through her mind it swept, that her fainting was some cause of it. She could not really believe that that could have brought so much abhorrence to his mind; yet she tried it. To say anything, to propose any cause, she struggled for that in order to know the why.

"It was because I fainted?" she said quickly. "You hate a woman to be weak; I know I was weak; you hate scenes of that sort. Do you think I can't understand it?" She worked herself into the belief that this was the reason, and her spirit of defence rose with it. "Of course I can understand. If I were a man, I should hate it too! But you're quite wrong if you think I shall get unnerved again, as I did this—"

"It's not that at all!" he said firmly. "Do you think I'm such a fool, do you even think I'm such a brute as to blame you, to think poorly, inconsiderately of you for something that was entirely my own fault? I shouldn't have let myself be carried away by the excitement of that fight. There are many things I shouldn't have done beside that. I shouldn't have stopped as I passed along King Street that night. When I saw that little gold head of yours in the window, I should have gone on, taken no notice. I shouldn't have followed, I shouldn't have spoken to you as I did."

"But why?" she entreated.

He gripped the bowl of his pipe in his fingers. "For the very reason you gave me yourself, on the 'bus that day, and afterwards when we were having lunch together."

"What was that?"

"That I didn't know you."

She looked her bewilderment. "I don't understand," she said simply.

"Then I can explain no further. We must leave it at that."

"Oh! but why can't you explain?" She had nearly added, "When it means so much to me," but shut her teeth, drew in her breath on the words, inducing the physical act to aid her in preventing their utterance.

"I think you would be—perhaps sorry—perhaps hurt—if I did."

"I'm sure I wouldn't—and I'd sooner know."

He looked at her fixedly as the pendulum of decision swung in his mind. To tell her would be to crush it, kill it utterly, the blow of the sword of Damocles falling at last—falling inevitably. He knew how she would take it; just as she had taken his advances to her on the 'bus that night. Did he think that of her? Was that all the depth of their acquaintance! Oh, she loathed him! Therefore, why let it end that way? Why not with this little mystery in her mind, which would not prevent their sometimes meeting again, even if she never came to his rooms?

He stood up from the table, crossed the room to where her hat was lying and picked it up.

"It's nearly eleven," he said quietly. "You'd better think of getting home."

She took the hat from him, then the pins. He watched her silently as she secured it to her head, not even appealing to him if it were straight. Slowly she drew on her gloves, shivering as her fingers fitted into the cold skin.

"I'm ready," she said, when all these things were done.

Traill went the round of the candles, blowing them out one by one, until the scent of the smoking wick was pungent in the air. Before the last, he stopped.

"You get to the door," he said.

Instead of obeying him, Sally walked firmly across to his side.

"We're not to meet again?" she asked.

"I didn't say that."

"But you will never bring me up to your rooms here again? As far as that goes, it finishes here?" She did not even stop to wonder at herself. The fears of losing him were spurs in her side.

"Yes."

"Then if you have any respect for me, you'll tell me why?"

"It's because I have respect for you, I suppose, that I don't tell you."

She stepped back from him. "Is it anything about me?" she asked, "or—or about yourself that you cannot tell me?" Then it was that she feared he had discovered her love for him and loathed her for the disclosing of her secret.

In this persistent determination of Sally's, Janet would scarcely have recognized her. But she was driven, the hounds of despair were at her heels. In such a moment as this, any woman drops the cloak and stands out, limbs free, to win her own.

"Is it about yourself?" she repeated.

Another suspicion now that he was married—engaged—bound in some way from which there was no escape—was throbbing, like the flickering shadow that a candle casts, in a deeply-hidden corner of her mind. She dared not let it advance, dared not let it become a palpable fear, yet there it was. And all this time, Traill was looking at her with steady eyes, behind which the pendulum was once more set a-swinging.

Should he tell her, should he not? Should he rip out the knife that would cut this knot which circumstances seemed to be tying?

"You want to know exactly what it is," he said suddenly. "Then it's this. I'm not the type of man who marries. I've seen marriage with other men and I've seen quite enough of it. My sister's married; marriage has the making of women as a rule, it gives them place, power, they want that—so much the better for them. With marriage, they get it. My sister has often tried to persuade me to marry, drop my life, adopt the social entity, and worship the god of respectability. I'd sooner put a rope round my neck and swing from the nearest lamp-post. And so, you see, I'm no fit company for you. I don't live the sort of life you'd choose a man to live. I'm not really the sort of man you take me for in the least. At dinner, this evening, you called me a gentleman. I'm not even the sort of gentleman as you understand him; though I've been trying to live up to my idea of the genus, ever since you said it. My dear Sally"—he took her hand—she let him hold it—"you don't know anything about the world, and I don't want to teach you the lesson that I suppose some man or circumstances will bring you to learn one day. Take my advice and have no truck with me."

He blew out the last remaining candle, took her arm and led her to the door. They walked down the one flight of stairs together, their footsteps echoing up through the empty house; out on the pavement he called a hansom, held his arm across the wheel as she stepped in; turned to the cabby, gave him his fare, told him Waterloo Station; then he leant across the step of the cab and held out his hand.

"Good-bye, Sally," he said.

She tried to answer him, but her words were dry and clung in her throat.

E. Temple Thurston

# CHAPTER XVIII

The hour of twelve was tolling out across the water from the little church on Kew Green, when Sally fitted her borrowed latch-key into the door. She had performed the journey back to Kew Bridge in a stupor of mind that could hold no single thought, review no single event with any clearness of vision. It was as if not one evening, but three days, had passed by since she had left the office of Bonsfield & CO.—the day they had dined together—the day on which they had watched that terrible fight—the day, the last of all, when she had awakened from unconsciousness, had struggled through a cruel agony of mind, and had finally said good-bye to him for ever. How was it possible, with the length, breadth and depth of three days all crushed into the microscopic space of five hours—a dizzy whirling acceleration of time—how was it possible for her to think logically, consecutively, to even think at all? She could not think. She had lain back in the carriage, her head lax against the cushions, and simply permitted the whole procession of events, like some retreating army with death at its heels, to stagger across her brain. Down the old river-path to the Hewsons' house, she had walked as if asleep, the glazed eyes of the somnambulist, staring in front, but seeing nothing. Up to her bedroom she had climbed with but one thought in her mind, the fear of waking any one. She had struck a match outside the door, lest the scratching of it in the room should rouse Janet. Such considerations as these her mind could grasp. It needed a night of sleep to nurse her comprehension back to all that she had been through. As yet, she was unable to realize it.

One by one, she took off her clothes, in the same mechanical way as she would have done if she had returned exhausted from working overtime at the office. When she put on her night-dress, she knelt down unpremeditatedly upon the floor, held her hands together, and looked up to the ceiling, watching a fly that was braving the cold of winter, as it crept in a sluggish, hibernated way across the white plaster. When she rose to her feet and blew out the candle, she was under the vague impression that she had said her prayers. Then she climbed into bed, pulled the clothes about her, and, as her hand touched the pillow, its softness, the remembrance of the many nights when in loneliness she had wept herself to sleep, all rushed back with their thousand associations, and the dam against her soul broke. The flood of tears poured through, and she sobbed convulsively.

Suddenly then, with a grasp of the breath, she stopped, though the tears still toppled down. She had heard her name.

"Sally—"

It was Janet. Before she could resist, before she could explain, two thin arms were clasped round her breast and a close, warm body was next to hers.

"What is it, Sally—little Sally? tell Janet—tell Janet—whisper—"

The passionate sobbing, which had begun again immediately Sally knew it was Janet, commenced now to break into uneven, uncontrolled breaths, that by degrees became quieter and quieter as Janet whispered the fond, meaningless things

E. Temple Thurston

into her ear. Meaningless? They would have had no meaning to any who might have overheard; but in Sally's heart, as it was meant they should be, they were charged to the full—a cup beneath an ever-flowing fountain that brims over—with such kindness and sympathy, as only a woman of Janet's nature knows how to bestow to another and more gentle of her sex.

"Are you unhappy, Sally?" she asked, when, from the sounds of her weeping, she had become more rational.

There was no answer.

"Are you, Sally?"

"Yes, frightfully—frightfully! Oh, I wish I hadn't got to go on." It was rent from her heart, torn from her. All the spirit in her was broken—crushed.

"But why, my darling? Why?" The thin arms held her tighter, warm lips kissed her neck and shoulders. "Did he treat you badly—did he?"

"No!"

Janet gleaned much in the directness of that answer.

"Doesn't he care for you?"

She knew then that Sally cared for him.

"I don't know. How could I know?"

"He hasn't told you so, one way or the other?"

"No."

"But you think he doesn't?"

"Oh, I don't know."

"Then what makes you so frightfully unhappy?"

"Because I'm never going to see him again."

The words were thick, choked almost in her throat.

"Oh, then he doesn't care," said Janet, softly.

"Yes, he does!" retorted Sally, wildly. "He does care, only—only—"

"Only what?"

"Only, he thinks too little of himself and—and too much of me. He says he's not the sort of man I ought to have anything to do with"—the words were rushing from her now—the torrent of earth that a landslip sets free. "He never wants to marry, he hates the conventionalities and the bonds of marriage like you say you do. And he asked me to forgive him for thinking I was different—different—to what he had expected. He said he ought never to have spoken to me in the first instance, and that it was his fault, and he blamed himself entirely for what had happened. Then he took me downstairs and put me in a hansom and said good-bye. And—I'm not to see him—any more."

It was a pitiable little story, pitiably told; punctuated with tears and choking breaths, with no heed for effect, nor attempt to make it dramatic or sadder than it already was.

When she had finished, she lay there, crying quietly in Janet's arms, all courage gone, all vitality sapped from her.

For a long time Janet waited, thinking it all through. Then she whispered in Sally's ears.

"And you love him, Sally?"

The heavy sigh, so deep drawn that it seemed to strain down to her heart—that was answer enough. What further answer need she give? Sighs, tears, the catch in the breath, the look in the eyes, the look from the eyes—those are the language in which a woman really speaks. Words, she uses to hide them.

# CHAPTER XIX

If you look into life, you will find that the key-note of every woman's existence is love—the broad, the great, the grand passion. She may take up a million causes, champion a thousand aims; but the end that she reaches—is love. To fail in such an end—to lose the grasp of it when once it might have been hers—this is the most bitter of aloes; gall that eats into her blood and corrodes her clearest vision. A man, forging destinies, is a king, to be mated only with a woman who loves.

There are exceptions; but these are not needed to prove the rule; for there hangs even some doubt, like a fly in the amber, in the history of Jeanne D'Arc, the most patent an example of them all. Yet whether, as some chronicles would say, she was never burnt as a witch, but smuggled into the country, and there mated in love—and it would seem a shame unpardonable to rob history of a great martyr and the Church of Rome of a saint—it makes no odds in the counting. Great women have loved greatly—lesser women have loved less—but all who are of the sex have made the heart their master, and obeyed it whenever it has truly called.

So it had come to Sally. Beyond all doubt, she loved; beyond all question, she was prepared to obey the faintest call that her heart prompted. Janet, tender to her that night, fondling

E. Temple Thurston

her and caressing her, answering to her with the very heart that she had tried to stifle within herself, was Janet herself again the next morning. But Sally was unchanged.

She dressed herself silently before the mirror, looking out through the window at the grey river-fog that fell gloomily across the water and Janet lay in bed, her hands crossed behind her head, a cigarette hanging between her lips and the smoke curling up past her eyes. The school of Art did not open until eleven o'clock that morning. Sally had to be at the office at nine.

"There'll be a fog up in Town," said Janet. She did not take the cigarette out of her mouth. It jerked up and down with the words.

"Sure to be," Sally replied.

"Suppose Mr. Traill will come and take you out to lunch?"

Sally turned quickly. "I told you last night," she said bitterly. "We shan't see each—"

"Oh yes, I know that. But do you think he means it?"

"I'm sure he does."

"I'm not."

Sally unpinned a coil of her hair and re-arranged it more carefully, unconscious that she did it because Janet had suggested the vague hope in her mind that he might come.

"Why are you so different this morning?" she asked.

Janet brushed away a piece of glowing ash that had fallen

like a cloud of dust into one of the hollows below her neck.

"Didn't know I was very different."

"You are."

"Well, I've been thinking—" She threw the end of her cigarette away and jumped out of bed, walking on her heels over the cold, linoleumed floor to the washstand. "I've been thinking," she repeated as she poured out the cold water into the basin—"and as far as I can see"—she dipped her face with a rush into the icy water, and her words became a gurgle of speeding bubbles—"there was really no need for all your crying and misery—heavens! this water'd nip a tenderer bud than I am. Ain't I a bud, Sally?" She laughed and shivered her shoulders as she struggled to work the soap into a lather.

"I never can understand you when you talk like that," said Sally. "I never know whether you really mean what you say."

"Well, I mean every word of it. It's the only time I do mean things, when I talk like that. Where'd you put the towel? We want a clean towel, Sally. I sopped up some tea I spilt with this last night. No—but can't you see, there's no need for you to be so miserable as you think. Men only make a sacrifice when they really love a woman. He'll come back to you, like a duck to the water. You know he will. Do you think if he'd cared for you at all, he'd have given tuppence whether he taught you what most men teach most women. The only woman a man thinks he has no real claim to, is the woman he loves; he believes he has a proprietary right to nearly every other blessed one he meets, and has only got to assert it."

"How do you know these things, Janet? What makes you

E. Temple Thurston

say them?"

"You mean who's taught me them—eh? What man has ever taken a sufficient interest in me to show me so much of his sex? Isn't that what you mean?"

"No!"

"Oh, I know I'm ugly enough. That glass has a habit of reminding me of it every morning. I could smash that glass sometimes with the back of a hair-brush, only it might break the hair-brush."

"Janet, you're cruel sometimes! Things like that never enter my dreams!" Sally exclaimed passionately.

"Bless your heart," said Janet, "facts never do. You take facts as they come; you act on them instinctively, but you don't realize them. I *am* ugly. There's no doubt about it. You don't think I'm ugly, but you see I am. That prompts your question without knowing it. But men have made fools of themselves—even over me. There was one man at the school last year—took a fancy to me, I believe because I was so ugly. Just like James II. and the ugly maids-of-honour. I was going to live with him. Can you believe that? And one night at one of the dances, we were kicking up a row a bit—dancing about as if we were lunatics—and my hair fell down—there's not much for a pin to stick into at the best of times. I remember laughing and looking across the room at him. Well, I saw an expression in his eyes that settled it. He looked as if he could see me—just like I know I am—in the mornings when I first wake up—all frowsy and fuddled, with this little bit of a mat I've got, sticking out in tails, about as long as your hand, on the pillow. It takes a bit of courage for a man to even go and live with a woman after he's seen her like that. I assure you it didn't take me much courage to tell him I'd changed my mind."

Sally watched her and the pain that she felt as she listened furrowed her brow into frowns. She knew that there was more than this, more than the bare statement behind this little story. That was Janet's way of putting it, the way Janet made herself look on at life, the apparently heartless aspect in which she viewed everything. To sympathize would only sting her to still more bitter sarcasm. Sally said nothing, the pity was in her eyes.

"I've never told you that before, have I?" said Janet.

"No."

"And I suppose you're terribly shocked because I even ever thought of living with a man?"

"No, I'm not. If you loved him and—and he couldn't marry you."

Out of the corner of her eyes Janet watched her, rubbing her face vigorously with the towel to conceal her observation. In that moment then, she saw the end of Sally, drew the matter out in her mind, as, with hurried strokes, she might have sketched a passing face upon the slip of paper.

"Well, you run on down to breakfast," she said. "You'll be late; it's five minutes to eight."

A whole week passed by, and Sally heard no more of Traill. Every day, when she went out to lunch, or left the office after work was over, she looked up and down King Street in the hope, almost the expectation, of seeing him waiting for her to come. Then the expectation died away; the hope grew fainter and fainter, like a shadow that the sun casts upon the sundial until, at an hour before setting, it is scarcely discernible.                                          .

Another week sped its days through. It was as the unwinding of a reel of silk, each day a round, each round and the body of the reel grew thinner and thinner, and the coils of silk lay wasted—entangled on the floor.

Deep shadows settled under Sally's eyes. The disease of love-sickness has its common symptoms, the whole world knows them; the hungry self-interest that wears itself out into a hypochondriacal morbidity; the perverted power of vision, the hopeless want of philosophy; not to mention the hundred ailments of the body that beset every single one who suffers from the complaint.

Janet watched Sally closely through it all until, as the time passed by, even she began to think that her calculations had been at fault.

At last, one morning, there lay on the breakfast-table in the kitchen, a little brown-paper parcel addressed to Sally. She picked it up eagerly and the flame flickered up into her cheeks as she laid it down again, unopened, in her lap. Janet smiled across at her, but said nothing. When breakfast was over, she let Sally go away by herself up to her bedroom, while she remained behind and talked to Mrs. Hewson. Ten minutes, she gave her; then she mounted the stairs as well. She did not knock. She walked straight into the bedroom and there she found Sally, seated near the window, the tears coursing down her cheeks, while she held out her wrist and stared at a woven gold bangle that bore on it her name in diamond letters. By the side of the empty box was a letter, well-folded, so that it could fit within, and on the floor lay the string and the brown paper, just as it had been torn off.

Janet stood in front of her, hands on hips, warmed with the sense of being a prophet in her own country.

"Are you satisfied now?" she asked.

Sally looked up; the pride of the woman in the bauble blent in her eyes with the disappointment of the woman in love.

"Isn't it lovely?" she said pathetically. "Oh, it is lovely. I've never had anything so beautiful before. But I can't keep it. How can I keep it?"

"Can't keep it!" exclaimed Janet. "What are you talking about? Do you think it was given to you to look at and then return? Why shouldn't you keep it? It's got your name on. He can't give it to anybody else, unless there's more than one Sally down his alley, which I should think is very doubtful. What do you mean—you can't keep it? You make me feel like Job's wife."

Sally unclasped the bangle and laid it back in the little velvet box with lingering fingers. Then she picked up the letter.

"Read that," she said.

Janet swept her eyes to it. To her, as she read, it seemed to be the condensation of more than one letter that had been written before. A man, she argued, who gives such a present, is more than probably in love; and a man who is in love, cannot write so directly to the point in his first attempt.

This was the letter:—

"DEAR MISS BISHOP—"

(To call her "Sally" in diamonds and "Miss Bishop" in ink,

E. Temple Thurston

was ridiculous. Ink was infinitely cheaper; and if he could afford the one, then why not the other?)

"I make it a habit to discharge debts. With this to you, I wipe out my debit sheet and stand clear. You remember my bet on the Hammersmith 'bus. I hope you were none the worse for my foolishness of our last evening. I have regretted my thoughtlessness many times since.

"Yours sincerely,
"J. HEWITT TRAILL."

"What foolishness?" asked Janet, looking up quickly at the end. "What did he do?"

Of the fight and her fainting, Sally had told her nothing. She told her nothing now. The fear that Traill might be thought selfish—a thought which love had refused to give entrance to in her own mind—had led her to defend him with silence. Now she told the deliberate lie, unblushingly, unfearingly.

"He did nothing," she replied; "that's only a joke of his. But you see, I can't keep the bangle," she went on quickly, covering the lie with words, as Eugene Aram hid the body of his victim with dead leaves. "I must send it back to him. I never knew he really meant it when he made that bet. I never even thought he meant it when he reminded me of it that day after lunch."

"No more he did mean it," said Janet, sharply. "If he'd seen you again and again—he'd never have paid it—not as he's pretending to pay it now."

"Pretending?"

"Yes."

Sally took up the bangle in her fingers.

"You don't call this pretence, do you?" she asked. "Why, it's worth even much more than he said in his bet. He paid more than ten pounds for this."

"Exactly," said Janet, shrewdly; "doesn't that prove it? If he was only paying his bet, you can make pretty sure that he'd have sent the money and not a penny more than he owed."

"Yes; but do you think he'd do a thing like that?" said Sally, with pride. "He'd know I wouldn't accept it that way."

"Well, perhaps not," Janet agreed; "but then he wouldn't have bought a thing that cost a penny more than ten pounds, if so much. You don't know men when they're parting with money that they've had to whip some one else to get. You say he's not so very well off. At any rate, he wouldn't have given you a thing that cost fifteen or twenty pounds—those diamonds aren't so small—when he only owed you ten."

"But he didn't owe it to me!" Sally interrupted.

"Very well, he didn't. Then why do you think he's sent you this?"

"Because he thinks he does."

"Very well, again; then why does he send you something that's worth so much more?"

Janet folded her arms in a triumph of silence. For a long time Sally could frame no reply. It had seemed, only an hour before, that she would have been so willing to seize at any straw which the tide of affairs should bring her, and now that the solid branch had floated to her reach, she could not find

E. Temple Thurston

the confidence to throw her whole weight upon it. It was the letter that thwarted her; the letter that warned her from too great a hope.

"But read the letter," she said at last. "Read the letter again. Would he ever have written as abruptly as that if—if what you suggest is right? He might have asked me to—to think sometimes when I wore it—"

"Why? Is he a sentimentalist?"

"My goodness! No!"

"Well, then, he wouldn't. That's a stock phrase of the sentimentalist. The sentimentalist is always thinking, that's all he does, and he breaks his heart over it if other people don't act what he thinks."

"Well, he's not a sentimentalist, certainly."

She even smiled when she thought of his exclamations during the fight.

"What are you smiling at?" asked Janet, quickly. "Something he said?"

"Yes."

"That wasn't sentimental?"

"Yes."

"Well, he certainly wouldn't have told you to think about him when you wore it. I imagine I can guess exactly what sort he is."

"How can you guess?"

"Well, because I know what sort you are, and I fancy I know just the type of man whom you'd fall in love with as rapidly as you've fallen in love with this Mr. Traill. He's hard—he can bend you—he can break you—he can crush you to dust, and there'll still be some wind or other that'ud blow your ashes to his feet. He's all man—man that's got the brute in him, too—and you're all woman, woman that's got the mating instinct in her, and will go like the lioness across the miles of desert, without food and without water, when once she hears the song of sex in the hungry throat of her mate. Oh, it's a pretty little story, too strong for a drawing-room; but Darwin'll tell it you, Huxley'll tell it you. But you'll never read Darwin, and you'll never read Huxley—except in a man's eyes. Oh, I know you think I'm a beast, I know you think I've got no sense of refinement at all, that I might have been a man just as well as a woman. Lord! how your friend Traill would hate me, 'cause he's got all I've got and more— in himself. But I don't care what you say about that letter— the letter's nothing. It's the gift that's the thing. That's the song of sex if you like; and whether you return it, or whether you don't, you'll answer it, as he meant you to. You'll go creeping across the desert, and you won't touch water, and you won't touch food, till you've reached him."

She stood there, shaking the words out of her, the revolutionary in her eyes and God's truth fearlessly in her breath. Then she lit a Virginian cigarette and walked out of the room.

E. Temple Thurston

# CHAPTER XX

There were occasions, as he had said, when Traill met his sister. They were infrequent, as infrequent as he could make them. And they were seldom, if ever, at her house in Sloane Street.

One evening, some three weeks or less after his parting with Sally, he took her out to dinner. He donned evening dress, loudly cursing the formality, and brought her to a fashionable restaurant, where he gently cursed the abject civility of the waiters beneath his breath.

"They're not men," he said to his sister; "they're worms of the underworld, waiting for the corpse to be lowered its regulation six feet."

Mrs. Durlacher shuddered. "You make use of horrible similes sometimes, Jack," she said.

"I see some horrible things," said Traill. "Look at that waiter, hovering like a vulture, while the fat old gentleman from Aberdeen goes through the items of the bill. He might just as well shut one eye and stand on one leg to make the picture complete. That's rather a pretty girl, too, at the same table."

His sister looked in the direction. "Why, he's not from

Aberdeen," she said, daintily. "That's Sir Standish-Roe; he sits on boards in the city."

"A vigorous exercise like that ought to reduce his bulk," said Traill. "Do you know them, then?"

"Yes."

"Who's the girl?"

"That's his daughter. I'll introduce you after dinner if they're not hurrying off to a theatre."

"No you don't," said Traill; "baited traps don't catch me, however alluring they are."

So they talked, all through dinner, criticizing in idle good-humour the various people about them. Whenever he was in his sister's company Traill sharpened his wits. Putting on the social gloss, he called it, whenever she laughed at his remarks and told him he would be a God-send at some of her dinners.

"Is it quite hopeless?" she asked him that evening.

"Quite! As far removed from possibility as I am from a seat in the Cabinet."

"But you might if you took up politics."

"Exactly, the point of absolute certainty being that I never shall."

She waited awhile, letting the conversation drift as it liked; then she dipped her oar again.

E. Temple Thurston

"Do you ever hunt or shoot now?"

"Hunt, yes, for jobs. I've made that feeble joke before to somebody else. No—neither."

"We had some rather good days with the pheasants this year down at Apsley."

"Did you?"

"Yes, Harold got sixty-seven birds one day."

"Lucky dog! Have you finished? Well, look here, we'll come along to my rooms—I'm on the first floor now; I hate talking in these places. You won't have to climb up all those stairs this time, and I'll give you some more of that coffee."

She needed no second persuasion. In the drift of her mind, she fancied she saw impressions floating by, first one and then another, impressions that he was more tractable this evening, more likely to be won a little to her side; for social though she was—the blood in her veins to the finger tips—she still cared for this Bohemian brother of hers; considered it trouble well spent to bring him to her way of thinking. We are all of us apt to think thus generously of those whom we hold dear.

"There aren't many women who come up these stairs in evening dress, I can assure you," he said, as they mounted the flight together.

She laughed. "And I suppose the ones who do are on their way to see you?"

"Dolly, I'm ashamed of you," he replied.

"Well, you've made yourself the reputation; don't grumble at it or shirk it."

"Shirk it? Why should I?" He stood aside to let her pass in. "I've nothing to be ashamed of. I don't wear the garment of respectability, but then I'm not stark naked. Every man clothes himself in some article of faith, virtue if you like." The name of Sally and Sally's face swept across his mind. There was one virtue at least which he could put on. "You people, the set you want me to join, the hunting set, the country house set—all you wear—I don't mean you particularly. God! If you were like that!" He was too intent upon what he was saying to notice the smile of ice that twisted her pretty lips. "All you wear is the big, comprehensive cloak of respectability, and sometimes you're not particular whether that's tied up properly."

Dolly broke into low laughter. "If you'd come down to Apsley," she said, "one week end, I'd get a certain number of people down there, and when they are all congregated in the drawing-room after dinner, you could stand with your back to the fire, command the whole room and, at a signal from me, make that speech. You'd be the lion of the evening."

"What does being the lion of the evening mean?" he asked, with the ironical turn of the lip. "That your bedroom door is liable to open, I suppose, and admit whatever lady is most hampered in the way of debts."

"Jack!" She sat upright in the chair she had taken, eyes well lit with a forced blaze, breath cunningly driven through the nostrils.

"What?"

"How dare you talk to me like that?"

"Don't know," he replied, imperturbably. "It is daring, I suppose, seeing that I'm not one of you. You'd listen to that on the hunting field from a man whom you'd met once before. But it was daring of me; I'm only your brother, and not in the crew at that."

Her eyes glittered more vividly, the breath came quicker still. Then it all blew away like sea-froth, and she shook with charming laughter.

"You talk like a Jesuit," she said. "Do you really feel those things as keenly as that?"

"Me?" He laughed with her and went for his pipe. "I don't feel them at all. What's there to feel about in them? I only want to show you that I'm not totally ignorant of what your set is like, the set you want me to become a lion-of-the-evening in. Lion-of-the-evening, beautiful lion, eh? Have a cigarette?"

"Thanks. Then why are you so hard on us?"

"Hard! I'm not hard." He lit a match for her, watched by the light of it her lineless face, deftly made up with its powder and its dust of rouge, the eyebrows cunningly pencilled, the lashes touched with black. None of it was obvious. It was only by the match's glare, held close to her face, that he could see the art that, in any less vivid an illumination, concealed the art. He smiled at it all, and her eyes, lifting, as the cigarette glowed, found the smile and sensitively questioned it.

"Why the smile?" she said, quickly.

"Why? Oh, I don't know. A comparison. I suppose you people really are artists. Mind you, I don't mean you. I'm not talking about you. If it were you—well, I shouldn't talk about it."

For the first moment in all their conversation of that evening, she looked ill-at-ease. A cloud passed over the sun of her self-assurance. It seemed, on the instant, to turn her eyes from blue to grey.

"What do you mean by—a comparison?" she inquired, "and saying we're artists? Artists at what? I believe you like to talk in riddles. That's another thing too that 'ud be in your favour. People 'ud think you so awfully clever. But what do you mean by comparison?"

He blew through his pipe, set it burning comfortably—took his favourite seat on the table with his legs swinging like a schoolboy's.

"A comparison—I mean a comparison between the women of your set, and the women who toil at the same job in the streets of London."

"Yes, but you said that when you looked at me, when you smiled while I was lighting the cigarette." The words hurried out of her lips, dropping metallically with a hard sound on his ears.

"I know, but I told you I didn't refer to you. Good God!" He gripped the table. "Do you think I could think about you like that? Look here, it's no good having this nonsense; I won't say another word if you think I am."

"Very well; all right. But tell me, at any rate, why you said it when you looked at me."

"Because you're made-up—made-up to perfection. I should

E. Temple Thurston

never have seen it if I hadn't held the match up to your face. And there's the difference—there's the comparison. The women in your set are artists. There's all the difference in a Sargent and a man with half a dozen coloured chalks on the pavement, between them and the women you'll find in Piccadilly at night. But they're both workers in the same dignified profession. When you think of the way those poor wretches shove on their rouge—a little silk bag turned inside out with eider-down on it and rouge powder on that, then the whole thing jammed on to the face before a mirror in one of Swan & Edgar's shop windows; any night you can see 'em doing it—and then look at a society woman done up, with a maid in attendance and a mirror lighted up, as if it were an actor's dressing-table—my heavens, you're liable to make a comparison then."

Dolly shuddered at the picture. "I think you've got a loathsome mind, Jack," she said with conviction.

"Of course you do, and you're quite right. It is a loathsome idea to think that a man of the type of Sargent is of the same noble profession as the pavement artist. You can only disinfect its loathsomeness in a degree by assuring people that they don't work in the same street. But it always is loathsome in this country to see facts as they really are, and when you know of society women who send nude portraits of themselves—"

"Jack!"

"—Up to wealthy men whom they have not had the pleasure of meeting, it's naturally a beastly conception of life to compare them with those unfortunate women whose exis-tence of course we all know about, but would much rather not discuss. I really quite agree with you, I have a loathsome mind."

Dolly rose with perfect dignity to her feet. "Do you think you ought to talk about things like that to me, Jack?"

"I don't know. I suppose it is questionable whether one ought to treat one's sister as a simple innocent, or talk to her, as undoubtedly you do talk in society to other men's wives and other men's daughters. I think myself that it doesn't really matter. You're not thinking of the impropriety of it. That doesn't worry you in the least. Many a man has talked to you sympathetically on similar subjects before. You've listened to them. The fault in me is the gentle vein of irony. Irony's an insidious thing when you grind it out of the truth. Sit down, Dolly; I won't talk about it any more. I'll pour the sweetest nothings you ever heard into your ears. Come on—sit down. It's not much after nine. I only wanted to show you why I don't appreciate society. I wouldn't mind it, if it admitted its vices and called them by their names; I think I'd permit myself to be dragged into it by a woman who was clean right through; but as it is, and as it describes itself, I prefer the pavement artist with his little sack of coloured chalks. There's not much reality, I admit, in his portrait of Lord Roberts or his beautiful pink and blue mackerel with its high light, that never shone on land or sea, except on the scales of that fish; there's not much reality in them, when they're finished, but there's a hell of a lot of it in the doing of them."

He sat and puffed at his pipe, while she remained standing, looking down into the fire.

The silence was long, then it was broken abruptly. A knock rattled gently on the door. It was soft, timid, but it rushed violently through their silence. Traill slid to his feet. His sister stood erect. Her eyes fastened to his face, and she watched him calculating the possibilities, as if he were counting them on his fingers, of whom it might be.

Then it came again.

"Who do you think it is?" she whispered. She was beginning already to shrink at the thought that some woman had come to see him. He heard that in her voice and casually smiled.

"It's all right," he said quietly. "I shan't let any one in who'd offend your sense of propriety. However I talk, we're related. Stay there."

She watched him cross to the door; turned, so that she could still observe him and yet with one twist of the head, if any one entered, seem to have been untouched by any curiosity.

He opened the door. It cut off his face from view; but she heard his sudden exclamation of surprise, and allowed a thousand speculations to travel through her brain.

"You!" he said.

"Yes," a woman's voice replied in a nervous undertone. "I came to see you, to see if you were in. I—I wanted to see you." The words were stilted with nervous repetitions.

"Of course, of course; come in; let me introduce you to my sister. Oh—you must—come in—please; we've been dining together and came on here—for coffee—"

He threw the door wide open, and Sally walked apprehensively into the room.

# CHAPTER XXI

Superficially, training is everything. The heaven-born genius comes once in a century of decades to remind us, as it were, that there is such a thing as creation; but beyond the heaven-born genius, training, on a day of superficialities, must win.

This moment, when Sally stood but a few paces within Traill's room, and looked—half-appealing, half-guardedly—at Mrs. Durlacher, the perfect woman of society—perfectly robed, perfectly mannered, perfectly painted, was a moment as superficial as one, so charged with possibilities, could be. And through that moment, over it, almost as if it were an occurrence of her daily life, Mrs. Durlacher rode as a swallow rides on an upland wind—pinions stretched straightly out—the consummate absence of effort; all the training of numberless years and numberless birds of the air in its wings.

"Dolly—this is Miss Bishop—my sister, Mrs. Durlacher." Traill stamped through the ceremony, like a man through a ploughed field.

In the minute fraction of time that followed—so short that no one in reason could call it a pause—Mrs. Durlacher had moulded a swift impression of Sally. Two facts—guide-ropes across a swinging bridge—she held to for support in

E. Temple Thurston

her sudden calculation. Firstly, Sally's appearance—the quiet, inexpensive display of a gentle taste. The blouse, showing through the little short-waisted coat—home-made—that, seen at a glance. The hat, with its quite artistic and unobtrusive colours—self-trimmed—the frame-work a year behind the fashion. The gloves, no holes in them, but well-worn. The skirt—not badly cut, but obviously a cheap material. The person, herself—more than probably a milliner's assistant. Secondly, the fact that she was in her brother's rooms. She knew Jack's dealings with women—did not even close her eyes to them—admitted them to be human and natural so long as he refrained from tying himself up with any one of them and thereby irretrievably separating himself from her and her set. With these two facts, then, she made her ultimate deduction of Sally's identity—a milliner's assistant, with a pardonable freedom of thought in the matter of propriety—and on that deduction, she acted accordingly. Ah, but it was acting that was finished and superb!

Her manner was gracious—she was compelled to accept her brother at his word, that he would let no one in who could offend her sense of propriety—yet it was graciousness which you saw through a polished glass, but could not touch. When Sally half-ventured forward with hand tentatively lifting, she bowed first—made it plain to Sally that in such a manner introductions were taken—then generously offered her hand, palpably to ease Sally's confusion.

Dressed as she was, looking as she did, in comparison with Sally, she held all the weapons. She could play them, wield them, just as she wished. Well-frocked, looking her best, a woman is a dangerous animal; but throw her in contact with another of her sex who is but poorly clad, socially beneath her, and in training her inferior, and you may behold all the grace, all the symmetry of the cobra as it unwinds its beautiful, sinuous body before the eyes of its panic-stricken prey.

The fact that her brother had admitted Sally to the room, made Mrs. Durlacher realize that he held her in special regard. Notwithstanding that Miss Bishop called upon him at his own rooms at half-past nine at night, when all young ladies who valued their reputations would be either playing incompetent bridge in the suburban home, or going respectably with relations to a harmless piece at the theatre, she took the other fact well into consideration—gave it full weight—and all in that brief moment of a pause, realized that as yet there was no intimacy between these two.

She did not look upon women as a class—the class he mixed with—as dangerous to her brother's ultimate salvation; but coming across the individual in Sally, quiet, unobtrusive—the type that valued its own possessions, and would certainly expect substantial settlement, if not marriage itself—she felt called into action and answered the call, as only such women with her training know how.

When she had shaken hands, she leant back again with one graceful elbow, bared, upon the mantelpiece—the pose of absolute ease. Sally, who, except for the students' balls, to which Janet had sometimes taken her, had not been in the presence of people in evening dress since she left home, stood, hiding her nervousness, but not hiding the fact that it was concealed. Traill's heart warmed to her. He knew his sister through and through—guessed every thought that was taking shape in her mind. But Sally—even her presence there alone—was more or less of an enigma and, seeing her almost pathetic perturbation of manner, he paid all the attentions he roughly knew to her.

"Here—you must sit down," he said easily. "We're not going

E. Temple Thurston

to let you rush away before you've come."

For that plural of the pronoun, Sally thanked him generously in her heart; for that also, Mrs. Durlacher smiled inwardly and saw visions of the power by which Jack would eventually win his way.

"Will you have some coffee?" he added, when she had accepted the chair he proffered. "We've just had some. Good—wasn't it, Dolly?"

"Excellent."

"Will you have some?" he repeated.

"No, thank you—well—yes,—yes, I think I will."

Even to take coffee is action—action that it is an aid to conceal.

"Some milk?"

"No, thank you—black, please."

She trusted that he would not remember that she had taken it with milk before. She always did take it with milk, but the eyes of that woman by the mantelpiece were on her, and she knew well enough how coffee ought to be taken.

All that Traill had told her of his sister, was racing wildly through her thoughts. She knew she was being criticized, knew that her position there was being looked upon in the least charitable light of all. She should never have come into the room. The fact that her voice had been heard, would have made no difference. But who thinks of such things when the moment is a goad, pricking mercilessly? Now she was there, her position could scarcely be worse. She would have given her life almost, in those first few moments, to sink into obscurity, no matter what peals of ironical laughter might ring in her ears as she vanished. But the thing was done now, and for every little attention he paid her, she thanked Traill with a full heart.

"What on earth have you got in that parcel?" he asked her, as he crushed down the saucepan of coffee to heat upon the fire.

Her cheeks reddened—flamed. It felt to her as if the eyes of his sister were lenses concentrating a burning sun upon her face.

"Oh it's nothing," she said, mastering confusion; "only something that I was taking home."

His eyes questioned her, noting the flaming cheeks while his sister studied the muscular development and forbidding features of James Brownrigg—heavy-weight champion in the fifties, whose portrait hung over the mantelpiece.

"Isn't this the type of man you'd call a bruiser?" she asked, with a pretty trace of doubtful confidence in her technical knowledge on the last word.

"That chap—Brownrigg? No. I should call him a gentleman. I'd have given a good deal to see him fight. He always allowed his man to have his chance, though there wasn't one in England he couldn't have knocked out in the first round. He used to keep that glorious left of his tucked up, as quiet as a pet spaniel under a lady's arm, till he'd given his man time to show what he was worth. Then he'd shake his shoulders, grin a bit with that ugly mouth—never with his eyes—and plant his blow, the kick of a mule, and his man curled up like a caterpillar on a hot brick. That stroke got to

E. Temple Thurston

be known as James Brownrigg's Waiting Left. I've met him. He kept a public house up in Islington. Died about four years ago, with both fists clenched, and his left still waiting. It's quite possible he kept it waiting till he got to the gates of heaven."

Mrs. Durlacher looked up at the portrait again and then half-shuddered her graceful shoulders.

"I suppose a man can be a gentleman and look like that," she said. "But some one ought to have told him to grow his hair a little longer. As it is, it has a fatal suggestion of three years' imprisonment for assault and battery."

"Or the army," suggested Traill, with a laugh.

She took that well and laughed with him. "Yes, quite so; or the army; but they don't look so much like convicts as they used to. What do you think, Miss Bishop? Would you say, to look at him, that James Brownrigg was a gentleman?"

This, in a period of ten minutes, was the first remark that she had addressed to Sally. Coming, as it did, after that space of time, pitched on the casual note, the eyebrows gently lifted, there was a whip in it that stung across Sally's sensitive cheeks. The words in themselves, of course, were nothing. Traill, in fact, thought that this icicle of a sister of his was beginning to thaw, and looked towards Sally for her answer in encouraging expectancy.

Sally rose to her feet and crossed to the mantelpiece. The spirit in her prompted her to considered lethargy, as though the remark were as inconsequent to her as it had been to the maker; but the gentleness of her nature made it impossible for her to give insult for insult. Her steps were not slow— they were almost eager—and her lips smiled. She gave the very impression that she would have died rather than create—the apparent sense of pleasure in which she felt in being addressed at all.

For a moment she stood looking into the impassive, brutal face of James Brownrigg. Her expression was one of studiousness and consideration; yet the face of James Brownrigg was completely blurred in her vision. She had to force her eyes to see, and spur her mind to think. Then she turned, facing Mrs. Durlacher.

"I think if you're going to judge everybody by their outward appearance," she said, "you certainly might feel inclined to say that he wasn't a gentleman. But outward appearances always seem to me so terribly deceptive. I should never let myself be led away by them."

This was a declaration! Even Sally, in her own gentle way, could declare war. The perfect curve of her upper lip grew thin as she said it, like a bow that straightens itself after the arrow has sped. Traill cast a swift glance at her, comprehending that there lay some meaning behind her words, yet knowing nothing of the duel that was being fought under his very eyes.

Mrs. Durlacher smiled. She took the thrust as gracefully as she had given her own.

To the trained hand and to the practised eyes, these things can not only be done with dexterity, they can be done with ease and with style. There are many who imagine that the days of romance are over because gentlemen do no longer saunter through the salons of the rich with pointed rapiers tapping at their heels. But romance did not go out with the duel. The duel itself has never gone out. Words, looks— these are the weapons of romance now. They are sheathed in

E. Temple Thurston

their scabbards of velvet politesse, but just as easy of drawing, just as light to flash out and tingle in the air as ever were the dainty little Toledo blades of some odd two hundred years ago.

"Jack," said Mrs. Durlacher, "you've introduced me to a diplomatist. She says what she means without telling you what she says."

Traill thought that it all alluded to the portrait of James Brownrigg—imagined that Sally agreed with him, yet did not like to contradict his sister, and he laughed with amusement at the smartness of her retort. But Sally returned to her seat, conscious that she had made an enemy. She could think of no reply that had not a lash of bitterness in it and, clinging to the dignity of silence, rather than the vigour of attack, she said nothing.

When Traill had handed her her coffee, his sister moved slowly across the room to the settle where her fur coat, scarf and gloves were lying.

"You're not going?" he asked, looking up.

"Yes, I must, my dear boy. It's getting on for ten. Harold's got some people coming in after the theatre, and I believe we've got a supper. Do you think you could get me a taxi?"

"There's not a stand here. But you can get any amount of hansoms."

"Yes, but I want to get home. You're sure to find heaps of empty ones in Piccadilly Circus just at this time. Run and see—do. I'll be putting on my coat."

Traill went—obedient. They heard him taking the stairs two

at a time in the darkness. Then the door slammed.

"One of these days he'll break his neck down those stairs," said Mrs. Durlacher. "Do you live in Town, Miss Bishop?"

She ran one sentence into the other inconsequently, as if they had connection.

"Well—not exactly," said Sally. "I live in Kew."

"Oh yes—Kew—it's a very pretty place. There are some delightful old houses on the Green—the gardens side—I believe they're King's property, aren't they?"

"I know the ones you mean," said Sally; "they are very nice, but I don't live there." She added that with a smile—a generous admission that she made no pretension to what she was not. Upon Mrs. Durlacher it was wasted, as was all generosity. She had not the quality herself; understood it as little as she possessed it.

"Oh, I wasn't supposing that," she replied easily. "I was thinking that that was the only part of Kew I had noticed. I think I've only been there once or twice at the most. Have you known my brother long?"

Sally's fingers gripped tight about her little parcel. "Oh no, not so very long."

"He's a quaint, int'resting sort of person. Don't you find him so?"

To Sally, this description sounded ludicrous. The fashionable way of putting things was utterly unknown to her. To think of Traill as quaint, in the sense of the word as she understood it, seemed preposterous. She could not realize that the

E. Temple Thurston

Society idea of quaintness is anything which does not passably imitate or become one of itself.

"Interesting—yes, I certainly think he is. This room alone would show that, wouldn't it?"

"Oh, well, I don't know so much about that. He'd have this sort of room anywhere, wherever he lived. It's the fact that he chooses to live here and slave and work that I think's uncommon—so quaint. But he'll give it up—he's bound to give it up after a time. You can't wash out what's in the blood. Do you think you can? He'll drop the Bohemian one day—it's merely a phase. I'm only just waiting, you know, to give the dinner on his coming out." She drew on her long gloves and smiled in her anticipation of the event.

None of the value of this did Sally lose—none of the intent that lay behind it. She perfectly realized that it was meant to convey a candid warning to her; that if she had pretensions, she might as well light their funeral pyre immediately, burn all her hopes and ambitions, a sacrifice before the altar of renunciation. But ambitions, she had none. With her nature, she would willingly have consented to their burning at such a command as this. What hopes she possessed, certainly, were shattered; but the flame of her passion, that was only kindled the more. Now that she realized how utterly he was beyond her reach, how immeasurably he was above her, she made silent concessions to the crying demands of her heart which she would not have dreamed of admitting to herself before.

Irretrievably he was gone now. All Janet had said, strong in truth as it may have seemed at the time, had only been based upon her extraordinary view of life in general. Some cases, perhaps, it might have applied to; it did not apply to this. Janet was utterly wrong; she was not winning him. In this chance meeting with his sister, brief though it may have been, she knew that she had lost him; arriving at which conclusion, she probably reached the most dangerous phase in the whole existence of a woman's temptations.

When Traill returned, he found them both in preparation for departure. Sally had replaced the little feather boa about her neck and one of her gloves, which she had taken off when he gave her the coffee, she was buttoning at the wrist.

"You're not going, are you?" he exclaimed.

"Yes; I must."

"But you haven't told me what you wanted to see me about yet."

"No, I know I haven't; but that must wait. I can easily write to you."

Mrs. Durlacher picked up her skirts, the silk rustling like leaves in an autumn wind. As she lowered her head in the movement, the dilation of her nostrils repressed a smile of satisfaction. "You mustn't let my going force you away," she said graciously.

"Oh, but I must go," said Sally.

Traill shrugged his shoulders. Let her have her way. When women are doing things for apparently no reason, they are the most obstinate. But at the door of the room as his sister passed out first, he caught Sally's elbow in a tense grip and for the instant held her back.

"I shall wait here for you for half an hour," he whispered.

# CHAPTER XXII

"Is there anywhere that I can take you, Miss Bishop?" Mrs. Durlacher offered, as they stood by the side of the shivering taxi. "I'm going out to Sloane Street."

"Oh no, thank you; it's very good of you. I'm going to catch a train at Waterloo." She shook hands, then held out her hand quietly to Traill.

"Good-bye, Mr. Traill."

He took her hand and held it with meaning. "Good-bye."

She turned away and walked down Waterloo Place, her head erect, her steps firm, but the tears rolling from her eyes, and her breast lifting with every sob that she stifled in her throat.

Mrs. Durlacher looked after her; then her eyes swept up to her brother's face.

"Is she going to walk all the way to Waterloo Station?" she asked incredulously.

"Expect so."

Mrs. Durlacher looked above her in a perfect simulation of

amazement. Then she stepped into the cab.

"Jack," she said, when she was seated.

"What?"

She prefaced her words with a little laugh. "I wouldn't be a little milliner at your mercy for all I could see."

Traill snorted contemptuously. "She's not a little milliner," he said, cutting each word clean with irony. "Neither in your sense, nor in reality. Fortune has cursed her with being a lady and withheld the necessary increment that would make such things obvious to you. Good night."

He stood away, and told the chauffeur the address in Sloane Street. They did not look at each other again, and the little vehicle pulled away from the kerbstone without the final nod of the head or shaking of the hand which usually terminated their meetings.

The last sight she had of him, was as he stood looking down Waterloo Place, his eyes picking out the people one by one, as the miner sifts the dross from the dust of gold. Then she leant back in the cab and a low, sententious laugh lazily parted her lips.

For a moment, Traill stood there; but Sally was out of sight. It crossed his mind to run down into Pall Mall—coatless, hatless, as he was—in the hope of finding her; but an inner consciousness convinced him that she would return, and he walked back into the house, upstairs to his room to wait for her.

When the mind had been made up to a critical sacrifice, it hates to be thwarted. The more difficult the sacrifice may be,

E. Temple Thurston

the more the mind is revolted by the hampering of circum-stances. Having brought herself through a thousand temptings to the determination that she must not keep the bangle which Traill had given her, Sally felt incensed with circumstances, incensed with everything, that she had been hindered in the carrying out of her design. All that Janet had said about her ultimate going back to him, she had wiped out with a rough and unrelenting hand during that hour when she had been in his sister's presence. But the sting of the other remained, while she firmly believed that her desire to see him once more, herself in the frail attitude of hope, had vanished—was dead, buried, almost forgotten.

The working of the mind is so like that of the body, that comparisons can be drawn at every point. When the body needs nourishment, or exercise, or rest, and is denied all of these things, it circumvents its own master and steals its needs with cunning. So is it precisely with the mind. When the mind craves a certain expression of itself, needs a certain relief, and is denied its craving, then it, too, circumvents its own master, and, by the crafty displacement of ideas, hoodwinking the very power that governs it, it attains its end.

Sally, yearning in her heart for one more sight of Traill, the putting to the touch of her last hope, and then crushing out the desire into an apparent oblivion, was trapped, deceived, outwitted by such subtle suggestions as that she had been thwarted in her determination of sacrifice.

At the bottom of Waterloo Place, she hesitated. He had said he would wait half an hour. She would be back almost immediately if she returned at once. Her steps took her onwards down Pall Mall, but they were slower and more measured than before. At the Carlton Restaurant, she stopped again. She wanted to give him back the bangle herself; to tell him herself how utterly she knew it was at an end. She could write, certainly; she could send the little box by post. She had said she would. But a romance, the only romance she had ever had in her life, to end through the tepid medium of the post—the letter dropped in through the black and gaping slit—just the one moment's thrill that now he must get it! Then, nothing; then, emptiness and the end. She wanted more than that. She would cry, perhaps, break down when she saw him put it aside where she could never touch it again. But what were tears? They were better than nothing; better than the hollowness of such an end as the writing of a letter would bring.

With half-formed decision, she turned up Haymarket instead of crossing towards Trafalgar Square and so, slowly, by indecisive steps, she found herself, some ten minutes later, once more knocking gently upon Traill's door.

The sound from within, as he jumped to his feet, set her heart beating through the blood, and though she steadied herself, her lips were trembling as he opened and made way for her to enter.

She walked straight into the room, did not turn until she heard him close the door; even then, she refused to let her eyes meet his in a direct gaze. This was not easy for, having once shut the door, he stood with his back to it, looking intently at her as if, securing her at last, he would not willingly let her free.

"What made you come?" he asked, slowly—"and, having come—then, why on earth did you go away? In the last few minutes before you arrived, I almost began to think that you weren't coming back again."

She tried to hide her nervousness by taking off her gloves, but her fingers fumbled at the buttons, and in her awkwardness the seam of one of the fingers slit from top to bottom. She looked at it ruefully; was about to make use of the incident to lessen the tension of the moment when he came across to her. Standing in front of her, he looked down at the broken glove, and her white skin laid bare by the rent stitching.

"You'll let me get you a new pair," he said under his breath. In that instant he wanted to give her the world. The proffer of the gloves tried to express the sensation.

She looked up into his face with a very small smile—half refusal, half gratitude. When her eyes met his, she realized that her senses were swimming. She was standing on a giddy height, to throw herself from which, became an almost imperative inclination. She felt that she was losing her balance and in another moment would be pitching forward into his arms. She wanted to tell him to kiss her, and words of violent strength, which she had never dreamed of before, shouted suggestions through her—even to her lips. He seemed to be waiting for her to do all this, but made no move to accelerate it; then she swung backwards—turned blindly to the table, laying down her gloves and the little brown-paper parcel.

"You're going to take off your hat now," he said; "this room's too hot for accessories."

She showed hesitation, was about to refuse, when he made it plain to her that he would not have it otherwise.

"I've taken it off before, you know," he said with a smile. "I'm by no means a novice at the art. You can't call me an amateur."

"When—?" she began; "oh, of course, I remember."

She did not consider her refusal now; she obeyed. He took the hat from her and her feather boa. Then he insisted on the removal of the little short-waisted coat. She demurred again, and again was obedient. He laid them all down on the settle, then sat for a moment and watched her while she poked her fingers into her hair and pulled it lightly out where the hat had rested.

"Now you look as if you'd come to see me." he said.

"What did I look like before?"

"I don't know. As if you had been and were going away. But what *did* you come for? What have you got to tell me? I assure you, when I opened that door and found you standing there—"

"Yes, I'm sure you must have been surprised," she joined in.

"I was—considerably. What do you think of Dolly?"

"Your sister?"

"Yes."

"I know she doesn't like me," she answered evasively.

"What makes you think that? I don't think you're correct. She hasn't got you right—that's all."

"No, she hasn't got me right. I know she thought I was quite a different person to what I really am."

"But how do you know that? She didn't tell you so when I'd gone out to get that taxi, did she? What did she say to you then?"

E. Temple Thurston

"Oh no, she didn't tell me what she thought. Under the circumstances, I'm sure she really treated me very well."

"I don't know about that," said Traill. "You must admit she was a bit icy at first. That's her social way—the way of the whole set when they meet strangers. One ought to bring a blast furnace when one goes calling at their houses, instead of a visiting card. My God, I've been to them myself, and I'd sooner undertake a job as look-out on a ship bound for the north pole. They'd freeze the very marrow in your bones."

Sally smiled—pleased—at his violent antipathy. "Don't you think you'll ever become one of them, then?" she asked. "I expect you will."

"No, not in fifty lifetimes. Did she say I would?"

"She said she expected it."

"Did she? Well, I wouldn't give a brass farthing for her expectations. Just like her to say that. I wonder what her game was. I wonder did she think you could persuade me to it."

He looked up at her; but Sally said nothing. She could have told him—told him to the letter what he wanted to know—but she said nothing. Then he asked her again why she had come that evening to see him.

"Is it anything to do with that parcel?" he asked suspiciously.

Her eyes turned to the little box in its wrapping of brown paper. She reached out her hand and took it from the table.

"Yes," she replied.

"Oh, the bracelet?"

"Yes."

Her fingers attacked the knots on the string with half-hearted enthusiasm.

"Doesn't it fit?" he questioned.

"Oh yes; it isn't that."

"Then what is it? You don't like it. Here—" he was growing impatient of her fingers' futile attempts; "cut the string. You'll never untie those knots. Here's a knife." He handed her one from his pocket. "You don't like it, eh?" he repeated.

She looked straightly at him, eyes unmoved by the steady gaze in his.

"Do you really think that?" she asked. "That I'm bringing it back because I don't like it?"

"I don't know, I'm sure. But if not that, then why?"

There was irritation in his voice; he made little attempt to conceal it. It was his imagination that he had come to dealings with the type of feather-brained woman who knows least of all what she wants when she gets it. It may be seen from this that his knowledge of Sally was supremely slight. He had a broad judgment for all women, a pigeon-hole in his mind into which he threw them without discrimination. When, therefore, he came across the exception in Sally, he did not recognize her, flung her in with the rest, folded more carefully perhaps, tied even with a little distinguishing piece of ribbon. But into that same receptacle in his mind she went, nevertheless. Yet Traill was not without shrewdness in his wide judgment of the sex. He could read his sister as you read a book in which the pages only need cutting, and the glossary sometimes referred to.

On this evening, certainly, he had failed to see the point towards which she drove; but in her dealings with another of her sex, a woman is most inexplicable of all to a man. For this edition de luxe, he needs reference, dictionary, and magnifying glass, with a steady finger always to keep his place on the line should his eyes for one moment lift or wander from the print.

Sally, as yet, he had classified broadly. In the very next moment he was to learn more of her, to take her down from that indiscriminating file in his mind, and scrutinize her afresh.

She took the bangle out of its velvet case and clasped it—with pride even then—upon her wrist.

"You see it fits—perfectly," she said, looking up pathetically.

"Then—Good Lord! why do you bring it back?"

She unclasped it, letting it lie in the palm of her hand, half-stretched out towards him.

"Because I mustn't accept it—I can't. If, after the last time I was here, when you said good-bye, you'd said to me you were going to buy it, I should have told you that I would not take it."

He paid no attention to her outstretched hand. At her eyes he looked.

"Why not? Why particularly after I'd said good-bye?"

"Because you have no right to give it me, and I have less right to accept it."

He half-laughed. "Isn't that rather childish?"

"I don't think so."

"But do you like it? Isn't it a sort of thing you'd like?"

"A sort of thing? I think it's beautiful. I've never had a present like it in my life—never had anything that was so valuable."

"And you're going to refuse it?"

"I must."

He still made no offer to take it from her, but looked persistently at her eyes.

"If I asked you quite straight," he said, "would you tell me quite straight—why?"

Now it must be the truth or the lie. No silence, no half-measures could answer here. She knew that he was at the very door of her heart, when it must either be slammed, bolted, locked in his face with a lie or flung, with the truth, wide open for him to enter if he chose.

She hesitated, it is true; but it was not the hesitation of indecision. When, only a few moments before, her senses have been giddily balancing upon a precipice, saved from the hopeless downfall, only because the man put out no hand to pull her over, a woman is not likely to delay in doubt when at last he offers his hands, his eyes and his voice to drag her into the ultimate abyss of ecstasy.

Sally delayed, only with the natural instinct of reserve. Eventually, she knew she must tell him; if not in words, then by actions, looks—even by silence itself.

"I never thought you meant that bet," she began in timid procrastination.

"No—probably you didn't—but I did. And that's not the reason why you're returning it now. Supposing we sponge out the debt and I tell you to look upon it as a gift—would you keep it then?"

"No."

"Well—it's the wherefore of that I want to know. Why wouldn't you?"

"Because you have no right, no cause, to make me presents. You practically told me so yourself—you said good-bye."

"But don't you take all you can get?" he asked, almost with brutality. So the passion was stirring in him. All that came to his lips found utterance.

At any time, she would have resented that. Now she knew instinctively what the brutality in it expressed.

"No," she replied under her breath—"you might know I don't."

"And so you're returning this because I said good-bye— you're returning this because I said I was not the type of man who hugs the idea of matrimony. How could you take a gift from such a man—eh? I suppose to you it savours almost of an insult. Yet, have you any conception what your returning it seems to me?"

She shook her head.

"It hurts. Do you think you'd feel inclined to believe that? You'd scarcely think I was capable of a wound to sentiment, would you? I am in this case. I gave you that, because I couldn't give you other things. That bangle was a sort of consolation to my thwarted wish to give. I'm quite aware that a woman gives most in a bargain; but a man likes to do a little bit of it as well. Half the jewellers' shops in London 'ud have to close if he didn't. Some of 'em 'ud keep open I know for the women who are bought and prefer the bargain to be settled in kind rather than in cash. And jewellery pretty nearly always realizes its own value. But this was a gift—a substitute for other things that I would rather have given you."

He paused and looked steadily at her, her head drooping, her fingers idly, nervously bending the woven gold.

"Have you any idea what those other things were?" he asked suddenly.

"No," she said—but she did not offer her eyes to convince him of her reply.

"They were the alteration of all your circumstances. The smashing of the chains that gave you to that damned treadmill of a typewriter—the unlocking of the door that keeps you mewed-up in that little lodging-house in Kew—rubbing shoulders with bank-clerks, being compelled to listen to their proposals of suburban marriage, with the prospect of feeding your husband as the stable-boy feeds the

E. Temple Thurston

horse when it comes back to the manger. Those were the things I wanted to free you from, and in their place, give you everything you could ask, so far as my limited income permits. I only wanted to give you the things you ought to have—the things you should have by right—the things you were born to. Your father was a clergyman—a rector. Why, down at Apsley, the rector comes and dines—for the sake of God—and respectability—and brings his daughters, dressed in their Sunday best—with low-necked frocks that make no pretence to be puritanical. And you slave, day after day, because your father, through no fault of yours, happened to come down in the world, while they sit in a comfortable rectory accepting the invitations of the county. I wanted to give you things that 'ud make your life brighter—*wanted* to give them—would have found intense pleasure in seeing you take them from me."

Sally rose with a choking of breath to her feet. She could bear the strain no longer. It was like an incessant hammer beating upon her strength, shattering her resolve, until only the desire and the sense were left. She crossed with unsteady steps to the mantelpiece. He rose as well, and followed her.

"Oh—don't!" she moaned. But he took no notice. The impetus he had gained, carried him on. She could not stop him now.

"They were not much, certainly," he went on; "not much compared with what I wanted in return. What I wanted in return, was what no gentleman has the right to expect from any woman who is straight unless she willingly offers it— and you had called me a gentleman. Do you remember that? I don't suppose you really knew when you said it, how much you were saving yourself from me. I wouldn't suggest that credit were due to me for a moment—it isn't. It was just the same as telling a man to do a brave act, when only the doing of it could save his life. I did it because I had to. To be a gentleman is often one chance in a lifetime, and the man who doesn't take it is not fit for hanging. Birth has nothing to do with it. You offered me my chance—I took it—that's all. But now you want to deprive me of my one consolation. You want to refuse that bangle. I refuse to take it back."

Sally turned and faced him. Her lips were set—her eyes had strange lights in them. She looked—as she felt—upon the scaffold of indecision, with the noose of fate about her neck.

"Oh, it is so hard! Why is it so hard?" she whispered.

"Why is what so hard?"

"This—all this."

He laughed ironically. Either he would not see, or he could not see. Men may not be so dense as they appear. Sometimes it is a subconscious cunning that aids them in forcing half the initiative into the hands of the woman.

"Surely, it can't be so difficult a job to just snap the catch of that bracelet on your wrist, and forget all about whether I ought to have given it you or not."

"Oh, I don't mean that," she exclaimed, "you must know I don't mean that."

"Then what?" His whole manner changed. Now she had told him definitely. Now he knew without a shadow of doubt. She cared. It was even swaying in her mind whether she could bear to lose him, notwithstanding all he had said. It did not seem to him that he had worked her up to it. In that moment, he exonerated himself of all blame. He had danced gentleman to the clapping of her hands and the stamping of

E. Temple Thurston

her foot; and if it came to this, that she cared for him more than convention, more than any principle, then it was not in his nature to force a part upon himself and play it, night after night, to an empty gallery. His hands caught her shoulders, the fingers gripping with passion to her flesh. "Then what?" he repeated. "Do you mean you care for me? Do you mean that it's so hard to go—hard to say good-bye because of that? Is that what you mean?"

She could not answer yet. Even then the rope was not drawn and she could still faintly feel the scaffold boards beneath her feet.

"If I've made a rotten mistake," he went on, content on the moment in her silence to misdoubt his own judgment. "If I've gone and jumped to this conclusion out of sheer conceit—misreading all I see in your eyes—translating all wrongly what I hear in your silence—you'll have to forgive me. I'm not trying to rush you into any expression of what you feel." He conscientiously thought he was not. "In fact, to tell you the honest truth, to me it seems that you—bringing back this bangle—holding from me your reason in doing so; you, stumbling over everything you say, and looking at me as you have done in the last few moments—that it's you who have dragged these things out of me. All my attitude has been in trying to avoid them, because of what I thought you expected me to be. And now I think differently. Am I right? Am I?" He turned her face to meet his eyes. "Am I?"

She raised her eyes once—let his take them—hold them—keep them. Then the boards of the scaffold slipped away from under her feet—one instant the sensation of dropping—dropping; then oblivion—the noose of Fate drawn tight—the account reckoned. She swayed into his arms and he held her—kissing her hair, kissing her shoulders, her cheeks, her eyes—then, gently putting his hand beneath her chin, he lifted her face upwards, and crushed her lips against her teeth with kisses.

END OF BOOK I

E. Temple Thurston

# BOOK II

## THE DESERTER

## CHAPTER I

Apsley Manor was one of those residences to be found scattered over the country, which are vaguely described as Tudor—memorials to the cultured taste in England, before the restoration with its sponge of Puritanical Piety wiped out the last traces of that refinement which Normandy had lent. Britain was destined to be great in commerce, and not even the inoculation of half the blood of France could ever make her people great in art as well.

It would be difficult to say the exact date when Apsley Manor was built. Certain it was that Elizabeth, in one of her progresses—the resort of a clever woman to fill a needy purse—had stayed there on her way to Oxford. The room, the bed even in which she was supposed to have slept, still remain there. Each owner, as he parted with the property, exacted a heavy premium upon that doubtful relic of history. None of them wished to remove it from the room where it had so many romantic associations; but they one and all had used it as a lever to raise the price of the property—if only a hundred pounds—beyond that which they had, in the first case, paid for it themselves. Once, in fact, the hangings had been taken down and the bed itself lifted from the ground before the very eyes of the intended purchaser; but that had been too much for him. He had given in. There is England's greatness! Can it be wondered—much as we pose to despise them—that we are the only nation in Europe which has given shelter to the tribes of Israel?

In spring-time, the Manor looked wonderful—the lawns cut for the first time since the winter, the hedges of blackthorn splashed thick with snow-blossom, and daffodils, as if sackfuls of new-minted gold were emptied underneath the trees and elves had scattered pieces here and there from out the mass. Birds were building in all the thickets, and the young leaves—virgin green—shyly hid their love-making. Everything alive was possessed with a new-found energy. The sparrows—most ostentatious of any bird there is—flew about, trailing long threads of hay, with an air as if they carried the Golden Fleece in their beaks each time they returned to the apple trees. But other creatures were as busy as they. Strange little brown birds—whitethroats and linnets perhaps, if the eye could only have followed them—flew in and out of the blackthorn hedges all day long. Thrushes and blackbirds hopped pompously about the lawns, and the starlings chattered like old women on the roofs of the red gables.

The house itself was modelled as are nearly all such residences of the Tudor period, the gables at either end making, with the hall, the formation of the letter E so characteristic of the architecture of that time. Only two additions had been made, oriel windows to enlarge the rooms at each end of the gables; but they had been executed, some seventy years before Sir William Hewitt Traill's occupation of the place, by a man who had respect for the days of King Harry and they had long since toned into the atmosphere. A great tree of wisteria lifted itself above one of the windows, and on the

E. Temple Thurston

other a clematis clung with its wiry, brittle shoots.

The huge cedars, holding out their black-green fans of foliage like Eastern canopies—the high yew-trees, to whom only age could bring such lofty dimensions, all surrounded the old, red building and wrapped it in a velvet cloak of warm security. Tulips in long beds—brilliant mosaics in a floor of green marble—were let into the lawn that stretched down the drive. Away on the horizon, the rising ground about Wycombe showed blue through the soft spring atmosphere, and in the middle distance, the ploughed fields—freshly turned—glowed with the rich, red blood of the earth's fulness. So it presented itself to the eyes of Mrs. Durlacher, when, one morning late in April, she drove up in her motor to the old iron-barred oak-door which opened into the panelled hall of her country residence.

She was alone. Her maid and another servant had come down by rail to High Wycombe and were being driven over in one of the house conveyances from the station, a distance of five miles. The chauffeur descended from the seat, opened the door of the car, and when she had passed into the house, beckoned a gardener who was at work on one of the tulip beds, to help him in with some of the luggage which Mrs. Durlacher had brought with her.

"She's coming to stay, then?" said the gardener.

"S'pose so," replied the chauffeur. "I'd understood yesterday as she was going to the openin' of a bazaar this afternoon—openin' by royalty; but I got my orders this morning to fill up the tank and come along at once, 'cos she was going out into the country. 'Ow's that ferret of mine going on?"

"First class," said the gardener.

"Well then, as soon as I get the car cleaned this afternoon, I'm going to have some rattin'. Here—put 'em in the 'all—here."

The gardener struggled obediently. The chauffeur did most of the looking on and practically all the talking.

From the mouths of babes and sucklings and from the lips of hired servants one gets wisdom in the one case and information in the other. All that the chauffeur had stated was quite true. Some five days before—and we have now three years behind us since that night when Sally Bishop tottered into Traill's arms—Mrs. Durlacher had received a letter from her brother, of whom she had seen nothing for almost six months, saying that he thought of going down to Apsley for the day. "But I make sure first," his letter concluded, "that the field is cleared. Down there, as you know, I prefer to be the only starter."

She had written in reply that she had only been down to Apsley once that year herself and, furthermore, on the day he mentioned, the place would be as deserted of human beings as London is in the heart of July—meaning thereby that any place is a wilderness which is empty of one's self and one's associates. That she had written by return of post; then, two days later, her mind had caught an impression—a wandering insect that the flimsy web of a spider clutches by chance. He had gone down to Apsley before this, many a time. She knew that he had a lingering fondness for the place which no amount of gluttony of Bohemianism could ever wipe out. But he had never taken these precautions before. He had chanced his luck; if he had found people there, then he had forced a retreat as soon as possible. But now he was going out of his way—writing a letter, an action foreign to the whole of his nature—to ensure that he should be alone.

E. Temple Thurston

The circumstance—for circumstance there must be, just as there is the puff of wind that drifts the wandering insect to the spider's web—that brought the impression to her mind, was the brief report of a cross-examination in the divorce courts, conducted by J.H. Traill. She knew that in the last two years he had, in a desultory way, been gleaning briefs from the great field where others reaped. That had stood for little in her mind; for though she had always realized that in temperament and intellect he would make an excellent barrister, she had never believed that he would throw aside the Bohemian side of his nature sufficiently to gain ambition. Now, in this stray report, she beheld between the lines the successful man. His cross-examination had won the case, for his side. Its ability was undoubted, even to her untutored mind, and from this, in that indirect method—taking no heed of the straight line—by which women come leaping to their admirable conclusions, she received the impression that when Traill came down to Apsley, he would not come alone.

It is scarcely possible to see how this is arrived at; yet, to the mind of a woman, it is simple enough. Her brother had, after all these years, breasted his way out of the slow-moving tide of mental indifference, into the rapid current of ambition. When a man does that, her intuition prompted her to know that it is more than likely that he brings a woman with him. It is always possible for a woman to recognize—apart from her own identity—that her sex is an encumbrance to most men which they cannot easily shake off. Witness the generous criticism of a woman upon any husband but her own. Combine with this intuitive knowledge the fact—hitherto unrecorded, even by Traill to Sally—that when he handed over Apsley Manor to his sister and took her ready money in exchange, Traill had made her sign a document granting him the right to repurchase possession with the same amount at any time that it might please him, and you have the appre-hension of the woman who knows that possession constitutes but few points of the law when there is ink and parchment to nullify the whole transaction.

Jack, with a woman at his heels; a woman, moreover, whom he had probably brought with him out of that dark abyss of the past; might quite easily be a crushing blow to all her social power. Five thousand pounds perhaps would be a difficult sum for him to raise—certainly to raise immediately—but she had the proof before her that he was striding into eminence and, as has been mentioned before in this chapter, England is the only country in Europe which is a safe harbour for the Jews.

So then she leapt to the conclusion. He was bringing a woman with him to see the place. She pictured the creature vividly in her mind—a woman with a large hat, red lips, a woman with a bold figure who knew how to dress it brazenly, with eyes that danced to the whip of his remarks; a woman who as mistress of Apsley, would make it impossible for her ever to go near the place again. There was only one way to meet the situation—a situation it had definitely become in the sudden workings of her mind—and that was face to face, at Apsley, in possession, with the servants at her command and the most gracious of speeches on her lips. Tramping through the house alone, that woman would be assigning rooms to their different owners, as if she were already in possession; but with Mrs. Durlacher, the perfect artist, as Jack had called her—she laughed unfeelingly when that phrase came back to her mind—with herself at the woman's heels, telling her what they did with this room and how in the hunting season they used that, there would be little scope for exhibition of the proprietary sentiment and, whoever the person might be, Mrs. Durlacher guaranteed she should not shine on that occasion before her brother.

For that day, then, she had cancelled all her engagements.

E. Temple Thurston

The opening of the bazaar, a function at which she had felt it her duty to be present, she crossed out of her book. From the dinner, to which she and her husband had been asked on the evening previous to Traill's visit to Apsley, she wrote and excused herself, saying she had been called out of Town; and on the next morning she had ordered the car to be round at the house in Sloane Street punctually at a quarter to ten.

"Can't see why you have to give up the dinner and drive me out of it as well because you have to go down to Apsley to-morrow," her husband had said when she had written to her hostess excusing their presence at dinner.

"The reason's obvious," she replied equably. "I haven't had a good night's rest for a week—I can't sleep after eight o'clock in the morning like you do, and I've got a woman to deal with to-morrow. You don't want to lose the shooting and the hunting down at Apsley, do you?"

"No—rather not—of course I don't."

"Then let me get a good night's rest."

One admires the woman who sees her plan of action and takes it like a sword in the hand. Certainly, there was a possibility that she might be wrong. There well might be no woman. But in her mind, she was confident, and this was the only method of defence. She did not hesitate to accept it, difficult though it were. The woman might be any one—a creature whose touch would be contamination. She placed no trust in her brother where women were concerned. He would not actually disgrace her; she could be certain of that. A calculation on the presence of Mrs. Butterick, the house-keeper, who was always left in charge of the Manor, would be bound to act as a certain restraint. But what he expected to present a quotient of respectability to Mrs. Butterick and the gardener if he happened to be about the grounds, might well represent sordid vulgarity to her. He had certainly taken every precaution to be alone. Yet having drawn all these facts into consideration, she was undaunted. The whole way down to Apsley, sitting comfortably in the corner of the car, her eyes unseeingly fixed upon the back of the chauffeur's neck, she rehearsed one scene after another with a precision of imagination that was worthy of a greater cause. Yet what cause could be greater to her? With the loss of Apsley, she fell irremediably in social power. Five thousand pounds would purchase another residence in the country. But what sort of a residence? She shuddered and, in a moment of relaxation, became aware that the chauffeur was in need of a clean collar.

The moment she arrived, she sent for Mrs. Butterick and went upstairs to her bedroom. The good, fat, little woman—her face a full harvest moon, to which the features adhered with regularity but no expression—soon followed her. She stood at the door of the long, lofty room with its three big, latticed windows and beamed upon her mistress. She loved the quality—the quality, she always called them. When the season of week-ends came round each year, she was the proudest of women in the country-side. At that very moment, she was wearing a silk petticoat, worth its weight in gold, five guineas at the utmost for it seemed like froth in the hand—which a French lady's maid had given her in exchange for silence over a little incident that scarcely calls for mention. The first return of her mistress to Apsley, then, was a sign of the nearing season—the lonely swallow that is seen scudding through the first break in the year by some enthusiastic ornithologist and recorded in the next morning's edition of the *Times*. She kept a diary, in fact, did Mrs. Butterick, and in about the middle of April of every year, might be noticed the comment, "Madame arrived—first time this year—" and then, more than probably the addition,

E. Temple Thurston

"House-party on the—" and thereafter the date, whatever it may have been.

Now, on this occasion, as she always did, she beamed in silence and waited.

"Good morning, Mrs. Butterick. You got my letter?"

"Yes, madam."

"These sheets are aired?"

"Dry as a bone, madam. I felt 'em myself."

"I shall only be staying the night," Mrs. Durlacher continued; "I go back to Town to-morrow morning."

Mrs. Butterick made no reply, If her features could have fallen into an expression of disappointment, they would willingly have done so; but nature had taken no trouble with them. They were an afterthought. It seemed as if they had been placed there at the last moment of birth, with no inner mechanism to answer to sensation. She just said nothing.

"To-morrow morning," Mrs. Durlacher repeated.

"Yes, madam."

"And now you can take the chintz covers off everything in this room and the drawing-room as well. There's rather a snap in the air; I think perhaps you might have the fire lighted in the dining-room. And tell one of the gardeners to pick me plenty of daffodils—not common ones—not those ordinary double ones, but the best he's got. White petals with the yellow trumpets—you know the ones I mean. Also some narcissi and a few tulips—pink ones for the drawing-room.

They must all be on the dining-room table when I come downstairs. I'll arrange them myself. And get my trunks sent up to me at once—I want to change my dress. Taylor and Mason are coming down by train; they'll be here any minute now. The trap went for them—didn't it?"

"Yes, madam—at half-past ten."

"Well, then, that's all, Mrs. Butterick. What time is it?"

The housekeeper extracted a silver watch with its flowery, ornamental dial from the recesses of an ample bosom. She drew it out by the chain and, once free, it swung violently to and fro till she caught it.

"A quarter past eleven, madam."

"Very well, there's not too much time. I expect my brother and probably a lady down here to-day. Oh yes, and by the way—when they come—well—I'll tell that to Taylor. You go and see about the flowers and the chintz covers at once—and my trunks—immediately. You'd better come up yourself and unpack for me until Mason arrives."

When once she heard the crunching wheels of the trap upon the drive, she rang her bell. Mason entered almost immediately.

"Tell Taylor I want her here at once," said Mrs. Durlacher, "and come and help me dress before you change your things."

The moment she had closed the door, her mistress called her back.

"And send Mrs. Butterick as well."

E. Temple Thurston

"Yes, madam."

Mason went downstairs with the report that something was in the air. She had a feeling, she said.

The interview with Taylor was shorter—more to the point.

"I'm expecting my brother—Mr. Traill, and probably a lady," she said. She laid no stress on the last word, much as the temptation assailed her. "It's quite likely they may be down to lunch. When they come, there is no need to say that I am here, unless, of course, Mr. Traill asks you. You'd better go and change your dress at once."

Then she turned to Mrs. Butterick.

"You've taken off the chintz covers?" she said.

"Yes, madam."

"Ordered the flowers?"

"Yes, madam."

"Well, now, what have you got in for lunch?"

"There's some lamb, madam."

"Well—that's no good—I'd better tell you what I want. A heavy lunch like that is impossible. I want all dainty little dishes—something out of the common, I leave it entirely to you. Four courses will be enough. And Sauterne and Burgundy. Tell Taylor we'll have coffee in the dining-room. Now my hair, Mason."

So she marshalled forces, occupied positions and concentrated artillery in preparation for the siege. The generalship of a woman is never so keen, so instinct with strategy, as when she gives battle against another of her sex. Her campaign against men, when once she takes up arms, is mimic warfare—a sham fight—compared to this. Against a man, she needs but a company of fascinations, and in one attack his squares—the stern veterans of determination—are driven to flight. But with a woman, whole regiments of cunning, whole battalions of craft, with all the well-trained scouts of intuition and all the dashing cavalries of charm, are needed to rout her absolutely from the field.

Within an hour Mrs. Durlacher descended to the dining-room. The gown she wore would not have pleased a man to infatuation; but a woman would have realized its beauty, known its value. With deft fingers, she arranged the flowers. In a chair by the fire, hiding herself from view to any one outside the window, she sat and watched the table being laid, giving orders how the vases were to be placed on the old oak table.

"Lay two places—that's all," she said.

Taylor looked up. "I thought you said there would be a lady with Mr. Traill, madam."

"I said—probably. You can lay another place if she comes." A vision crossed her mind of making so small a point as that, a moment of embarrassment for her unwelcome guest.

Then a sound reached her ears. Her eyes were arrested, fixed unseeingly to a point before her as she listened.

"Is that a motor, Taylor?"

E. Temple Thurston

Taylor looked out of the window. "It's a taxi-cab, madam."

"Can you see who's inside?"

"I suppose it's Mr. Traill, madam. Yes—it is."

"Any one with him?"

"Yes, madam—a lady."

## CHAPTER II

Circumstances will almost make a character in a day; in three years, a character can be moulded, bent, twisted or straightened, in the furnace of events; just as the potter, idling with the passive clay, will shape it, heedlessly almost, as the fancy nerves his fingers. But before he is aware, the time slips by, the clay gets set and there, in front of his eyes, is the figure as his fancy made it—brittle, easily broken into dust, but impossible of being moulded afresh until it shall again go back into the water of oblivion and become the shapeless mass that once it was.

So, in the three years that had passed since she had yielded body and soul into the keeping of Jack Traill, had Sally's character become set in the moulding of his influence. Happiness she had—that to the full. He cared for her the more when once he had her gentle nature under his touch; showed her all those little attentions of which such a mind as his is capable of conceiving—teased her, petted her, laughed like a schoolboy at her feminine whims and fancies.

For the first month of their relationship, they went abroad. He gave her money, more money than she had ever had in absolute possession before, wherewith to fit herself for the journey. She tried to refuse half of it—told him the sum was preposterous, that less than half of what he was giving would

E. Temple Thurston

provide her with the most expensive of frocks for the rest of her life.

"Sixty pounds?" he said. "My sister spends that in half an hour at a dressmaker's in Dover Street."

"Ah, yes, but that's your sister," she had objected pathetically.

"And you?"

"But thirty pounds will really be more than enough."

It lay deep in her mind, never offering to rise to the surface, to remind him that she was not his wife. But he would not give way. He had said sixty pounds—sixty pounds it had to be. So he mastered her, without effort, at every turn.

She went then with Janet to the shops—she, and her sixty pounds, gripped tight in brittle ten-pound notes in her purse. At that time she was still staying on at Kew, still attending her office in King Street; but at both places she had given notice to leave, and in a week's time would be free.

Her first intimation to Janet of all that had occurred and all that was to follow, was made, as usual, one night, when the darkness hid her face, and she could only tell by the sound of Janet's breathing what effect her story might have.

When she had finished, Janet made use of that remark— justified in her case—which every prophet, false or true, utters at one time or another—

"Didn't I tell you so?"

But then she went on, and they had talked far into the night;

and at every moment, when doubt or regret seized and shook Sally with a quivering remorse, Janet laughed at her fears.

"You've got the best bargain in the world," she exclaimed. "You want a man's love—you've got it—haven't you? And yet you're free—as free as air. If you should tire—"

Sally laughed bitterly.

"Very well, then, if he should tire, you're your own mistress. All this caging of wild birds seems to me to be futile. Morals? Oh, morals be hanged! Are you going to call yourself immoral because the man has no great respect for matrimony?"

"Yes; but I have."

"You have! That's only because you were dragged up in a rectory, just outside the church door. I can't understand you. You've shaken off your belief in lots of things—you don't believe in the actual divinity of Christ—yet you cling to an antiquated sacrament that dates back long before the time of a man whose statement that he was the actual Son of God you're prepared to doubt. It's only because you labour under the misapprehension—as nearly everybody does—that marriage is a convenience to a woman. It's the inconvenience of the thing that makes the morality or the immorality in your mind. You're only a conventionalist like everybody else-you're not a moralist."

Yet, notwithstanding all these arguments of Janet's, there were dark moments during that week before she left Kew, when all the force of dogma, all the waves of conventionality, beat against her breast; but it was her faith in love that held her to the end; just as his faith in the dogma itself, had held the Rev. Samuel Bishop to the teachings of his

E. Temple Thurston

Church. Love, she made the high altar of her worship; to that, unconsciously, she offered all prayers, made all sacrifice. These dark moments hung heavy in her heart so long as they were present; but one meeting with Traill was sufficient to drive them in a body from her mind—gloomy phantoms of imagination which, in the night, have vivid reality, and with the first welcome break of morning are stricken out of sight.

When forty-five of the sixty pounds had been spent and she had bought every conceivable thing that she required, purchasing from habit where things were cheapest, she had brought the remainder back to Traill.

He held her face, crumpling it, in his hands.

"What on earth sort of a child are you?" he asked.

"How do you mean?"

"Why—I give you a certain amount of money to spend on clothes and you bring me back fifteen pounds like the little girl coming back with change from the grocer's."

"But I've got everything I want," she replied, laughing.

"Have you got an opera cloak?"

"No, I don't want that."

"Have you got an umbrella?"

She laughed again—head thrown back, like a child at its father's knee.

"No, I have one of my own already."

"Did you get a—get a—oh, I don't know—did you get boots for tramping through the country with—boots for show, boots for wear, boots for comfort? How many pair of boots *did* you get?"

"Two."

"Well—go and get some more and an opera cloak—to-morrow evening, we're going to sit in the Comedie Francais and not understand a word that's said."

Then they had gone abroad, and life—wonderful—had passed from day to day like a pageant before Sally's eyes. The dark moments came with less frequency. After a time, they passed away altogether. She saw no end to it; she saw no sin in it. What sin could there be? Janet's arguments had penetrated more deeply into her mind than she had ever imagined. When, on rare occasions, she was alone in the hotel where they happened to be staying—and it was then that doubt, while there was any, oppressed her—she hugged Janet's sayings to her mind, forced them to support her. "You're only a conventionalist, like everybody else—you're not a moralist."

Now she was a moralist, or nothing. She had cut the last link with convention and, at a moment such as that, the realization that there was no returning, no getting back, obsessed her with a shuddering fear. She did not understand that she was conventionalist still at heart; she did not divine that she was not the great woman, loving greatly—only the lesser woman, loving, it is true, with all the utmost of her personality, but loving less.

There is no conventionality in greatness. Great natures make laws for lesser natures to obey; and, far though she had gone from the broad path where the little people huddle on their

E. Temple Thurston

way, the blood of the little people was in her veins and conventionality still held its claim upon her. She liked to think that she was married. It was beyond the strength of her mind to look upon herself as the mistress of the man she loved.

"It cannot end—it can never end," she told herself. "He loves me too much and I love him better still. It's as good—quite as good, as being married. The Church makes no difference." She thought of her father, remembering how, through the very precepts of that very Church, he had found retribution. So people, who married with the Church's sanction, found retribution too. Some lives were miserable; she had known them. What good had the blessing of the Church been to them? None!

Then Traill would return to her and doubts would vanish like shadows that a light disperses. They were happy. She had never conceived of such happiness before. Her mood was one of continual gratitude. She thanked him for everything— if not with lips, then with eyes.

"You remind me of a little starved gutter-arab, whenever I give you anything," he once said, when he had brought her back from a theatre in Rome and given her supper in the restaurant of the Quirinale.

"Not very complimentary," she replied without objection.

"Well—you look at me that way—as if I were giving you God's earth for God's sake. Have you never been happy before in your life?"

"Never."

"I don't mean particularly like this. Like this, I know you

haven't. But any other way?"

"No, I don't think I ever have. I went away from home when I was eighteen—I wasn't happy there. Then I had to work too hard."

"Then you are a little starved gutter-arab." He took her gently in his arms. "And what do I seem to you—eh? Sort of fairy prince, I suppose, in gold armour."

"You seem like God, sometimes," she whispered.

He put her away with a stab of conscience—seated her on a chair and looked down at her.

"It's silly to talk like that," he said evenly. "If there is a God—and I suppose there is—the world spends a heap of money in fostering the idea—then He's certainly more consistent in His being than I am—though consistency always seems to me His weak point. But you've not got to idealize me, you know. You remember what I once said to you—don't you?"

"What was that?"

"There's a beast in every man, thank God!"

"Yes—I don't think I shall ever forget that."

"Well—don't," he added.

But even this did not harbour in her mind. She wrote long, impulsive letters to Janet, pouring out a flood of description of all the places which they visited, opening her heart of its perfect happiness.

E. Temple Thurston

"You said he was hard once," she wrote from Florence. "You said you knew he was hard. He's never said a hard thing to me the whole time we've been away. He may be hard to other people. I've seen him awfully bitter sometimes, but never to me. We are in love, you see. We shall always be in love. Dear, dear old Janet, I wish you could be with us."

Janet took a deep breath when she had finished the reading of that letter, and when Mrs. Hewson pushed some shrimps on to her plate, she pulled the shells from them with impatient energy.

And so—slowly, even in that month—some little of the change in her character was wrought. Her nature began to set in the mould of luxury in which he placed her. Not for one moment was she spoilt by it; not for one moment made selfish. Whenever he gave her money for a definite object, she still made her purchases as cheaply as possible, still brought what was left over in the flat of an empty palm to him. But the enfranchising influence of those two years of hard work began to lose its effect. She lost independence at every turn and, by the time they returned to London, was beginning to lean on Traill, rely on him, submit subserviently to every wish he uttered.

Such had been her desertion from the cause, a conscript in which, she had so ill-understood. The falling back into luxury, the acceptance of those things which in her tentative, unrevolutionary way she had always imagined to come into her right of possession, had been very easy—very gentle— the drifting of a feather on an idle summer wind. She had let herself be borne on it, using it, not as an advantage, not as a step to lift her to a greater freedom and a wider independence, but as a fit setting, a worthy environment to this love which consumed the whole of her being and rode, the master, with an unslacking rein, over all her actions.

If she had taken the situation as it was, faced the meaning of it with firm lips and a steady eye, there would have been hope—more, there would have been salvation for her. But frail, sensitive, tender-hearted, little Sally Bishop was not of that blood, that breeding was not in her bone. She took the threads, coloured them one and all with that deceptive dye of the imagination, and wove a romance out of the materials of a stern reality.

To every intent, to every purpose in her mind, she was a married woman. The constant use of his name in the hotels where they stayed abroad had fostered the delusion in her mind. That, in reality, she was still Sally Bishop was a fact, obvious enough, patent enough, and one which she was not so foolish as to try and force herself to forget; but she was Sally Bishop only in name. So, in contrary comparison, other women were wives only in name, yet had no husbands.

The true, logical state of the case never made its appeal to her. She was too much of a romantic, living, as many women do, in a cloudland of hallucination, until a lightning circumstance tears its rent in the vaporous fabric and experience thunders in their ears. Had she consented to the reasoning that she had but left the plying of one trade in exchange for another; had she admitted the fact that she had but abandoned one master for the service of another, there would have been every chance that, if the end should come, she would be able to take up the threads where they had broken off and wring profit from the ultimate position. But no such thought entered her mind. Emancipation was no goal for her ambitions. She sought for chains to gyve about her soul and, in her relationship with Traill, she fondly dreamed that she had found them. If the real aspect of the case had forcibly made its way into her consideration, she would never have accepted the situation, never have laid seal to the compact.

E. Temple Thurston

All this delirium of reasoning, she showed in the first few moments to Janet when she had returned to London. Down at Kew she spent an evening, delighted, with a justifiable pride, to be seen in one of the dainty frocks that Traill had bought her.

"So you're married now, I 'ear," said Mrs. Hewson.

"Yes." Sally beamed with her reply, and Janet watched her with questioning eyes.

"I hope you're happy."

"I couldn't be happier," Sally answered; then she dragged Janet upstairs to the room they had shared together for two years, and throwing her parcels—presents that she had brought from abroad—on to the bed, she twined her arms round Janet's slender neck and covered the thin, drawn face with kisses.

One knows the endearments that such an occasion exacts. They come out of a full heart and bear no repetition, for only a full heart can understand them. They swept over Janet, for the moment blinding her in her fondness for this child, full of swift impulse in her gratitude, and drugged with romance in her mind. But once those endearments had been spoken, when once the presents had been divested of their paper wrappings—porcelain representations of the Bambinos from Florence—a marble statue of the Venus de Milo from Pisa— an ornament in mosaic from Rome—when once they had been set up, admired, paid for in kisses of gratitude, then Janet gave words to the questions that had been looking from her eyes.

"What sort of a settlement has he made on you?" she asked.

The inquiry, notwithstanding the fact that it had been spoken with a gentle voice, tuned to consideration for her feelings, struck the sensitiveness of Sally's mind, whipped the blood to her cheeks.

"There is no settlement. Why should there be?"

"Why? Well, for every reason in the world, I should think."

"There is none, then."

"You haven't even suggested it?"

"No!"

She rose, turning away from the bed where she had been sitting, with the tears smarting in her eyes. Janet looked after her, an expression of contemplation pursing her features, wrinkling her forehead.

"I think I'll go and see Mr. Traill," she said slowly.

Sally wheeled round, her heel a pivot to the motion.

"What for?" she asked.

"I think he'd better be told that he can't play indiscriminately with women like you."

"He's not playing," Sally retorted violently. "You're cruel, Janet. If you do go to him, I'll never speak to you again."

"That's quite possible; I should expect that," Janet replied imperturbably. "Whenever one tries to arrange the affairs of people who cannot arrange them themselves, one must anticipate that sort of treatment."

"Ah, but you don't understand," Sally pleaded piteously. "He would hate any interference of that sort. He would hate me through it. We don't look at the thing in the same light that you do. You make a business of it. Do you think if I had ever seen it in that light, I could have done what I have done? You know I couldn't. I should loathe myself too. I tell you, we love each other. There can be no question of settlement in such a case as that."

Janet looked at her with pity. It was hard for her to say all that she intended; but the mind of the revolutionary, however wasted its cause, has kindred with the mind of God. Justice and truth before all things is the cry of it, and let suffering be a means rather than a hindrance to the end.

"Never drown sorrow," Janet had once said from her pinnacle of enthusiasm, "the dripping ghost of it'll haunt you. Don't drown it—save it, learn of it."

Now, with a steady hand, she carried that precept into practice. It might make a rent in Sally's heart; it might bring separation between them; but she did not hesitate at that. The cause of justice and the desire for truth have no need of sentiment.

"And how long do you think that love is going to last?" she asked.

"Always; why not?"

"With you, perhaps; but with him?"

Sally looked out of the window across the river. The night that Mr. Arthur had proposed to her—offering her marriage —danced flauntingly across her memory. He had been ready to bind himself to her for the rest of his life. She let the memory go on, with its mincing steps, back into the dreary darkness of the river from whence it had come; but she said nothing.

"You can't answer for him?" suggested Janet.

"Yes, I can," she replied impetuously. "Why not always with him? He'll never marry. He's always said so."

"Yes, but you didn't answer at once. Sally—" Janet put a hand on her shoulder, "I believe you think you're as good as married. The way you answered Mrs. Thing-um-i-bob down-stairs—Mrs. Hewson—when she asked you, what we'd both agreed to tell her—that made me begin to wonder. But you're not married, Sally. He's only your master—that's all, and if I were you, I'd see that I got my settlement. He might want to leave you any day."

Sally moved herself free of the detaining hand and laughed, with a bitter absence of merriment.

"That shows how little you understand," she said. "He's told me over and over again that he never thought he would find any one who fitted in so perfectly to his life as I do."

"Most any pretty woman fits into a man's life when he wants, and so long as he wants her," Janet remarked. "It's only women like myself—ugly little devils like me—who have to meet the difficulty of finding a niche that'll hold them for more than the latter part of an afternoon before the lights are turned up. You fit into his life—of course you do. I'm not suggesting that you don't. I'm only questioning how long you're going to do it—only trying to remind you that it won't be for always. Why will you insist on being so romantic? Why can't you look at life through a plain sheet of glass—if you must look at it through something—instead of choosing

E. Temple Thurston

the red and the yellow and the purples—anything but the plain, the untinted reality. Go and get your settlement. Make him put it in black and white, and shove his name down at the bottom. Then you can look at it any way you like—forget about it—sit and nurse your romance all day long if you want to; but make sure of the reality first. He'll think twice as much of you if you do."

"You think that," said Sally. "You believe he'd think twice as much of me if I came to him in a mercenary spirit like that? And I thought you knew something about men."

"Mercenary!" Janet threw her head back and laughed. "You'd have to ask for a good deal more than that to seem mercenary, my dear child. You! Why, you've worked two years and you never knew your own value all that time. I've seen your finger-nails worn square on that old typewriter you used to pound; but you never dreamed of thinking that you were worth more than your twenty-five or your twenty-seven shillings a week, however much they made you stay at that office overtime. Mercenary's about the last word that could be applied to you. I don't want to worry the life out of you, or make you miserable, but when I see you rushing along—giving, giving, always giving, with both hands—"

"I'm not only giving," Sally exclaimed. "Do you think I get nothing in return? I've never been made so happy in my life before—never! Is that receiving nothing for what I give?"

Janet looked at her, steadying her eyes.

"You don't understand the proportion of things," she said slowly. "You don't realize the comparative ratio of one thing to another. Any man can give happiness to a woman who loves him—but that's no bargain! He merely gives her happiness by taking his own. Do you call that a fair exchange? To you, drunk with romance, perhaps it is. But in reality it's robbery. He has to pay higher for his pleasures than that. Why, even the women in the streets, he pays and takes all risks inclusive? Then what do you think he owes a woman like you? Why, in the name of God, can't you sweep all this mist away, that's in front of your eyes, and see it as a transaction? Sign it, seal it, make a deed of it, and then forget it if you like; but insure yourself against the worst if it should ever come."

To suppose that this reasoning would appeal to Sally, to expect that she would assimilate Janet's point of view, adopt Janet's attitude of mind, is beyond all imagination. The whole aspect that Janet had revealed, depressed her, weighed—a heavy drag—upon her spirits. But she was not convinced.

To call things by their names—albeit that language has been evolved these many thousands of years, and during all that time human beings have sat in the dust and worked and played with its cunning symbols—is no easy matter. For the evolution of language has achieved two ends, and the perfection of it has accomplished the one as thoroughly as it has the other. With language we give expression of our feelings; but also with language we have learnt to hide feelings, cloak thoughts, and dissemble before the very eyes that know us best. Janet, demanding the truth in all things, seeking in words the very highest aim of the words themselves, was a far higher type than Sally.

To Sally, the only means by which she could follow the true bent of her inclinations, was by wrapping up the matter in a cunning tissue of words. Herein she is no great woman, loving greatly. She could not bring herself to think of her position as that of a mistress. To still love and do that, was beyond her. And so she persisted in regarding herself as a

E. Temple Thurston

woman who has faced-out conventionality, dared the opinion of the world, and chosen to live with a man as his wife without the condescending sanction of the Church.

It is all pardonable, all this. It is an occurrence as common in big cities as are the lofty chimneys, and besmirching haze which, on the horizon, herald the approach of a place where men and women are gathered closely together. But it is a position which, with the present conditions of tortured conventionality, is impossible, untenable. Either a woman is the wife of a man, or his mistress; and if the latter then, as Janet has said, she had better see to her settlement first and build her romance, if so she chose, upon its foundations. A man may keep closed the gates of matrimony until the last moment, but when he finds that only through them can he gain the woman he loves, then no amount of principle and no desire of freedom will hinder him from swinging them wide and following her through. On the other hand also, he will make but little attempt to unlock those very gates, so long as there is a shadow of the prospect within his mind that she will meet him outside.

To Sally, such reasoning as this would have robbed her of all romance—the shattering siege gun that thunders through a town, and tumbles the images from their altars in the little church.

Two ways there were in which to view the matter truly. If she were the great woman, she would have loved for the love of love itself—let it end where it might. If she were the revolutionary seeking truth, demanding freedom, then she would have loved the transaction for the transaction's sake—let it end to-morrow if it willed.

But Sally was neither. She took a middle course. She neither loved wholly for the sake of love, nor could she make her transaction and be proud of it. Like thousands of other women, she liked to think that she was loved in return and that it would never end. Like thousands of other women, she believed that what the man had taken, that he would keep, because in the eyes of God and all the other phrases of romantic sentimentalism, they were one.

But this is conventionality, and conventionality has to be thanked for it. So women have been brought up; and until that army, of which Sally now is a deserter, has forced its marches and driven its enemy from the field, women will so continue to think, so continue to act, so continue to be broken into dust, the grains of which any wind may carry into the west where the sun sets in deep crimson.

That night when Sally returned from Kew, Traill had noticed her depression.

"What's Miss Hallard been saying to you?" he asked. "Telling you that you're leading a terrible life, I suppose."

"No, why should she? Do you think I am, Jack?"

"Me? I should hope not, since I'm the cause of it. Do you feel you're doing anything very terrible? Here—put your arms round my neck—kiss me—God bless your little heart—you couldn't do anything terrible. Now, are we going to sit and mope, or shall we go out to supper?"

That meant that they were going to supper, and in half an hour she was as happy again as a child.

For the first of the three years they passed through an incessant round of amusements, going abroad every few months, once bicycling all through France from North to South and then returning by train, spending a week in Paris.

E. Temple Thurston

Their method of living was frugal, and Sally's demands amounted practically to nothing. For the whole of that year, Traill had sunned himself in the warm delight of her simplicity. The years when he was alone had brought with them a certain amount of cynicism, a definite trace of bitterness. But with Sally, he forgot all that—threw from his shoulders the years that solitude had added to his age and became the man of thirty-six who still looks youth in the eyes without question.

Then he had shaken himself and awakened to the broad responsibilities of life. A small case was offered him in the courts. Such cases he had refused before; now Sally urged him to accept it and he obeyed, looking rather to the future than her immediate prompting. So began the seriousness of his career as a barrister. The second year only brought one other small brief with it; but both cases were won. Then he began to specialize in divorce and finally, contact with a well-known solicitor which had come through the medium of journalism, brought him his first brief in the probate and divorce division. The case was rather a big one and he was not the leading counsel, but the assistance he gave was deemed of such value, that the next brief from the solicitor was given entirely to him.

Sally came down to the courts and listened to his cross-examination of the woman who against a thousand incriminating circumstances was fighting, with white lips and piteously hunted eyes, to keep her name from the mud into which Traill was striving to drag it.

There she saw the cruelty in him again. It was impossible for her, listening with every sense taut to the uttermost, to obliterate the personal element, to think that he was merely a machine grinding, in the course of his duty, as the implacable mills crush the yielding grain into the listless powder of flour.

"Didn't it strike you at all," he asked the trembling woman, his voice barren of all feeling and edged with biting incredulity. "Didn't it strike you at all, when you kissed the co-respondent, that you were betraying your husband's confidence in you?"

"No, not when I kissed him. We—we cared for each other—I admit to that; but—but kissing did not seem wrong."

"You didn't consider kissing wrong?"

"No."

"At what point then in your intimate relations with a man—with the co-respondent in particular—would you have considered that wrong began and right ended?"

The wretched woman had looked pitiably at the judge. The judge looked unseeingly before him into the well of the court.

"At what point?" Traill had insisted.

"I don't know how to say it," she pleaded feebly.

"Then can I assist you? Would you have considered it wrong—having kissed you—for him to put his arms round you?"

"Yes, I think so."

"There is all the difference, then, in your mind between a man's kissing you and putting his arms round you. All the difference between right and wrong?"

E. Temple Thurston

"No, I suppose there isn't."

"Then you would not have considered that wrong?"

"No."

"Would you have considered it wrong to sit on his knee?"

Seeing how her case was weakening—realizing how he was belittling her scruples—she had admitted that she would not think it wrong, hoping that the ready admission of that would remedy the effect of her previous indecision.

"Then am I to understand—" asked Traill with a voice stirred in well-simulated anger, "am I to understand that because you loved the co-respondent, you kissed him, thinking no wrong in it and yet, thinking no wrong in sitting on his knee or having his arms about you, you yet—loving him—refused these things in which you saw no harm? Is that what you wish his lordship and the jury to understand?"

"I—I—may have let him put his arms round me—perhaps I did sit on his knee—once or twice."

"Then why," shouted Traill, "when the last witness affirmed that she had seen you sitting in the drawing-room with the co-respondent's arm round your neck, did you so vehemently deny it?"

Into the trap she had fallen—into the trap which with his cold cunning he had laid for her—and from that moment, rigidly denying her misconduct on her oath before God, the wretched creature was brought on the rack of his questioning to almost every admission but that of adultery. At last Sally had left the court. She could bear the strain of it no longer.

The thoughts which that incident had given rise to in her mind, had thrown their shadows upon all her lightness of heart for many days afterwards. There she had seen the keen acid of implacable justice separating, with undeviating precision, the dross from the gold. She had beheld the naked fact of adultery—stripped of all the silk of glamour, all the velvet of romance which once it had worn—held in its cringing shame before the unsympathetic eyes of twelve men in a public court of law. And he who had done it, he who had wrenched away the silken garments, torn off the folds of velvet and flung the naked deed before their eyes, was the man into whose keeping she had given her whole existence.

"You, who admittedly can play with passion at the fringe of adultery," she heard him crying out as she stole from the court, "do you expect a jury of men, who know the world, to believe that a mere scruple has withheld you from giving yourself to the importunate desires of this man—the co-respondent?"

Was that what he thought of her—was that what he thought she had done to her shame with him? Sally had cried out these questions to herself, as he had cried them to the woman; but when that evening, he asked her in a quiet voice what she had thought of the case, she had evaded any expression that would disclose the trouble of her mind.

"I couldn't stay till the end, you know," she said. "I had to go before the verdict. What happened?"

"Oh, we won—hands down; but upon my soul I'm not sure that she did actually commit adultery. There are some women—men too, for that matter—who'll play with fire till their hearts are burnt out—but conventionality drags 'em back from the one deed that will absolutely crush their conscience, and they think themselves confoundedly

E. Temple Thurston

ill-treated when they get their retribution. They whine, like that woman did to-day; but I'm inclined to believe that on the vital clause she was telling the truth."

Sally had looked at him, wondering and in amazement; but she had said nothing, mistrusting herself to speak.

The effect of this incident upon her mind had softened with time—in time she had practically forgotten about it. And then came round the end of the third year. The previous year he had given up journalism entirely, his time being fully occupied with legal business at the courts. He took chambers to himself in the Temple. Sometimes Sally came down there on a quiet day and they had tea together.

"We'll pretend," she would say, "that you've never met me before—and it's awfully unwise for me to come and see you in chambers—but I come and then perhaps—while I'm making the tea—you suddenly put your arms round my waist, and of course I'm awfully offended. Then you kiss me, and I begin to get fond of you—and then—" So she led him through a child's game to the outburst of a man's passion and he, amused with being the child, found in it all the burning zest of being a man.

In the Spring that followed the conclusion of that third year, she had reminded him of his promise to take her once to Apsley. He jumped at it.

"A day in the country 'll do me all the good in the world!" he exclaimed—"and you too. I'll write to Dolly at once and see that no one's down there on Friday. If there isn't, we'll go."

## CHAPTER III

They made a day of it. In Trafalgar Square at eleven o'clock the next morning, they stepped into a taxi-cab—the same little vehicle that Taylor, from the dining-room window, had seen spinning round the curve of the drive. The hood was put down; the warm sunshine, just touched with a light sting from the regions of cold air through which it had passed, beat upon their faces. To such a day, from the grey fogs and lightless hours of winter, one comes, finding life well worth its while. Sally sat with her hand wrapped in Traill's, giving vent to a thousand expressions of delight, drawing his sudden attention to the thousand things that pleased her eye—the faint wash of green from the buds upon the hedgerows, the bright clusters of primroses that struck light through the shadows in the wood, forcing life through the thick carpet of dead leaves that the trees had given back to earth.

"Does it worry you—my keeping on pointing out things?" she asked at last.

"Worry? Lord, no! Shout as much as you like. It reminds me of when I was a kid, coming back from Harrow to Apsley for the holidays."

When they came in sight of the Manor, could perceive

E. Temple Thurston

through rents in the cloak of cedars that enveloped it, the high, graceful Elizabethan chimneys and the points of the red gables on which the starlings congregated, Traill half rose to his feet with a straining of his neck—a light of excitement in his eyes.

"There it is!" he exclaimed. "That place through the dark trees there. Jove, I haven't seen it for more than three years."

She followed the direction in which his extended finger pointed, and her eyes took in, not only Apsley, but his life and the true gulf that lay between them. As she saw it from there, she recognized it as a place which, passing, even in those better days when her father had lived in the quaint little rectory at Cailsham, she might have exclaimed—"Oh, what a lovely place that is! I wonder who lives there?" And it had belonged to him—this man who had taken her life out of its dreary groove and placed it in a pleasure-garden of plenty; but the garden gate was not locked and the key was not in her keeping.

This mood was momentary. It passed, scudding across her mind, a fringe of rain cloud that the wind has caught hanging between the hill-tops and driven at its will. When Traill leant out of the car and gave peremptory orders of direction, she forgot about it. Then, in his almost boyish excitement, she realized how much the place really was to him; how much, notwithstanding all his Bohemianism, it counted in his life.

"You love this place—don't you?" she said, when he dropped back again into his seat.

"Yes—I should think so. I know every stick and stone for miles round here. See that little lane up there?"

"Yes."

"Had a fight there once with a gamekeeper. Much more exciting, I can tell you, than that show you saw that night."

"Were you hurt?" she asked, frowning.

"Oh, not much; not more than he was. It was stopped precipitously by a stick, wielded by my governor. He'd got wind of it. We hadn't much time to make a mess of each other."

"I suppose it must be full of memories," she said. "I can never understand why you should have given it up."

"Oh, I was a fool, of course. I wanted ready money, and I didn't want to sell the place—couldn't have sold it. So I let my sister take it over for what the pater had left her. That suited me at the time. I'm not sorry that I saw far enough to re-purchase if I wanted to."

"You can re-purchase?"

"Lord, yes!"

"But you did not tell me that."

"Didn't I? Oh yes, I can re-purchase; five thousand any day will make this place my own again. That's the sum I took from my sister."

Sally inclined her head to show that she understood, but she made no reply. The cloud had blown back again into her mind. She felt the shadow of it, the chill of it, even in the warm sunshine. It took no definite shape, it brought no definite warning; but she was oppressively conscious of its presence and its weight upon all her thoughts.

E. Temple Thurston

Then they entered the drive, swept up between the long beds of brilliant tulips until the house came full in view, and from that moment her little ejaculations of delight and admiration were a pleasure to him and a distraction to her.

"It's a wonderful old place!" she exclaimed. "And doesn't it make it twice as wonderful to think that Queen Elizabeth stayed here when it was just like it is now!" This fact he had told her as they came down, knowing that the childish enthusiasm of her mind would catch hold of it, drive it deep into her imagination and hang thereon a pretty raiment of romance.

"Does add a bit of colour," he admitted with a smile. "I expect she made it pretty expensive for the old gentleman who entertained her. He probably had to keep quiet for a few months after she'd gone, and lay restrictions on the house-hold expenditure."

Then they drew up before the hall door and Traill helped her to alight.

"I guess we'll make old Mrs. Butterick give us some lunch first. Are you hungry?" He opened the hall door and stood aside to let her enter.

"Yes, frightfully. I suppose it was the drive."

"All right, just a second; you go round there through the hall to the left—fine old hall, isn't it?—and the first door on the left, that's the dining-room. I shan't be long. I just want to see about getting this filthy coloured taxi out of the light and tell the gardener to get the chauffeur a meal—you wait in the dining-room."

He closed the door again. Sally stood for a moment looking

about her. The old square panelling of oak—black with age—the huge open grate with its logs of wood ready for the burning, the ornaments of pewter—old pewter jugs, old pewter plates with coats of arms embossed upon their surface, all the perfection of it awed her and, with a momentary wave of depression that beat over her feelings of admiration, she felt an interloper in a place that was beyond her wildest dreams of avarice. It was with no little sense of reluctance, even though the anticipation of meeting any one never for the moment entered her head, that she made her way slowly to the dining-room, hoping every moment to hear his footsteps following her—giving her, so it seemed, the right to her presence in so luxurious a place. No wonder he loved it. And then, the thought struck at her, would it be any wonder if he re-purchased, as he had said he had the right to do? And if that were to happen—he was making his name now, and it well might—would he bring her here to live with him? Would he perhaps make her his wife? Or would they live, as they lived together now? Or—and the thought drove blood that was cold and chilling through her veins—would it be impossible for them to live so publicly in such a way, and would he then live alone?

She tried to shake herself free of this mood of conjecture, took the handle firmly within her fingers, opened the door, and walked into the room.

The next moment her heart leapt, a live thing within her, then lay still. Every action through her body seemed suspended. She scarcely realized her physical existence at all. It was as though she were conscious only of mind, mind that was filled with perplexity, astonishment, consternation, a mind that was being buffeted by winds from every quarter of the compass of sensation. And through it all, she struggled to drive words together into sentences, words, that like a flock of witless sheep upon open ground, would not be driven, but

E. Temple Thurston

ran this way and jumped that in a frolicsome imbecility of purpose.

And there she stood, just within the room, while Mrs. Durlacher with slowly uplifting eyebrows of amazement rose gradually from the comfortable armchair to her feet.

"Aren't you Miss—Miss—?" She tried to catch the name in the air with her fingers.

"Bishop," said Sally, with dry lips.

"Yes, of course, Bishop—Miss Bishop?"

Sally half inclined her head.

"But what—?" she hesitated, knowing that the rest of her sentence must be obvious, yet gaining time to put the matter together—fit it to the whole from its separate parts. This was the girl whom she had met that night in Jack's room—the girl he had called a lady. They were still acquainted, still friends—greater friends than ever, since he had brought her down with him to Apsley. Were they married? Married secretly? She was a thousand times better dressed than she had been before. The thought tasted bitter. She swallowed the possibility of it with undeniable courage.

"Have you come down here with my brother?" she asked, still in assumed bewilderment.

"Yes," replied Sally. "We—we came down in a taxi-cab."

"But he never said he was bringing any one. He wrote. I—I thought he was going to be alone."

Nothing could be said to this. To apologize for her presence there would be ridiculous. Sally said nothing.

"Well," Mrs. Durlacher smiled, brushing away her surprise with that half-breath of laughter which throws a thin wrapping of amusement about a wealth of contemptuous resignation. "I'm afraid we haven't got much of a lunch to offer you. I expect you'll be very discontented with the slight fare I have provided for Jack and myself. He ought to have told me. Do come into the room, won't you? Wouldn't you like to take off your coat?"

So, with that ease of apparent hospitality, she made her guest as uncomfortable as possible, a glutton for the slightest sign of embarrassment from Sally. Her gluttony was well served. The poor child pitiably looked once through the door, straining eager ears for the sound of Traill's footsteps; then she closed it and came to the fireplace, taking the first chair that offered.

The sense that she had fallen into a trap, notwithstanding all the perfect simulation of Mrs. Durlacher's apparently genuine surprise, swept chillingly through her blood. When once she became conscious again of her bodily existence, felt the pulses throbbing in her forehead, and knew that her heart was beating like the muffled rattling of a kettledrum, she shuddered. Traill, she knew, had nothing to do with it. If that thought, with the force of conviction behind it, had entered her mind, she would have fled; driven with the curling lash of fear—fear of life itself, fear of everything. But she did not even contemplate it. It was the woman her instinct mistrusted. She had realized her an enemy before; now, in the purring tones of her tardy welcome, she recognized in her an enemy whose aggressiveness is active, brought into definite play.

Where lay the trap and how it had been set, she could not

E. Temple Thurston

conjecture; but that a trap was there, she was convinced, and as she had walked unthinkingly into that room, so she had unsuspiciously fallen into the cruel iron jaws of the relentless machine. She sat in that chair by the fire, gazing at the hissing logs as they spat at the flames that licked them, and felt all the powerlessness, all the impotence, that the frightened rabbit knows when it is caught in the device of the snarer.

"Did you come down from Town?" said Mrs. Durlacher, presently.

"Yes."

"It's a nice drive, isn't it?"

"Oh yes, it's lovely."

"Let me see, how long is it since we met last?"

"Three years, I think, perhaps a little more."

"Of course—yes—of course it must be. What a good memory you have! Would you care to see over the house before lunch? It's rather a charming old place, don't you think so? But of course it's terribly untidy now. I haven't started my house-parties yet, and everything's generally more or less upside down till my husband and I begin to come down regularly. Perhaps you'd prefer to wait till after lunch, though?"

Sally rose willingly to her feet.

"Oh no. Not at all—I should like to see it immensely. I think the hall is perfectly wonderful."

Mrs. Durlacher stood up, her eyes candidly criticizing Sally's dress.

"Yes, it is rather quaint. We'll go through to the library first."

Then, but not until that moment, not until she had passed through the white heat of the fire, and had felt her spirit charred, did any help come to her. Traill opened the door abruptly and came into the room. From the set line of his lips, both of them could see that his temper was loose. His shutting of the door, every action, was an expression of feeling to which an innate sense of politeness made him deny speech. He crossed the room without hesitation to join them, shaking hands with his sister.

"They told me you were here, Dolly," he said, all pleasure of meeting her stamped utterly from his voice.

"Well, I suppose they did," she replied with a laugh. "Besides, didn't you see the car? I motored over this morning. That reminds me—" She played with self-possession, it came so easily to her. "That reminds me. Garrett wants a clean collar. Did you see Garrett?"

"Yes."

"Well, did you ever see such a filthy collar as he's wearing in all your life?"

"I don't know—" He crushed her flippancy with the tone in his voice, the look in his eyes. "I don't go about looking at other people's linen."

"No, but you'd have to if you sat behind Garrett as I did this morning for something over an hour. You couldn't help noticing it."

"Well, you can't expect a servant to be clean, can you?" he retorted. "If he hides his uncleanliness that's all you can demand of him."

She broke into a light, ringing laugh at his ironical humour; but he took no notice of that.

"Where were you two going?" he added. He addressed the question to Sally, turning his eyes to hers.

Mrs. Durlacher interposed the answer. "I was going to show Miss Bishop round the house before lunch," she said. "I thought you might show her the grounds afterwards."

"She's much too tired to go tramping round the place before lunch," said Traill, abruptly. "Remember we've just been bumped down from Town—Trafalgar Square—in a jolting taxi. No, she's too tired. She'd better go and take off her hat, I think. Where's Taylor?" He moved towards the bell. "Taylor had better take her up to the Elizabeth room, or your room if you don't mind."

The outline of Mrs. Durlacher's lips tightened; but Traill took no notice. He turned to Sally. "Like to lay your hat on the spot where her gracious Majesty was supposed to have rested a weary head, aching with finance?" he asked.

Sally smiled. Admiration for him then was intense. Mrs. Durlacher smiled as well; but for one instant, she winced first.

"Let me do the honours, Jack, *please*," she said sweetly, "at any rate in my own house."

That was a foolish thing to have said—the first false step she had taken. But so far in the encounter, she knew she was losing, and it takes a greater woman than she to play a losing game. In the first clash of weapons, she had been well-nigh disarmed, and the sting of the steel in her loosened grip had touched her to that momentary loss of control. It was not so much the fact that she had spoken of Apsley as her house. That piece of boasting would have fallen from Traill's shoulders, shaken off by the shrug with which he would have taken it. It was the veiled insult to Sally, the ill-concealed suggestion as to what their relations had been when she had met Sally at the rooms in Regent Street, that whipped him to reply.

He rang the bell imperturbably. That little action, occupying the brief moment that it did, gave him ease to temper his feelings; then he turned.

"Don't let's worry about whose house it is," he said coldly. "Miss Bishop's tired—that's our first consideration. A taxi's not got the latest pattern of springs that your car has."

Taylor entered the room.

"Taylor," he added. "Show Miss Bishop up to the Elizabeth room."

He smiled at Sally as she departed; then, when the door had closed, he turned back to his sister.

Now she was a lost woman, losing a losing game. Her eyes sparkled with anger; she took her breath rapidly between her teeth.

"How dare you bring your mistresses down here and insult me in my own house!" she said recklessly. So a woman, the best of them, strikes when the points are turning against her. It is the rushing blow of the losing man in the ring. Its

E. Temple Thurston

comparison can be traced through all sports—all games. There is always force at the back of the blow, the brute force of desperation; but, with no head to guide it, it wastes itself in air. Once delivered, striking nothing, with all the weight of the body behind it, the body itself is unbalanced, loses equilibrium, becomes a tottering mark for the answering fist.

The moment she had said it, seeing the flame that it lit in her brother's eyes, Mrs. Durlacher wished it unsaid. For the instant he gazed at her, then his anger was spent. Knowing how wasted that blow was, he turned to the mantelpiece and laughed. It was the most bitter retaliation he could have made. She heard it echoing through her brain as the fallen man, dazed and helpless, just hears the seconds being meted out, yet cannot rise, can lift no voice to stop them.

"What Miss Bishop is to me," he said quietly, "is neither here nor there—only to be classed with one of those impulsive conjectures of yours—just the same as when you said that she was a milliner. You don't quite know what you're speaking about, and that gives you confidence. You're a woman. But you'll have to forgive me if I correct you when you talk about this house as yours—it's not—it's mine. You've scarcely what constitutes a tenancy of it."

"Haven't you to put down the sum of five thousand pounds before you can say that?" she asked, her voice steadied, her impulses all under the curb now. She must step lightly if she were to win after this.

"Do you think that would be a very difficult matter?" he questioned in return.

"Well, can you do it?"

"Oh no," he smiled. "As a matter of fact, I never carry more than four or five pounds in loose cash about with me. Don't be a fool, Dolly. Do you want to irritate me into doing something that you know would put your nose out of joint for the rest of your natural life? You know well enough, that I could find the money to-morrow if I wanted to. You've irritated me quite enough already."

"How?"

"By coming down here."

"Why should that irritate you?"

"Because I guess pretty well your reasons. You were expecting a lady—so Mrs. Butterick amiably told me." He turned and looked at her fixedly. "You're as cute as ten, Dolly, but I'm hanged if you know how to play with me."

"Mrs. Butterick told you that?" she said.

"Yes—she spoke like a book. Like the book of Revelations. Now, when I'd expressly asked you if I should be alone when I came down, what the deuce did you want to come for?"

"Don't you think you can speak a little more politely?" she requested.

"That won't help the discussion from your side or mine," he replied quietly. "But rather than give you cause for interruption—I'll do so. Why did you come down here?"

The mind of a woman works with amazing rapidity, but it is impossible to see the direction it will take. There are little insects known to our childish days as skip-jacks. Scratch them with the end of a piece of grass, and they reward you for your pains—they will jump—bound with one spasmodic

E. Temple Thurston

leap and vanish. So is the working of a woman's mind. You can be almost certain of the jump—but of the direction—never.

"Why?" Traill insisted, and then Mrs. Durlacher turned her gaze to the window, looked far away across the stretch of fields ploughed and green, beyond the blue, rising land that lifts above Wycombe, into that distance which holds all the intricate mysteries of a woman's being. When a woman looks like this, a man strains eyes to follow her. He realizes all the distance, but cannot with his utmost effort decipher what it contains. And that very inability in him is the strongest weapon that she holds. He sees the distance, yet there is none. No wonder that he cannot discern its contents. There is no distance. She is looking inwards—not outwards; searching her own mind, searching his, and only playing the game of contemplation to hide what she has found.

When Traill saw that expression of her face, he dropped the note of brass from his voice.

"Why?" he asked again, almost gently.

Her lips bound tight together as though she were keeping back her confession; her nostrils dilated, checking tears.

"I wanted to see you—that's all."

She said it with a shrug of the shoulders—the motion with which you shake an unwelcome thought from your mind.

He pressed her further. "But you apparently knew I was bringing some one?" he said.

She still looked towards her invisible horizon. "I guessed that—guessed that from your letter—the way you said you wanted to find no one down here. I thought you wouldn't mind my coming—besides—there was no one to order anything for you, and then—as I said—I wanted to see you."

"Yes, but why?" He took her arm, held the elbow in the cup of his hand.

She looked once more—looked long into her distance—then turned, petulantly almost, with a smothered sigh to the fireplace, rested her feet upon the fender, and redirected her gaze into the heart of the fire.

"Oh, it's no good talking about it now," she said. "Miss Bishop '11 be down in a minute."

"Aren't you happy? That it?"

"Yes."

"You aren't happy?"

"No."

"Harold?"

"Yes."

On the fender she beat out her thoughts.

"All the things she wants to say and is too proud," he said to himself as he watched the tapping of her dainty toe. That was precisely what he was meant to think.

"What's he done?" he asked.

"Tisn't what he's done—I don't think he's done anything."

E. Temple Thurston

"Then what?" He put his hand on her shoulder. "Poor old Dolly," he said softly. "But why did you say that about bringing mistresses down here?"

She looked up frankly—generously into his eyes. "Jealousy," she admitted.

He laughed lightly. It just caught the edge of his vanity to which she played. Then, bending down, he kissed her, and as Sally entered the room, she saw the kiss—to her, a kiss of Judas. In that instant, the intuition that it was she who was betrayed, shot upwards like a flame of fire, rushing the blood in a burning race to her temples.

# CHAPTER IV

You may jeer at the instinct of a woman, plant the straight line of logic beside it and ridicule the comparison as you choose, but it is a sense, a subliminal sense, number it as you like, upon which she can rely as surely as on touch or scent or sight.

"One of those impulsive conjectures of yours," Traill had said to his sister in reply to her intuition of his relations with Sally. "You don't quite know what you're speaking about, and that gives you confidence. You're a woman." In the face of her accuracy he had said that. It is only retaliation a man has when a woman betrays the amazing abnormality of that sense which he can never hope to possess. He resorts to one weapon, the scientific reliability of evidence.

"Where's your evidence?" he asks, and having none, he smiles at her. But she knows; a knowledge that will sweep her into the fire of action, whilst he is methodically buckling on his armour of conviction with the straps of logical evidence.

It was this instinct, the sixth sense in Sally, that had cast her mind forward, flung it beyond herself into the future, where she saw the Tragedy that awaited her. From the moment she had seen that kiss, she had known that she had an enemy

E. Temple Thurston

whose weapons were sure, whose wielding of them was quick and keen. From that moment, standing on the rise of so small, so insignificant an incident, she had seen ahead into the years and known what her end would be. With what evidence? None! With what reason? Little indeed of that. That they were standing with swords drawn when she had left the room and that when she returned the swords were sleeping in their scabbards and they were kissing to make friends—how much was there to be reasoned from that? Were not such incidents common to the relationship between brother and sister? Yet, beyond all that, Sally saw with a clearness of vision that penetrated every obvious deduction; saw away into the stretch of Time when his sister would have won him back to her side where she could have no place, no existence.

It might have been wrong, quite easily could have been false a thousand times, but it was knowledge to her, sure, fateful, undeniable knowledge; and from that day her instinct was keyed to find its proof. The cancerous disease of jealousy had dropped its first seed in the blood of her, and the vulturous growth began to spread its lean, clutching fingers about her heart.

"My sister's not hitting it off with her husband," Traill told her, that afternoon as they drove back to London.

"Is that what she was telling you when I went upstairs to take off my hat?" asked Sally.

"Yes."

"That was why you kissed her?"

"Exactly; did you see me kissing her?"

"Yes, when I came into the room."

"Yes; well, that's it. I always thought Durlacher was a fool," he added meditatively. "Used to tell her so before she married him. What in the name of God can you expect of a guardsman? He's one of those men who just lives through life—taking all, giving nothing. I doubt if the rotting of his body will be manure for the earth when he dies. He'd sell it if it were."

Sally closed her eyes, then opened them suddenly to study his face. Such stray phrases as these that fell from his lips always kept the knowledge in her mind of how hard he was.

"Has he been unkind to her?" she hazarded. She forced a spurious interest to please him.

"She says not—but then—she doesn't know. It's perhaps as well that she doesn't. My experience of divorce leads me to see that it's a dog's game; mountains are made out of molehills to weight the case one way or another, and he could probably retaliate with a lot of half-truths, quite unprovable; but the mere mentioning of them in the courts would leave a stain on her. No, it's perhaps as well that she doesn't know as much as I do. She just thinks they don't get on and a patch can settle a thing like that. Lord! The number of people nowadays who pull along all right, with marriage lines that are unrecognizable from their original condition because of the patches here and the patches there—why, they're legion!"

"Are you going to do anything about it?" she asked.

"Me? Oh, I suppose I shall have to be a sort of go-between. She's my sister, and as far as I can see, she's pretty miserable."

E. Temple Thurston

On this account, then, began his first visits to Sloane Street. There, the actors in this little play went through their parts— well trained, well rehearsed. There was never a note of the prompter's voice to reach the ears of Traill from the wings. He listened quietly, sympathetically to her tardy admission of the state of affairs. Three times he went to Sloane Street in the afternoon before he was placed in possession of all the subtle details and never once did he meet Durlacher. Durlacher, himself, was always away. It must be admitted that Traill was interested in these intricate details. They gave him insight into the vagaries, the pitfalls and the fallacies of the life with which he had to deal in the divorce courts. Undoubtedly they were of service to him; undoubtedly, moreover, blood is thicker than water, and he thought, he imagined, that he would be able to save his sister from an impending crisis.

On the third occasion, whilst they were sitting over tea in the drawing-room, the door opened and the man-servant announced—Miss Standish-Roe.

Traill stood up with a jerk and felt for his gloves.

Mrs. Durlacher's eyes lost no sight of that and she hurried quickly forwards.

"My dear child, how sweet of you!" She kissed her cheek affectionately. "Let me introduce you to my brother."

Traill turned and his mind was cast back to the night he had dined with his sister at the restaurant. This was the girl he had noticed; her father was the man who sat on boards in the city. He bowed with his eyes on her face.

"Surely you're not going to go yet, Jack," said Mrs. Durlacher. Her eyes were feverishly watching his hands as he began slowly to draw on his gloves. He hesitated. Miss Standish-Roe took the seat he had vacated and looked questioningly up into his face as though it were she who had made the request.

"Very well," he said. "Then I'll have another cup of tea with you."

From that moment, and Mrs. Durlacher's heart had leaped with exultation, she began to play for his humour, baiting the line that she cast with those little turns of phrase, those little feathers of speech which she knew would tempt him to rise to the surface of his mood. In a few moments, he was entertaining them with his tirades against conventional institutions.

"Conventionality," he exclaimed; "I'd sooner have the honest vice of the man who pleads guilty; I'd a thousand times sooner defend his case, than urge for a woman who just holds on to the virtue of conventionality with the tips of her fingers."

"You gave that lady a bad time the other day, Mr. Traill," said Miss Standish-Roe, admiringly.

"I did? Which one?"

"The lady who admitted to kissing the co-respondent."

"Why, you weren't in the court, were you?"

"No—but I read it in the paper—your sister told me about it."

Mrs. Durlacher looked apprehensively to her brother's eyes. From so small a thing as that he might unearth suspicion. But

E. Temple Thurston

a pardonable vanity was touched in him. He turned no ground to find the intentions that lay beneath.

"Well, *there* was a case," he said. "I've no doubt the woman was innocent of the worst; but that was an exact case of the virtue of conventionality. She'd just hung on to it, scraping her nails. She deserved all she got."

"And you persisted in trying to prove her guilty?" said Miss Standish-Roe, in amazement. "When you thought her innocent?"

"Why not?" he retorted. "Society wants to be purged of that sort of woman, and it's full of 'em."

Mrs. Durlacher deftly changed the subject.

"I've got a box to-morrow night, Jack, at some theatre or other," she said casually. "Harold's going out to dinner, will you dine with us and drag us along there?"

"Who's us?"

"Miss Standish-Roe and myself. We shall be all alone if you don't."

Sally's face rose in Traill's mind. If he went, this would be the first evening, except for those engagements which his profession demanded, on which he would have left her to dine at a restaurant by herself. But was he bound? Not in the least! The consideration that it might even seem to an outsider, decided him.

"Yes, I'll come," he said. "What time dinner?"

Again there was exultation in the heart of Mrs. Durlacher.

"Better be seven-thirty," she said.

He agreed. It never suggested itself to him that he wanted to go. He hated to seem bound. That was his reason. So he took it with an open mind, questioning nothing.

When he had gone, Mrs. Durlacher turned to her friend.

"You can come—can't you?" she asked.

Miss Standish-Roe nodded her head.

E. Temple Thurston

# CHAPTER V

That evening, Traill removed the first pillar in the structure which Sally had built—the Temple of her security. Notwithstanding all Janet's advice, heedless, utterly, of Janet's point of view which had been held before her eyes on almost every occasion on which they had met during the last three years, she persisted in believing more surely in the mooring of her life to Traill's, so long as no mention of settlement was ever suggested.

There was full reason on her side for this. Unable to accept conditions as Janet would have had her take them—the abandoning of one master for the service of another—she knew that so long as Traill kept her by his side without a word of agreement, his honour as the gentleman she always knew him to be would remain as binding as any sanction of the Church.

On this evening, then, when he returned from his visit in Sloane Street, they went together to the little restaurant in Soho where they had taken their first dinner together.

There was Berthe and Marie—there was Madame—there was Alexandre—all still working together with the precious regularity of the Dutch clock.

"Bon soir, monsieur—bon soir, madame." Not an inflection was changed, not a note was altered. The firm hand of necessity had wound them up day after day, all those three years, and they had ticked together and tocked together to the swing of the pendulum of fortune ever since.

"I shall always love this place," said Sally cheerfully, as they sat down at the same table—*sous l'escalier*.

"Why?"

"Because you first brought me here." She stretched her hand across the table and lovingly touched his fingers. She was happy, then.

"You're not sorry that I did?" he asked seriously.

"Sorry—no! How could I be?" Trouble came too quickly into her eyes. It left them slower than it came.

"Do you remember what you said to me"—he reminded her—"just before we went on to my rooms?"

"I said so many things."

"No—oh, you didn't. You said so few; but you said one that struck in—deep—straight home."

"What was that?"

"You said I was a gentleman."

"So I believed then, when I first saw you. So I know now, after these three years and more."

"You know it—do you?"

E. Temple Thurston

"Yes."

"Yet I've never said anything to you about what I intend to give you for yourself, in your own right."

Pain struck into Sally's eyes. Her lips parted in fear and anticipation.

"Have you taken all that on trust?" he continued. "If I were to die, suppose—death is a great deed that even the smallest of us are able to accomplish—Berthe!" He turned to the attendant who was waiting—"Consomme—Omelette aux fines herbes—et poulet roti aux cressons."

"Oui, monsieur—Consomme—pour deux, monsieur?"

"The whole lot pour deux."

Berthe laughed with her little cooing sound in the throat.

"Omelette aux fines herbes, et poulet roti aux cresson—oui, monsieur."

She departed and they listened to the repetition of it all—

"Deux consommes—deux—" as she shouted it through the little doorway to the kitchen.

"Supposing I were to die," Traill repeated. He leant his elbows on the table and gazed steadily into her eyes.

"Why should you talk like that?" she pleaded, and all the while through her brain scampered the questions—"Does he mean if he were to die? Doesn't he mean if he were to leave me?" They danced a mad dance behind her eyes. Had he looked deep enough, he might have seen their capers.

"Because that sort of thing has to be talked," he said gently. "You haven't the faintest idea whether I've made any provision for you or not. I've often wondered would you ask, but you've never said a word. Aren't you rather foolish? Do you think you take enough care for yourself? Do you think you look far enough into the future? Don't you think you treat life too much in the same way as you did my offer of the umbrella on the top of the Hammersmith 'bus?"

Many another woman would have had it out then; flung the questions at him, preferring knowledge rather than torture of mind. To Sally this was impossible. Again she showed those same characteristics of her father. She hoped against almost all absence of promise; she had faith in the face of the blackest doubt. He had said—if he died—perhaps he meant that. Yet the kissing of his sister lifted like the shadow in a dream before her eyes. She knew he had been with Mrs. Durlacher that afternoon. Could she have won him still further? Sally knew her own impotence—bowed under it, recognized fully how powerless she was to hold him if once the links in the chain of their caring began to lose their grip. And now, he was offering to make provision for her. Inevitably that seemed to be the beginning of the end. Before, she was his, with that emotional phrase in her mind—as God had made them. Now she was to become his, because he had bought her, paid for her. There lay in that the difference between two worlds in her mind; and she fought against it with what strength she knew.

"I don't want to look into the future," she said bravely. "I hate looking into the future. I'm happy in the present; why shouldn't I remain so?"

"How will this prevent you? Doesn't it appeal to you at all, that when we came to live together, I took up a certain responsibility with you? I've got to fulfil that responsibility.

E. Temple Thurston

This evening, when we go back, I'm going to draw out some form of settlement which I intend to place with you. I shall take it to my solicitor and get it legalized to-morrow morning."

She leant forward across the table and touched his hand again. Her lips were trembling; her whole face, which only a few moments before was bright with cheerfulness, was now drawn, pinched with the suffering and terror in her mind.

"Please don't," she said brokenly. "Please don't. I don't want any settlement as long as you care for me. What is a settlement to me if, as you say, you were to die? What good would it be to me then? Do you think I could bear to go On living?"

He searched her face with amazement. "You mustn't talk foolishness like this," he replied firmly, but not unkindly. "We've all got our own lives to get through. We've all got to answer for them one by one, and live them one by one as well. There's no condition of relationship in existence, which can make a man and a woman one person except in their imaginations and according to the fairy tales of the Church. You're a dear, simple, little child to talk about not being able to go on living if I were to peg out; but you would. You'd go on living. There's no doubt in my mind, but that you'd love some one else again."

"You little understand me," she exclaimed bitterly, "if you could ever think that."

"Well—in that respect, at least, I believe I understand human nature; and in that respect, too, I imagine it must be a surer criterion from which to judge of such matters. I don't insist upon it as a certainty—I only suppose it possible. But in any event you would want money to live upon, and my mind is quite made up that I ought to make a settlement on you. Why should you not want me to—eh? Why?"

She hung her head. To tell him, when she had no definite proof that he had thought of leaving her, might be to put the thought into his mind. She could not tell him. But pride did not enter the matter in the least. If it could have served her purpose in any way, she would willingly have let him know that she counted it possible for him to desert her. But the fear that it might create a suggestion to his consciousness which hitherto had not existed, locked the words in her lips. She would not have uttered them for a crown of wealth.

"Why?" he repeated. "Eh?"

"I'd rather you didn't," she said, with trouble in voice. "I'd rather you didn't—that's all."

"Well—I'm afraid it's got to be," he replied finally. "In my mind it's not fair to you, and I'm determined that where you're concerned, I shall have nothing with which to reproach myself. I shall draw it up this evening when we go back."

She looked pitiably about her. Now it seemed that the little Dutch clock, which had been ticking so merrily, so much in unison with life, all went out of time. It seemed a farce then, that little Dutch clock. All the romance went out of it—it was only a trade—a trade machine for the making of money, no longer the counting of happy hours. Everything seemed a trade then—everything seemed a trade.

# CHAPTER VI

That evening the settlement was drawn up. When he had finished it, Traill held it out to her.

"You'd better just read it through," he said; "the substance of it is there. To legalize, merely means to write the same thing at greater length and in less comprehensive English."

"I don't want to read it," she replied.

"But why?"

"It doesn't interest me. You've written it to please yourself, not to please me. Please don't ask me to read it!"

He was unable to follow the reasoning of this, and he shrugged his shoulders with a sense of irritation. "As you wish," he said quietly and put the paper away in a drawer of his bureau. "I'll give you a copy of this, at any rate."

Before they had gone abroad, Traill had taken a lease of the floor above his chambers, which contained rooms similar in shape and size to those in which he lived. These, he had decorated and furnished according to the slightest wish that he could induce Sally to express. In the room which she used as a sitting-room, he had given her a piano with permission to play on it whenever he was not in the rooms below. Most of the daytime, then, she was at liberty to make what noise she liked and, at all times, free to have any friends she wished to see, on the strict understanding that he was not to be bothered by them.

There was only one friend. Janet came to see her on every occasion when Traill had to be out for the evening—at a Law Courts dinner or some such public function, but she never met him.

"Why doesn't he want to meet your friends?" Janet once asked her.

"I have only one," Sally had replied, laughing.

"Well—why won't he meet me? I suppose you've shown him that photograph you've got of me? It's enough to put any man off."

"I shall never take any notice when you talk like that," said Sally.

"Very well—don't! But why is it?"

"I think I know—but I'm afraid you'll be angry."

"No, I shan't. Come along—out with it!"

"Well—I told him once—that first day I dined with him— that I should love you two to meet. I said I'd love to hear you argue—"

"Oh, God!" exclaimed Janet. She cast her eyes up to the ceiling. "That did it! What did he say?"

"He said he could love a woman, but he couldn't argue with her."

"Yes—of course he did. A woman has to be confoundedly pretty before a man's going to let her have a point of view. Even then, if she isn't fairly cute, it's his own he gives her. Then I suppose when you came to live here, he saw my photograph?"

"I suppose he—yes, I think he did. I showed it to him; or he asked who it was."

Janet broke out into a peal of harsh—strident laughter.

"It's a wonder he risks your bringing me as near as the next floor," she had said. "Lord! A woman with a face like mine, who argues! God help us!"

But once she had understood that point, Janet had never alluded to it again; had made no effort to catch a glimpse of the man who so filled Sally's life. So much, in fact, had she endeavoured to avoid their contact that, on one occasion, when she and Sally had been climbing up to the second floor, and the door of his room was opened, through which his voice had sounded, calling to Sally, she had run hurriedly up the stairs out of sight, her heart thumping with excitement when he had shouted out—

"Who the devil's that?"

The inclination to shout back—"What the devil's that to you?" she had clipped on the tip of her tongue; but only for Sally's sake.

On this evening, then, that the settlement was drawn up, Sally had slowly climbed the stairs to the floor above, and once in her little sitting-room, with the door closed behind her, she had seated herself upon the settee near the fireplace and gazed into the cheerless, unlighted fire with dry and tearless eyes.

To her, the shadow of the end fell on everything. Just a little more than three years and a bend in the road had shown it stretching across her path. True, it was only a shadow. He had said nothing whatever about leaving her; had not even suggested it in the slightest word he had uttered. She must pass through the shadow, then; but what lay upon the other side was beyond her knowledge, though not beyond her fear.

To drive the apprehensions from her mind, she rose suddenly, shrugging shoulders, as though her blood were cold, and went to the piano. Without thinking, she sat down, began to play; then her hands lifted from the keys as if they burnt her touch. She had as suddenly remembered. Traill was below. For a moment longer she sat there, just touching, feeling the notes with the tips of her fingers—listening to the sounds in her mind—then she rose, standing motionless, attentive to all the little noises in the room below.

She heard the clink of a glass. He was taking his whisky. The sound indicated that he would soon be going to bed. She glanced at the clock, ticking daintily on her mantelpiece. It was just after eleven. Thoughts, calculations began to wander to her mind. Downstairs, he had said good night, kissed her—gently, as he always did—and opened the door for her as she came upstairs. But then he did that every night. Every evening he kissed her, every evening he said good night; but then perhaps, some half-hour later, she would hear him mounting the stairs to her room, and her heart would hammer like steel upon an anvil until he had knocked at her door and she had whispered—"Come in."

E. Temple Thurston

Would he come up that evening, she wondered. Two weeks now had passed since he had been to her thus, and so her mind—searching, as it would seem, for its trouble—intuitively connected the circumstance with this event of the settlement. So she drove herself to judge him by the lowest standards—those standards to which a woman at last resorts when she thinks she sees the waning of her influence. That in the heart of them they seldom put first, but last. Yet in the ninety-nine cases out of a hundred it is, in a man, the soonest to come and the soonest to go, while fondness, caring and affection may remain behind, untouched by its departure. The beast in the every man has little to do with the intellect, and it is with his intellect, above all things, that he loves truest and most of all.

But here Sally fell into that most common of women's mistakes. She judged him by his passions. If she did not hear his footsteps on the stairs that night; if his knock did not fall upon the door and startle the silence in her heart into a thousand pulsating echoes, then she knew that she would be one step nearer to the realization that it was the end indeed.

She looked again at the clock and then, with sudden decision, went into the other room and began to undress. From a drawer in the Chippendale chest which he had bought her, she brought forth a new nightdress, in-let with dainty openwork, which a few days before she had purchased. This she put on. Then she went to the mirror, scrutinizing herself in its polished reflection. Her hair was untidy. She took it all down and put it up afresh, curling the long strands around her fingers as he had often said he had loved to see them. When that was finished, she sprayed herself with scent—on her hair, her arms, her breast, turning the spray, before it spluttered into silence, in the direction of the pillow upon which she slept. Finally, she knelt down by her bedside and prayed—

"Oh God—let him love me—always—always; show me how I can keep him to love me—always—always."

So she prayed for a way, having already chosen it, as once before she had prayed for guidance, well knowing what course she was about to adopt. So most of us pray that we may know those things on which we have decided knowledge already. It helps us in the throwing of blame on to the shoulders of God. It consoles us—the deed being done—when we think that—at least—we prayed.

When she rose to her feet, she stood listening—listening intently. Then she moved to her bedroom door and opened it. She could hear him still moving in his room below; but now it was in the room beneath hers—beneath her bedroom. He was going to bed. She crept to the top of the stairs. Every sound she could hear there, the dropping of his boots on the floor, the opening and shutting of his cupboard doors as he put his clothes away. Then, last of all, the creaking of the springs of his bed as he got into it and moved to right and left, seeking the comfortable groove.

A heavy sigh forced its way through her lips. She had to swallow hastily in her throat to check the sudden rising of the tears. At last, with impulsive decision, she went back to her room, took a silk dressing-gown from the wardrobe, fitted her feet into little silk slippers and, without hesitation, without pausing to formulate her definite plan of action, she crept down the stairs again, opened the door of his sitting-room and stole in.

"Jack," she whispered. "Jack!"

Her throat was dry and the low voice found no resonance from the roof of her mouth. There was no answer. He had not heard her.

E. Temple Thurston

"Jack!" She said it again and tapped faintly on his door.

"That you, Sally?"

"Yes."

"What is it? Come in. I'm in bed. Believe I was asleep. What is it? Come in."

She opened the door gently. He sat up in bed, found matches, struck one and lit a candle.

"Lord!" he exclaimed, "you'll catch your death of cold. What do you want, child?"

"I can't get to sleep," she murmured, blinking her eyes at the sudden glare of the candle.

"Why not?"

He sat there, looking at her, his eyes dazed, half awake.

"I don't know."

"Thinking too much?"

"Yes, I suppose so."

"Well, count sheep going through a gate. A hundred's the prescribed amount."

She tried to smile because she knew that if she did not, he would think she was unhappy or depressed.

"No, I want you to let me have a book," she said; "I think perhaps if I read—"

"Of course, take anything you like, and try smoking a cigarette. That may make you drowsy."

He lay back on the pillows. For a moment, she stood, undecided as to what to do; then she went into the other room, taking up the first book that her hands touched in the darkness. There, again, she waited in silence. At last she undid the fastenings that held her dressing-gown tight about her and came back again into the room.

"What did you get?" he asked.

She looked for the first time at the cover.

"Macaulay's 'History of England.'"

The springs of the bed creaked to his chuckle of laughter.

"You'll go to sleep all right now," he said.

"But I think I'd like a cigarette, if I might."

"Yes, why not?"

"Where shall I find them?"

"In the case, in my waistcoat pocket. It's hanging over the back of the chair. What a ridiculous child you are to let that dressing-gown flap open like that. You'll catch your death of cold. Fasten it up—go on!"

She reluctantly did as she was bid; then searched for the case. When she had found it, she came down to the side of his bed and stood there, picking nervously at the cigarette in her fingers.

E. Temple Thurston

"Would you like me to blow out the candle?" she asked.

"Oh no, that's all right. I can blow it out from here. You get to the door and see your way out first."

She sat down slowly on the bed by his side, then bent forward, winding one arm around his neck, leaning the full weight of her body upon him.

"Good night," she whispered as her lips touched his.

"By Jove, you do smell of scent!" he exclaimed. "Do you always drown yourself in scent before you go to bed?"

"No." Her mouth was dry, her tongue like leather, scraping against her teeth. "Not always."

"Well, good night, little woman; you read half a page of Macaulay and you'll soon get to sleep. Kiss me."

She kissed him, longingly and then, as he half tried to turn, she felt conscious of her dismissal and rose hurriedly from the bed.

"Can you find your way upstairs without a candle?" he asked, when she had opened the door.

"Oh yes," she said stridently, "quite easily." And she departed, closing the door behind her. With a glimmer of wonder in his mind, he blew out the candle, just listened until he heard her footsteps pattering overhead, then turned over and fell asleep.

But there was no sleep to be found for Sally. When she was once within her room, she flung book and cigarette upon the bed and her body, just as she was, across them. Then came the deluge of her tears. If he had waited, listening to the sounds one moment longer before he went to sleep, he would have heard the choking sobs that broke between her lips.

E. Temple Thurston

# CHAPTER VII

When Traill came back early from the Temple the next evening and told Sally that he was dining with his sister at the house in Sloane Street, she took the announcement in silence, eyes lifting to his in a steady question, her heart wearily adding one more figure to the column of events which she had already compiled against her hopes of happiness.

As yet, openly, she dared question nothing. She knew too well the outlook of his mind where freedom of his own action was concerned. Now she was beginning to realize the full extent, the full impotence of her position as his mistress. Had she been legally his wife, he had given her no cause to complain, created no right for her criticism. As his mistress, she was still less justified in questioning his actions and to do so would, she knew to a certainty, bring down his wrath, more surely than ever draw to a close their relationship, the termination of which was shadowing itself upon the surface of her suspicion.

"Is your sister getting on better with her husband?" she asked.

"Somewhat, I think. I don't really know—it's difficult to say. I haven't seen him yet. She doesn't want me to speak to him about it. She thinks it might only make things worse. Says I've got a blunt way that 'ud ruffle what little patience he's got."

Sally looked directly, deeply into his eyes.

"You really think it is serious?" she said. "I suppose it wouldn't have been possible for her to have imagined it?"

"Imagined it? No! Why? What should she have imagined it for? We Traills haven't got an ounce of imagination between us. How could she imagine it? What good would it do her? A woman doesn't hesitate and stumble and drag a thing out of her with tears in her eyes, hating to talk about it, when the whole business is only a tissue of her imagination. Besides, what would she gain by it?"

"Your sympathy," Sally replied.

Traill walked into his bedroom with a laugh.

"A deuced lot she really cares about my sympathy," he exclaimed. "I assure you Dolly's not a sentimentalist. She only wants to cling to her rung of the ladder, that's all."

That was all, and Sally knew it; but she could say no more. She had tried to plant the seed of suspicion in his mind. She had failed. The ambitions which were a motive to all his sister's actions, he could see well enough; but to the means she used in gratifying them, he was blind. And Sally, though she knew nothing, dared not attempt the opening of his eyes.

"Are you going to change now?" she asked.

He mumbled an affirmative. She realized, sensitively, that his mind was pre-occupied with other things and, quietly, she

E. Temple Thurston

crept out of the room, upstairs to the other floor where she stood, looking out of the window, finding her eyes watching the women who were wheeling round the corner of the Circus into Piccadilly, with skirts tight gripped about them, little reticule bags swinging with their ungainly walk, heads alert to follow any direction that their eyes might prompt them.

When Traill looked into his sitting-room a few moments later, looked through the opening front of a white shirt which he was in the process of dragging over his head, she had gone.

"What are you going to do with yourself this evening, Sally?" he asked, before his head was free of the folds of the stiff, starched linen. No answer was given him. Then, when he found he was alone, he cursed volubly at the intractable shirt. The words steadied on his lips as a knock fell on the door. He marched across the room as he was, holding up his garments with one hand and flung it open—one of his characteristic actions—he cared little how he appeared or whom his appearance affected.

"You? Come in!" he said.

A tall, well-featured man, well-dressed, well-groomed, walked in through the open door. With a certain amount of care—customary enough in him to hide the obvious—he laid his silk hat, brim upwards, upon the table, pulled off his gloves, threw them carelessly into it, and turned round.

"You're going out?" he said.

"Yes."

"Can't come and have dinner with me?"

"No, couldn't."

"Taking the little lady out, I suppose?"

"No, she's upstairs."

The man's eyes passed across Traill's face as they wandered to the portrait of James Brownrigg over the mantelpiece.

"Well, I'm at a loose end," he said. He took a gold cigarette-case from his pocket and extracted a cigarette. Traill continued his gymnastics with the shirt, forcing studs through obdurate holes, fastening links and muttering under his breath.

"I thought we might have dined together and taken the little lady to a music hall, like we did before. How long ago was that?"

Traill tramped into the other room and came out, struggling with a collar.

"Oh, last September, wasn't it?"

"Something like that, getting on for a year. How is she?"

"Oh, first rate. Will you have a drink?"

"No, thanks, old man. Where are you going to?"

"I'm dining with my sister. Going to some theatre, I believe."

"Ah, I saw your sister the other day, about a couple of weeks ago." He seated himself, hitching his trousers above the uppers of his boots. "Prince's, I think it was. Yes, she was skating with that Miss Standish-Roe."

"Yes, she's coming with my sister and me this evening."

"Is she?" Again his eye lifted to Traill's face. "Damned pretty girl."

Traill did not reply. Had he made some casual answer in the affirmative, the man's eyes might not have followed him as he walked back into his bedroom; the humorous twist of the man's lips might not have been visible. There would have been no thought to create it.

"What theatre are you going to?" he asked unconcernedly.

Traill mentioned the name, and began the singing of a hymn tune with impossible crescendos and various deviations from the melody.

"'Can a woman's tender care
Cease toward the child she bare?
Yes, she may forgetful be ...'"

"I say!" he called out with unceremonious interruption to himself.

"What?"

"You say you've got a loose end?"

"Yes, there's Time got to be killed somehow."

"Well, take Sally out to dinner."

"What, the little lady?"

"Yes, she'll be lonely by herself. I gave her such damned short notice about this engagement of mine that she didn't have time to send for that friend of hers—that Miss Hallard. Would you mind doing that? Don't hesitate to say if you would."

"Oh no, I wouldn't mind in the least. But how about her?"

"I'll call out to her."

The visitor could hear him opening the door that led into the passage, then his voice—

"Sally!" The clattering of feet above reached them, the hurried opening of another door, as though the person called for had been waiting eagerly for the summons.

"I'm coming," she replied. Her heels tapped loudly—the quick successive knockings as on a cobbler's last—as she ran down the stairs.

"Mr. Devenish has come in to ask me to dinner, Sally," he said, before she reached the bottom. "He's going to take you instead; I can't go, of course."

The footsteps stopped.

Devenish, within the room, half-closed his eyes, bent his head in an attitude of amused attention. He heard many things in the silence that followed.

"Had I better go and dress?" she asked, after the moment's pause.

"Oh no, he's not changed. He's in here; come along."

Sally entered and Devenish moved forward to shake hands.

E. Temple Thurston

"Good evening, Miss Bishop; don't you hesitate to say if you'd thought of doing anything else. I just had a loose end, nothing to do—so I looked in here, hoping he might come out to dinner."

"It's very kind of you to think of it."

"Oh, not a bit. I shall be delighted. You say where you'd like to dine; it doesn't make the slightest difference to me. I'll go back and change if you prefer to dress."

"Oh no, thanks. Really, I think I'd rather not. If you don't mind my coming as I am."

"Not a bit."

She turned to Traill.

"Shall I go up and put on my hat, Jack?" There was no interest in her voice, no enthusiasm. This was a child doing the bidding of his master. Devenish saw through every note of it. He gathered—erroneously—that Traill had told her he was taking Miss Standish-Roe to the theatre; fancied that perhaps she may have seen or heard of the girl's undeniable prettiness, and was piqued with jealousy. Certainly it was not for love that she was coming out to dine with him. But that was no deterrent. He looked forward to it all the more.

"Yes, run up and put on your hat; we can all go out together if you're quick."

She went away quietly. They heard her mounting the stairs, but only Devenish noticed the difference in the way she had come down and the manner in which she returned. He also read its meaning.

"How long has she been living with you here?" he asked, when Traill had closed the door and returned to the continuance of his dressing.

"A few months over three years."

"Of course—I remember your telling me."

They fell into silence, Devenish watching his friend with half-conscious amusement as he clumsily tied a white tie, then shot his arms into waistcoat and coat, one after the other, with no study of the effect and apparently but little interest.

Lest it should seem unaccountable that this man, seemingly a stranger, walking casually one evening into his rooms, should be apparently so intimately possessed of the circumstances of Traill's relationship with Sally, it were as well to point out that men in their friendship are bound by no necessity of constant meeting. In a while they meet and for a while see nothing of each other; but when they meet—no matter what time may have elapsed since their last coming together—they are the same friends whose conversation might just have been broken, needing only the formalities of welcome to set it going on again, as you wind a clock that has run out the tether of its spring. To account then for the friendship of these two so diametrically opposed in character—for in Devenish's regard for appearances and Traill's supercilious contempt of them, there are the foundations of two utterly opposite characters—it is necessary to say that their friendship had been formed at school, after which, a train of circumstances had nursed it to maturity. At school, Devenish had been an athlete, superior to Traill in every sport that he took up. You have there the ground for approval and a certain strain of sympathy between the two men. The fact that at the 'Varsity Devenish had developed

E. Temple Thurston

taste for dress was outweighed by the fact that he was a double blue, holding place in the fifteen and winning the quarter-mile in a time that justified admiration.

These qualities had left a lasting impression upon Traill. He disliked the dandy with a strong predisposition to like the man. Knowing little of his life in society, refusing to meet his wife—where he assured Devenish all friendships between man and man ended—he had retained that predisposition towards friendship and in the light of it had spoken, as every man does to another who is his friend, in an open yet casual way about his life with Sally.

"She lives with me," he had admitted. "If you'd rather not meet her, say so. If you'd like to, don't look down on her—I don't suppose you would, but I never trust the virtue of the married man, he's compelled to wear it on his sleeve. Anyhow, she's the best. I've never met any woman for whom I'd so readily contemplate the ghastly ceremony of marriage. But I suppose every one lays hold of what he can take. I'm absolutely satisfied as I am. The strange woman has no fascination for me now."

Two years and a half had passed since Traill had said that. Now Devenish had dropped in again for the third or fourth time and found them, still together, but with a vague and subtle difference upon it all, to which his astute mind had assigned the reason which Sally only, beside himself, was aware of. Traill was tiring. If Devenish did not know it instinctively, then he made his deductions from the fact alone that brought about the mentioning of the name of Coralie Standish-Roe. To him, with his own social knowledge of that young lady, the fact in itself was sufficient.

By the time that Traill was ready, Sally came down prepared

to go out. They all descended the stairs together, parting in the street, where Traill held Sally's hand affectionately, then called a hansom and drove away.

With apparently casual glances, Devenish watched Sally's face as she looked after the departing cab. She followed it with her eyes as they walked up into the Circus; followed it until it welded into the mass of traffic and was lost from sight.

"Where shall we go?" he asked, when her features relaxed from their strain of momentary interest.

"Really, I don't mind," she replied indifferently.

He mentioned the restaurant in Soho. She shook her head definitely.

"Not there?"

"No, anywhere but there. I don't—" she hesitated.

"You don't care for the place?"

"Oh yes, I do. But—"

"Well, then—" He mentioned another and she agreed to anything rather than that which held so many happy associations.

When they were seated at their table, he leant back in his chair and looked at her pleasurably.

"You know, it's mighty good of you," he said, "to keep me company like this."

She was too impervious to outer sensation then to find repugnance at the tone of his voice; at another time she might have resented it. Now, scarcely the sense of the words reached her.

"Which would you prefer, a theatre or a music hall afterwards?"

"Whichever you like."

"Oh, we'll say a music hall, then. In a theatre, you're so bound to listen for the sake of the other people who want to hear. We'll go to the Palace."

She nodded her head in assent. There was no concealment of her mood, no hiding of her unhappiness. Even with this man above all others, whom she well knew was thoroughly aware of the relationship that existed between Traill and herself, she could not shake off the entangling folds of her depression, lift eyes that were laughing, throw head back and face it out until the ordeal of being in his company was over. At moments she tried—drove a smile to her lips for him to see; but she felt that it did not convince him; knew that it utterly failed to convince herself. When he began to speak about Traill, it faded completely from her expression.

"Jack's gone to a theatre to-night, hasn't he?" he asked ingenuously, when they had half struggled through the courses.

"Yes—"

"Duke of York's, isn't it?"

"Yes—I think it is."

He watched her closely, but her eyes were lowered persistently to her plate, or wandering aimlessly from table to table, never meeting his. The thought that this man might guess the running of the current of events, stung her to some show of pride that yet was not keen enough, not great enough in itself to master, even for the moment, the despair within. All the making up for the part it lent; but the acting of it was beyond her.

"You've met his sister, Mrs. Durlacher—haven't you?" he asked presently.

She saw no motive in this. She felt thankful for it—glad to be able to say that she had.

"She was at Prince's the other day when I was there and she told me that Jack had taken you down to Apsley."

"Yes, I went down with him in April."

"Lovely place—isn't it?"

"Yes, I thought it was wonderful. Did Mrs. Durlacher talk to you about me at all?"

She could not hold herself from that curiosity. Into her voice she drilled all the orderliness of casual inquiry; but give way to it she must. Devenish thought of all the things that Traill's sister had said to him; he thought of the many others, far more potent, that she had left unsaid in the silent parenthesis of insinuation.

"She said how pretty she thought you were," he replied.

Had he thought that would please her? Scarcely. If he knew her mood at all, he must have realized that this was but the

E. Temple Thurston

sponge of vinegar held to the lips, softened but little, if at all, with the gentle flavour of hyssop.

They had finished dinner now and were just sipping coffee preparatory to departure.

"Is that all she said?" Sally asked, imperturbably.

"Oh no, I'm sure it wasn't. But that girl—Miss Standish-Roe—who's gone with them to-night—she was there, and she kept on breaking into our conversation so that really I can't quite remember."

Had he watched Sally's face then, as closely as he had watched it all through dinner, he would have seen the colour of ashes that swept across it, tardily letting the blood drain back into her cheeks.

"Miss Standish-Roe?" she repeated, almost inaudibly.

"Yes—Coralie—she's the youngest daughter of old Sir Standish-Roe. All the others have paired off. Didn't you know Jack was going with them to-night?"

"Not with her."

"By Jove—I'm sorry, then." He shrugged his shoulders to free himself from the sense of discomfort to his conscience. "I suppose I ought not to have mentioned it."

"Why not?"

It is hard to prevent a woman, in the stress of emotion, from becoming melodramatic. Tragedy twists her features, strikes unnatural lights in her eyes. She has but little understanding of the drama of reserve. She acts with her heart, not with her brain—with her emotions, not with her intellect. In a moment of Tragedy, it is possible for a man to think consciously in his mind of the appearance he presents. With a woman that is impossible. Considerate at every other time of the impression which she gives, a woman, with the full light of emotion upon her, throws appearances to the winds. She will cry, though she knows there is nothing less prepossessing; she will distend nostrils, curl her lip with an ugly turn, fling herself utterly into the grip of the situation, and lose dignity in the tempest of her feelings, unless it be, as in some cases, that the imperiousness of anger should add a dignity to her stature.

So, in that moment, it became with Sally. From the instant that she knew there was another woman in Traill's life—and it needed even less than instinct to show her that this girl was trying to steal him from her—the whole flame of jealousy licked her with a burning tongue. Quiet, sensitive, tender-hearted little Sally Bishop blazed into a furnace of emotion. She did not even know that she was melodramatic; she did not stop to think what effect her expression or her action would have on this man beside her. When he questioned the advisability of having told her that which came so near to the whole system of her being, she let reserve go, and feelings—a pack of sensations unleashed—raced riot across her mind, twisting her childish face into a haggard distortion of jealousy.

"Why not?" she repeated under her breath—"Why shouldn't you have mentioned it? Did he tell you not to?"

Before him, within the next few moments, Devenish could see the rising of a storm, and so he set his sails, kept a clear head, talked gently, almost beneath his breath, as if the matter were not of the import she found it. The jealousy of women was not unknown to him. He had met it often before;

E. Temple Thurston

knew the tempest it called forth; had sailed through it himself with canvas close-reefed and tiller well-gripped in his hands. In Sally's eyes, as she branded her question on his mind, he could discern that unnatural glint which presages the driven action of a woman who is goaded to desperation. For Traill's sake, for her sake also, for his own sake too, it was essential to keep a steady head—move warily and take no risks.

"Did he tell you not to?" she asked again, before the plan of action was settled in his mind.

"Not at all—of course not. Why should he? Besides, if he had, should I have spoken to you about it? I thought you knew."

"No—I didn't know. How old is she—this girl?"

"About twenty-one, I suppose. Twenty-two—twenty-one."

"Is she pretty?"

Devenish screwed up his lips—lifted his shoulders.

"Is she?" she reiterated.

"Many people might not think so."

"But you do?"

"Well—I suppose—well, she's not what you'd call plain."

"Ah, you won't tell me. She is pretty—very pretty. Is she fair?"

"Yes."

"Fairer than I am?"

"Well—she has red hair, you see."

"Is her father wealthy?"

"I shouldn't think so. Of course they're by no means poor."

"He's a knight—you said."

"He's Sir—he's a baronet."

"That means the title's in the family."

"Exactly."

"Is she a nice girl? You know her—you said so."

"Oh yes, she's quite nice. Nothing very particular, nothing very wonderful."

She looked full to his eyes, her own starved for knowledge.

"You're not telling me the truth," she exclaimed suddenly. "You're telling me all lies. You're trying to save Jack. You know you've said too much in telling me that he was going with her to-night, now you're trying to smooth it over."

"My dear Miss Bishop—" He smiled amiably at her distress of mind—"Surely Jack can go with his sister and some other lady to a theatre without your being so unreasonably put out about it. You can't wish to tie him down."

"I don't wish to tie him down. That's the last thing I should dream of doing. But you know as well as I do that he hates that set in society, would never have gone near the house in

Sloane Street if it had not been for his sister's unhappiness about her husband!"

Devenish looked up at her quickly with a swift change of expression.

"What unhappiness?" he asked.

"Why, that they're not getting on together."

The moment she had said it, a rush of fear that she had betrayed Traill's confidence, overwhelmed her with a sense of nausea.

"Please don't say I've said that," she begged.

"Certainly not; but, how on earth can you say it? Captain and Mrs. Durlacher may not be lovers in the passionate sense of the word, but I know of few married people who get on as well as they do."

She looked at him with increasing amazement.

"Some time ago—yes—perhaps. But not now?"

"Yes, now. I know it for a fact. They hit it off admirably."

Hit it off—Traill's very words! Then it was a lie. A lie of Mrs. Durlacher's that day when they were down at Apsley, a lie to win his sympathy at a moment when she had all but lost it. She had come down there to Apsley with the intention of estranging them. Traill had seen through that. Sally had realized at the time that that was what had stirred him to anger when he had come into the dining-room, finding his sister there with her. Mrs. Durlacher had failed then. She remembered her smothered feelings of delight at the attitude he was taking when she left the room; but it was after that, after she had gone upstairs, that Mrs. Durlacher, with this lie of her unhappiness, had won him to her side.

"Are you absolutely sure of that?" she whispered.

"Why, of course! If anybody's spreading that report about, it's a confounded lie."

Sally looked piteously about her. The iron teeth of the trap she had seen were surely fast in her now. As yet, she was unable to discern the deeper motive in Mrs. Durlacher's mind in which the proprietorship of Apsley Manor played so vital a part; but she was none the less certain of the designs that were being carried out so effectually to wrest Traill from her side. She was an encumbrance to his career. Had he told her that himself she would, with bowed head, have accepted the inevitable; but, coming to her in this way, this deep-laid plot and all the machinations of a woman whom, from the very first, she had had good reason to despise, a devil of jealousy was wakened in her. Obedience she might have given; her life she would willingly have offered; yet when it was a subtle poison that was being dropped into his mind to eat away his love for her, all force in her nature rose uppermost and she was driven to ends so foreign, so inconsistent with her whole being, that from that moment Devenish scarcely recognized her as the same woman.

"I can't come to the music hall with you," she said suddenly.

He looked at her suspiciously.

"Why not?" he asked.

"I couldn't—I couldn't sit there—I—"

It was impossible not to feel sympathy for her. The hardest nature in the world must yield its pity when the scourge of circumstance falls upon the weak. Devenish only knew in part what she was suffering. The mistress—deserted—is a position precarious enough, undesirable enough for any man to realize and feel sympathy for. To her mind, seeing that before her, he offered all such pity as he possessed. But of the love wrenched from her life, the heart aching with its overwhelming burden of misery, he saw nothing. She would get over it. He knew that. Women did—women had to. She would settle down into another type of existence. She would become some other man's mistress. She would pull through. He looked at her childish face and hoped she would pull through. The thought crossed his mind that it would be a pity—a spoiling of something not meant to be spoilt—if she lost caste and went on the streets. She deserved a better fate than that. But it would never come to that.

"What are you going to do, then?" he asked quietly.

"Oh, I don't know—anything—I don't know."

"You won't do anything foolish?"

"Foolish? How? Foolish?"

He leant his elbows on the table, bearing his eyes direct upon hers. The slight catch in her voice was breaking almost on a note of hysteria.

"You're excited, you know," he said gently. "You know, you're imagining things. You've got no grounds for them—I assure you you've got no grounds. Come to the music hall with me and forget all about it."

She shook her head.

"I couldn't," she replied; "I couldn't. I—I shan't do anything foolish, but I think I'll go now—now—if you've finished."

"Yes, I've quite finished. But I'm going to say something first."

"What?"

"Don't let your imagination run riot with you; and if I can do anything for you—there's nothing to be done, I mean—but if I can, you let me know. Will you?"

She nodded her head vaguely. It meant nothing to her; but she nodded her head.

　　　　　　E. Temple Thurston

# CHAPTER VIII

Mrs. Durlacher had asked one of her guests to come early.

"Come at seven," she had said; "before if you can." And Miss Standish-Roe had arrived at a quarter to the hour.

When she entered the drawing-room, Mrs. Durlacher kissed her affectionately, then held her at arm's length, her hands on her shoulders and gazed pensively into her eyes.

"Why do you look at me like that?" Coralie asked.

Mrs. Durlacher shrugged her shoulders and turned away to her chair.

"For no reason at all, my dear child, and for a million reasons. I wish I was as pretty as you are."

"What nonsense!"

"Yes, isn't it? But if I had that red hair of yours, and those eyes, I'd be happy for the rest of my life. You can't grow old with that hair as long as you keep thin. Do you mind my telling you something?"

"No, not a bit; what?"

"You've got a little too much on that cheek, and your lips as well; do you mind?"

"Heavens! No! Was that one of the million reasons?" She crossed the room to a well-lighted mirror and, by the aid of its reflection, rubbed her cheeks and lips with a handkerchief taken from the front of her dress. "Was that why you stared at me?" she asked, turning round, looking at Mrs. Durlacher, then at that part of the handkerchief that her lips had touched.

"One of the reasons? Oh no. I only noticed it. That's all right now. I believe you look better without it."

"Well, I felt so fagged this evening."

"I know; that's wretched. If you were a man, you'd drink; being a woman, you make up. It's much more respectable really. By the way, you don't see anything of Devenish now, do you?"

"No, nothing. We saw him that day at Prince's—I hadn't seen him for two or three months before that—I haven't seen him since. I don't think you can ever rely on a married man. Don't you know that line of Kipling's?"

"Which?"

"In 'Barrack Room Ballads'—'Fuzzy Wuzzy,' I think."

"Nothing about a married man, surely?"

"No; but it fits him."

> ""E's all 'ot sand and ginger when alive,
> An' 'e's generally shammin' when 'e's dead.'"

E. Temple Thurston

Mrs. Durlacher broke into a peal of laughter. "What a quaint creature you are!" she said. "Whatever made you think of that?"

"Well, he is like that—isn't he? I mean, you never know the moment when his wife isn't going to hear a rumour. Then he shams dead, and the next time he sees you, he just manages, with an effort, to recognize you by your appearance."

"Is that what happened to Devenish?" asked Mrs. Durlacher with amusement.

"I expect so. I never heard that his wife knew anything; but from the way he suddenly fell in a heap, I should think it's quite likely. And he's shamming still."

"Well, let him sham. I don't think he's worth anything else." She paused, watching the effect of her words. "Oh, and you never told me what you thought of my brother yesterday?"

"I think he's rather quaint."

"Yes, isn't he? I'm glad you like him."

"But why haven't I met him before? Don't you ever ask him down to Apsley? I never realized you'd got a brother, you know, till the other day you showed me that case in the paper."

"Very few people I know do," replied Mrs. Durlacher, whereby she created a sense of the mysterious, raised curiosity and played a hand that needed all her skill, all her ingenuity. "I shouldn't have told you about him, even then," she continued, "if it hadn't been fairly obvious to me that he was becoming a different sort of person."

"Why, what sort of an individual has he been?"

Mrs. Durlacher told her. Ah, but she made the telling interesting. A man who owns such a place in the country as Apsley Manor, yet prefers to live the life of the Bohemian in town, shunning society, reaping none of the benefits that should naturally accrue to him from such a position, can quite easily be surrounded with a halo of interest if his narrative be placed in the hands of a skilful raconteur. Mrs. Durlacher spared no pains in the telling of her story. Led it up slowly through its various stages to the crisis, the crisis as she made it. He owned Apsley Manor, not they! It was his property, capable of repurchase at any moment! And—she leant back in her chair, covering her face with her hands as though the blow were an unbearable tragedy to her—he had said that he would take the place back. Five thousand pounds was nothing to him. He could find it at a moment's notice. So would any one, when such a place as Apsley was in the balance.

"You can imagine," she concluded—bearing it bravely with the resignation of martyrdom—"what a catastrophe that'll be to us."

"Poor Dolly; I never knew of that. I always thought the place was yours. You always said so."

"Yes; why not? With every right. It is ours—till he repurchases. You see he's beginning to nurse ambition now. I suppose there's no doubt that he'll come up to the top of the ladder. I always knew he'd make a splendid barrister if he once caught hold of the ambition. Now, of course, he'll find that the possession of Apsley's of value to him. He'll have to entertain. A Bohemian can't entertain any one but a Bohemian. Then, I suppose, he'll marry—get a house in Town like we have—and use Apsley, as we've done, for his friends."

"But, my dear Dolly—what on earth will you do?"

"Do?" Mrs. Durlacher rose with a sigh. "Well—there's prayer and fasting; but there'll be considerably more fasting than prayer, I should imagine. I assure you, I do pray that he doesn't make a fool of himself and marry some woman out of the bottomless pit of Bohemia."

"Well, I should think so. It 'ud be an awful pity, wouldn't it?"

"A considerable pity—yes. Here he is." She turned quickly to her friend, but her voice was cleverly pitched on a casual note. "Don't say anything to him about Apsley," she remarked. "He never admits to possession of it—that's one of his peculiarities. I don't suppose he will until he planks down his five thousand pounds. He has what he calls a legal sense of justice. Makes sure of a statement before he delivers it. You'll never catch him out. That's the Scotch blood on the mater's side of the family. I should think it's saved him out of many a difficulty."

Traill strode into the drawing-room as unconscious of the fate that Mrs. Durlacher had so deftly woven for him as is the unwieldy gull that, tumbling down the wind, strikes into the meshes of the fowler's net and finds itself enchained within the web. Coralie, herself, set to the task of winning him, was as unconscious of the subtly diaphonous mechanism of the trap as he. Yet she was versed well enough in human nature in her way. Innocence could not be laid at her door with the hope of finding it again. But it needs the long training of social strategy for any one to realize the cunning knowledge that things are not obtained in this world by asking for them, but by the hidden method of suggestion. That Mrs. Durlacher was in search of a suitable sister-in-law was obvious to the most untrained eye. It was no capable deduction on Coralie's part to have made certain of that. But she hesitated when she came to the wondering of whether she was considered suitable to fill that position herself. The hesitancy was of but little duration. The first time she had seen Traill, he had attracted her; now the attraction was increased a thousandfold. She had often stayed at Apsley Manor. Once her father had gone down for the shooting and had returned glowing with enthusiasm.

"Place I should like to have," he had grunted, "place I should like to have." And after dinner he sat over his port and amused himself with breaking the tenth commandment.

But there was no certainty in Coralie's mind that Mrs. Durlacher, with all her outward show of friendship, would consider her to be the eligible one. Yet here the chance offered. She determined to take it—hand open, ready for the gift.

From the moment then, that he arrived, she began the outset of her campaign. The social manner she knew he hated. That she cast off. The astute woman of the world, he despised. Mrs. Durlacher had well grounded her. She wrapped herself in the simplicity of a girl whose eyes have scarcely opened to a knowledge of life and whose inner consciousness is as yet untouched.

If she had given him any impression of a want of innocence the day before when they discussed the case in the divorce court which he had won, she now swept it from his mind. He found her ingenuousness charming. Her eyes helped her. They were big, grey, wide-open like a child's. He found himself looking interestedly for the simple questions that they turned upon him. In the box at the theatre, they leant back in their seats and talked in undertones through the acts

E. Temple Thurston

and Mrs. Durlacher, leaning out to watch the piece, heard not a word that the actors said. Her ears were strained to catch the progress of their conversation. During the intervals, she levelled her glasses at the house and was apparently too pre-occupied to interrupt their enjoyment. In the interval that followed the second act, her glasses, roaming aimlessly across the stalls, became riveted to her eyes. After a moment, she looked hastily away, then stealthily looked again. Finally she turned round to her brother, curbing the surprise which, notwithstanding her efforts, forced itself into the expression of her face.

Then she beckoned to him. He rose from his chair and came to her side.

"In the interval after the next act," she whispered, "look through the glasses at the third row in the pit. Not now—not now! It might be noticed now."

"Who is it?" he asked.

"I don't know—I'm not certain."

The lights in the theatre were put out just as he was about to turn his head in the direction. He went back to his seat and in five minutes had forgotten about it.

When that act was over and the lights revived again, Mrs. Durlacher handed him the glasses. He came to the edge of the box. Coralie followed him, looking down on the rows of heads below her.

"Look round the house first," Mrs. Durlacher whispered.

He swept the glasses right and left, about the theatre in an indiscriminate manner—seeing nothing. Then he turned them in the direction his sister had indicated. From one face to another he passed along the third row of the pit, seeing only clerks and their young girls, shop-keepers and their wives. At last he stopped. There was a girl sitting by herself. Her head was down, her face hidden; but he recognized her. Then she looked up quickly—straight to the box—turned direct to his glasses a pair of dark eyes that were burning, cheeks that were pale, almost unhealthy in the pallor, and white lips, half-parted to the breaths he could almost hear her talking.

It was Sally!

Directly she thought that he had seen her, her head lowered guiltily again. She kept it bent, hidden from him, lifting a programme to shield her utterly from his gaze.

He put down his glasses on the ledge of the box.

"Do you allow that sort of thing?" Mrs. Durlacher whispered as she took them up.

"My God—no!" he exclaimed.

She smiled in her mind. That word—allow—was chosen with discretion.

# CHAPTER IX

As the curtain fell Traill proposed supper at a restaurant. They readily agreed. Mrs. Durlacher, in the best of spirits, thanking Providence for the weakness of human nature that had driven Sally to follow Traill to the theatre, still thrilling with the sound of his exclamation in her ears, would have lit the dullest entertainment in the world with the humour of her mood. There was a part for her to play. She played it. All her remarks, bristling with the pointed satires of spiteful criticism, were a foil to the gentle temper of Coralie's conversation.

"My God!" said Traill, as they walked down one of the passages to the *foyer*, and he listened to his sister's verdict upon a woman who had gone out before them. "Do you women allow a stitch of respectability to hang on each other's backs?"

"She'd want more than a stitch," Mrs. Durlacher replied, "if she's not going to put on more clothes than that."

Traill shrugged his shoulders, half conscious of a comparison between his sister and the quiet reserve of this girl beside him. He had thought her pretty, seeing her at a distance on the night when he had dined with Dolly. Meeting her the day before, in the dim light of the drawing-room at Sloane Street, he had found her still more attractive; but on this evening, in the glamour of bright lights—young, fresh, charming as she seemed to him—his senses were swept by her fascination.

At all times a beautiful woman is wonderful—the thing of beauty and the joy for ever; the phrase that comes naturally to the mind. But when, conscious of her own attractions, she lends that beauty to the expression of pleasure which she finds in the company of the man beside her, then, to possibly that man alone, but certainly to him, she is doubly beautiful. Nature indeed had been generous with Coralie Standish-Roe. Nature has her moods and her devilish humours. She was more than amiable when she bestowed her gifts upon Coralie. You may talk about the value of a noble heart beating in an empty corset, shining out of pinched and tired eyes; but it is a value, unmarketable, where the good things in a woman's life are given in exchange. Janet Hallard and her like have learnt the realization of that. And of the qualities of noble-heartedness, Coralie possessed but very few. Her disposition was intensely selfish. She took all the admiration that she could get—and it was infinitely more than some women dream of—with a grace of gratitude whose parallel may be found in the schoolboy galloping through one helping of food that he may begin another. Her hunger for it was insatiable, but she was too young as yet for any such reputation to have fastened itself upon her; too young for the manner which becomes the natural expression of women of this type to have blotted out her undeniable charm of youth. Youth saved her from Traill's critical appreciation of women. Two years later he would have passed her with a momentary lifting of interest which she herself would unconsciously have dispelled at the first touch of acquaintance. Now, he was not only thrilled, he was interested. She was a child. He found her so—as much a child as Sally had been. Add her beauty to that—a beauty unquestionably greater than the simple charm of Sally's baby features—and add still again that fallacious sense of social position by which Traill realized that such a girl he could not ask promiscuously out to dinner, could not casually persuade to come to his rooms, and you have, besides the unavoidable comparison between the two in his mind, that subtle difference which a life of ease and a life of labour makes in the position of women to a man's conception of the sex.

Immediately they stepped outside the theatre into the blaze of light where the attendants were rushing for carriages, and men and women, in a confused mass, jostled each other to fight free of the crowd, Traill's eyes searched quickly for a sight of Sally. Mrs. Durlacher also was alert to the possibility of finding her watching their movements. But they saw no trace of her.

In the mouth of a little alley, deep with shadows, on the other side of St. Martin's Lane, she was standing, her heart throbbing, half timidly, half jealously, yet secure in the knowledge that she was safe from observation. With eyes, burnt in the fever of a fierce emotion, she watched them as they stepped into the car that drew up beneath the lighted portico. When she saw Mrs. Durlacher's gesture inviting Traill to sit between them on the back seat; when she saw him willingly accept, notwithstanding that there was more room, more comfort in the seat opposite, she drew in a breath between her teeth, and the nails of her fingers bit into the palms of her hands. Now, from what little she had seen in the theatre, and taking into greatest consideration of all the proof of her own eyes that the woman was beautiful, eclipsing herself at every point of attraction, Sally was full-swept into the mad whirlpool of unreasoning jealousy. Every action and every incident that her starved eyes fed upon were distorted, embittered to the taste as though the taint of aloes had crept into everything.

She thought she saw him lay his hand upon hers as he took the place beside her. In that position she knew that they would be wedged close together, their limbs touching, thrilling his senses as she well knew she herself had thrilled them by even slighter proximity than that. Here, too, she judged again by the lowest of standards, if judgment it can be said of a wild flinging of thoughts—vitriol hurled in a moment of madness. Yet against him she could find no bitterness. The woman, kissing the hand that strikes her, to shield it from the falling of the law, is a type that has made no history; but in the hearts of men she is to be found with her ineffaceable record.

It was against the two women, against Mrs. Durlacher with her damnable cunning, against the other with her still more damnable fascination, that all the blinding acid of Sally's thoughts was cast. The woman who had hoodwinked him with her lies about her husband, the woman who had crept in, seizing the moment of his blindness—these were the two people in the world whom she could willingly have strangled with her little hands that gripped and loosened in the mad emotion of her rage. Under her breath she muttered—hissing the words—the vain things that she would do. All the civilized refinement of humanity was burnt out of her. She was not human. She had lost control. The thoughts that revelled in her brain were animal; the savage fury of the beast starved of its food and then deprived of the flesh and blood that are snatched from the very clutching of its claws.

It is not so far a call, even now, for this divine humanity, weaned upon the nutritious food of intelligence, nursed in the refining lap of civilization, to hark back, driven by one rush of events, to the lowest forms of nature that exist. If, in the hour of death, seeking immunity from peril, there live men who have trodden down the bodies of women, beaten them with naked fists, severed arms from their bleeding

E. Temple Thurston

hands that held to safety in order that they might find their own escape; then, surely it is no very wonderful thing for a woman, threatened with the destruction of all her happiness, to give herself over to the mad riot of murderous intent that shouts the cry of bloody revolution through her brain!

In these moments nothing human could have been accounted for in Sally. In these moments the fire of the enraged animal glittered in her eyes, the incoherent mutterings of dumb passion vibrated in her breath.

A man passing down through the dark shadows of the alley into the street, turned and gazed at her. She took no notice. Did not even see him. The car was just beginning to move out into the traffic. As it turned, too eager to follow it, she stepped on to the pavement.

Traill's eyes caught her then, saw her begin to quicken her steps, break even into a run following their tardy progress as they squeezed a way through the press of other vehicles. He looked out through the small, square window in the back of the hood and could still see her, forcing her way through the crowds of people, sometimes jostling them upon the path, then running in the gutter for the greater freedom of passage.

"God!" he muttered under his breath, as he turned back again.

"What is it?" asked Coralie.

"Oh, nothing," he replied; "nothing."

Mrs. Durlacher caught her lips between her teeth to crush the smile that rose to them. Now she was sure at least that Sally's power was broken. Her subtle use of that word "allow" had served its double purpose. Not only had it delicately questioned the possession of that authority which she knew he held above all things; but also, in permitting it, the admission had been deftly drawn from him that Sally was his mistress. She had known it before, as women do know things. Now she was certain of it and, in her certainty, realized that this was the moment—to strike when he was weakest. A man, shaken free of the ties that bind him to one woman, is more ready than another in the reaction of indifference which follows to fetter himself again in order that life may seem less void, less hollow than he finds it.

To Coralie, then, in the dressing-room of the restaurant, as they took off their cloaks, she said—

"My dear girl, you're making that brother of mine in love with you."

And to Traill, she jested as they said good night—

"My dear boy, considering your obligations to other women, do you think it's fair? The girl's losing her heart to you, or will be if she sees you again."

E. Temple Thurston

# CHAPTER X

The congestion of the traffic, the knotted lines of carriages conveying to their houses the thousands of people whom the theatres had disgorged into the streets, enabled Sally to keep Mrs. Durlacher's car in sight until it passed through the wide portals of a restaurant in the Strand where, from the street, she could see them dismount and pass into the building. They had gone to supper. Traill had told her nothing about that. Then it had only been decided since he had met them; he must be enjoying himself in the society of these very people whose society he professed to abhor. That they might have pressed him to accompany them so that he found it impossible to refuse, did not enter the argument in her mind. All thoughts tended in one direction—instinct guiding them—instinct, drunk with the noxious ferment of jealousy, whipping her mind down paths where no reason could follow, yet bringing her invariably to the truth with that same generosity of Providence which watches over the besotted wanderings of a drunken man.

For some moments she stood there, watching the doors which a powdered flunkey had swung to after their entrance. Wild suggestions flung themselves before her consideration. She would go back to her room, dress herself in the best frock that Traill had given her and go to supper there herself. She would wait there an hour, an hour and a half if necessary, to see if he went home with them. That she had almost decided on, when a man of whose presence, passing behind her once or twice upon the pavement, she had been unaware, stopped by her side.

"Waiting for some one?" he said, with that insinuating tone of voice which disposes of any need for introduction.

She drew away from him quickly in horror, fear driving cold through the hot blood of her jealousy. Then she turned, as he laughed to conceal his momentary embarrassment, and hurried off in the direction of Trafalgar Square.

That incident proved her waiting to be impossible. She walked slowly home, all the spirit within her sinking down into an impenetrable mood of depression from which not even the persistent hope that love must win her back her happiness in the end had any power to raise her. Now she was crushed—burnt out. Only the charred cinders and the ashes of herself were left behind from the flames of that furnace which had torn its way through her.

Lighting just one candle, she sat in his room waiting for his return. An hour passed, and at last she blew the candle out. He might think it strange to find her there, sitting up for him; he might suspect, and as yet she was sublimely unconscious that he had seen her. She was sure when she had covered her face with the programme in the theatre that the action had been in time; moreover, she was by no means certain that from that distance his glasses had covered her at all.

Mounting the uncarpeted stairs from his room to the floor above, she stopped once or twice, thinking she heard a hansom pulling up in the street. Her heart stopped with her and she held a breath in suspense; but on each occasion it jingled on, losing the noise of its bells in the murmuring

E. Temple Thurston

night sounds which never quite die into silence in that quarter.

When she reached her room, she lit a candle, holding it up before the mirror on the dressing-table and gazing at her face in its reflection.

"My God!" she whispered.

Truly, in the light of that one candle, she hardly recognized herself. Violent sensations, deep emotions, these are the accelerations of time. They produce—momentarily no doubt—the same effect as do the passing of years over which such intensity of feeling is more evenly distributed. In those few hours, since she had heard from Devenish that another woman was claiming the attentions of Traill's mind, Sally had aged—withered almost—in the fierce stress of her passion of jealousy. It had passed over her like the sirocco of the desert, leaving her parched, dried, shrivelled, as a child grown old before its years. No colour was there in her cheeks, no vestige of the sign that beneath a mere fraction's measurement of that white skin, the blood was flowing through her veins. Yet the skin was not really white. It was an ugly grey, smirched with a colour that bore but the faintest resemblance to animation. Beneath the eyes deep shadows lay, smeared into the sockets. She lifted the candle to their level, but they did not disappear. Pain had cast them, and no shifting of material light would wipe them out. But it was the eyes themselves that startled her. When she looked into them—deep into the pupils—she realized how close she had drifted to the moment beyond which control is of no account—the moment of absolute madness. Even then, they glittered unnaturally. A gleam from the candle again? She moved it once more—this way and that—but still the light flickered there, frightening her into a sudden effort of restraint. She tried to pull herself together; put down the candle hurriedly and, feeling the leathern dryness in her mouth, caught at a carafe of water, drinking from it without use of the glass.

That steadied her. Thoughts drifted back into their channels and, coming with them, looming with its portentous realization above the others, the remembrance that only the evening before, he had drawn out the settlement upon her life. Now she knew why he had done it. Now she found the absolute trending of his mind. He had said if he died! That was only to blind, only to tie a bandage about her eyes in order to conceal from her the true motive that had instigated him. But she saw the true motive now. Under the bandages she had already tried to peer; now circumstance itself had wrenched them from her.

With feverish movements, she opened a drawer and took from it a little slip of paper. This was a copy of the settlement as he had drawn it out. He had presented it to her.

"You'd better keep it as a memorandum of the details," he had said and, without glancing at its contents, she had thrust it into this drawer. Now she hurriedly spread it open.

"In the event of my death, or the discontinuance of the relations which now exist between Miss Sally Bishop and myself—"

These were the first words that met her eyes. Her fingers closed automatically over the paper, crushing it into her palm. Could she need any more proof than that? That a settlement and dealing with a relationship such as theirs must be worded in such a way, carried no weight with it to her mind. She knew then, that when he had alluded to the event of his death, it had been farthest from his thoughts. He had meant their separation. In three years—a little more than three years it had come. He was tired of her. She knew well then how useless had been her efforts to move him to passion the night before. Her cheeks flamed, thinking that it had not been because he was unconscious of her attempt. He had seen it. There was no doubt in her mind that when he had told her to fasten her dressing-gown, when he had noticed the perfumes of scent from her hair, he had realized the motive that was acting within her. But he was tired—satiated. And how he must have loathed her! Yet no greater than she, at that moment, loathed herself. He knew—of course he knew—that her coming down to get the book had all been an excuse. He had probably thought that her desire had been for herself. How could he possibly have known that she felt no desire, had been frigid, cold, without a strain of passion in her thoughts, seeking only to tempt him to her side, for his pleasure alone, with the delights of her body? How could he have known? He did not know! Of a certainty he must have thought that it was her own satisfaction she was seeking. The blood raced back from her cheeks, leaving her shivering and cold. Oh, how he must have loathed her! Why had she done it? Why was there not some illuminating power to point out the intricacy of the ways when people came to such a maze in life as this?

In a torture of shame that blent with all her misery, she flung herself, dressed as she was, on to the bed. Let him find her there—what did it matter! She realized that she had lost everything. And there she lay, eyes burning and dry, heart just beating faintly in her breast. But when she heard his footsteps mounting the stairs, she suddenly got up. If he knew that she had followed them, he would never forgive her. So, in the midst of her misery, she still found the strength to hope. Jumping up from the bed she stood before her mirror and began to take off her hat as though she had that moment returned.

When his knock fell on the door, she forced fear from her voice, drove eagerness into the place of it, and called him to enter.

The door opened. In the mirror's reflection, she could see him stop abruptly as he came into the room. With hands still lifted, extricating the pins from her hat, she turned. His lips were tight closed, his eyes merciless. So he had looked that day at Apsley when he had returned to find his sister with her in the dining-room. So he had directed his gaze upon the woman whom she had heard him cross-examine in the Law Courts. The suspicion leapt to her mind that he knew, that he had seen her; but having steeled herself to tell the lie, she did not attempt, in the sudden moment, to reconstruct her mind to a hasty admission of the truth. She must tell the lie, clinging to it through everything.

"Have you only just come in?" he asked.

The tone in his voice seemed to question her right to come in at all. And she was no actress. Another woman in her place, even knowing all she knew, suspecting all she did, would have turned to him in amazement; questioning his right to speak to her like that; covered her guilt with a cloak of astonished innocence and paraded her injury before him. Sally took it for granted; did not even argue from it the certainty that he had seen her. Her mind was made up for the lie and she did not possess that agility of purpose which, at a moment's notice, could enable her to twist her intentions—a mental somersault that needs the double-jointedness of cunning and all the consummate flexibility of tact. He might know that she had followed them, but she must never admit it. It seemed a feasible argument to her, in the whirling panic of her thoughts, that her admission would be fatal—just as the prisoner in the dock pleads "not guilty" against all the damning evidence of every witness who can be  brought

E. Temple Thurston

against him.

"I've been in about half an hour," she replied.

"Did you dine with Devenish?"

The same direct form of question, thrown at her with the same implacable scrutiny of his eyes.

"Yes," she replied.

"Where?"

She mentioned the name of the restaurant in Shaftesbury Avenue.

"Where did you go afterwards?"

It was all prepared on her tongue. She did not hesitate.

"To the Palace," she replied.

"To the Palace?" He repeated it. His eyes burnt into her. Then she knew that he had seen her in the theatre; but only in the theatre where she could still swear to him that he was mistaken. Every instinct she possessed forced her to deny it until the last; beyond that if breath were left her.

"Did you see it out? Did you see the performance out?" he continued.

"Yes—we waited till the end."

A note of warning despatched to Devenish would ensure his confirmation of all she had said. He had told her that if ever she needed a friend—now indeed she wanted one.

"What did you do then if you only came in half an hour ago? It's just one o'clock."

A thought rushed exultingly to her mind that he was jealous—jealous of Devenish. He had not seen her at all. This was jealousy. Her heart cried out in thankfulness. She crossed the room to him, all the whole wealth of her love alive and bright in her eyes.

"Jack"—she whispered—"you're not jealous of Devenish, are you?"

A laugh broke out from his lips, striking her with the sting of its harshness.

"Where did you go afterwards?" he repeated.

"To supper—we went to supper—the same place where we had dined. Why wouldn't you tell me if you were jealous? Do you think I should mind?"

"Jealous?" He took her arm and led her nearer to the light of the solitary candle. There he faced her, looking down into the weary pupils of her eyes. "All these things you've been saying," he said brutally—"are lies—the whole—blessed—pack of them. You never went to the Palace Theatre, you went to the Duke of York's. You sat in the third row of the pit and covered your face with a programme whenever you thought we were looking in your direction. You never went to supper afterwards. You tracked Dolly's car into the Strand—running in the gutter to keep pace with it. Jealous? Great God! No! What have I to be jealous about? What did you think you were doing—eh? What did you think you were going to gain by it?"

Up to a moment, she met his eyes; but when he railed at her

thoughts of his jealousy, then all courage fell from her. "Jealous? Great God! No!" She knew it was finished when he had said that and, beneath the weight of his contempt, she crumbled into the dust of pitiful obsession.

"Did you imagine," he went on mercilessly—"that I undertook the arrangement of this life with you with the thought for a moment in my mind that you would institute a close vigil over all my actions?"

"It was only because I knew you were being deceived," she said brokenly.

"How being deceived? By whom?"

"By your sister."

"How has she deceived me?" He forced her eyes to his. "How?" he repeated.

To defend her case, just as the woman in the Courts had done, she told him of what Devenish had said; notwithstanding that she herself had pleaded with Devenish to repeat nothing of what had passed between them. Then, in the cold glittering of his eyes, she saw how she had doubly wronged her cause.

"So you speak to outsiders," he said quietly, "about the things which I have told you in confidence. My God! It's well that you and I are not married; well for you and well for me that we haven't to smirch our names in order to get the release of a divorce."

"Divorce?"

"Yes. Great heavens! Do you think I'm going to live on with

you now? Do you think I'm going to be followed in all my actions—tracked, trapped—and dandle the private detective on my knee?"

"Ah, but Jack!" She flung arms around his neck, her head bent close to his chest. "I was jealous—can't you see that? I was jealous of that girl."

He put her firmly away from him. "Oh, that be damned for a tale!" he exclaimed.

She shuddered. She had sought for pity—the last hope. In his voice there was none. If only she had had some one to guide her, some one to show her that it would all lead to this. She would have held him longer; she would still have held him, had she not given way to let jealousy wrestle with her soul, flinging it at his feet for him to trample on. Whatever had been the attitude of his mind before, she had afforded him no reason to leave her. Now there was cause—cause enough. She could only see the enormity of her guilt with his eyes, so completely did he dominate her. That a thousand circumstances had mitigated her action, had goaded her, as the unwilling beast is driven through the noise and smoke of battle, until, in the fury of fear, it plunges headlong towards the murderous cannonade—that these things should be taken into account did not enter her conception of the situation. She had wronged him. That was all she felt. And now, clutching his hand, raising it to her lips, drenching it with her tears and kisses, she begged his forgiveness, humbling herself down to the very dust.

He took his hand away. "What's the good of talking about forgiveness?" he said unemotionally. "The thing's done. I was not the only person who saw you."

"Your sister?"

"Yes; she pointed you out first."

"I might have guessed that!" Sally exclaimed bitterly.

"Why?"

"Because she hates me. She knew it 'ud make you angry if you saw me there."

"Oh, that's nonsense! Why should she hate you?"

"Why, because she wants you for that other girl. And you do care for her now, don't you—don't you?"

Traill turned away with annoyance. "We'll leave that matter alone," he said. "I haven't the slightest intention of discussing it. To-morrow morning I shall see about letting my rooms. According to the terms of the settlement I drew out last night, you retain these—rent free—to the expiration of the lease. That's three years. But you mayn't sub-let."

Sub-let! He could talk about sub-letting! The irony of it dragged a laugh through her lips.

"Do you think I shall want to sub-let?" she said stridently. "Do you think I shall care what I do, where I live, how I live?"

"You'll be a fool if you don't," he remarked.

The hysterical note in her voice had jarred through him. Once before in his life he had had a woman screaming about his ears. There was no desire in his mind to relish the enjoyment of it again. He turned slowly towards the door. This was the worst of women. A man's relations with them were bound to end something after this fashion. In common with most men, he shared a hatred of that termination of all intimacies which one calls a scene.

But, really, he had no cause for apprehension. The tears now were streaming down her face, sobs were choking her, convulsive shudderings that shook her body in a merciless grip. Her spirit was utterly broken. No worse could happen to her now. But through all her misery, she could still think first of him. That tentative drawing away, the hand stretching out for the door, she knew the meaning of that; she saw that he had had enough—enough of her weeping, enough of her despair. Just as when, watching the fight, she had struggled against her weakness lest it should spoil his pleasure, so now she fought down the hysteria of her mind to give him ease. Very wearily she crossed the room and stood beside him, forcing back tears with lips that were trembling and contorted. It was no show of bravado, no spurious bravery, aping self-respect, taking it well, as the phrase has it. She was not brave. She felt a coward to all of life that offered. Her heart was that of a derelict—numbed, inert, no spirit left in it—just lifting its head with sluggish weariness above the body of the waves. But simply out of love for him she could not bear to see him annoyed by her suffering.

"You needn't hurry to go," she said finely; "I shan't make a fool of myself—the way you think. I shan't be a drag on you—I promise you that. And if you're going to-morrow, wouldn't you stop just a little while and talk?"

At any other moment the simplicity of that would have touched him; but the affection that Devenish had seen to be tiring had been snapped—a thread in a flame—when he had found her watching his actions, dogging his footsteps. His liberty—that which a man of his type most prizes when he finds it being encroached upon—had been threatened. There was no forgiveness in the heart of him for that. In the sudden

E. Temple Thurston

freedom of his affections—just as Mrs. Durlacher had so deftly anticipated—he had let them drift—a moth to the nearest candle, a floating seed to the nearest shore—and Coralie Standish-Roe had claimed them.

"Can anything be gained by talking?" he asked, quietly.

"Yes—perhaps it's the last time."

"But nothing can be gained by it. You'll only make yourself more miserable. What is the good of that?"

"Do you think I could be more miserable?" she asked.

He shrugged his shoulders.

This scarcely, without seeking defence for Traill, is the most difficult part for a man to play well. He had never offered, in the first beginning of their acquaintance, to deceive her. He was not a man who had respect for marriage, he had said quite honestly. He had told her to go—have no truck with him; and if she had gone, if she had not taken upon herself to return his present, he would have seen no more of her. She had known of his love of liberty, and she herself had threatened it; yet now, seemingly, he was playing a mean part, deserting her, casting her off, when she loved him with every breath her trembling lips drew through her body. It is hard to play such a part well. Even the least sensitive of men, conscious of their own cruelty, will seek to end it as quickly as may be. Wherefore, how could he be expected to see the good gained by staying and talking? What good, in God's name, did talking do? With the agony prolonged, the strain drawn out, how were they—either of them—to benefit? Here, indeed, is a judgment of the head. But it was with her heart alone that Sally craved for its continuance. It was the last she was to see of him; the last time that he would be in her bedroom where all the passionate associations of her life would always lie buried. Can it be wondered that she would willingly have dragged the misery of it through all that night, if only to keep him for the moments as they passed, by her side?

Yet he was driven to play the mean part—the part for which there never will be—perhaps never should be—any sympathy. And he must play it with the best grace he could. A man is always a spectator to his own actions; a woman, in her emotions—never. So women lose their self-respect more easily than men.

But Traill was not the type to allow these abstract considerations to worry him. The love in him she found to be dead. He was not even moved by the piteousness of her appeal. There, then, it must end. It was not his nature to choose the most graceful, the kindest way to end it. He snapped it off as, across the knees, you break a faggot for the burning. And that, too, is the only way to do it.

"I didn't come up here," he said, "to discuss anything. The whole thing's discussed in my mind. When I saw you running after the car, pushing your way along the gutter— that ended it. You'd better read through your settlement now and if you don't think I've been generous enough, tell me to-morrow morning. I shall be downstairs till eleven."

He opened the door—passed through—closed it. She listened to each one of his steps as he descended the stairs, her mouth hanging open, her eyes struck in a fixed glare at the spot where he had stood. Then, when she heard him close his door below, she just crumpled up in an abandoned heap upon the floor, and with each breath she moaned—"Oh— oh—oh."

E. Temple Thurston

Traill, undressing below, heard it. With a muttered exclamation, he dragged his shirt over his head and flung it violently into the corner of the room amongst the bundle of dirty linen.

## END OF BOOK II

# BOOK III

## DERELICT

## CHAPTER I

Virtue is the personality of many women. Rob them of it, those of them whose value it enhances, and you prize a jewel from its setting, you wrench a star out of the mystery of the heavens and bring it down to earth. It is a common trend of the mind in these modern days to make nobility out of the women whose personality needs no virtue to lift it to a pedestal of fame. But really, it is they who make the nobility for themselves. Phryne of Athens, Helen of Troy, Catherine of Russia, Mary of Scotland—these are women who have ennobled themselves without aid of eulogy. Personality has been theirs without necessity for the robe of virtue to grace them in the eyes of the world. But with the seemingly lesser women, the women of seemingly no vast account—with those whose whole individuality depends upon the invaluable possession of their virtue, no great epic can well be sung, no loud paean sounded. You may find just a lyric here, a rondel there, set to the lilt of a phrase in an idle hour and sung in a passing moment to send a tired heart asleep. But that is all. Yet they are the women upon whom the world has spent six thousand years in the making; they are the women at whose breasts are fed the sons of men. The whole race has

E. Temple Thurston

been weaned by them; every country has been nursed into manhood in their arms. But they are too normal or they are too much a class to have men sing of them. There is not one mother of children in the vast calendars of history who stands out now for our eyes to reverence. Upon the stage of the world their part is played, and what eye is there can grasp in comprehensive glance the whole broad sweep of power which their frail hands have wielded? Only upon that mimic platform of fame, raised where the eyes of all can watch the figure as it treads the boards, have women stood apart where the recorder can jot their names upon a scroll of history for the world to read. There is no virtue essential here; virtue indeed but adds a glamour with its absence.

There is some subtle attraction in a Catherine of Russia or a Manon Lescaut which tempts the cunning lust of men to cry their praise for the nobility of heart that lies beneath. But what elusive charm is there in the mother of children whose stainless virtue is her only personality? None? Yet to the all-seeing eye, to the all-comprehending brain—to that omni-science whom some call God, be it in Trinity or in Unity, and others know not what to call—these are the women who lift immeasurably above fame, infinitely above repute.

So, therefore, rob them of their virtue and you prize a jewel from its setting, you wrench a star from the mystery of the heavens and bring it down to earth, you filch from the generous hand of Nature that very possession which she holds most dear. For without virtue, these women are nothing. Without virtue, you may see them dragging the bed of the streets for the bodies they can find. It is the last task which Nature sets them—bait to lure men from the theft of that virtue in others which they can in no wise repay.

And this very virtue itself needs no little power of subtle comprehension to understand; for intrinsically it is a fixed quality while outwardly it changes, just as the tide of custom ebbs or flows. Intrinsically then, it is that quality in a woman which breeds respect in men—respect, the lure of which is so often their own vanity. And the pure, the chaste, the untouched woman, whether it be vanity or not, is she whom men most venerate. Of these they make mothers—for these alone they will live continently. And however much love a man may bear in his heart for a woman whom some other than himself has possessed, the knowledge of it will corrupt like a poison in the blood though he forgive her a thousand times.

Such a woman, pure, chaste, and untouched, had been Sally Bishop. But to one man alone can a woman be this, and then, only so long as she remains with him. Once he has cast her off, when once she is discarded, she becomes to all who know her, a woman of easy virtue, prey to the first hungry hands that are ready to claim her. This, in an age when the binding sacrament of matrimony is being held up to ridicule both in theory and in practice, is perhaps the only reasonable argument that can be utilized in its defence. It is surely not pedantic to hope that the purity of some women is still essential for the race, and it is surely not illogical to suppose that marriage is the means, in such cases as that of Sally Bishop, to this humble end.

Pure, certainly, she had been, even in the eyes of such a man as Devenish; but in the light of a discarded mistress, all her virtue vanished. Innate in the mind of the worst of men is the timid hesitation before he brands a virtuous woman; but when once he knows that she has fallen, conscience lifts, like a feather on the breeze. With a light heart, he reaps the harvest of tares which some other than himself must be blamed for sowing, and with a light heart he goes his way, immune to remorse.

E. Temple Thurston

This then is the Tragedy which, like some insect in the heart of the rose, had eaten its way into the romance of Sally Bishop.

For three days after Traill had left her, she broke under the flood of her despair. For those three days she did not move out of her rooms, taking just what nourishment there was to be found in the cupboards where they stored the food for their breakfasts. On the side of her bed she sometimes sat, biting a dry piece of bread—anything that she could find—in that unconscious instinct with which the body prompts the mind for its own preservation. But these meals—if such they can be called—she took at no stated times. Crusts of bread lay about on the table, showing how indiscriminately of order she had fed herself. For two hours together, she would sit in awful silence, with eyes strained staringly before her. Of tears, there were none. Sometimes a sob broke through her lips when a sound downstairs reminded her of him; but no tears accompanied it. It was more like the complaining cry of some animal in its sleep.

For the first two nights she just flung herself on her bed when the darkness came. She did not undress. The nights were warm then, or cold might have driven her between the clothes. But, on the third evening, she disrobed. This was habit reasserting itself. She did it unconsciously, only remembering as she crept, shuddering, between the sheets, that for the two previous nights she had not gone to bed at all.

The toppling fall of reason would soon have ended it; that merciful potion of magic which can bring a torturing misery in the guise of a quaint conceit to a mind made simple as a little child's. Another day or so, and the frightened agony that glittered in her eyes—fusing slowly towards the last great conflagration—would have burnt up in the sudden panic-flare as the reason guttered out, then smouldered down into that pitiable lightless flickering where all glimmer of intelligence is dead.

Inevitably this must have followed, had not Janet visited her late in the evening of the fourth day. Two days before, she had written saying that she would come if Traill were not likely to be there.

Her note finished abruptly, characteristic of all her letters.

"If I don't hear from you to the contrary," it concluded, "I shall arrive."

She heard nothing to the contrary. The letter had lain, since its arrival, in the box downstairs. Sally had not moved out of her room. The possibility of a letter from Traill might have drawn her forth; but she knew that such a possibility did not exist. The woman who attended to their rooms she had sent away.

"I shall be able to look after these two rooms myself," she had thought vaguely. Then she had locked herself into her bedroom, taken up a duster to begin the morning's work and, after five minutes, idly lifting each thing in her hand, she had seated herself by the side of the bed, allowing the duster to fall limply from her fingers. Then, throwing herself on to the pillows, had given way with tearless eye to her despair.

When Janet's knock fell, she was lying in bed, eyes gaping at the ceiling above her in a gaze that scarcely wandered or moved from the spot upon which they were fixed. At the unexpected sound, she sat up. Intelligence struggled for the mastery in her mind. There, in her eyes, you could see it fight for victory.

E. Temple Thurston

"Who's that?" she called out querulously in a thin voice.

"Janet! Do you mean to say you're not up yet?"

"No."

"Well, come and unlock the door. I can't get in."

Sally drove the energy into her limbs with an effort and tumbled from the bed. As her feet touched the floor, she lurched forward with weakness. She clutched at the clothes and held herself erect; but her knees trembled, knocking together like wooden clubs that are shaken by reckless vibration.

With a little moan of weakness she stumbled to the door, holding to the end of the bed, the back of a chair, the handle of the door in her uncertain progress.

As soon as she heard the key turned, Janet entered and found Sally in her night-dress, a white ghost of what she was, swinging unsteadily before her—so a dead body, swung from a gallows, eddies in a lifting wind.

"Sally!" she exclaimed.

Sally stared at her. Her dry lips half-parted to make Janet's name. Her eyes, burnt out in the deep black hollows, flickered with a light of thankful recognition. Then she swung forward, a dead weight on to Janet's shoulder.

For a moment, Janet held her there, looking over the shoulders that crumbled against her thin breast, at the disordered room before her. She saw the crusts of bread, she saw the bed-clothes hanging to the floor. She gazed down at the unkempt head of hair that dragged lifelessly on her shoulder, and her eyes were wide in bewildered amazement.

"Great God!" she exclaimed.

And she realized how inadequate that was.

# CHAPTER II

For three weeks Janet stayed with her, sleeping with her, arms tight-locked about her yielding body as they had often slept together in the days at Kew. With her own hands, she fed her; in the warmth of her big, generous heart, she nursed her back to life, as you revive some little bird, starved and cold, in the heat of your two hands.

During the first fortnight, she asked no questions. What had happened was obvious. She learnt from the people on the second floor in the office of the railway company that Traill had left his rooms; but under what circumstances and why, she made no inquiries. Brought face to face with the exigencies in the lives of others, there is a fund of common sense to be found in the character of the revolutionary woman. That Janet Hallard was an artist, now with a studio of sorts of her own, says nothing for her temperament and less for her art. She had no conception of the higher life, and to her mind the inner mysticism was a jumble of confused nonsense—the blind leading the blind, for whom the ultimate ditch was a bastard theosophy. As a matter of fact, Janet had no mean ideas of design; but they were vigorous and, for her living, she had to struggle against the overwhelming senti-mentalism of the *nouveau* art.

In dealing with Sally then, a subject needing tact, common

sense and an unyielding strength of purpose, she was more than eminently fitted to save her from the edge of the precipice towards which she had found her so blindly stumbling. It was just such a moment as when one sees one's dearest friend walking blindly to the verge of an abyss and knows that too sudden a cry, too swift a movement to save them, may plunge their reckless body for ever into eternity. In this moment, Janet kept her wits. With infinite care, with infinite tenderness, never weakening to the importunate demands that were made of her, giving up her work, giving up every other interest that she had, she slowly drew Sally back into the steady current of existence; saw day by day the life come tardily again into the bloodless cheeks, and watched the smearing shadows beneath the hollow eyes as they disappeared.

Then, at the end of a fortnight, she learnt in quavering sentences from Sally's lips, trembling as they told it, the story of her desertion.

"You shouldn't have followed him, Sally," she whispered gently at its conclusion.

"I know I shouldn't—I know I shouldn't. And so I know of course he isn't to blame. It's that woman—his sister. I always knew she hated me—knew it! She used to look at me like you look at soiled things in a shop! She pointed me out to him in the theatre. I can guess the things she said. She brought the other—the other one to see him. Oh, wasn't it cunning of her? Mustn't she be a brute! Think what she's done to me! Look how wretched she's made my life! And she's got every single thing she can want. Oh, I don't wonder that people have their doubts about this marvellous mercy of God! I don't see any mercy in what's happened to me. I never saw any mercy in what happened to father; and yet he only did what he ought to have done."

E. Temple Thurston

The excitement was rising within her—a steady torrent lifting to the flood. Janet watched its progress steadily in her eyes. When it reached this point, she adroitly changed the current of her thoughts.

"What did your father do?" she asked with interest.

Sally looked up and the expression in her eyes changed.

"Have I never told you?"

"No."

"He consecrated too much wine one Easter Sunday where he was taking a *locum tenens*—and afterwards, when he had to drink it—it went to his head."

She told it so seriously that Janet was driven to choke the rush of laughter rising within her.

"Why did he have to drink it?" she asked.

"They have to. Consecrated wine mustn't be kept."

"But why not? Does it go bad?"

"Janet! No—but, don't you see?—they do keep it in the Roman Catholic Church—on the altar—that's why the little red lamp is always burning in front. That's why the people bow when they first come into the church. And don't you see they're afraid in the Anglican Church, that if the Bread and Wine were kept, people might venerate it as the real Presence, which of course it isn't."

"Isn't it?"

"No."

"Why not?"

"I couldn't tell you."

"Then he had to drink it all himself?"

"Yes."

"Why didn't he get somebody to help him?"

"He did try. He asked the warden—but the warden was a total abstainer."

Janet looked sternly out of the window.

"Then he asked a man he saw outside the church—but he was apparently an atheist. At any rate, he didn't believe in that."

"P'raps he thought the wine wasn't good?" Janet suggested.

"Oh no—he offered to drink it; but of course as he didn't believe—"

"Didn't believe in what? He believed it was wine, didn't he?"

"Oh yes—but he didn't believe in the Communion. So father had to drink it himself. And then, the Bishop came into the vestry and found him."

"What happened then?"

"Nothing then—but a few months later, he was appointed to the chaplaincy of a Union—of course a much smaller

E. Temple Thurston

position than the one he had occupied."

"Didn't they give any reasons?"

"Oh yes—in a sort of a way. They said that they thought the rectorship of Cailsham was rather too responsible a post for him. They asked him to accept the other in such a way that it would have been hard to refuse. Of course, they couldn't actually turn him out. But mother hated him for going. It was soon after we left there that I came up to you in London. They were getting so poor. My brother couldn't be kept up at Oxford. The governess had to go. Father died not long after I left. I know what he died of. They called it a general break-up."

"Oh—I know that," said Janet. "There's the shot-gun prescription—all the pharmacopoeia ground into a pill and fired down the patient's throat. It must hit something. That general break-up is the double-barrelled diagnosis. You believe it was the resignation of the rectorship that finished him."

"Yes—I'm sure of it. I remember, the day I went away from home—when I came in to say good-bye to him, he was writing a sermon for Easter. It was just Easter then, don't you remember? I went to the little church on Kew Green. He read a bit of it out to me—something about there being the promise of everlasting life in the rising of Christ from the dead—and yet I know, in his heart, he was cast down in the very lowest depth of despair."

Janet shook her head up and down. Not one of us is too old to learn some new mystery in the inner workings of the human machine. To Janet it was a fairy tale, what had been life and death to the Rev. Samuel Bishop. But she had achieved her object. Sally was quieter after the relation of that little story and, seeing in her mood a good opportunity for suggesting some plans about the future, Janet said quietly—

"What are your mother and sisters doing now?"

"They've gone back to Cailsham. They've got a school there for little boys—sons of gentlemen—preparatory for the Grammar School at Maidstone. The sort of thing that nearly every woman takes up when she gets as poor as mother is."

Janet left it at that, and set about the getting of a meal, talking all the time in a light and flippant way about her studio; pointing humorous descriptions of the managers of firms with whom she had to deal in her business of designing.

"There's one man," she said. "You know the place up the Tottenham Court Road—he weighs seventeen stone if he weighs an ounce, and he comes up to business in the morning, all the way from Turnham Green in a motor-car that makes the noise of thirty horses galloping over a hard road, with the power of six of them in its inside. He asked me down to dinner one night; I went. It meant business. His wife weighs the ounce that he ought to weigh if he didn't weigh seventeen stone, and they sit at each end of a huge table in a tiny room filled with maroon plush against a green carpet, and all through dinner they talk about carburetters and low-tension magnetos, and Mr. Cheeseman discusses what friend living in the row of houses, of which theirs is one, they would get most out of in return for a drive in the motor next Sunday. 'There's one fellow I know,' I remember him saying. 'He's something to do with the stage—his brother's in the booking-office at Daly's. He might get us some seats if we took him out.'"

Sally laughed. The first moment that her lips had parted to

E. Temple Thurston

the sound since Janet had been with her.

"It's true," said Janet. "I'm not making it up. He got that car—allowing for his trade discount—for a hundred and thirty-five pounds—cape-cart hood and all. It only costs him thirteen pounds a year in tyres—and it can do twenty-five miles to a gallon of petrol with him inside, and he reckons he's been saved five shillings a week regularly in dinners since he got it. Well, what else do you think a man buys a motor-car for if he can't afford it? Some one has to pay for it—why not his friends? That's the English system of hospitality—what I buy you pay for; what you pay for I get, and what I've got I must have bought, otherwise I shouldn't have it. It's the principle of the *reductio ad absurdum*, if you know what that is. Everybody gets what they want, everybody else pays for it, and everybody's happy. I'll do your washing if you'll do mine. Can you have a more generous hospitality than that?"

Sally laughed again, and then Janet launched her boat of enterprise.

"You're fond of kiddies, aren't you, Sally?" she asked suddenly.

A tender look crept into Sally's eyes. "You know I am," she replied.

"Well—why don't you go down to your people at Cailsham and help them for a little while in the school?"

The look of tenderness died out. Her eyes roamed pitiably about the room.

"I couldn't leave here," she said powerlessly.

"Why not?"

"I couldn't. It's all reminding me I know; but I couldn't be happy anywhere else. I should be miserable away from here."

The meeting of such obstacles as this, Janet had anticipated. She knew well that slough of the mind which sucks in its own despair, and with all the concentration of her persuasion, she strove to lift Sally out of the morass. Failing on that occasion, she turned the conversation into another channel—let it drift as it pleased; but the next day she led it back again. At all costs Sally must be removed from the association of her surroundings, and no means offered better than these. Yet at the end of three weeks, notwithstanding all the patient persuasion that she employed, her object was as far from being reached as at the beginning.

"If you spoil your life, Sally," she said, as she was going, "it'll be the bitterest disappointment to me that I can think of. No man is worth it to a woman—no woman's worth it to a man. Can't you get some ambition to do something? All your time's your own, and you haven't got to work for your living. He's been generous enough—I'll admit that. Let me give you lessons in drawing."

"I could never learn anything like that," said Sally, wearily. "Haven't got it in me."

This mood of wilful depression, bordering upon melancholia, can be perhaps the most trying test to friendship that exists. To throw life into the balance of chance—to fling it absolutely away in a moment of heroism for a friend one loves, is a simple task compared with the unwearying patience that is needed to face the lightless gloom of another's misery. It taints all life, discolours all pleasures, tracks one—dogs one, like a shadow on the wall. Yet Janet passed the test with love the greater, even at the end of the gauntlet of those three weeks.

"I'll be with you all day, the day after to-morrow," she said, as she departed; "and think about teaching the kiddies—I would if I were you. You'd get awfully fond of them—as if they were your own. Sons of gentlemen! Think of them! Dear little chaps! My God—the mothers bore them, though."

# CHAPTER III

It should not be lightly touched upon, this heroism of Janet Hallard's in sacrificing three weeks of her work—every hour of which meant some living to her—in order to save Sally from that ultimate dark world of dementia towards which she was inevitably drifting. It was not the sacrifice of time alone, not the fact that on her return she was compelled to sell some of her valued possessions in order to meet the rent of her studio which the work she had left undone would have amply supplied. Much rather was it the noble perseverance of effort through the dim, impenetrable gloom of Sally's wide-eyed misery, her own spirits never cast down by the seeming impossibility of the task, her resources never exhausted by the persistent drain that was made upon them. Here was the strength of her masculinity united with the patient endurance of the woman in her heart. No man, of his own nature alone, could have won through the sweating labour of those three weeks—few women either. But that very combination of sex, that very duality of her nature which, as a woman, made her unlovable to any man, and endeared her so closely to Sally's life, had succeeded where a thousand others of her sex would have failed.

She left Sally, it is true, a woman with a wounded heart to nurse, an aching misery to bear; but she left her with a sanity of purpose which can take up the tangled threads and,

E. Temple Thurston

however blinded be the eyes with weeping, with fingers feeling their way, can unravel the knotted mass that lies before her.

So she slowly returned to the common factors of existence, and in six weeks from the time of Traill's departure, was ready to smile at any moment to the humour of Janet's dry criticisms of life. But to move from her rooms, to disassociate herself from the past with every sorrow and every joy that it contained, was more than she could bring herself to do. Through all Janet's persuasions, Sally remained obdurate.

"I've only got the rooms for three years," she replied finally. "I can't think of it as really past until that time's gone by; Then, I will. I'll go anywhere you like. I'll come and share your studio with you."

They entered into a formal agreement on that and, knowing the Romance in Sally's nature, Janet pursued her quest of success on the other point no further.

But circumstance, with an arm stronger than Janet could ever wield, succeeded where she had failed.

One evening, as Sally was preparing to go out alone to dinner, she heard footsteps mounting the stairs to her floor. On the moment, her heart leapt, beating to her throat. Her hands, raising the hat to her head, so trembled that she had to put it back upon the dressing-table. A cold dew damped her forehead. She put her hand up and found it wet. Then the knock fell and, shaking in every limb, she set her lips and walked as firmly as she could to the door. There she stopped, taking a deep breath. Then she swung it open.

It was Devenish.

He took off his hat and held a hand out to her. She accepted it, confused in her mind as to the reason of his coming. Did he know? Or was he utterly unconscious? He must have known; he had come to her door.

"Do you mind my coming in?" he asked.

"No, not at all."

She made way for him to pass into her sitting-room. There followed an awkward pause which he tried to fill with the laying down of his hat and the discarding of his gloves. Sally stood there where she had closed the door, waiting for him to explain his presence. Had he brought a message for her from Jack? Had he come to see Jack—knowing nothing—and, finding the rooms below occupied by another tenant, had he come to learn the reason of her? Why had he come? And at last he turned frankly to her.

"Miss Bishop, I saw Jack the other day. He told me."

Sally lifted her head with an assumption of pride, a strained effort to show the pride that Janet had urged her to possess. She crossed the room and dropped into a chair.

"Aren't you going to sit down?" she asked.

"Thanks." He took the nearest chair, winding his watch-chain about his finger to convey the air that he was at ease.

"Did Jack send you to see me?" she asked then.

"No."

"You've no message from him?"

"No."

"Then, why do you come here?" She wanted to put the question firmly, but in her ears it sounded wavering; in his, touched only with surprise.

"Do you remember that evening we dined together?" he asked in reply.

Could she forget it? She nodded her head in silence.

"If you recollect, I said I wished to offer my friendship?"

Her head nodded again. She did not make it easy for him; but the social training inures one to the difficulties of forging conversation. He ploughed through with a straight, undeviating edge that in no way displeased her.

"Well, I don't want to distress you by going over the whole business which, as you might quite justly say, was none of mine. I thought you might find it a bit lonely, and so, as I'd taken you out to dinner before"—he raised his eyes, finishing the sentence with a smile and lifting eyebrows. "Were you going out to dinner now?" he added, before she had time to reply.

"Yes, I was."

"Then will you come with me?"

She met his gaze with frank speculation. What did it matter where she went? Who was there to care? Janet, the only one, would urge her to it if she knew. There was no doubt in her mind that friendship had prompted him. It was a considerate thought on his part to come and offer to take her out because he had imagined she might be lonely. She felt grateful to him, but with no desire to show it. If it pleased him to be generous on her behalf, why should she refuse to profit by it? But here was no thought of giving in return. A woman seldom meets but one man in the world to whom she will give without a shadow of the desire for the value in return. What was there in the world now to prevent her from taking what life offered of its small, distracting pleasures? A moment of recklessness brought a deceptive lift to her spirits.

"I shall be very glad to," she said.

In her mind was no unfaithfulness to the memory of Traill. Unfaithful, even to a slender memory, it was not in her nature to be. The benefit of the Church now was the only door through which she could pass out of his life. She considered no likelihood of it; for, in common with those of her sex in whom the strong waters of emotion run deep in the vein of sentiment, she felt—being once possessed by him—that he was the lord of her life.

"But I warn you," she added, with a pathetic smile, "I shan't be good company. You'll have to do all the talking. You'll have to make all the jokes."

"I'm prepared to do as much and more," he said lightly.

"Then you must wait while I put on my hat. Play the piano—can you?"

"No—not I. Can you?"

"Yes—just a little."

"Sing?"

E. Temple Thurston

"Yes—sometimes."

"Ah, that settles it. We come back here after dinner, and you sing every song in your repertoire."

She laughed brightly at his enthusiasm. "You're really fond of music?" she said.

"Yes, passionately. And I suffer little for my passion because I know absolutely nothing about it. That's a promise, then? You'll sing to me after dinner?"

"Yes, I should love to."

So much had her spirits lifted in this deceptive atmosphere of diversion that Devenish even heard her humming a tune in the other room. And he smiled, looking up to the ceiling with hands spread out and fingers lightly playing one upon the other.

At a restaurant in Great Portland Street, shut off from the rest of the room by the astute arrangement of a screen—ranged around every table, presumably to ward off the draught—they dined in comparative seclusion. Into the selection of that dinner Devenish put a great part of his ingenuity. The man who knows how to choose a meal and savour those intervals between the courses with anecdote, has reached a high-water mark of social excellence. Devenish was the type. He was not hampered with the possession of intelligence. Wit he had, but it was not his own. The man, after all, who can echo the wit of others and suit its application to the moment is a man of no little accomplishment. The least that can be said of him is that he is worthy of his place at a dinner-table where conversation is as empty as the bubbles that shoot through the glittering wine to the frothy surface. To suffer from intelligence in such an atmosphere as this is a disease—the silent sickness—of which such symptoms as the lips tight bound, the heart heavy, and an aching void behind the eyes, are common to all its victims. Later, in the course of its development, if the attack is acute, comes the forced speech from lips now scarcely opened—forced speech recognizable by its various degrees of imbecility. The man, for instance, who asks you if you have been to a theatre lately when you have just deftly foisted upon the company the latest joke you heard in a musical comedy, has reached that stage of the disease when retirement is the only cure. Like quinine in fever districts, there is one drug which may ward off the icy fingers of the complaint—champagne—but it should be administered at frequent intervals.

From such a malady as this, Devenish was not only immune, but he carried with him that lightness of spirit which may go far to relieve others of their suffering. Add to this a face well-featured, a figure well-planned with all the alertness of an athlete, an immaculate taste in dress, and you have the type which the 'Varsity mould offers yearly to the ephemeral needs of her country. The impression remains, stamped upon the man until he is well-nigh forty. He knows how to get drunk in the most gentlemanly way and his judgment about women is sometimes very shrewd. A knowledge of the classics is of service to him if he does nothing. If, on the other hand, he sets about the earning of his living—a drudgery that some of these youths are compelled to submit to—the classics are only the peas in the shoe which, as a pilgrim to the far-off shrine of utility, he is compelled to wear.

Not having to earn his own livelihood, or rather, having already earned it in the profession of matrimony into which he had entered in partnership with a wealthy woman, Devenish was a pride to the college which had turned him out.

E. Temple Thurston

He knew most of those people in London who range in the category of—worth knowing. Anecdotes of them all—those little personal insights into private domestic relations of which surely there must somewhere be an illicit still, hidden in the mountains where gossip echoes—he had at the tips of his fingers.

"Surely you've heard that last thing that Mrs.—said at the first night of—;" and thereafter follows some quaint conceit—smuggled, God knows how, from the illicit still in the mountains, stamped with a fictitious year to give it flavour—which the well-known actress in question would have offered her soul to have said on the occasion alluded to in the story, but which she had never even thought of.

It may be concluded, then, from these apparently needless digressions that Devenish was good company. He did his best to amuse Sally—he succeeded. When they were halfway through the dinner and he had casually refilled her glass with champagne, she was prepared to see humour in everything he said.

There is a mood of recklessness—wild determined reckless-ness—that strikes, like a light in the heavens, across the face of despair. In such a mood was Sally then. Her mind, empty of the vice which so often accompanies it, was echoing with the cry—What does it matter? What does it matter? When he filled her glass a second time, she half raised a hand from her lap to stop him. But what did it matter? It would put her in good spirits, and in good spirits she felt the strong desire to be. Between this and the harmful result of the wine, so far a call was stretched in her mind that she never let it enter her consideration. Let him fill her glass a second time! She was to return to rooms empty but of the bitterest of associations. The whole long night had to be passed through with that haunting speculation—which now so frequently beset her—the wondering of what Traill was doing, the questioning in what woman's arms he was finding the joy of desire which he had found in hers.

What did it signify then, this evening in which she let go the strained reserve which at any other time she would have retained? What did it signify, so long as the deepest beating of her heart was unmoved by the quickened pulses and the eyes alight with a reckless laughter?

It mattered nothing to her who knew its meaning; but to Devenish, seeing the colour lifting to her cheeks, watching the sparkling in those eyes which had met his but an hour or more ago, when disappointed hope had thrown them into deep shadows, there was a tentative significance. It appealed to the lowest nature of his senses to see her, whom he had long desired, unbending in her reticence. Her laughter was a whip about his body; her lips, parted—losing that expression of restraint—were becoming an obsession to his eyes. But he guarded all his actions with a steady hand.

When her glass was empty for the second time, he stretched out his hand to refill it again.

"Oh—I'd better not have any more," she said lightly. "Whatever would you do with me if I took too much?" And she laughed. Laughed, he imagined, at the possibilities that rose to her mind, and it was on the edge of his lips to say the things he would do.

"Another glass can't hurt you," he said, laughing with her. "Here—I'll fill mine—there"—he held up the bottle for her to see—"Now you have the remainder. You don't want me to drink it all, do you? I should like to know what you'd do—I suppose you'd give me in charge of the head waiter? I guess you'd shirk your responsibilities more than I would." And as

E. Temple Thurston

he talked, he emptied the bottle into her glass beneath the fringe of the conversation.

"Ever hear that story," he began again, and caught her attention once more with an idle tale that had worn its way through half the clubs in Town. His yarns were all fresh to her, and, moreover, he spun them amazingly well. There was none of that disconcerting fear of their staleness to thwart him—no need for the tentative preface—"You'll say if you've heard this before." One suggested another—they rolled off his tongue. And while she sipped her champagne, he kept her amused; never allowed her the moments of inaction in which to relent. He amused himself. The old, worn-out story has all the humour still keen in it for you—if *you* tell it. It was no effort, no strain to Devenish. He laughed as heartily as she did over the stale old jests. Their novelty to her made them new to him. She leant her elbows on the table and watched his face as he told them.

"Now," he said, when they had finished their coffee, "how about the songs? I've done my share of the entertainment. As soon as I've got the bill, we'll go back, and you can supply the more serious items of the programme."

"Really—I'm afraid I couldn't. I believe you think I sing well—I don't. I did think of going on the stage once—into musical comedy—but not because I was musical."

"Well—of course not. It isn't a refuge for the art. But I have my belief in your being able to sing. You're not going to shake that."

"Very well—I suppose I'll try." Her hands lifted to her face. "My cheeks are burning. Do they look very red?"

"No—not particularly—the room's warm, I think."

She permitted herself to be satisfied with that explanation. Had a mirror been near at hand, she would have realized in its reflection that the warmth of the room was not the only cause for the flushed scarlet of her cheeks, or the light that glittered in the expanded pupils of her eyes.

When Devenish had paid the bill, they departed. A hansom conveyed them back to Sally's rooms in Regent Street. Once seated in it, she leaned back in the corner, and her eyes closed.

"I do feel so awfully sleepy," she said, ingenuously.

He glanced at her swiftly. Was that simplicity, or a veiled request for him to close his arms about her? How could she be simple? The mistress of a man for three years—what simplicity could be left in her now? Undoubtedly she must know—of course she knew by now—the thoughts that were travelling wildly through his mind.

"Poor child," he said considerately—"I suppose you are."

Her eyes opened to that. She sat a little straighter in the corner. There was a tone in his voice more subtle than friendship. Her ears had heard it, but her senses were too drowsy then to dwell for long upon its consideration.

He would have said more—in another moment, he would have slipped his arm around her waist, had it not been for her sudden movement of reserve. That warned him. Unconsciously a woman gives out of herself the impression of whether she be easy of winning or not. With Sally, notwithstanding all the circumstances that ranged against her in his mind, Devenish realized that an inconsidered step would be fatal to his desires. That did not thwart him. He admired her the more for it; wanted her the more.

E. Temple Thurston

When they reached her rooms and, taking off her hat, she seated herself at the piano, creating in the susceptibility of his mind a greater sense of the intimacy of their relations, he stood at the other side of the room watching her, content to let his anticipations slowly drift upon the quiet stream of events to the ultimate cataract of their realization.

This is the true nature of the sensualist. Woman or man, whatever sex, you may know them by their feline delight in the procrastination of the moment. It is an evolution of the intellect. The raw, unbridled forces of nature have no dealings with such as these. They are people of pleasure. They have taken the gifts that Nature has offered and, with the subtle cunning of their minds, have torn the inviolable parchment of her laws to shreds before her face. With no inheritance of the intellect, Devenish possessed all the other qualities. Sensualist as he was, with that strain of refinement induced by the easy circumstances of life, the paid women disgusted him. Of mere animalism, he had none. Here in this widest essential, his nature marked its contrast with Traill. To admit the beast in every man would have been beyond him; simply because the admission of a generalization such as that, would most directly have implied himself. In Traill's concession of it, such an admission may easily be read. And this is the type of man, such as Devenish, most dangerous to society.

If the threadbare hypocrisy of this country of England could but bring itself to don the acknowledgment that the hired woman has her place in the scheme of things, such men as Devenish would find the virtuous woman more closely guarded from their strategies than she is.

When her first song was finished, Sally turned in her chair, laughing frankly to his eyes.

"You needn't suffer on account of your passion for music by having to criticize," she said. "I know it was awful."

He crossed the room to her side. "As you like," he said, bringing his eyes full to hers. "You can call it anything you please—but I want some more." He picked up the pieces of music that lay on the top of the piano. "Do you sing that song out of the Persian Garden—Beside the Shalimar? I forget the words of it?"

Her fingers ran through the pile of music. "'Pale Hands I Loved.' Is that it?" She lifted her face and looked up at him.

"Yes—yes—sing that!"

"I'm afraid I haven't got the music—can't play without the music."

He drew a deep breath. "That's a pity," he said.

"Well—listen—I'll sing this."

She placed the music before her on the rest, and with one hand on the back of her chair, the other resting on the piano, he bent over her, eyes wandering from the gold of her hair to the parting of her lips as she sang. It was just such a song as he had asked for; filled with the abandoned sentimentalism of decadent passion—

> "Lord of my life, than whom none other shareth
> The deep, red, silent wine that fills my soul—
> Take thou and drain, till not one drop remaineth
> To wet thy lips—then turn thou down the bowl.
>
> "Lord of my heart—this boon I crave—this only,
> That all my worth may be possessed by thee;

E. Temple Thurston

Make thou my life a chalice, drained, that lonely
Stands on the altar of Eternity."

She looked up at him as her fingers wandered to the final chord. His lips were set in a thin line, and he was breathing quickly.

"Why did you sing that?" he asked.

She blindly shrugged her shoulders. "I don't know—why shouldn't I? The music's a good deal nicer than the words, I think. Don't you find the words are rather silly? They are of most songs, I think."

"And you call that silly," he said. "I suppose it's a woman's song—but, my God! do you know I could sing that to you?"

His arm was round her then, dragging her towards him in a lithe grip, the fierce strength of which she too well under-stood. She struggled, breathing heavily, for her freedom; but he caught her face in his hand, dragged it to his lips and covered her with kisses.

Then she broke free, rising to her feet, overturning the chair behind her, pushing back the disordered hair from her forehead.

"How dare you!" she breathed.

Countless women have said it, in countless moments similar to this. And with it, often, seeing all the circumstances that have led up to it in their different light, comes the knowledge—as it came also to Sally—the understanding of how the man has dared. Recklessness had led her. In her heart, she blamed herself. She might have known men now; known them from her knowledge at least of one man.

Undoubtedly she was to blame, taking everything into account—the defencelessness of her position, the fact that he had known of her relationship with Traill and its termination; yet her eyes flamed with contempt as they met his.

"Your hat is over on that chair." she said presently in a strident voice. "Will you go?"

He crossed the room quietly—no want of composure—and picked it up.

"Would you rather I didn't come and see you again?" he asked, brushing the hat casually with his sleeve.

"I never want to see you again!" she exclaimed.

He smiled amiably. "Don't you think you're rather foolish?"

"Foolish!"

"Yes—the unmarried man who keeps a woman is bound to leave her some time or other—that's not half as likely to be the case with—"

"What do you mean?" She was white to the lips.

He looked puzzled. "I'm afraid I can't understand you," he said.

She tried to answer him, but the words mingled in a stammering of confusion before she could utter them.

"You don't think there's a chance of Traill coming back to you, do you?" he went on. "I shouldn't be here, I assure you, if there were."

Sally's knees trembled with weakness. An overwhelming nausea shook her till she shuddered.

"Did he tell you to come here?" she whispered.

"Heavens, no! I don't suppose he'd do that. He wouldn't do a thing like that. But I'm pretty sure he's in love with that Miss Standish-Roe—the beautiful Coralie. He knows it. He won't admit it; but I'm certain he is, and I rather think I'd better open his eyes a little."

That last remark did not fall within her understanding. She took no notice of it.

"And so you came here of your own accord?"

"Yes—why not? I had an apparently erroneous idea that you liked me. When you let me come back here after dinner, I was sure of it. I saw no reason why we shouldn't get along together just as well as you and Traill did."

"Oh!" she exclaimed, and she hid her face in her hand.

"Oh yes—I see my mistake by this time," he said easily. All passion was cooled in him now. "I'm sorry. There was no intention of insulting you in my mind." He moved to the door. "I—I thought you understood it."

Sally dropped into a chair, her face still covered; shame—the deepest sense of it—beating through all her pulses.

"Well—I must only hope you'll excuse my—my ignorance of women, though I must admit you're a bit different to the rest. Well—I suppose I'd better say good night, then."

She heard him take the step forward. She could see in her

mind the hand held out, but she did not look up. He turned again to the door. She heard it open. She heard it close. She heard his footsteps slowly descending the stairs. And still she sat there with her face close-buried in her hands.

E. Temple Thurston

# CHAPTER IV

You are never to know how deep the iron has entered your soul until Fate begins to draw it out.

When Traill had left her, Sally's mind had been numbed with misery. The despair of such loneliness as hers is often a narcotic, that drugs all power of thought. In the beating of her pulses, when she had first heard Devenish's footsteps mounting the stairs, she was forced to the realization that hope was not yet dead in the heart of her. That undoubtedly was why, despite all Janet's efforts, she had refused to leave her rooms. The hope that Traill would one day return, that one evening she would hear his steps on the stairs, his knock on the door, had needed only such a coincidence as the unexpected visit of Devenish to stir it into vivid animation. Just so had the Rev. Samuel Bishop hoped, in the fulfilment of his duties as chaplain, that one day the rectorship of Cailsham would return to his possession; just so had he been imbued with faith, the same as hers, when he had shuddered at his narrow avoidance of sacrilege in the vestry of the little church at Steynton. To him, at that moment, it would have been as impossible to pour back the consecrated into the unconsecrated wine, as it had been for Sally to lose assurance that Traill would one day return to her.

But now it was different. The iron, in the sure grasp of the fingers of Fate, was being torn out of her. She could feel it wrenching its way from the very depths. Traill would never come back. It was not so much because she had heard he was in love, that she realized it; that—even then—her faith, in its ashes, repudiated. But when Devenish had said—alluding to the faintest chance of his return—"I shouldn't be here, I assure you, if there were," she had been made conscious of Traill's tacit permission—unspoken no doubt—to Devenish which had prompted his visit to her rooms.

But last and most poignant of all in the bitterness of this lesson that she had learnt, was her understanding of the place she held in the eyes of such men as Devenish. With those who knew of her life, no friendship was possible. One relationship, one only could exist—a relationship, at the thought of which her whole nature shuddered in violent disgust.

Janet was right. Janet had seen things from their proper point of view. As a trade she should have looked at it. As the leaving of one master to labour in the service of another she should have weighed its issue. Yet, even now, the cruelty of that outlook revolted her. Had she viewed it thus, those three years of absolute happiness could never have been and she could not even forego the memory of them.

But the knowledge that had come to her, brought decision with it. She could stay no longer where she was. The thought of meeting just those few people whom she knew, who knew her, in the streets, drove the blood burning to her forehead. She must go away—away from London—away from every chance incident that might fling back in her face the tragedy of her existence. Away from all its associations she would be able to hide it; not from herself, not from the biting criticism of her own thoughts. But from others; she could hide it from them.

E. Temple Thurston

That night she wrote to Janet asking her to come and see her; and the next day they sat opposite to each other at a table in a quiet restaurant up West.

"I'm going to take your advice," Sally began.

"You're going away?"

"Yes."

"When?"

"At once; in a day or two, as soon as I hear from mother. I wrote to her this morning."

"What did you say?"

"I said that I'd saved up some money and, as I hadn't been very well, I wanted to come down and stay with her for a change. I suggested that I might be of some use in the school."

"Yes, that's all right. But for goodness' sake don't let her see that you've got a lot of money. The wives of clergymen, as far as I've ever seen, are weaned on the milk of suspicion. They'll never believe anybody's properly married but themselves; I suppose that's because they're in the trade. I know Mr. Cheeseman thinks nobody's furniture genuine, except his own. That's always a little business failing. But you ought to be careful."

"But I haven't any too much money," said Sally quietly.

Janet gazed up at her in unsympathetic surprise. "That's rather unlike you," she said abruptly. "I think he was very generous. A hundred and fifty a year, free of rent for three years, is more, I imagine, than most men would drag out of their pockets. You could make what living you liked beside that, if you chose to. I know I should jolly-well think myself a Croesus with that capital."

Her tone of voice was hard with criticism.

"But do you think I take all he's offered me?" asked Sally.

"Do you mean to say you don't?"

"No, I take the very least I can. A pound a week is all I want for my food; what else should I want? I wouldn't touch another penny of it but that till the three years are over. I have all the clothes I could possibly want. You thought I was mean, didn't you, Janet?"

Janet looked up at the ceiling, then impulsively held out her hand.

"God help me!" she exclaimed, "if I find my own sex an enigma; but what on earth made you decide?"

"Mr. Devenish."

"Who?"

"Mr. Devenish, the man I told you I was dining with that night, six weeks ago."

"Why him, in the name of Heaven?"

"He came to see me last night."

"Well?"

"He took me out to dinner."

"Very good thing too. You want a little of that sort of entertaining. Did he advise you to go?"

"No—"

"Then what?"

She could see the colour mounting and falling in Sally's cheeks and her suspicions sped to a conclusion.

"He made love to me," said Sally. Her hand went to her eyes. She covered them.

"Oh, I see. You want to get away from him? You don't like him? Think he's going to be a nuisance?"

"No, it's not that." She still hid her face. "I don't think he'd ever come and see me again, now."

"Then what?"

"It was what he said."

"What did he say?"

"He wanted— Oh!"

Janet leant forward on the table. "To take Traill's place— eh?"

"Yes."

Janet leant back in her chair and looked scrutinizingly at Sally's head, bent into her hands, and from what she knew by this time of Sally's nature, there came the understanding of what such a proposal must have meant.

"And what else did you expect?" she asked gently. "Most men are the same. News that there is a woman to be found situated such as you are spreads through the ranks of them like—like—like a prairie fire. It goes whispering from one lip to another. You can never tell where it starts. You can never tell where it ends. As soon as a man knows that money can buy a woman he wants, he'll scrape the bottom of the Bank of England to get it. I told you before, it's a business! Why in the name of Heaven can't you give up all your romanticism? If you don't want to go on with it, to be absolutely brutal, if you don't want to make it pay, why can't you take all the money that Traill's given you and go away from here altogether? Well—you are going—thank the Lord for that much sense! But go, and take all you can get with you. Save it up if you won't spend it; and that's better still. But, for God's sake, take it, it's yours! Surely you've earned it. I should think you had."

Sally dropped her hands and looked up. "I don't know why you and I have ever got on together, Janet," she said brokenly. "I could never conceive two people more absolutely opposite. I sometimes hate the things you say, but I nearly always love you for saying them. I loathe the things you've said now. If I thought like that, I can't see what there would be to stop me from sinking as low—as low as a woman can. Do you really mean to say that you'd do like that if you cared for a man, as I do for Jack? Would you grasp every penny he'd left you?"

"I don't know. I should either do that, or not take a farthing of it. Make my own living, earn my own way, be independent at any cost."

E. Temple Thurston

"Do you mean I ought to do that?"

"I don't mean you ought, because I know you couldn't. You could no more go and earn your own living now—now that you've learnt the ease and luxury of living in a man's arms—than you could fly. You aren't the type, Sally; you never were."

Sally's lips pressed together. "You think I love the ease and luxury?" she said bitterly. "You think as poorly of me as that?"

"I don't think poorly at all. You were never meant to work. Your curse is the curse of Eve, not Adam. You ought to have a child. You wouldn't be wasting your soul out on a man then. You'd take every farthing that Traill's left you, as it's only right you should. You don't see any right in it now; but you would then. Every single thing in the world is worth its salt, and a child 'ud be the salt of life to you. When do you think you'll hear from your mother?"

"To-morrow, perhaps."

"Well, then, directly you hear you can go—go! Don't stop in London another second. It's a pitiable purgatory for you now. Go and look after the little kiddies in the school. You'll know quick enough what I mean about the curse of Eve, when you find one of them tugging at your skirts for sympathy."

## END OF BOOK III

# BOOK IV

## THE EMPTY HORIZON

### CHAPTER I

Cailsham—one of those small antiquated towns which, in its day, has had its name writ in history—sits at the feet of the hills, like an old man, weary of toil, and gazes out with sleepy eyes over the garden of Kent. In the spring, the country is patched with white around—white, with the blossoms in the fruit plantations. Broad acres of cherry orchards spread their snow-white sheets out in the sun—a giant's washing-day. The little lanes wind tortuous ways between the fields of apple bloom, and off in the forest of the tree stems, lying lazily in the high-grown grass, dappled yellow with sunlight, you will find in every orchard a boy, idly beating a monotonous tattoo to scare away the birds. A collection of tin pots in various stages of dilapidation, each one emitting a different hollow note, are spread around him, and there he lies the day through till nightfall, eating the meals that are brought him, humming a tune between them to pass away the time; but ceaselessly beating a discordant dominant upon his sounding drums of tin. This is Cailsham in the spring. Cailsham at any time is more the country that surrounds it. All its colours, all its life, all its interests, it takes from those great, wide gardens of fruit as they break

E. Temple Thurston

from leaf into blossom, blossom to fruit, from fruit to the black, naked branches of winter, when Cailsham itself sinks into the silence of a well-earned, lethargic repose. Then they talk of the fruit seasons that are past, and the fruit seasons that are to come. The lights burn out early in the windows, and by ten o'clock the little town is asleep.

This is Cailsham. The narrow High Street and the miniature Exchange, the square of the market-place and the stone fountain that stands with such an effort of nobility in the centre, bearing upon one of its rough slabs the name of the munificent donor, and the occasion on which the towns-people were presented with its cherished possession—these are nothing. They are only accessories. The real Cailsham is to be found in the apple, the plum, and the cherry orchards. From these, either as owners or as labourers, all the inhabitants draw their source of life, with the exception of those few shopkeepers whose premises extend in a disorderly fashion down the High Street; the Rector, who has his interest in the fruit season as well as the rest; and lastly, Mrs. Bishop, headmistress of that little school in Wyatt Street, where the sons of gentlemen are fitted for such exigencies of life as are to be met with between the ages of four and eight.

With the name of Lady Bray to conjure popularity, she had set up her establishment immediately after her husband's death. Then the old lady herself had fallen asleep—in her case a literal description of her disease. One night they had put her quietly to bed as usual, and in the morning she was still asleep—a slumber which really must be rest.

Fortunately for Mrs. Bishop the school was planted then. Twenty pupils sat round the cheap kitchen tables in the schoolroom—all sons of gentlemen—whose mothers paid occasional visits to the house and peeped into the schoolroom, after they had partaken of tea with Mrs. Bishop in the drawing-room. Whenever this incident occurred, the little boys rose electrically from their forms in courteous deference to the visitor; and the boy, whose mother it was, would blush with pride and look away, or he would frankly smile up to his mother's eyes. Then Mrs. Bishop would inevitably eulogize his progress as she sped the parting guest, making inquiries from her daughters afterwards to ascertain how near she had gone to the truth. One boarder only she accepted into the establishment. It had not been her intention to have any. But one day a lady had written from Winchester to say that through a friend of a friend of Lady Bray's, she had heard of Mrs. Bishop's preparatory school for the sons of gentlemen. She was compelled, she concluded in her letter, to go for some little time to live in London and, though she knew that Mrs. Bishop only accepted day pupils at her house, she would consider it a great favour if, for a term or so, she would consent to the admission of her son as a boarder. If such an arrangement were possible, she would be glad to know the terms which Mrs. Bishop would deem most reasonable.

For the rest of that day there had been unprecedented excitement at No. 17, Wyatt Street. Until late that evening Elsie and Dora Bishop, in consultation with their mother, went into all the financial details of the undertaking. Little Maurice Priestly could sleep in the small room at the top of the house, used then as a box room. The smallness of the window in the sloping ceiling could easily be disguised by lace curtains at six three-farthings a yard.

"Put that down," Mrs. Bishop had said; and the item of capital outlay had gone down on a half-sheet of note-paper.

To Cailsham they had brought with them an old armchair convertible, at considerable risk to the fingers, into a

E. Temple Thurston

shake-down bed.

"We needn't buy a bed, then," said Mrs. Bishop.

"No; but it'll need some sort of coverlet to make it look decent. I've seen them at Robinson's in the High Street for two and eleven-three."

"Put that down," said Mrs. Bishop.

By ten o'clock the list of expenses had been compiled. By eleven o'clock it was decided what would be the cost of board and lodging for an adult—a little being added on to that for visionary extras—soap, light, towels, and suchlike, less visionary than others, but extras nevertheless.

When Mallins, the constable on night duty, passed down Wyatt Street at quarter-past eleven and saw a light in No. 17, he stopped in amazement and gazed through a chink in the old Venetian blind.

"It's 'ard on that Mrs. Bishop," he said to his wife the next morning, "the way she 'as to work."

That same morning a letter had been despatched to Mrs. Priestly, and by return of post came the reply—

"I suppose what you ask is quite reasonable. I am bringing Maurice to you the day after to-morrow."

"Suppose!" said Elsie.

"We couldn't do it for less," said Mrs. Bishop.

"And the box room'll look really quite comfortable," Dora joined in. "I've just put the bed up. I never thought it was such a nice little room."

Two days afterwards Mrs. Priestly and little Maurice had made their appearance. The slowest of the three flies in the town of Cailsham drove them up to the door and, for the moment, all work in the schoolroom had been suspended. The twenty sons of gentlemen, left to themselves, behaved as the sons of gentlemen—of any men, in fact-will do. There was an uproar in the schoolroom which Dora, before she had obtained a proper view of Mrs. Priestly from behind the door of the pantry at the end of the long hall, was compelled to go and reduce to silence. Having been deprived of the grati- fication of her curiosity, her effort had been with unqualified success. Between the ages of four and eight a boy can be quelled by a look. That look, the twenty sons of gentlemen received.

Mrs. Priestly was a tall woman, graceful and, for one who lived in one of the smaller of the provincial towns, elegantly dressed. Her face and its expression were sad. The quietness of her manner and the gentle reserve of her voice added to that sadness. The patient gaze of her deep grey eyes suggested suffering. Undoubtedly she had suffered. To the sympathetic observer, this would have been obvious; but to the calculating mind of Mrs. Bishop it presented itself in the form of a social aloofness which she was morbidly quick to see in any one.

Mrs. Priestly was dark. Little Maurice was fair—the Saxon stamped on his head, coloured in his blue eyes. He was six years old, abundant in extreme animal spirits, which his mother beheld with a love and pride in her eyes that was almost pathetic to see in one so possessed by the apathy of unhappiness, and which Mrs. Bishop observed with the silent resolve that Master Maurice was on no account to be allowed into her drawing-room.

E. Temple Thurston

When it had come to the moment of leaving her son to the glowing promises of Mrs. Bishop's tenderness and affection, Mrs. Priestly broke down, winding her arms tight about his little neck and pressing him fiercely to her bosom. Mrs. Bishop stood by with an indulgent smile.

Then Mrs. Priestly had looked up with tears heavy in her eyes.

"I'll come and see you, Mrs. Bishop," she had said with control—"I'll come and see you when I've said good-bye, before I go."

Mrs. Bishop had wisely taken the suggestion and departed to the end of the hall where her daughters were standing expectantly.

"Of course the child is spoilt," she said, in an undertone.

"Why?" they asked in chorus.

"Well, she's saying good-bye to him—crying over him. I call it very nonsensical. I came away. That sort of thing annoys me."

And in the drawing-room, mother and son were saying a long farewell that was to last them for a few weeks. It would be some time before she could come down from London, Mrs. Priestly had said. The tears were falling fast down their cheeks.

"You won't love any one else but mummy, will you, Maurie?"

"Shan't love her," he had said, with a thrusting of his head towards the door which Mrs. Bishop had just closed.

"And you'll say prayers every night and every morning?"

"Yes, mummy."

"And you'll say, 'God help mummy'"

"Will I pray for father?"

She took a deep breath as she looked above his head. He was too young to feel the weight of the pause. It meant nothing to him. He thought she had not heard.

"Will I pray for father?" he repeated.

"Yes," she said slowly; "pray for father, pray for him first, and then mummy, just before you go to sleep. God bless you, my little darling—" and in the fierce blinding passion which a mother alone can understand, she caught him again in her arms and crushed his yielding little body to her heart.

Such was the arrival of Master Maurice Priestly at No. 17, Wyatt Street.

When she arrived, some three weeks after this event, Sally found a little fair-haired boy with sad blue eyes whom at night, in the room next to hers, she sometimes heard crying. She had mentioned this to her mother.

"Oh, take no notice of it, Sally," she said. "It's probably a noise he makes in his sleep."

Sally had become a welcome addition to the household. She had offered to pay liberally for her board while she stayed there and, during that visit, however long it should prove to be, they had been able to dispense with the services of Miss Hatch, the music-mistress, who came regularly every morning from ten till twelve and was a considerable drain on the net profits of the establishment. Sally, unconscious of the change, filled her place. From a quarter-past ten, until half-past, her pupil was Maurice, and on the day she had spoken to her mother about his crying, she also questioned him.

"I wasn't crying," he said proudly. "I couldn't cry."

He found it easy to say that in the bright light of the morning. But it was a different matter at night. That very night again he wept. She could hear his sobs stifled in the pillow. She was going to bed. When the sound reached her ears, she stopped, listening. It *was* crying! She opened her door gently. Certainly it was the sound of crying! Then, half-undressed, not thinking to cover her shoulders, she crept across the passage to his door, opened it and peered inside.

"Maurie," she whispered.

The crying stopped.

"Maurie," she repeated, "you are crying."

He admitted it—sadly; they had found him out. Now they would think he was a baby. That was the inevitable accusation in the mind of these people who were grown up—in the mind of every one, except his mother.

"But I'm not a baby!" he exclaimed.

Sally knelt down by the side of his bed. "Who said you were a baby?" she whispered.

"You were just going to."

"No, I wasn't. I don't think you are a baby. I cry sometimes."

"Do you?" There was a thin note of amazement in his voice. "What do you cry for?"

"Oh, lots of things. What do you?"

"For mummy—it's so cold in bed without mummy."

"Do you sleep with mummy, then?" she asked, and she slid a warm arm around his sturdy little neck.

"Yes—always. Mummy's so warm and she lies so tight. Your arm's warm—I like your arm." He felt it with his fingers. "What's that?" he asked suddenly.

"What's what?" said Sally.

"Something wet fell on the back of my hand. Why, it's you—it's you. You're crying. Aren't you? You're crying. Oh, I wonder if you're a baby. I don't see why you should be, if you don't think I am. Why are you crying?"

"I don't know."

"Oh, but you must know! I always know why I'm crying. I cry at nights when it's all dark, and you can't hear anything. I cry then because I want mummy. Mummy cries sometimes though, and she doesn't know why."

"Do you ask her, then?"

"Yes; and she says she doesn't know. So I suppose ladies don't know sometimes, but boys always do. But you won't say I cried, will you? Promise!"

"I promise," she said firmly.

"Because the others 'ud think I was a baby if they knew, and I'm not really a baby—not in the morning, am I?"

"No; not a bit."

"You wouldn't think I was a baby when you give me my music lesson, would you?"

"No; I always think you're very brave."

He twisted about in the bed. "Put your other arm round my neck, will you?—like mummy does. She always puts both arms—it's much warmer."

She clasped him with both arms.

"Ah; that's better," he said. "I hope mummy wouldn't mind, because she said I wasn't to love any one else but her. But, of course, I don't really love you, you know. I like you because you're warm."

"You don't love me, then?"

"No; how could I? I could only love mummy, really. Oh, there it is again! You're still crying, you know."

"Yes; I know I am."

"I suppose you wouldn't come into bed and cry—it's much warmer."

A sob broke in Sally's throat.

Here now it had come—so soon as this—the fulfilment of Janet's prophecy. The curse of Eve was no mystery to her now. She knew. She knew what life lacked.

"No; you must go to sleep now, Maurie," she said thickly. "You must go to sleep now. You mustn't cry any more."

"Very well, then," he said resignedly. "You must promise you won't too."

"I promise I won't. Good night."

And so, to keep her promise, lest he should hear as she had heard, she lay on her bed and buried her face in the pillow. But she cried.

E. Temple Thurston

# CHAPTER II

That night began their friendship. In that night was sown the seed of the new idea in her mind, which neither the wild passion of her love for Traill, nor all the stern preaching of Janet's philosophy had caused to take root before. A child— she knew that now—a child would save her. A child would make this life of hers worth while. And, having none, she set her heart, as you set a lure with cunning hands, to win the love of little Maurice Priestly.

At the age of six, a boy-child is constituted of impressions— soft wax to the working of any fingers that touch his heart. In their ramblings together, through the orchards where the ripening apples turned up their bonny faces, peering through the leaves to find the sun; up the side of the hills, exploring the hidden dangers of the hollow chalk-pits—climbing always to see what the world looked like on the other side— they came to know each other; Sally to know all his little faults, sometimes of pride, sometimes of lovable boast- fulness; he to know that her heart was aching—aching for something—something that he could not comprehend. But fancy wove the story for him. He must have a story with which to realize that her heart really was aching.

"If there's no story," he said, "I shan't really believe you're sad."

So they sat on the side of the hills, looking out over the head of the tired old man—the little town of Cailsham—and seeing with their eyes what the tired old man saw all day long—the abundant garden of England. There Maurice told her the story of her misery, in which fairies and goblins and giants and witches moved in quick and sudden passage across the vistas of his vivid imagination.

"And that's why you're sad," he said at its conclusion. "If only the prince had not done what the witch told him, you'd have been perfectly happy, wouldn't you?"

Sally put her arm round his neck, lifted the soft, smooth little face to hers, and kissed it.

"Yes, that's why," she said gently; "but you must never tell any one."

"Mayn't I tell mummy?" he pleaded.

She took her arm from his neck and looked straight before her. The moment of jealousy sped through her—shame rode fierce behind.

"Yes," she replied, "you can tell mummy."

The weeks of the summer flew by. No sympathy was lost between her mother and herself. Her sisters frankly were jealous of her. She had better clothes than they, knew more of the world, was more interesting to strangers in her conversation. The people of Cailsham, treating her first as one of the Bishops—the one who had lived in London, earning her living—came to find that she was a different type of person to the rest of her family. The women admitted her to look smart; the men—at the weekly teas which some member of the tennis club always provided—sought out her company.

And then, to compensate for all the unpleasantness in her home, there was Maurie—Maurie whom every night since that first occasion of their friendship she said good night to. With arms round each other's necks, they said their prayers together—Sally who had offered no supplication on her knees since the night when Traill had left her.

"I scarcely thought it possible to be so happy," she wrote to Janet. "I absolutely look forward to the waking in the mornings now, because then I go in and wake him up, kiss his dear, brave little face as it lies on the pillow fast asleep; and then he kneels on the bed, puts his arms round my neck, and we say our prayers together. That means nothing to you, I expect; but don't laugh at it. Oh, Janet, I wish he were mine."

She was woman enough, too, to find some consolation in the attention which the people of Cailsham paid to her. She was gratified by the interest which the men in the little town, and principal amongst them, Wilfrid Grierson, showed in her whenever they met. He was the eldest son of the largest fruit farmer in the town—a man, therefore, in much request, conspicuous at every party to which it was thought considerate to ask Mrs. Bishop and her daughters. To Sally's mind, nauseated still whenever she thought of it by the light in which Devenish had seen her, the possibility of a man falling in love with her was remote from her consideration. She was brought abruptly to its realization by a remark which Dora, her younger sister, dropped for her benefit.

"If Mr. Grierson wasn't so eminently sensible," she said one evening after a tea which Mrs. Bishop had given at the tennis club, "one would feel inclined to think that he'd lost his head over you, Sally."

A flame of colour spread across Sally's cheeks. "Let's be

thankful that he's eminently sensible, then," she replied.

"What—do you mean to say you wouldn't marry him?"

"He hasn't asked me—surely that's sufficient. He never will. My position in life is not the position that he's ever likely to choose a wife from."

"Your position, Sally," said Mrs. Bishop, looking up from the writing of a letter at the other end of the room, "so long as you are with us, is the same as ours."

"Yes, I'm quite aware of that, mother. So I say it's quite unlikely that he will ever ask me to marry him."

Then she left the room, and they discussed the advisability of keeping her with them. The fact that she saved the expense of Miss Hatch's services as music-mistress weighed ponderously in the balance, swung down the scales. They tacitly passed the matter over.

Upstairs Sally was saying good night to Maurie. "I only want you, my darling," she whispered in the darkness. "I don't want anybody else now—say you know I don't want anybody else."

"But you can't," he replied simply; "I'm mummy's."

Sally stood up from the bed. "Yes—you're mummy's," she repeated under her breath, and she repeated it again. She went into her bedroom, beginning slowly to undress, still repeating it.

From that day onwards, whenever possible, she avoided Mr. Grierson as you skirt a district where fever rages. He was too good a man, too honourable, for her to throw her life in his way. All the outlook of men upon a woman such as herself, which Devenish that evening had shown her, rose warningly to thwart her from taking the opportunity which circumstances seemed generously to be offering. The love of Traill was in no wise lessened in her heart; but now, lifting beside it, had come this love of a child, and with the knowledge that Maurie could never be hers, the insensate desire to bear children of her own rose exultantly within her. If she were to marry, this would be her portion. If she were to marry for that reason, above all, would she separate herself for ever from the hope—the still flickering hope—that Traill might one day return?

Whilst one impulse, then, pressed her forward to the seeking of the better acquaintance with Wilfrid Grierson, the fear that she was unfit to be the wife of any so honourable as he withheld her.

But fate, circumstance—give it any name that pleases—was in its obstinate mood. That better acquaintance, it was determined, should be made.

One afternoon, while Maurie was at his lessons, and her own work for the day was over, she was walking through those apple orchards which spread up to the side of that little lane which leads down off the London Road. Supremely unconscious of whose property it was in which she was wandering, she suddenly became aware of a figure descending from one of the apple trees. The first thought that some one was stealing the fruit was driven from her when she recognized Mr. Grierson.

Before he had seen her, she had turned and hurried back in the direction in which she had come. A break in the hedge had given her entrance from the lane. She made as quickly as possible for that. But the sound of footsteps running over the soft ground, the hissing of the grass stems as they lashed against leather leggings, then the sound of her name, showed her that it was too late. She turned.

"I saw you getting down from the tree," she said evasively, "but I thought it was a man stealing fruit."

"So you made a bolt for it?"

"Yes; was it very cowardly?"

"Not at all. If it had been a thief, and he'd thought you were suspicious, he might have turned nasty. But are you sure you didn't recognize me, and come to the conclusion that I was even less desirable than the man stealing the apples?"

She laughed nervously, knowing what was before her.

"No; why should I?"

"Because you've been avoiding me for the last ten days, ever since that tea-party your mother gave at the tennis club."

She looked to the ground; she looked to the forest of leaves above her head, where the rosy apples peered at her, beaming with their bright, healthy cheeks.

"You don't say anything to that," he said, striking his leggings with the little switch in his hand.

"I didn't know I had been," she replied, glancing up to the open candour of his eyes.

"But you have. I was going to write to you."

"You were?"

"Yes; I'm not much of a hand at it, but I was going to make a shot. I was going to ask you if you—if you were preferring—oh—you understand what I mean—if you didn't like my thrusting my attentions on you—well—as I—as I had been doing. I was going to write that to-night."

She looked up with wide eyes—the eyes that Traill had first loved—but she said nothing.

"Well?" he asked, pressing her to the answer. "What would have been your reply?"

"I really don't know," she said honestly.

"You don't care for me?" he exclaimed. "I'm not the sort of chap who—"

"Oh, it's not that!"

"Then, what?"

She met his eyes steadily. "It's—am I the sort of woman?"

He came close to her side, took her hand reverently as though its preciousness made him fear the harm his heavy grip might do. And there, under the network of apple branches interwoven with the patches of a deep, blue sky, with now and then the sound of an apple tumbling heavily to the ground, or a flight of starlings whirring overhead, and in the distance the hollow monotonous beating on the tin drums of the boy who scared the birds, he told her roughly, unevenly, in words cut out of the solid vein of his emotion, what kind of a woman he thought she was.

"No," she kept on whispering; "no, no."

But he paid no attention. He scarcely heard the word in the gentleness of her voice. When he had finished, she took away her hand.

"That means nothing to you, then?" he said bitterly.

She gazed away through the lines of apple trees that hid the greater distance from view.

"It means more than you think," she replied. "But I can't let you say it—I can't let you continue to think it, until—until"—she took a deep breath—"until I tell you."

"Tell me what?"

"I'll write to you."

"But you can tell me. Why can't you tell me?" His lips were white. The little switch snapped in his fingers. Neither of them noticed it. Neither heard the sound. "Why can't you tell me?" he repeated.

"I can't, that is all. After what you've said—after what you've been so generous to tell me that you thought of me, I—couldn't. I'll write it."

He threw the pieces of the switch away into the grass.

"You're going to be married?" he muttered. "You're in love, you're engaged to some one else?"

"No, no, it's not that. Please don't ask me. I'm not engaged to be married."

"You're married already?" He leant forward, bending over her, the words clicking on his tongue.

"No—no—not even that."

"Then, what is it?"

She looked up to his eyes and let him read them. Then he stood upright—slowly stood erect. His cheeks were patched with white, there was a sweat on his forehead. He wiped it off with his hand.

"My God!" he whispered. "You, you? Great God, no!"

He turned, strode a few steps away from her, and stood looking down into the grass. She could hear him muttering. For a little time she waited, head bent, expectant of the sudden bursting of his revolt against the truth. But it never came. His silence was more pregnant with rebuke than speech could ever have been. She bore with it until she thought she had given him full opportunity to rail against her had he wished, then she walked slowly away, the unconquerable sickness in her heart. She walked slowly; but she did not look back. Would he follow her? Would he? Would he? She reached the gap in the hedge. Then she turned her head. He was still standing where she had left him, gazing down into the forest of grass stems.

# CHAPTER III

This ended her life at Cailsham. How could she remain, how face the reproach, no matter what effort she knew he would make to conceal it, which at any moment she might find herself compelled to meet in the eyes of Wilfrid Grierson? Cailsham was too small a place, the little set in which her mother moved too narrow and confined to ever hope of avoiding it. This must end her life at Cailsham.

With the readiness of this realization, then, why had she told? Cry the woman a fool! She was a fool. Most good women are. But just as the matter is vital in the mind of a man, so is it in the woman the crucial test of honour. A thousand reasons—her happiness—the happiness of content,—the sheltering of her name, the sheltering of her position, all the cared-for security of her life to follow— these can be placed in the scale, weighty arguments against that little drachm of abstract honour, to plead for her silence. A thousand times she could have been justified in saying nothing; but had she done so she would have been a different woman. Fine things must be done sometimes; mean things will be done always. There are men and women to do them both.

That no passion was in the heart of her may have been an aid to her honesty. With passion to lift the scale on to the agate,

E. Temple Thurston

there would have been a deed worthy of eulogy then! But even as it was, she sacrificed much; she sacrificed her all. For now she knew that she must go; and there could he no more joy in life for her in the love of little Maurice. To face that, she clutched her hands that afternoon as she walked back into Cailsham. How it was to be accomplished, how endured, was more than she could realize, more than the listless energy of her mind could grasp.

"I am leaving Cailsham almost immediately," she wrote that evening to Grierson. "You will understand my reasons. I am sorry to have caused you the pain that I did. As you realized, I tried to avoid it. I am not presuming at all in my mind that you will ever wish to see me again; but if your generosity should make you think that you owe me any explanation of your silence this afternoon, please believe me that I already understand it, expected it and sympathize from my heart with the position in which I placed you. All that you said to me before you knew, which, of course, I know you cannot think now, I shall treasure in my mind as the opinions of a generous man which were once believed of me. What I have told, or what I have left untold, I know you will hold in your confidence. Good-bye."

Grierson read that letter the next morning in his bedroom. He sat down on the bed, and read it through again; then he railed at women, railed at life, railed at himself that such things should mean so much.

A scene no less dramatic than this was being enacted over the breakfast table at No. 17, Wyatt Street. There, it was the custom for Dora to read such pieces of information from the newspaper as were considered essential to those who, ruling the lives of the sons of gentlemen and being pioneers of education in Cailsham, must be kept up with the times. On this morning, she had given extracts from the foreign intelligence, had read in full the account of the latest London sensation. Then she stopped with an exclamation.

"Mother!"

"What?"

"Mrs. Priestly!"

"Mrs. Priestly?"

"Yes."

"What about her?"

"She's—she's in the divorce court!"

Mrs. Bishop slowly laid down her egg-spoon. "Pass me the paper," she said.

"Yes; just one minute. The case came on—"

"Dora—the paper!"

The printed sheets were handed to her across the table, and Sally's eyes—pained, terrified—watched her face as she read. When she had finished, she laid down the paper, took off her spectacles and laid them glass downwards on the table. The long steel wires to pass over the ears stood upright, formidably bristling.

"I always had my suspicions about that woman," she said, with thin lips. "Oh, it's monstrous, it's abominable! That boy can't stop here another minute."

"Oh, but, mother—why?" Sally exclaimed importunately.

E. Temple Thurston

"What's he done—he's done nothing."

"If you had a little more understanding about the laws of propriety, you wouldn't ask a ridiculous question like that. The boy must go at once. I've often thought since you came down here that the effect of London upon you was to make you extremely lax in your judgment of other people's morals. I've noticed it once or twice in different things you've said. But you'll kindly leave this matter entirely to me. That boy— I feel ashamed to think he's ever been under this roof—is illegitimate!"

"Mother!" exclaimed the two girls.

"So I gather from this report," she said coldly.

Sally said nothing.

"And to think that I've allowed the wretched little creature to live in my house and mix with my boys—a contaminating influence."

"It's horrible!" said the two girls.

"Oh, how unjust you all are!" exclaimed Sally, rising from the table with burning cheeks. "How can a boy of that age be a contaminating influence? How can he affect the innocence of all those other little wretches whom you simper over just because their mothers have it in their power to lift you in the society of this wretched little place?"

Mrs. Bishop had risen from her chair with white lips and distended nostrils. The two girls were staring at Sally with wide eyes and open mouths. For a moment there was a silence that thundered in all their ears.

"Sally," said her mother, biting her words before she foamed them from her, "if you weren't a daughter of mine, I'd—I'd say you were a wanton woman. You know in your heart, as your father always taught you—as you could read in the Bible now—if you ever do read your Bible—that the sins of the fathers, yes, and the mothers too, will fall on the children until the third and fourth generation; and do you think that child of sin isn't contaminated by the vice of his mother's wickedness?"

Elsie came to her mother's side with the proper affection of a daughter and laid her hand gently on her shoulder.

"Don't worry yourself, mother," she said. "He can't stay, of course he can't stay. Sally doesn't know what she's talking about."

"Certainly, he can't stay," reiterated Mrs. Bishop. "If I have to put him in the train myself to-day, and pack him off to London."

"But who'll meet him?" asked Dora.

"Oh, of course, I suppose I shall telegraph to her. I've got her address."

"But that's a terrible waste of money," Elsie objected. "If you wrote now and sent him by a later train, wouldn't she get it in time?"

"It can be charged to her bill," said Mrs. Bishop.

"And are you going to send Maurie alone, all the way up to London?" Sally exclaimed, forced at last to break her silence.

"Of course," said Mrs. Bishop, with surprise. "You don't

think I'm going to afford him the luxury of a travelling companion, do you?"

"You may not; but I shall."

"What on earth do you mean?"

"I shall go with him myself."

"If you do—if you associate yourself with those disreputable people at all—you shall never enter this house again."

Her voice thrilled with the terror of her threat.

"I can look forward to the prospect of that with no great reluctance," said Sally quietly.

"Oh!" Mrs. Bishop exclaimed. "Oh!" Then her daughters wisely led her from the room.

"I've left my egg unfinished," she said brokenly as she departed.

They fondly believed that Sally could not face the ominous threat of her mother until they beheld her trunks ready packed in the hall. Then Elsie came to her.

"Sally," she said, with the voice of one who carries out implacable orders, "do you realize that mother meant what she said?"

"Realize it? I suppose so. I haven't thought about it."

"You don't mean that. You must have thought about it. Do you realize that you'll never see her again?"

"Yes, quite. But not particularly because she says so. I'd never come back again if she were to beg me to. It means a lot to you perhaps, it means nothing to me."

Elsie looked at her in horrified alarm, as at one sinking into the nethermost hell.

"I could never have believed you'd say anything like that," she murmured under her breath. "Can't you see that you're breaking the fifth commandment?"

"Can't mother see," retorted Sally, with vehemence, "that she's breaking all the unwritten commandments of charity— love your enemies—do good to them that hate you? I'd break the fifth commandment fifty times rather than come back and live with all of you again. You're narrow, you're cruel, you're hard, and you save yourselves from your own consciences by calling it Christianity."

When this was all repeated, as inwardly she hoped it would be, they could not believe her to be the same Sally. Mrs. Bishop came out into the hall where she and Maurie were waiting for the vehicle which was to convey them to the station.

"You're not going to say good-bye, Sally?" she asked, drawing her aside into the dining-room.

"I saw no necessity. Wouldn't it be a farce?"

"You can talk like that when you're never going to see me again?"

"I don't see why stating a fact should be unsuitable to the occasion. It would be a farce. You hate me—I'm not fond of you. Yet you would be willing to kiss me—make a sentimental good-bye of it, because you want to do what you know is wrong—cruel, unkind—in the most Christian-like way."

Here indeed was the spirit of Janet speaking from Sally's lips. The contrast, in fact, which induced Janet to preach her philosophy to Sally, was now apparent to Sally herself, between her and her mother. She saw through all the little petty sentimentalities, all the false self-deceits with which the worldly mind of many a clergyman's wife shields itself from rebuke.

"How dare you say such things to me, Sally?" she whispered. "Do you absolutely forget that I'm your mother; that in pain and agony I brought you into the world, and nursed and fed you to life?"

"No, I don't forget that," said Sally, quietly. "But why do you think so much of yourself? Why can't you think a little of that poor woman up in London, trying to shield Maurie from all the horror of this divorce case which now so easily may come to his ears? Why can't you let her leave him here in peace? She suffered just the same agony as you; but she's suffering it still—and you—you're as hard as you can be."

Mrs. Bishop paled with anger. Accusations, epithets, abuse, were the only words that bubbled to her lips.

"You're just as much a fool as your father!" she said chokingly. "He reduced us to this because he was a fool!"

"You know where it's written," Sally remarked, "'He that calleth his brother a fool.'" In a text-quoting atmosphere, she felt that a remark of this kind would carry more weight.

"Yes; but are you my brother? That's identically the same

sort of remark that your father would have made."

"I see," said Sally, "you read your Bible literally. All good Christians do—sometimes. And you could call father a fool! If you had half the Christianity in you that he had in him, I shouldn't be shocking Elsie by breaking the fifth commandment."

The rumbling of the old vehicle outside mercifully put an end to that interview and, once in the train, Sally took Maurie in her arms, pressing his head silently to her breast.

"We're going to see mummie," she kept on telling him. "Mummie'll be at the station to meet us;" and she had to listen to the exclamations of delight that fell mercilessly from his lips.

From a photograph that Maurie had had upon the mantel-piece in his little room, she recognized the tall, stately lady as the train slowed down into the station. Maurie had been leaning out of the carriage and was frantically waving a handkerchief as she walked after them.

"That's mummie—that's mummie!" he said repeatedly, looking back into the carriage at her.

Each time she nodded her head and said to herself, "Now it's all over—now it's all over;" and standing behind him, holding him gently back until the train stopped, she waited stoically for the last moment.

Directly it came to a standstill, Maurie jumped out of the train, and when, a moment later, she descended from their carriage, she could see the little fair head half hidden in the mother's arms.

E. Temple Thurston

Nervously, reticently, she approached them. Then Mrs. Priestly looked up and the sad grey eyes rested on Sally. She held out her hand in hesitating embarrassment.

"You are Miss Bishop?" she said.

Sally inclined her head.

"Maurie talked about you in every letter he wrote me."

"I—I think we were friends," said Sally.

Mrs. Priestly called a fourwheeler, told Maurie to get inside. Then she turned to Sally.

"I received a telegram this morning," she said, "saying that Maurie was coming up to London by this train. But I've had no explanation."

"Didn't you guess the reason?" said Sally, softly.

"Yes; I guessed it, but—" She did not know how much to say, how much to leave unsaid.

"Well, that is it," Sally replied, evasively. "My mother read about your case in the paper this morning."

"And she packed him off, like this, the same day?"

"Yes; my mother is a Christian. She sees things in that light."

"Did she send you with Maurie, then?"

"No; she forbade me to go. She was going to send him alone."

"Then why—?"

"Because I suppose I'm not a Christian."

"You came with him all the same?"

"Yes; I love him." She looked up into Mrs. Priestly's eyes. "Perhaps that sounds an offence to you? But he doesn't love me. You needn't be afraid that I've stolen his love from you. We always used to say our prayers together, and he always used to pray for you. One night I asked him to pray for me, and he said, 'Would that mean that I loved you?' And I— well—I wanted him to love me—you must blame me for that if you wish—I said 'Yes,' because I thought he was going to do it. And then—he said"—Sally stared hard at a stoker shovelling coals into the furnace of one of the engines—"he said he mustn't—because he only loved you. I only told you that because—"

"You thought I'd be jealous?"

"Yes; I should have been."

"And now you've come up to London," said Mrs. Priestly, straining back the tears in her throat. "What are you going to do? Are you going back to Cailsham?"

"No—I'm not going back."

"Then will you come with us? The rooms I've taken are not very comfortable—but—"

"No, I won't come with you—thank you for asking me. I have rooms in London myself. I shall go to them. Good-bye."

E. Temple Thurston

"But, Miss Bishop, you can't leave us like this. I must thank you properly for all your kindness. You can't leave us like this!"

"It's the best way," said Sally; "I'd sooner this way. Good-bye."

They shook hands silently. Mrs. Priestly got into the cab. Sally wondered would she tell Maurie that he would not see her again. Then, as the lumbering old vehicle drove off, a little fair head shot suddenly out of the window and a large white handkerchief flapped like a beating flag against his happy little face.

# CHAPTER IV

When she had left her trunks at the rooms in Regent Street, Sally drove straight to Janet's studio, situated in the environments of Shepherd's Bush.

In the apron of the art-student, her hands unwashed, her hair dishevelled and untidy, she opened the door to Sally's summons.

"Heavens!" she exclaimed. "Why aren't you at Cailsham?"

"I came up this afternoon."

Sally entered the room, crossed to the drawing-board, where the design for a figure of lace was slowly materializing in white paint upon brown paper under Janet's hand. With an apparent concentration of interest she gazed into that. Then Janet closed the door.

"When are you going back?" she asked, climbing slowly to her stool.

"I'm not going back."

Janet grunted, dipped her brush into the porcelain palette and painted in a line that meant nothing. Then she laid down the brush and looked up.

"I've been expecting this." she said. "Why aren't you going back?"

"Mother doesn't want me—I don't want to go."

"Does your mother know?"

"She knows nothing."

Janet stared. "Then what?" she asked abruptly.

Sally dropped into a chair. "Mrs. Priestly—Maurie's mother—is being divorced. They found it out to-day in the papers. Maurie's not her husband's child. They packed him off at once; weren't even going to send any one with him. I said I'd go. Mother said if I did, she'd never have me in the house again. That didn't make any difference to me. I was going in any case."

"Why?"

"A Mr. Grierson down there, asked me to marry him. I couldn't consent without telling him."

"You told him?"

"Yes."

"What did he say?"

"Not very much. Just that at first he couldn't believe it. Then, when he saw I was telling the truth, he said nothing."

"Why did you tell him?"

"Because—it was only right—it was only fair."

Janet gazed at her, eyes softened with a gentle admiration.

"Do you remember what you told me about your father?" she said.

"Yes, why?"

"I expect you must he very like him. Only, instead of being a slave to a Church, you're a slave to your heart. You're just as much the type of woman whom the world wants and treats damned badly—I don't care if I do swear—as he was the type of man whom an institution like the Church of England requires—and treats damned badly too. I guess you're exactly like your father."

"That's what mother said; but she didn't put it in that way. She said I was a fool—like father was."

"Hum!" said Janet, and picked up her brush again. For a time she worked in silence, eyes strained to the fine lines, breath held in to steady her hand, then liberated with a sudden grunting sound.

"Would you have married the man?" she asked presently.

"Yes."

Janet painted in a few more lines. "Do you mean to say you didn't realize that he wouldn't be able to stand what you told him?"

"I expected it."

"Then why—?"

"Simply it wasn't fair. You couldn't make it fair, however much you tried. You'd have done the same yourself. I think I could have been happy with him if he knew. I'd have worshipped his children. But I should have been miserable if he didn't know."

"So you've learnt at last what I told you?" said Janet. "Did Traill never wish you to have a child?"

"No; I don't think so. He never said anything about it."

"And you?"

"No; I don't think I did. I was too happy."

Janet bent down over the drawing-board. "You would now?" she said without looking up. In the delicate operation of painting in the petals of a rose, she did not realize that her question had not been answered. A minute slipped by and with breath strained in the holding of it, she repeated her question. "You would now?"

When the rose had bloomed under her brush, still receiving no reply, she sat upright and looked round. Sally's body was bent forward, her elbows were on her knees, her face in her hands.

Janet clambered down from her stool. "Crying?" she asked.

Sally gazed up at her with tearless eyes. "No; I can't cry now. I try to. I can't."

"God! What a difference it 'ud make to you!" said Janet.

"What would?"

"If you had a kiddy. What was this little Maurie like? He sounded sweet in your letters. Why don't you see as much of him as you can? I'm sure he's fond of you. Isn't he?"

"Yes—in his way—in his dear little way. But you don't want fondness from children."

"What do you want, then?"

"Love. If you want anything at all. There were some of the little boys down at Cailsham who were loathsome: horrid little wretches, who'd put out their tongues at you."

"Sons of gentlemen," said Janet.

"One of them spat at me once when I was giving him a music lesson. You couldn't want anything from them. But I could almost have believed that Maurie was mine."

"Then why don't you go and see him? Take care of him for Mrs. Priestly till the case is over. He's bound to be in the way. When will it be over?"

"The case?"

"Yes."

"I don't know."

"Is she likely to win?"

"I'm afraid not, and I don't believe she minds as long as she's got Maurie."

"What counsel has she?"

E. Temple Thurston

"Oh, I don't know. I didn't read the paper."

"Well, why don't you go and take care of him till it's over?"

"I don't believe she'd like me to."

"Why on earth not? Here, let me get at that stove. We're going to have some tea. But why on earth not?"

"I know she was jealous. Maurie used to write her lots of letters about me. She was afraid he was getting to love me. I could see that this afternoon. I could see it so plainly that I told her. I admitted that I'd tried to get him to love me and failed."

"You did try?"

"Yes; I suppose it was about the meanest thing I've ever done."

Janet laid down the kettle silently on the stove, then came and sat on the arm of Sally's chair. One hand she laid on her shoulder, with the other she raised her face.

"I haven't appreciated you sufficiently, Sally," she said in a toneless voice. "You're not the sort that gets appreciation. But, my God! I think you're wonderful. Do I keep saying 'God' too much, d'you think?"

## CHAPTER V

That night Sally sat in her old rooms once more and wrote a letter to Traill. The return to them had for one moment surged back in a rushing flood of memories; but it did not overwhelm her. She threw herself into no quagmire of despair. Her eyes were tearless. All her actions were such as those of a person dazed with sleep. One hope she had in her heart which animated her, just as the hope of ultimate rest will give sluggish life to the person whose eyes are heavy with fatigue.

Towards the realization of that hope, she seated herself at her desk and wrote to Traill.

"DEAR JACK,

"Will you come and see me to-morrow afternoon at about half-past four? I will give you some tea. I want to speak to you. Please do not think that I am going to begin to pester you with unwelcome attentions. My silence over these two or three months should convince you that I would not worry you like that for anything.

"Hoping that I shall see you,
"Yours sincerely,
"SALLY BISHOP."

E. Temple Thurston

When she had posted it, she went to bed and slept fitfully till morning. There was no letter waiting her from Traill, but an envelope addressed with a scrawled, uneven writing lay in the box. She tore it eagerly open, her heart beating exultantly.

"DEAR SALLY," it read,

"Mummy has gone out I am to write to you  I am to say good bi proply I am very fond of you but I doant luv you Mummy ses you have been very kind I wode luv you very much if you was my mummy but mummy ses she is she is I am afrade this is not spellt rite but I have got a very bad pen.

"Yours affagintly,
"MAURIE."

If the tears could have come then; but she laid the letter down on the table, and her eyes were aching and dry. The quaintness of the spelling, the almost complete absence of punctuation. That queer little repetition, of words—"she is she is"—none of these things moved her, even to smile. Maurie had said good-bye properly. That, and that he was only just fond of her, was all that reached her understanding. Had the letter been from a lover, dashing all her hopes into fragments, she could not have read it more seriously. But one prospect was left her. She never took her eyes from that. The fact that Traill had not written did not convey to her mind any fear that he would not come. She knew that he would not needlessly lead her to expect him and disappoint her at the last.

At four o'clock she had the table laid for tea. The dainty china that she had bought with him when abroad was brought out. The kettle was beginning to sing on the gas stove in the grate. When everything was ready, she tried to sit quietly in a chair, but her eyes kept wandering to the little Sevres clock. Again and again she rose to her feet, looking out of her window into the street below.

At last footsteps echoed up the stairs. She caught her breath, and a sound broke in her throat. They came nearer, and she trembled; her hand shook; her whole body was chilled with searching cold. She had not seen him for three months—more. Now she began to think that she could not bear it. Then the knock fell on the door. A cry was on her lips. She forced it back, turned, holding as naturally as possible to the mantelpiece, and said—

"Come in."

He entered. He closed the door after him. Then she looked around.

The situation was as strained, as tautened, as is the gut of a snapping fiddle-string. Every sound seemed to vibrate in itself. For an instant he stood still, coming forward at last, hand outstretched to relieve the tension.

"Well, how are you, Sally?" he asked.

The random speech, jerked out—any words to break the silence. Even he felt it beating on his brain.

She shook hands with him. For the brief moment he touched her cold fingers in the grip of his; then she withdrew them.

"Let me take your hat," she said.

He gave it her. Watched her as she crossed the room to lay it on the chintz-covered settee, turned then to the fireplace,

E. Temple Thurston

biting a nail between his teeth.

"Do you know the kettle's boiling?" he forced himself to say.

"Yes; I'm just going to make tea. You'll have some tea?"

"Oh, rather. You promised that."

He looked up with his old jerk of the head, courting the smile to her lips. She had no smile to give, and a shrug half tossed his shoulders.

"Are you comfortable here?" he asked, as she poured out the boiling water.

"Oh yes. Very."

"God!" he said casually within himself, feeling the weight of the strain. Then he struggled for it once more.

"I'm dining with Devenish this evening," he said lightly. "You remember Devenish, don't you?"

"Oh yes—I remember him. He came up to see me here a few weeks ago."

"Did he? He's a gay dog," he said lightly. "Do you like him?"

"I haven't thought about it."

"Oh, then you don't. And haven't you seen him since?"

"No; I've been away."

"Away?"

"Yes; down at Cailsham—staying with my mother."

"Oh, very nice, I should think. I'm glad you're moving about a bit. I was rather afraid, you know, that you'd hang about in town all through the summer, and that 'ud be bound to knock you up."

She handed him his cup of tea. "Why were you afraid?" she asked.

"Why? Do you think I'd be glad if you were knocked up?"

He looked up at her, with raised eyebrows, not understanding.

"I don't suppose you'd be sorry, would you?"

She said it gently—no strain of bitterness. The emotion which had swept her at first was passed now. All her mind concentrated to the one end.

"Of course I should," he replied. "Of course I should be sorry. Do you paint me in your mind the little boy dropped in and out of a love affair?"

"Oh no."

"Then why say that? Of course I should be sorry. Because you and I couldn't fit things properly together—"

"Is that how it seems to you now?" she interrupted.

"Well, could we? Is it any good going over it all again? Did you ever imagine me to be the type of man who would consent to being followed, as you followed me that night? I can't suppose you did; otherwise, would you have tried to hide it from me? But I don't lose any friendly regard for you because of that."

"You don't object to being here, then?" she asked eagerly.

"No; certainly not! Why should I?"

"Would you come again if nothing of that were ever mentioned any more between us—would you come again?"

"Yes, willingly. Now that I see that your intention is to be
perfectly reasonable, I would—willingly. Why not? I don't
see why we should be enemies."

"No," said Sally quickly; "neither do I—neither do I."

He drank through his tea. One mouthful—they were such
tiny cups; but that is the way a man takes his entertainment.

"Have a good time down at Cailsham?" he asked presently.

He felt more at his ease. She was taking it well—so much
better than he expected.

"Oh, not very good. I have told you, haven't I, that I don't get
on very well with my people."

"Of course; yes. Isn't that rather a pity?"

Possibly conscience was plying its spurs. There was some
suggestion underlying the quietness of her manner which he
found to bring a sense of uneasiness. He would have
preferred that she had got on well at Cailsham. He would
rather that she had taken a fancy to Devenish. But she was
reasonable—extremely reasonable. He had nothing to
grumble at. Yet he could not get away from the sense of
something that made each word they said drag slowly,

unnaturally into utterance. He tried to shake it from him.

"Well, what is it you've got to speak to me about?" he asked in a fresh tone of voice, as if with a jerk they were starting again over lighter ground.

"Won't you wait till you've finished your tea?" she asked.

"I have finished."

"No more?"

"No, thanks. Do you mind my smoking?"

She lit a match for him in answer—held it out, waiting while he extracted the cigarette from his case.

"Now tell me," he said, when she had thrown the match away.

She gazed for a moment in the grate, at the kettle breathing contentedly on the gas stove.

"I'm lonely," she said, turning to his eyes.

He met her gaze as well as he could. He knew she was lonely. Conscience—conscience that no strength of will could override—had often pricked him on that point. But what was a conscience? He would not have believed himself guilty of the weakness at any other time. He gave no rein to it.

"But you'll get over that," he said. "You'll get over that."

"I don't think so."

"But why not? Perhaps you give way to it. Find yourself plenty to do. Keep yourself moving. You won't be lonely then."

"I know. But do what?"

"Well," the question faced him. He had to answer it. "Well, you're fond of reading, aren't you?"

"Reading!"

"And you've got these rooms to keep straight. A good many women if they thought they'd got to tidy up two rooms every day would grumble at the amount of labour, because it took up so much of their time."

"Yes; but they'd do it."

"Probably they'd have to."

"And then they wouldn't be lonely."

"Quite so. Isn't that what I say?"

"Yes; but don't you forget one thing?"

"What's that?"

"They'd be doing it for some one else. They wouldn't be doing it for themselves. And don't you think they get the impetus to do it from that?"

She leant forward—no sign of triumph in her face—and watched his eyes. She knew he could not reply to that. He knew it too. He pulled strenuously at his cigarette, then flung it into the empty fireplace.

"Then what is your point?" he asked firmly. He beat around no bushes. That was not the nature of him. This was a difficulty. He faced it. This was the scene she had deftly been leading up to. Let her have it out and he would tell her straight, once and for all. "What is your point?" he repeated. "You want me to come back—go through the same business all over again?"

"No!"

Now he was puzzled. His eyes frowned straight into hers.

"Then what? Come along, Sally, out with it."

She turned her head away. He heard the sound in her throat as she began to form the words. But she could not say it. Then her hands covered her face, for a moment stayed there; at last she took them away and met the beating gaze of his eyes.

"If I had a child," she said quickly.

His forehead creased, line upon line. He took a deep breath and leant back in his chair.

"What do you mean?" he asked.

"If I had a child," she repeated, "I shouldn't be lonely then. I should have some one to do all these things for then. I should have something to live for."

Traill stood abruptly to his feet. "You're—you're crazy!" he exclaimed.

She stood beside him. Her hand stretched out nervously, touching his coat.

E. Temple Thurston

"No, no, I'm not. I mean it. Can't you see what it would mean to me, here alone, night after night, night after night, no one, absolutely no one but myself."

He studied her in amazement. "If it were any other woman than you," he said suddenly, "I should think this was a put-up job to compromise me—a cunning, put-up job. But you! It's amazing! I don't understand it. Why, you'd brand yourself to the whole world. It'd be a mill stone round your neck, not a child."

"Don't you think I'm branded plainly enough already? What do you think a man like Devenish thinks of me?"

"Oh, Devenish be damned! There are other men than Devenish in the world. Men who know nothing; men who'd be ready to marry you."

"Yes, I found one—one who thought me everything—everything till I told him."

"You told him?"

"Yes."

"In the name of God, what for? You must be crazy. What the deuce did you want to tell him for?"

"It was the only fair thing to do," she said quietly.

"Fair? Rot! That's chucking your chances away. That's playing the fool! What's he got to do with your life before you met him?" This was flinging the blame at him.

"Would you rather that the woman you were going to marry kept silent, risked your not finding out afterwards? Would you think she'd treated you fairly if she said nothing, and you were to discover it when it was too late?"

He had no answer. He tried to make one. His lips parted; then, in silence, he turned away.

"It might have made your mind easier," she said quietly, without tone of blame, "but it wouldn't have been fair."

He twisted back. "There's no need for my mind to be made easier," he said hardly. "I've treated you fairly from the beginning to the end. I warned you in the first instance; I told you to have no truck with me. I sent you away. You came back. I didn't ask you to come back."

Janet's words flashed across Sally's memory; the words she had said when they were talking over the bangle: "I don't care what you say about that letter, the letter's nothing! It's the gift that's the thing. That's the song of sex if you like, and whether you return it, or whether you don't, you'll answer it, as he means you to."

It was on the edge of her mind to repeat them then to him, but she refrained. It was better then, at that moment, to let him think that he had no cause to blame himself.

"No, my mind's perfectly easy," he added. "Thank God, I don't pose for a paragon; I've got the beast in me all right, but I've treated you square—absolutely square."

Her fingers clutched. To win her desires she must let him think so. And perhaps he had treated her square; she supposed he had.

"Then help me not to be lonely now," she begged. She could see the wave of repulsion beat across his face, but even that did not deter her. "Oh, I don't mean that you should come back and live with me," she went on. "It isn't for that. You can't—you surely can't hate me as much as all that." It was not in her knowledge to realize that he must love her, greater than he had ever loved, if she were to win. To the woman needing the child it is the child alone; to the man, the child is only the child when it is his.

"I don't hate you," he said. He picked up his hat from the settee, and her heart dropped to a leaden weight. "You seem to harp on that. But what you ask, you surely must realize is frankly impossible. I don't wish to be responsible for a child."

"You needn't be responsible," she said eagerly. "You need never see it. You've been generous enough to me in what you've given me. I shan't ask for a penny more—I shan't use the child to extract money from you. You'll never hear from me again. After all, you have loved me," she said piteously. "You did love me once."

He turned angrily away. "My God!" he exclaimed. "You talk as if you were out of your mind! If I did have a child, I should want to see it. I shouldn't want to be ashamed of it; I shouldn't want to disown it, as you'd have me do."

"Well, then, you might see it as often as you wished."

He strode to the door. She must have it now. He had meant to say nothing, wishing to save her feelings; but she must have it now.

"Then I'm engaged to be married," he said firmly. "Do you see now that it's impossible?"

She dropped into a chair, staring strangely at his face.

"You—married?" she whispered.

"Yes; and I've no desire to have things cropping up in my life afterwards, just in the way that this Mrs. Priestly in the divorce courts—"

Sally struggled to her feet.

"Mrs. Priestly?"

"Yes; what about her? Do you know her?"

"What do you know about her?" she asked.

"I'm counsel for her husband."

"You're cross-examining her?"

Straight through her mind leapt that scene in the divorce court when she had witnessed his attack upon the miserable woman whom the law had placed out for his feet to trample on.

"Yes," he replied. "What *do* you know about her?"

She sank back into her chair saying nothing.

"You won't say?"

She shook her head.

"Well, it's of not much interest to me. I shouldn't have you subpoenaed, if you did know anything. You know the case, at any rate. Well, I don't want that sort of affair in my life; so you never need mention this matter again. I'll come and see you sometimes, if you want me to; but only on condition that we have none of this. When I'm married, of course, then it'll have to stop."

Sally raised her head. Her eyes were burning—her lips were drawn to a thin colourless line.

"You—who never were going to marry!" she shouted. "You who didn't believe in it—who wouldn't fetter yourself with it! Oh, go! Go!"

# CHAPTER VI

That same evening there might have been seen two men seated opposite to each other at a small table in the corner of the grill-room of a well-known restaurant. Throughout the beginning of the meal, they laughed and talked amiably to each other. No one took particular notice of them. The waiter, attendant upon their table, leant against a marble pillar some little distance away and surreptitiously cleaned his nails with the corner of a menu-card. A band played on a raised platform in some other part of the room. From where they sat, they could see the conductor leading his orchestra with the swaying of his violin. He tossed his hair into artistic disorder with the violent intensity of feeling as he played, and his fingers, strained out till the tendons between them were stretched like the strings upon which they moved, felt for the harmonics—shrill notes that pierced through the sounds of all the other instruments.

In the midst of the rattling of plates, the coming and going, the buzz of conversation, these two men chatted good-naturedly over their meal. At its conclusion, they ordered coffee, cigars and liqueurs, and leant back comfortably in their chairs. Hundreds of others there, were doing precisely the same as they—thousands of others in all the restaurants in London. There was nothing remarkable about their faces, their dress or their manner until one of them suddenly leant

E. Temple Thurston

forward across the table, and his expression, from genial amusement, leapt in sudden changes from the amazement of surprise to the fierceness of contempt and anger. Some exclamation in the force of the moment probably left his lips, for a woman at a table near by turned in her chair and gazed at them with unconcealed curiosity. She kept strained in that position as he brought down his fist on the table. She could see his fingers gripping the cloth. Then the other man put out his hand with a gesture of restraint.

From that they talked on excitedly—one or them driving his questions to the tardy replies of the other. Here and there in their speech the name of God ripped out, and the waiter, placing the card back on one of the empty tables, stood more alert, listening.

Their cigars burnt low, their coffee was drained; yet still they continued, voices pitched now on a lower key, but none the less intense, none the less spurred with vital interest. The man apparently most concerned had ceased from the urging of his questions. His elbows were resting on the table, his face was in his hands. Now and again he nodded in under-standing, now and again he ejaculated some remark, pressing his companion to the full measure of what he had to say. Obviously it was a story—the relation of some incident, reluctantly dragged from the one by the persistent, unyielding demands of the other.

The woman at the near table put up her hand to her ear, shutting off the conversation of those with her, striving to catch a word here and there in the endeavour to piece it together. It was about some woman. She—was continually being alluded to. She—had done this—at a later date she had done that. Gathering as little as she did, the woman who listened was still strangely fascinated to curiosity.

Then at last a whole sentence reached her ears in a sudden hush of sound.

The man took his elbows from the table, as if the climax of the story had been reached.

"I know!" he said excitedly; "I know—the type of woman who never breaks a commandment because she daren't, yet never earns a beatitude because she can't; but, my God, if this isn't true—"

Then the other began his reply—

"My dear fellow—should I come and—"

She heard no more. A renewed deafening clatter of plates from the grill drowned the remainder of his sentence.

"There's a little tragedy behind us," said the woman, leaning forward, speaking under her breath to one of her companions. They all turned and gazed in the direction of the table. Then the two men stood up. One of them picked up the bill.

"Pay at the desk, please, sir," said the waiter obsequiously.

He half followed them down the room. They had forgotten to tip him. It was quite obvious that they forgot. Yet his face was a study in the mingling of disappointment and contempt. He stood there looking after them; then he chucked up his head in disgust, and catching the eye of some distant waiter, he made a sign of a nought with his fingers, and looked up at the ceiling.

As they passed the woman's table, she heard one of them say—

E. Temple Thurston

"There's not a straight woman in the whole of that damned set—not one!" Then they passed out of hearing.

"I think it's a marvellous thing," said the woman when they had gone, "to think of the thousands of exciting tragedies, romances, crimes perhaps, that are being acted out to their ends all round one, and except for a stray little bit of conversation like that, one would never realize it. I remember hearing a woman in a crowd say something to a man in the most awful voice, full of horror, that I've ever heard. I just caught her saying, 'If he finds it out to-night, either I'll kill myself or he'll do it for me,' and then they got out of the crowd, called a hansom and drove away. Positively, I didn't sleep that night, wondering if he had found it out, wondering if he had killed her, wondering if hundreds of other people had found out hundreds of other horrible things. But it all went in the morning. Cissy had a terrible toothache, and I had to take her to the dentist's."

# CHAPTER VII

It was nine o'clock in the evening of the same day on which Traill had been to see Sally. The lights were burning in her room as Janet approached the street door. Opening it, she walked along the passage and began the ascent of stairs. Halfway up the first flight she stopped. The voices of two men, talking rather excitedly, came up to her from the street as if they were nearing the house. Another moment and she heard one bidding the other good night in the passage. Evidently he was coming in. She walked on up the flight of stairs. His footsteps sounded behind her. She took but little more notice of the fact until, when she stopped before Sally's door, he stopped behind her. Then she turned round. Her eyes opened a little wider. She began to say one thing; then she changed her mind and said another.

"Aren't you Mr. Traill?" she asked.

He looked at her more closely in the dim light from the landing window.

"Yes; how did you know?"

"I'm Miss Hallard."

"Oh, oh yes! You're Sally's friend."

E. Temple Thurston

"'Bout the only one she has." said Janet. There was no flinching in her eyes from his.

"You mean that for me?"

"Yes."

"Would it surprise you to hear me say I deserve it?"

"Yes, considerably. Isn't it a pity you didn't realize that a bit sooner?"

"Well, we must all have disagreeable times in our lives," he said rigidly. "Sally's had hers, but I guess it's over now. I fancy I've just come from school and learnt my lesson."

"What do you mean?"

"Do you expect me to answer that to you?"

Here, in the first moment, they came to their antagonism, as Janet had always realized they would.

"No, I don't expect it in the least" she replied.

"Well, if you're going in—?"

"Yes, I'm going in." She opened the door and entered the sitting-room. All the lights were burning. Sally's hat lay untidily on the table.

"One moment," said Traill.

Janet turned round.

"I should be glad if you'd allow me to see Sally alone as soon as possible. I want to talk to her. I've got a lot to say."

"I'll go now," she replied.

"No, oh no, see her first. She's probably been expecting you. Didn't she send for you this afternoon, some time after five o'clock—eh?"

"No, I haven't seen her since yesterday. I'll just knock at her door. Sally!" She called the name gently and knocked. Traill walked to the mantelpiece. There was no answer.

"She must be in," he said, "there's her hat."

Janet knocked again. There was no reply. She turned round.

"I wonder can she have gone to bed and be asleep? She looked terribly tired when I saw her yesterday."

She knocked again and tried the door; then bent down and examined the keyhole. The key was inside, and a light was burning in the room. Janet stood up suddenly. Her lips were shaking; her cheeks were white.

"Mr. Traill," she said in a hollow voice, but raising it as though he were some distance away. "This door's locked from the inside, and there's a light in the room."

He took it quite casually. "Better let me try it," he said. "It can't be locked from the inside unless she's there."

Janet stood aside, trembling, as he tried the handle. Then he, too, bent down and examined the keyhole.

"Good God! You're right!" he said thickly.

E. Temple Thurston

Janet's eyes roamed feverishly from his face to the door. When he stood back and called out Sally's name, her senses sharpened to a quivering point to catch the slightest sound of a reply. She must be inside—she must be inside! Then why didn't she answer? Why? She recalled Sally's face as she had last seen it, white, drawn, the eyes hollow, the lips but faintly tinged with pink. Now it was in that room, the face that she had lifted and kissed before she had said how wonderful she was. But what was it looking like now? What was it looking like now, alone in that awful silence?

Traill strode back into the room.

"What are you going to do?" asked Janet. "Something's got to be done! What are you going to do?"

"Break down the door," was his answer.

He searched in the fireplace. He searched round the room.

"Take that chair! Take that chair!" cried Janet.

He picked it up by its heavy arms, stood back and then charged the door. There was a shuddering noise, a splintering sound of wood giving. Then it was all quiet again.

He got ready to do it again.

"Wait!" said Janet. In a quivering voice she called Sally's name again.

There was no reply.

"Do it now!" she said, almost incoherently. "Do it now! I believe one of the panels is giving."

He charged it once more, and then again.

"The panel's giving," said Janet.

He flung down the chair from his shoulders. The panel had splintered from its joining at the bottom. He could just push it forward a little, making a slight aperture.

"Get the poker!" he said firmly.

She ran obediently and brought it to him. He prized it into the gap, levered it forward until there was room for his fingers to squeeze through; then he thrust them in and used the strength of his arm, an additional lever, to push an opening down towards the key inside.

"Mind your arm," said Janet; "you're tearing the skin."

He made no reply—forced his hand still further through the gap until the splinters of wood were cutting into the flesh and the blood was dripping down in red blotches on the white paint of the door. She glanced at his face. It was grey. The pupils of his eyes were large with fear. His breath was hunting through his nostrils as he strained to reach the key.

"Now I've got it," he whispered. "Prize that open with the poker as far as you can or I'll never get my hand back."

She leant all her fragile weight against it, aided with the strength of maddening fear. Her ears were strained for the sound in the lock. When she heard the bolt click, she gasped and pressed forward again with redoubled vigour as he slowly drew out his lacerated hand from the crevice.

Then they both stood upright. Together they both drew a deep breath as Traill turned the handle and opened the door.

A physical sickness made them weak. Janet half tumbled, half ran into the room. The length of Traill's strides brought him even with her.

Sally was there. Sally was in the room. She lay crumpled on the bed, her legs drawn up, twisted, bent; one arm thrown out covering her face, her other hand gripping a corner of the bed-clothes, stretching out from her in tautened creases. She looked as though some giant hand had knotted her fragile body with fingers of iron.

With a cry, Janet bent over the bed. At her feet, Traill picked up a little bottle, hurriedly read the label, and blindly put it in his pocket.

"Uncover her face," he whispered; "take her arm away from her face—she's choking herself."

"Choking herself!" Janet gently bent the arm back. Every feature was twisted in the same grip, the lips caught in the same iron fingers and dragged in her suffering, baring the teeth—the whole expression of her face was as though she had died, emitting one last scream of unbearable agony. "Look! Choking herself? She's dead!"

With a muffled sound, Traill forced himself to her side. He put his arm round her. He lifted her up. The body dragged against him, the head swung from the loose neck.

"Sally's had her bad time," said Janet, hoarsely, "and, my God, it's over now!"

### THE END

# Choose from Thousands of 1stWorldLibrary Classics By

A. M. Barnard
Ada Leverson
Adolphus William Ward
Aesop
Agatha Christie
Alexander Aaronsohn
Alexander Kielland
Alexandre Dumas
Alfred Gatty
Alfred Ollivant
Alice Duer Miller
Alice Turner Curtis
Alice Dunbar
Allen Chapman
Alleyne Ireland
Ambrose Bierce
Amelia E. Barr
Amory H. Bradford
Andrew Lang
Andrew McFarland Davis
Andy Adams
Angela Brazil
Anna Alice Chapin
Anna Sewell
Annie Besant
Annie Hamilton Donnell
Annie Payson Call
Annie Roe Carr
Annonaymous
Anton Chekhov
Archibald Lee Fletcher
Arnold Bennett
Arthur C. Benson
Arthur Conan Doyle
Arthur M. Winfield
Arthur Ransome
Arthur Schnitzler
Arthur Train
Atticus
B.H. Baden-Powell
B. M. Bower
B. C. Chatterjee
Baroness Emmuska Orczy
Baroness Orczy
Basil King
Bayard Taylor
Ben Macomber
Bertha Muzzy Bower
Bjornstjerne Bjornson

Booth Tarkington
Boyd Cable
Bram Stoker
C. Collodi
C. E. Orr
C. M. Ingleby
Carolyn Wells
Catherine Parr Traill
Charles A. Eastman
Charles Amory Beach
Charles Dickens
Charles Dudley Warner
Charles Farrar Browne
Charles Ives
Charles Kingsley
Charles Klein
Charles Hanson Towne
Charles Lathrop Pack
Charles Romyn Dake
Charles Whibley
Charles Willing Beale
Charlotte M. Braeme
Charlotte M. Yonge
Charlotte Perkins Stetson
Clair W. Hayes
Clarence Day Jr.
Clarence E. Mulford
Clemence Housman
Confucius
Coningsby Dawson
Cornelis DeWitt Wilcox
Cyril Burleigh
D. H. Lawrence
Daniel Defoe
David Garnett
Dinah Craik
Don Carlos Janes
Donald Keyhoe
Dorothy Kilner
Dougan Clark
Douglas Fairbanks
E. Nesbit
E. P. Roe
E. Phillips Oppenheim
E. S. Brooks
Earl Barnes
Edgar Rice Burroughs
Edith Van Dyne
Edith Wharton

Edward Everett Hale
Edward J. O'Biren
Edward S. Ellis
Edwin L. Arnold
Eleanor Atkins
Eleanor Hallowell Abbott
Eliot Gregory
Elizabeth Gaskell
Elizabeth McCracken
Elizabeth Von Arnim
Ellem Key
Emerson Hough
Emilie F. Carlen
Emily Bronte
Emily Dickinson
Enid Bagnold
Enilor Macartney Lane
Erasmus W. Jones
Ernie Howard Pie
Ethel May Dell
Ethel Turner
Ethel Watts Mumford
Eugene Sue
Eugenie Foa
Eugene Wood
Eustace Hale Ball
Evelyn Everett-green
Everard Cotes
F. H. Cheley
F. J. Cross
F. Marion Crawford
Fannie E. Newberry
Federick Austin Ogg
Ferdinand Ossendowski
Fergus Hume
Florence A. Kilpatrick
Fremont B. Deering
Francis Bacon
Francis Darwin
Frances Hodgson Burnett
Frances Parkinson Keyes
Frank Gee Patchin
Frank Harris
Frank Jewett Mather
Frank L. Packard
Frank V. Webster
Frederic Stewart Isham
Frederick Trevor Hill
Frederick Winslow Taylor

Friedrich Kerst
Friedrich Nietzsche
Fyodor Dostoyevsky
G.A. Henty
G.K. Chesterton
Gabrielle E. Jackson
Garrett P. Serviss
Gaston Leroux
George A. Warren
George Ade
Geroge Bernard Shaw
George Cary Eggleston
George Durston
George Ebers
George Eliot
George Gissing
George MacDonald
George Meredith
George Orwell
George Sylvester Viereck
George Tucker
George W. Cable
George Wharton James
Gertrude Atherton
Gordon Casserly
Grace E. King
Grace Gallatin
Grace Greenwood
Grant Allen
Guillermo A. Sherwell
Gulielma Zollinger
Gustav Flaubert
H. A. Cody
H. B. Irving
H.C. Bailey
H. G. Wells
H. H. Munro
H. Irving Hancock
H. R. Naylor
H. Rider Haggard
H. W. C. Davis
Haldeman Julius
Hall Caine
Hamilton Wright Mabie
Hans Christian Andersen
Harold Avery
Harold McGrath
Harriet Beecher Stowe
Harry Castlemon
Harry Coghill
Harry Houidini

Hayden Carruth
Helent Hunt Jackson
Helen Nicolay
Hendrik Conscience
Hendy David Thoreau
Henri Barbusse
Henrik Ibsen
Henry Adams
Henry Ford
Henry Frost
Henry James
Henry Jones Ford
Henry Seton Merriman
Henry W Longfellow
Herbert A. Giles
Herbert Carter
Herbert N. Casson
Herman Hesse
Hildegard G. Frey
Homer
Honore De Balzac
Horace B. Day
Horace Walpole
Horatio Alger Jr.
Howard Pyle
Howard R. Garis
Hugh Lofting
Hugh Walpole
Humphry Ward
Ian Maclaren
Inez Haynes Gillmore
Irving Bacheller
Isabel Cecilia Williams
Isabel Hornibrook
Israel Abrahams
Ivan Turgenev
J.G.Austin
J. Henri Fabre
J. M. Barrie
J. M. Walsh
J. Macdonald Oxley
J. R. Miller
J. S. Fletcher
J. S. Knowles
J. Storer Clouston
J. W. Duffield
Jack London
Jacob Abbott
James Allen
James Andrews
James Baldwin

James Branch Cabell
James DeMille
James Joyce
James Lane Allen
James Lane Allen
James Oliver Curwood
James Oppenheim
James Otis
James R. Driscoll
Jane Abbott
Jane Austen
Jane L. Stewart
Janet Aldridge
Jens Peter Jacobsen
Jerome K. Jerome
Jessie Graham Flower
John Buchan
John Burroughs
John Cournos
John F. Kennedy
John Gay
John Glasworthy
John Habberton
John Joy Bell
John Kendrick Bangs
John Milton
John Philip Sousa
John Taintor Foote
Jonas Lauritz Idemil Lie
Jonathan Swift
Joseph A. Altsheler
Joseph Carey
Joseph Conrad
Joseph E. Badger Jr
Joseph Hergesheimer
Joseph Jacobs
Jules Vernes
Julian Hawthrone
Julie A Lippmann
Justin Huntly McCarthy
Kakuzo Okakura
Karle Wilson Baker
Kate Chopin
Kenneth Grahame
Kenneth McGaffey
Kate Langley Bosher
Kate Langley Bosher
Katherine Cecil Thurston
Katherine Stokes
L. A. Abbot
L. T. Meade

L. Frank Baum
Latta Griswold
Laura Dent Crane
Laura Lee Hope
Laurence Housman
Lawrence Beasley
Leo Tolstoy
Leonid Andreyev
Lewis Carroll
Lewis Sperry Chafer
Lilian Bell
Lloyd Osbourne
Louis Hughes
Louis Joseph Vance
Louis Tracy
Louisa May Alcott
Lucy Fitch Perkins
Lucy Maud Montgomery
Luther Benson
Lydia Miller Middleton
Lyndon Orr
M. Corvus
M. H. Adams
Margaret E. Sangster
Margret Howth
Margaret Vandercook
Margaret W. Hungerford
Margret Penrose
Maria Edgeworth
Maria Thompson Daviess
Mariano Azuela
Marion Polk Angellotti
Mark Overton
Mark Twain
Mary Austin
Mary Catherine Crowley
Mary Cole
Mary Hastings Bradley
Mary Roberts Rinehart
Mary Rowlandson
M. Wollstonecraft Shelley
Maud Lindsay
Max Beerbohm
Myra Kelly
Nathaniel Hawthrone
Nicolo Machiavelli
O. F. Walton
Oscar Wilde

Owen Johnson
P.G. Wodehouse
Paul and Mabel Thorne
Paul G. Tomlinson
Paul Severing
Percy Brebner
Percy Keese Fitzhugh
Peter B. Kyne
Plato
Quincy Allen
R. Derby Holmes
R. L. Stevenson
R. S. Ball
Rabindranath Tagore
Rahul Alvares
Ralph Bonehill
Ralph Henry Barbour
Ralph Victor
Ralph Waldo Emmerson
Rene Descartes
Ray Cummings
Rex Beach
Rex E. Beach
Richard Harding Davis
Richard Jefferies
Richard Le Gallienne
Robert Barr
Robert Frost
Robert Gordon Anderson
Robert L. Drake
Robert Lansing
Robert Lynd
Robert Michael Ballantyne
Robert W. Chambers
Rosa Nouchette Carey
Rudyard Kipling
Saint Augustine
Samuel B. Allison
Samuel Hopkins Adams
Sarah Bernhardt
Sarah C. Hallowell
Selma Lagerlof
Sherwood Anderson
Sigmund Freud
Standish O'Grady
Stanley Weyman
Stella Benson
Stella M. Francis

Stephen Crane
Stewart Edward White
Stijn Streuvels
Swami Abhedananda
Swami Parmananda
T. S. Ackland
T. S. Arthur
The Princess Der Ling
Thomas A. Janvier
Thomas A Kempis
Thomas Anderton
Thomas Bailey Aldrich
Thomas Bulfinch
Thomas De Quincey
Thomas Dixon
Thomas H. Huxley
Thomas Hardy
Thomas More
Thornton W. Burgess
U. S. Grant
Upton Sinclair
Valentine Williams
Various Authors
Vaughan Kester
Victor Appleton
Victor G. Durham
Victoria Cross
Virginia Woolf
Wadsworth Camp
Walter Camp
Walter Scott
Washington Irving
Wilbur Lawton
Wilkie Collins
Willa Cather
Willard F. Baker
William Dean Howells
William le Queux
W. Makepeace Thackeray
William W. Walter
William Shakespeare
Winston Churchill
Yei Theodora Ozaki
Yogi Ramacharaka
Young E. Allison
Zane Grey